GLADYSS OF THE HUNT

Gladyss of the Hunt

ARTHUR NERSESIAN

DARK PASSAGE

Dedicated to my mother, Honora Agnes Burke

A Dark Passage book
Published by Verse Chorus Press
PO Box 14806, Portland OR 97293
info@versechorus.com

Cover design by Mike Reddy
Interior design and layout by Steve Connell/Transgraphic
Dark Passage logo by Mike Reddy

Printed in the USA

Library of Congress Cataloging-in-Publication Data

Nersesian, Arthur.
  Gladyss of the hunt / Arthur Nersesian.
     pages cm
   ISBN 978-1-891241-39-0 (pbk.)—ISBN 978-1-891241-99-4 (e-book)
   1. Detectives—New York (State)—New York—Fiction. 2. Serial murder investigation—Fiction. I. Title.
PS3564.E67G53 2014
813'.54—dc23
                         2013047864

Come now, son, you must understand what sort of island this is. No mariner approaches it by choice, since there is no anchorage or port where he can find a gainful market or a kindly host. This is not a place to which prudent men voyage.

—Sophocles, *Philoctetes*

CHAPTER ONE

Bernie Farrell wasn't one of the nineteen who died the night Sandy hit Staten Island. In fact he survived nearly a month after that lethal storm surge. He'd been in bad shape when he retired, because of injuries he'd suffered on the job, and since he was too damn bullheaded to get proper treatment, let alone physical therapy, I'm sure his health had declined further over the years. Reports indicated that for three excruciating weeks after the storm he had camped out in his ramshackle home in New Dorp Beach without electricity, a charged cell phone, or any kind of heat, foraging for whatever food he could find. Apparently he became isolated toward the end. I still don't know why he ever moved out of his spacious, rent-controlled Manhattan apartment—or how he wound up down there, in the middle of nowhere. No one I knew kept in touch, let alone visited him. Still, you couldn't feel sorry for him. I'm sure he wanted it that way. Even his immediate neighbors seem to have avoided him. His body was finally discovered when a FEMA housing inspector, after repeated attempts to check for damage, peeked below his window shade, past the can filled with empty liquor bottles, and saw his legs splayed out on the filthy kitchen floor.

I wish I could've cried for him. I should've felt bad, but after the Blonde Hooker case we went our separate ways, and I was in an awful place. A self-help book I read on depression at the time said it was important to avoid triggers, so I put a big red traffic cone in front of him and everyone else who'd been involved in the whole affair.

Shortly after hearing of Bernie's death—during the family New Year's Eve party, before I could welcome in 2013—I had a major falling out with my bipolar brother. It wasn't so much the fight that bothered me, it was realizing how bad things had gotten. That night I did something I never do—I went home and got seriously drunk. And that was when I found myself carefully piecing together the whole fucked-up mess that had begun almost a decade earlier. Ultimately it really was all Eddie O'Ryan's fault.

We were both rookies, and after graduating from the police academy O'Ryan and I had been dumped into the Neighborhood Stabilization Unit attached to the One-Four in Midtown South. It wasn't a bad area, but crowd control on Times Square during New Year's Eve of 2003 was stressful enough—everyone was still waiting for that next big terrorist attack.

Afterwards, in his studio apartment, we had our own little count-down and popped the cork on a small bottle of champagne. Though Eddie was a little bland, he had rugged good looks and at work he always had my back. The single detail I found most appealing about him was the fact that he was taller than me—at six foot two, I found it difficult to find men I could look up to. He wasn't a bad kisser and the mood was perfect.

Slowly clothes came off: my shirt, bra, pants, panties. His fingers migrated subtly southward. I had made up my mind to finally get it over with. Quickly we moved from his tiny sofa to his king-size bed, a shiny brass affair that looked like some kind of sexy chariot. As his giant spear rose over me, I started backing away nervously.

"This is actually my first time," I confessed.

"First time at what?"

"*It!*"

"Gladyss, are you kidding me!"

"I wish I were."

"Wow! Not many virgins around nowadays," he murmured.

"Why don't I . . ." He slithered down and proceeded to lick me where I was already wet enough. I told him that now I was ready for the kill, and reached down to find that he had gone soft.

Suddenly my cellphone chimed. My brother Carl calling from California. Back then, he was the only person I'd always pick up for.

"Why don't we take a break?" I suggested, since O'Ryan obvi-ously needed a moment. I hadn't spoken to Carl in a while and fig-ured he just wanted to quickly wish me a Happy New Year. As Eddie headed into the bathroom, my brother launched into his rant of the day about "Bush's rape of Iraq." Soon I heard the toilet flush, and the door opened.

"You're going to feel foolish when they *do* find Saddam's cache," I told Carl.

"Who?" O'Ryan mouthed.

Since my wallet was on the side table I held it up, showing him the plastic window with a photo of my brother and I hugging. O'Ryan took the wallet out of my hand and gasped at it in amazement. He had never seen or met my twin, though I had told him about Carl's anti-war sentiments.

"Is he back on his 'leave it to the UN' spiel?"

I didn't respond. It was best just to let Carl exhaust himself, then I could say goodbye and O'Ryan and I could get back to the business at hand. But my would-be lover shouted out: "If Saddam really had nothing to hide, he'd just give the weapons inspectors full access!"

"Let me speak to that guy," said Carl.

Within seconds, O'Ryan had my cell pressed to his face and the two were going back and forth about Iraq's nuclear capabilities. "Saddam was within six months of weapons-grade production back in '91!" O'Ryan yelled.

I vowed never to answer my brother's calls again. I should've expected this. As twins, the closest thing Carl and I had to a psychic bond was his uncanny ability to call me at the worst possible moments. And yet I'd always answer—perhaps because he always seemed distressed.

I don't remember falling asleep that night, but when I woke up early the next morning O'Ryan was passed out next to me, snoring loudly. When I delicately tried to revive him, he only rolled to the far side of the bed. For a couple of fidgety hours I tried to go back to sleep. Eventually, unable to get past his kazoo-like snoring, I quietly dressed and went home.

Later that day I decided that my continued virginity was officially Carl's fault. I left a message on Eddie's voice mail apologizing for tiptoeing out, adding that I had New Year's chores awaiting me. I expected that he would quickly call me back, and we'd pick up where we left off, but the call never came. In fact, though I saw him every day at work, over the days and weeks that followed he didn't say a single word about the aborted act—it was as if the evening had never happened. I finally called Carl and complained about his phone call interruptus. Without apologizing, he said, "You know, this is exactly what I suspected would happen. I knew you'd go out and do something crazy on New Year's Eve, and I was right!"

"Give me a break! You're not my father!"

"No, I'm your older brother and . . ." He took a deep breath. "And you don't need to rush into this, is all I'm saying."

"I'm not rushing! I'm the last virgin in this city and Eddie O'Ryan happens to be a really good guy. We work together."

"That's no reason to jump in the sack with him."

"We get along. In fact, he's my most compatible sign—a Scorpio."

"Trust me, I saved you from getting stung by a scorpion!" he said, compelling me to hang up on him.

Some winters New York got off easy, but that year it was unforgivably cold. In fact if it hadn't been so damn cold, I probably would've requested a new assignment and a new partner, but the frost seemed to freeze all insecurities. With wind chills hitting minus ten, it was all I could do just to stay on the job. This was before we knew that global warming meant manic cold as well as hot weather. After a barrage of storms that dropped over four feet of snow in a single month, everything froze into mini glaciers. I'd always get a thrill when I heard that alternate side of the street parking had been suspended—it meant a day I didn't have to write tickets. Unfortunately, those days were few.

I was in the habit of grabbing a venti cup of Starbucks chai when I started my morning tour. Usually I'd spot a violation before I was halfway through drinking it, and I'd have to toss the remainder so I could write the ticket. That day, still feeling a little sleepy, I made the mistake of ordering a coffee. As if that wasn't bad enough, I was able to down the entire twenty ounces without writing a single ticket and I soon found myself in desperate need of a bathroom. The only sanitary establishment on Forty-second between Ninth and Tenth was an expensive restaurant called DiCarlo's, and I was pleasantly surprised to see it was open that early. I went in and asked the maitre d' if I could use their facilities. She pointed to the rear.

As I headed back there, I overheard a waiter addressing the place's only customer: "Sir, I truly regret having to ask, but cigarette smoking in New York restaurants is no longer permitted."

When I returned a couple minutes later, I heard the maitre d' saying, "I'd hate to have to ask you again . . ."

"All right, just one autograph."

Now that my eyes had adjusted to the dark room, I realized the customer in question was none other than motion picture star Noel Holden, sitting in a corner booth. Of all the celebrities in the pantheon of tabloid gods, he was the one my next door neighbor Maggie was most obsessed with. She had clipped photos of him from various magazines and taped them around the mirror above her armoire.

"It's the cigar, sir," the maitre d' replied. "I believe the waiter just explained—"

"The waiter only said *cigarette* smoking was prohibited."

"No smoking is allowed of any kind," the maitre d' said politely.

"Look, this is a hundred dollar cigar." Holden held it up. "I can't just put it out."

"We're in the process of getting a smoking van that will be parked out front," she told him. "Right now though, all we have is a Bloomberg bucket near the front door."

Restaurant smoking was the first casualty of the new mayor's health crusade, which would eventually lead to the banning of trans fats in restaurants and the creation of a city-wide bike system.

"It's twenty degrees below outside. Let me just have a minute and…" He took another thick puff.

"Either put out the cigar right now or I'll write you a ticket," I said, stepping in. Technically it was the job of the Cabaret Unit to monitor illegal smoking, but I owed the maitre d' a favor.

"This cigar probably cost more than your ticket," Holden said, looking me over. "But if you're leaving, I'll go with you and smoke it outside."

"Fair enough," I replied, staring back at him. His zero-fat body and aching good looks were a genuine anomaly. A couple hundred years ago, such absurd perfection would've gotten him shunned as a freak.

"You know, I have an even better idea," he said. "Why don't I put out the cigar and you join me for an early lunch?"

"Because I'm on duty."

He stood up and escorted me outside, then—despite the fact that he was wearing only a light sports jacket—followed me into the arctic chill.

I suppose I should've been flattered, but I knew from Maggie's constant chatter about him that Holden was already involved with someone. a surgically enhanced airhead heiress called Venezia Ramada. She had worked briefly as a fashion model, but her breasts were so salined up that they crowded the return lane on the catwalk. Recently she'd completed her first movie—with co-star Noel Holden.

"How about a quick drink?" he persisted as he followed me up the frozen block. "A wholesome cup of cocoa. What do you say?"

"I'm on duty, sir."

"Surely an Amazonian princess like you can do anything you want."

O'Ryan must've spotted us leaving the restaurant. Sneaking up behind us, he suddenly shoved the actor up against a closed storefront. The icy sidewalk forced Holden to grab hold of O'Ryan to regain his balance, at which point O'Ryan slipped backwards on the ice and fell right on his ass.

"I'm so sorry," the actor said, unable to avoid a snicker as he extended a hand. "I'm Noel Holden."

Slapping it away, O'Ryan sprang to his feet and yelled, "I know who you are, asshole! That doesn't give you the right to harass a police officer!"

"Pardon?"

"It's okay," I told O'Ryan.

"If you *ever* disrespect a cop again," O'Ryan said, shoving his long index finger into the man's pretty face, "I don't care *who* you are."

"Was I disrespecting you, my dear?" the handsome one asked me innocently. Of course he wasn't, but I couldn't say that. You were supposed to back up your partner. I simply turned away and walked east. O'Ryan followed.

Female civilians are constantly flirting with male cops—I couldn't count how many times I'd seen O'Ryan enjoying this—but when a guy did it, apparently it was harassment. Nearly a month had passed since Eddie's failed deflowering of me, and he still hadn't so much as mentioned it.

It wasn't until we turned down Ninth Avenue that I finally said, "What the hell is your problem, Eddie?"

"It's just—I thought he was coming on to you."

"What if he was?"

He looked away, red-faced. "I saw you coming out of that restaurant with him trailing you," he said contritely, "and I thought you might be in trouble."

"Did I look like I was trouble?"

"What were you doing in there anyway?"

"I had to use the goddamn bathroom."

We proceeded silently down Ninth Avenue, searching for quality-of-life violations or anything that might put the awkwardness behind us.

"Help! Police!" we heard as we reached the corner of Thirty-fifth Street.

We turned to see our sergeant grinning at us from his patrol car. Warm air seeped from his half-lowered window as he asked, "So which one of you wants your first big murder case?"

"What do you mean?" O'Ryan asked.

"I got a crime scene needs protecting." Sgt. McKenner said.

Security guard work. O'Ryan didn't say anything, so I said, "I'll take it."

O'Ryan often bragged about his pals in City Hall and was hoping for some big administrative appointment in the Mayor's office sooner or later. He had offered to take me with him when it came through, but back then all I wanted was to be in homicide. Still, he usually would've fought to be on a murder scene, so I figured he was trying to make amends.

"Pick up some lunch. You're going to be there a while."

"Where?"

"The Templeton, southeast corner of Forty-second and Ninth."

"We just passed there." The hotel was half a block east of the pricey restaurant where I had just peed. It was a dive.

"The body was called in this morning, but the murder probably took place last night," the sergeant explained. "I need you to go and relieve the first on the scene."

I grabbed another tea on the way. Rookies always caught the jobs no one else wanted. We were constantly being tossed into line-ups or watching investigation sites. And if we were lucky, we occasionally guarded a murder scene.

Several police cars were parked out front of the Templeton. In the lobby was a sloppily dressed clerk who silently pointed to the metal gate to his right. When I went over to it, he buzzed me in, then I went up a flight of stairs.

The browning wallpaper looked more like flypaper. The lighting was permanently dim, and the floor tiles were worn down or missing altogether.

A yellow ribbon sagged loosely across the end of the second-floor corridor. As I stepped over it, I heard a police radio and traced it to Room 236. A big, middle-aged patrolman named Lenny Lombardi was leaning in the doorway finishing a hotdog.

"What's up?"

"It's the Blonde Hooker thing," he replied. Somebody had killed two prostitutes within the past two months, both of them tall and blonde. I didn't know exactly what had happened, but there were rumors that the murderer had mutilated the bodies horribly.

"So what exactly does he do?"

"Believe me, you don't want to know. And you don't want to go in there." He pointed behind him with his half-eaten hotdog.

"I've seen bodies before," I replied, although actually I had only seen new ones. At that point, childbirths were my one claim to fame. I had driven one bursting mama to Roosevelt Hospital, and on another occasion I'd arrived in the middle of a labor in process and helped in the delivery.

"The killer pulled this one apart limb by limb, numbered the pieces, then taped her back together." An annoying strand of sauerkraut was hanging from Lenny's large right cheek.

"Numbered her?" Inside I could only see the back of one of the gloved and masked CSU investigators. He was on his hands and knees, going over the worn carpet with a lint brush. Since the window was open and it was about thirty degrees, he had kept his Northern Exposure parka on. The other technician had Crime Scene

Unit printed on the back of his jacket, and was dusting the end table for fingerprints. Their metallic suitcases were open in the corner of the room.

When I took a step inside the room, I saw the vic. With her blood-splattered arms and legs thrust in the air, it looked as if she'd died in the Happy Baby yoga pose. I couldn't understand how the limbs were defying gravity until one of the forensic people moved away. Several tight coils of transparent tape glistened in the sunlight. The tape encompassed the victim's elbows and wound its way up her wrists. A black bracelet with large onyx-like pieces dangled from her left wrist, and between her slightly curled fingers the killer had apparently slipped a business card for some local establishment. Another spiral of tape was wrapped around her knees and connected her ankles. More tape tied her upper and lower limbs together.

Not until I looked closely did I see the full barbarity of the crime. The victim had been raggedly decapitated. Nestled on her abdomen, within the tightly woven confinement of taped-up arms and legs, was her head. I slipped back out to the hallway.

"Anyone know who she is?"

"Pross."

As I watched the technicians dusting the surfaces and the bedside lamp, I asked, "When did they find her?"

"Maid found her this morning," Lenny said.

"No one saw the john?"

"The desk clerk said the girl signed for the room. A guy was with her, but he couldn't even give an age or race," Lenny explained. I knew he was tired of talking about it.

"So whose case is it?"

"Hernandez already came and went." He was one of the precinct homicide detectives.

When a murder occurred, the precinct detectives came first. If it was an isolated killing, as it usually was, it belonged to them. After they ran it through the database, if a preexisting pattern turned up—an open case—they would call for homicide investigators from Manhattan South. They caught everything south of 59th Street.

As he pulled on his scarf and buttoned up his coat, Lenny said, "About ten minutes ago, the guy at the desk was going to send someone up with a chair. I'll remind him on my way out."

I thanked him and he was gone.

When one of the techs finally exited the room, I peeked inside as the other guy was carefully putting away his tools and chemicals and asked if they'd found anything.

"Yeah, a sperm archive of every man born in the last century. I don't think they ever changed the sheets." He nodded toward the body. "No sign our killer had sex with this one, though."

"How old was the victim?" I asked.

"Early twenties," he read from his report. "Blonde hair. Several identifying tattoos that could have been done in prison."

The maid, an older black woman in a torn wool sweater, appeared at the end of the hallway. She was pushing a broom cart out of one room, heading toward another.

"Excuse me!" I called, walking over to her. "Are you the one who found the body?"

"Hell yeah, and I'll never forget it. Never saw no one with no head before." She spoke with a faded island dialect. "And some policeman took my fingerprints, but I was telling them, I didn't do nothing wrong."

"They'll just be elimination prints, to make sure we can rule you out. Did anyone interview you?"

"Yeah, some guy with a bushy mustache." That was Hernandez. "Oh, and the cop who was just here. He took my name and the name of a tenant who's lived down the hall a long time."

"Did you ever see the victim before, when she was alive?" I inquired. I wasn't supposed to question anyone, but I was alone and I had time to kill.

"Yeah, I told the other officer. She came here from time to time."

"Are you sure?"

"Yeah. I remembered her 'cause she tipped me once, when the room was a real mess."

"How'd you know it was her?"

"The cop let me look at her face," she said. "I remembered her tattoo."

"What tattoo?"

"She had a tiny tear drop near her eye." I had noticed it.

"So when was the last time you saw her?"

"A month or so ago, I guess. I don't really remember. The old desk clerk, Sam, he used to have deals with some of the girls."

"What kind of deals?"

"He'd give the girls a room, just for an hour or so. After a guest checked out, but before I'd clean them. He died a while back, before the big sweep. Maybe the new guy does it now."

"Would you recognize any of the johns who were with her in the past?"

"Maybe, if I saw them, but I didn't know her regulars."

"Does this place have any exits other than through the lobby?"

"The fire escape out front," she replied.

Some detective, a young guy in a Gucci knock-off, came in with a uniform cop named Ray. I sensed they were only there for a little sightseeing.

I thanked the cleaning lady, and followed them into the room. The sightseers fell silent when they saw the vic, so I asked them to watch the scene a minute while I dashed out.

I thought there was at least a chance the killer had left some trace behind, on his way to and from the room. Flicking on my Maglite, I pointed it at the floor as I headed down the hallway. Stopping myself, I paused, closed my eyes, and took some quick shallow breaths—a technique I had recently learned that was designed to heighten my awareness. After a moment my heartbeat quickened. I knew I was ready.

I continued to the staircase and looked down all the way to the lobby—nada. I went back up. On the half landing, just above the murder scene, I spotted a double A battery in the corner. Let it be relevant to the case, I thought as I bent over. Almost through sheer force of will, it became a tube of lipstick. When I rolled it up, and saw the color was bright orange, I realized I had stopped willing too soon. It didn't quite match the color worn by the victim. Still, I held it by its edge as I returned to the room.

"We gotta dash," one of the sightseeing cops said when I returned.

An old wooden folding chair was now leaning against the hallway wall. I opened it, unlidded my cold tea, and waited for the Johnny-come-lately from Homicide South.

Ten minutes later a surprisingly young guy showed up, a cigarette between his yellow teeth and a gold shield dangling from a leather wallet that was wedged in his jacket pocket.

"How's it going?" he greeted me.

"You're a detective?" I asked astonished. With his fuzzy post-adolescent mustache, he couldn't have been much older than me.

"What do we have?"

"I only looked inside," I said, in case he was testing me. "Her head is cut off, and her limbs were taped together."

"Holy shit!" he said, then snapped a photo of the victim from the doorway. "Do we have a name?"

"Not to my knowledge. Seems like she was a hooker."

"So how many murders does this make it?"

"You're the detective, you tell me," I replied. "Are you allowed to smoke in here?"

When he grinned, I realized I hadn't been following proper procedures. I flipped open my memo book and told him that if he wanted to enter the room, he had to sign it first, since I was technically in charge of the scene. I should've gotten the earlier sightseers to do likewise.

"Let me finish my cig first," he said and walked back down the stairs.

It took me a minute or two before I realized he wasn't coming back. Whoever that kid was, he wasn't a detective. Probably a reporter, damn it. They were constantly monitoring police radios.

Twenty minutes later, I heard coughing in the distance. The cough slowly grew louder and was accompanied by an odd thud. Finally a rugged, older man emerged from the stairway, panting for air. He walked with a distinct limp. This guy had detective written all over him.

As soon as he saw me, he nervously planted an unlit cigarette between his lips.

"My fucking foot is killing me."

"Who exactly are you?" I asked.

He took his wallet from his pocket and flipped open his gold shield. "Detective Sergeant Bernie Farrell. Is the rest of the squad here?"

"Just me, sir."

"Who are you again?"

"Officer Chronou."

"First name, dear heart?"

"Gladyss, with two esses."

"Tell me no reporters came by, Gladyss."

"Actually this young guy just came by . . . He said he was a detective, but he kept asking me questions."

"Make me glad, Gladyss with two esses, and tell me he didn't snap a picture."

"He took a picture."

"Shit! Exactly what does 'protect the crime scene' mean to you?"

"I'm really sorry, sir," I said.

"No, I shoulda told . . . See, some asshole reporter got ahold of the mugs of the last vic, as well as the crime scene of the first vic, and has been running stories on the case."

Detective Farrell went over and stared down at the body. He hung his hand forward and pursed his lips like a gargoyle. "Shit," he said. He walked around the room until he came to the window, then stared up at the surrounding buildings silently for several long minutes.

"Why don't you warn him off?" I said, if only to awaken him.

"We tried, but there wasn't a byline on the stories, they were just credited to a special correspondent," Farrell said. "And surprise, surprise, the newspaper's editor refused to reveal their sources."

"The real fear," he continued, "is that killers sometimes like to return to the scene of the crime. And this killer does this whole weird human sculpture thing."

"I remember this guy's face pretty clearly."

"Well, he probably *isn't* the murderer. The killer is obviously smart, or we would've caught him by now. And this murder officially makes him a serial killer."

"This is the third?"

"The third that we know of, but I wouldn't be surprised if there are others we don't know about. Look at this weird shit." He pointed to the corpse.

"They're all tall with blonde hair."

"Maybe his ex was tall?"

"I think the reason he looks for tall gals is because of this whole structure he makes." He pointed to the bound limbs. "He wants them nice and erect."

"She's holding a card in her hand."

"Yeah, the last one had an expired Metrocard, and some tacky bracelet on her other wrist, too—but it really varies here." He pointed to the poor woman's skull. "In the first murder, he moved the head up over there, and he carved the number 9 on the vic's forehead. The second one, he cut the number 2 on her forehead and put the head over there." He pointed to the right.

"It's like some perverse work of art, isn't it?"

"Shit! I definitely should've had this joint staked out."

"How could you know he'd bring her here?"

"It's one of the only three places he *could've* brought her."

"Isn't this area loaded with fleabag hotels?"

"Not anymore. Everything's either been zoned or priced up. Ten, fifteen years ago you could rent rooms by the trick, screw, strangle, and be out in twenty. But all the streetwalkers and car johns have moved online or up to Hunts Point."

"I've seen streetwalkers around here," I said.

"Yeah, you still get a few desperadoes along Lex—but all our vics are from escort services. And the hotels around here are strictly all-night affairs. Some of the rooms are three, four times the price of the girl. But aside from being one of the cheapest, this crap-ass dive is one of the last three hotels in the area that doesn't even have a video setup in the lobby."

He let out a big sigh and muttered, apparently to himself. "Fuck, Bert would've had them all staked out—at least for a week after the last girl. Course, he had the power to authorize that and I don't."

"Someone must have seen something."

"The clerk here said he had no recollection of the john, just the girl. We were luckier at the last scene. The clerk there clearly remembered the vic *and* her john."

The detective pulled out a creased sketch that looked eerily similar to the one I remembered of the Unabomber. He could've been anywhere from forty to sixty, and wore dark sunglasses and a loose hoodie.

"How'd he pay for the room?'

"A stolen credit card that didn't lead anywhere."

"So what now?"

"Well, now he's going to have to leave his hunting ground—'cause we're going to be waiting for him in all the old familiar places."

Looking at his wristwatch, Farrell said, "The medical examiner is still at a murder scene up in East Harlem. After he's been here and checked out this body, you can call the morgue to come collect her. Then it's the ME's job. You can seal up the room."

"No one's going to relieve me?"

"You're on a regular daytime shift, right?

"Yes, sir."

"We'll be done by the end of your shift."

Hopefully I could still make my evening yoga class.

The detective snapped on a pair of latex gloves, took out his notebook, and started scribbling notes as he walked carefully around the room. Finally he took out a magnifying glass and inspected the floor.

"This guy must've used a fucking drop cloth," the detective said. "Forensics told me, but I had to see it for myself. Except for right here, there ain't a drop of blood."

"Wouldn't a lot of blood have pumped out when he decapitated her?"

"Not when they're already dead," Bernie replied. "This guy drugs them, strangles them, and then beheads them. That's a lot of time and energy."

"What does he slip them, roofies?"

"Nah, you only use roofies if you want to keep them alive, and he doesn't want to screw them. He gives them some cheap over-the-counter shit, then once they're nodding off, he strangles them with his hands."

After a moment he asked, "So how long you been out of the academy?"

"Six months."

"So you're still a proby."

"Yes, sir," I replied. Then I asked him back, "Do you always work on your own, sir?"

"My squad was here earlier; they're supposed to come back soon. I had the same partner for nearly twenty years. Bert died recently."

I suddenly remembered. "Oh! I might've found a clue."

I showed him the lipstick I'd found on the stairs. "It doesn't match anything she's wearing, but I thought it might possibly be evidence."

Still wearing his latex gloves, he carefully took the lipstick.

"But you found this outside the room?"

"Yes."

21

"You're a crazy little go-getter, aren't you? I like that."

He tossed the lipstick into the trash. "There's a reason we have a crime scene. You can go crazy if you start on an endless scavenger hunt. Unless of course you find a gun. Those are always keepers."

"Sorry." I'd hoped that my Kundalini had finally been turned on.

"Most cops are fat and lazy, so you get points for trying."

"You said the other victims were all blondes?"

"Yeah, why?"

"And this girl's pretty tall."

"Even without her head," he joked.

"So he must be calling escort services and asking for tall blondes."

"You figured that out, did you?"

"I'm a tall blonde," I said.

"Chronou," he read my name plate. "What are you, Greek?"

"Yeah, why?"

"Greeks are usually brunette."

"Not necessarily. If you read histories of ancient Greece, they are usually described as a blonde race."

"But how do I know you're a natural blonde?" he said, sliding his unlit cigarette back into the pack.

"Does this look like a dye job?" I said, plucking off my hat and ear warmers.

"I don't know how he knows," the detective said earnestly, "but with all the vics, the carpet has always matched the drapes."

I wasn't sure if he was kidding me, so I didn't say anything. When I saw the helpful maid passing by, I introduced her to Detective Farrell without making eye contact with him.

"You look familiar," Farrell said. "I never hauled you in for anything, did I?"

"No sir."

He gave her a slight grin and thanked her for her help, then turned back to me.

"So how'd you like a juicy ninety-day assignment?" he asked.

"Sure," I shot back.

The PBA had a rule that cops couldn't get temporary transfers to homicide for longer than 90 days, because these short assignments rarely led to promotions. Still, it was a chance to get my foot in the door.

"Prove to me you're a natural blonde and the assignment's all yours," he said.

I lifted my right leg, yanked up the cuff of my pants along with my long johns, and showed him the two-week growth of yellowish stubble on my upper calf.

"I ain't showing you my carpet, but you can see my welcome mat."

The detective broke out laughing.

"A female cop who shaves her legs that infrequently deserves to be brought in from the cold."

It crossed my mind that if he did get me a transfer, I'd have a conflict. I was scheduled to have laser surgery on my eyes in little more than a month, to fix my nearsightedness. An eye-glassectomy, as my neighbor Maggie called it. But I'd only be out of action for a day or so.

Detective Sergeant Bernie Farrell wrote down my name and badge number, and asked why my first name had two esses instead of one. I explained that it was an old Welsh spelling.

"I thought you were Greek."

"I am. My mom named me after an old family friend."

Two other detectives from Farrell's squad came by, a rotund black man and a slim white woman, both in their forties. He quietly reviewed several points with them and they all left together.

Over the next hour or so, several other cops dropped in to see the murder scene. I copied down their names and badge numbers. Toward the end of the shift, O'Ryan finally made an appearance.

"So this is your big murder case?" he asked, peeking inside.

"Guess what?" I said. "The lead detective said he was going to consider me for a ninety-day homicide assignment."

"Whose case is it?"

"Detective Farrell's."

"Burnout Farrell!" He burst out laughing. "Oh, you drew the short straw on this one!"

"Why?"

He carried on chuckling like I had just been pranked.

"Aside from the rumor that he killed his partner, he is one nasty SOB."

"What do you mean he killed his partner?"

"The guy had some lingering disease, and Farrell was the last to see him alive at the hospital."

"As long as he wasn't shot in the back."

"Anyway, they might give you a thirty-day, but that's it."

"Hey, thirty days in homicide is fine."

O'Ryan looked closely at the body. Probably because we were amateurs at this, we talked like seasoned detectives. I relayed what I'd seen and what I'd been told, and we hypothesized about the killing just as they had taught us in the academy.

"If he didn't screw her, why'd he kill her here?" O'Ryan said, trying to get inside the killer's head. I shrugged. "It'd be so much easier to pick her up in a car, then he could just dump her body in the river. That's what I would do."

The Caribbean maid appeared in the hallway.

"Where's that other guy?" she asked.

"What other guy?"

"That older guy that was here with you."

"He left."

"I saw him with her before, that's why I'm asking."

O'Ryan gave me a funny look and asked her, "You saw the lead detective with the victim on a previous occasion?"

"Yes sir."

"When?"

"A few weeks ago. They were in here together."

"Are you sure?"

"Pretty sure. Game leg. Smoker's hack. He was pretty rough with her, too."

"Lucky he didn't recognize you," O'Ryan said.

"He probably did. That's why he asked me if I had a criminal record. He was trying to 'timidate me."

"Was he *with* her?" O'Ryan asked.

"What do you mean?"

"Was the detective her john?"

She shrugged.

"Was he alone or with another cop?" I asked.

"You know what? Maybe I'm wrong. Forget it," she said nervously and left.

If she was right, I thought, that could account for Farrell's weird reaction on seeing the victim's body.

"Most detectives look like johns, though." O'Ryan always defended cops automatically. "And there are a lot of vindictive people in this job."

"Believe me," I said staring at him with arched brows, "I know."

"Listen," O'Ryan said slightly jerkily. "I'm sorry about earlier today."

"You should be."

"Hey, if he was just another guy, I wouldn't have said anything, but I read enough gossip columns to know Holden's a real sleazebag."

"Like what, exactly?"

"Like he slept with the director's fiancée! And the guy was supposedly his best friend."

The ME finally showed up and began his examination of the body. If it had taken him this long to get here during the worst of the summer heat, it would've been decomposed by now. Feeling self-conscious, O'Ryan checked his watch and said he'd better get back to work.

Half an hour later, when the ME was done and was signing the paperwork, I radioed for the morgue. The ME left, and twenty minutes later the meat wagon arrived and took all the parts of the ravaged body away, leaving a bloody spot in the middle of the carpeted floor, where the killer had evidently done all his cutting. I carefully sealed the room with a BY ORDER OF THE NYPD sticker, and locked the door, taking the key with me.

CHAPTER TWO

I told the Templeton clerk that the room was off limits until further notice and stepped out into the freezing air. I stood still for a minute and began taking deep, lucid breaths. Just as the Renunciate had taught me, it felt like water filling my lungs. I thought about the poor Jane Doe I'd spent the whole day watching, wondering how her entire life had somehow led her to that awful room that she wouldn't leave alive. Continuing to breathe from my abdomen, I focused on the thought that my entire purpose was to find her killer. Then I looked across the street and saw a slim, handsome guy who was checking me out. As he stepped under a street light, I couldn't believe what I was seeing: Noel Holden, megastar, was just standing on the northwest corner of Forty-second and Ninth, grinning at me like an idiot.

I remembered O'Ryan shoving him that morning and smiled, slightly embarrassed. He started crossing the street toward me. As he approached, I wondered what the odds were of running into the same Hollywood hulk twice in one day.

"Forgive me if I was rude earlier. And please allow me to properly introduce myself. I'm Noel Holden." He extended his hand.

"Gladyss Chronou," I replied, although part of me wanted to ask him something—like if he'd really had sex with Britney Spears, as one gossip column had recently implied. We shook hands briefly and I pulled my coat tightly around me.

"So you're dating that other cop?" he asked.

"No, but..."

"All I was suggesting is that we grab a quick coffee."

If I hadn't spent the whole day looking forward to a late night yoga class, I would've agreed. As a compromise, I said, "I'm walking back to my precinct. Instead of getting coffee, why don't you walk with me and we can talk."

"Sounds good," he replied.

Aside from the novel sensation of being with a celebrity, it struck me as odd that Holden just happened to be lingering outside a murder scene. As Detective Farrell had reminded me, it was something that murderers have been known to do.

As we carefully walked the dark and icy streets to the precinct, he asked me a slew of questions: Where was I born . . . and raised . . . and educated. Did I have a boyfriend . . . a girlfriend? Had I ever dated another girl?

"Why don't we talk about you for a while?" I finally interrupted.

"Sure," he said, and without any further prompting gave a quick rundown of his film and TV work. He didn't say anything about his high-profile romances that were eternally being gossiped about, but I was aware for the first time that juicy tidbits of his life had been slipped into my memory anyway, almost against my will, thanks to the media machine.

And I now had some insight into my neighbor's skittish mind, and even an inkling about how Maggie could be deluded into thinking that just because she had learned intimate details of some celebrities' lives, a sentimental osmosis had mysteriously occurred: She must've thought that they had come to know, and more specifically care, about her.

Finally Noel got to his current endeavor, a crime flick called *Fashion Dogs*. It was his twelfth starring film, he told me; it co-starred Venezia Ramada and was directed by Crispin Marachino. He told me he was meeting the two of them shortly, then talked about his role in the new film.

"Let me get this straight," I said, after listening to his summary of the plot. "You play a male fashion model who is also an undercover cop?"

"He's only an *amateur* model," Noel said earnestly.

"Oh, *that* sounds likely," I said. Cops were notoriously unfashionable.

"Actually, Crispin has got me doing the catwalk for Anton Rocmarni during Fashion Week to publicize the movie."

"Wow."

"I just read in the newspaper that they finally convicted the Green River Killer after all these years," he said out of the blue.

"Yeah, I read about that too."

"He killed forty-eight hookers in the 80s and only just got caught 'cause of DNA testing."

"I heard he pled to forty-nine murders. Did he get sentenced yet?"

"Yeah, it was a plea bargain, life imprisonment." He sounded almost gleeful. "Forty-nine murdered girls and not even the death penalty."

"That is unbelievable." Sentencing in America did frequently seem arbitrary.

"The thing is: forty-nine murders and suddenly he just stops? I mean he hasn't murdered anyone in nearly twenty years." Noel said blithely. "God, he must have been attending Murderers Anonymous meetings to keep from making it a round fifty."

I could've pointed out that the killer actually claimed he'd killed many more than fifty women. Instead I said, "I find it a little distressing that you find that so amusing."

"Come on, this country is obsessed with crime. It's entertainment. *Law & Order* and all those shows are huge. Isn't that one of the reasons you became a cop?"

He had a point.

"Would you mind if I asked you some professional questions?" I asked.

"Like what?"

"Like why were you having lunch at DiCarlo's at nine this morning?"

"It was closer to ten, and I was hungry."

"It looked like you were finishing a dinner."

"You know, as a movie actor I can have all the sex, drugs, and rock & roll that I want, but I can't eat a thing. I basically have to starve myself. But every so often I lose it and go on a binge."

"You're kidding."

"Nope. And this morning I totally lost it."

"Something to share at your Overeaters Anonymous meeting."

"No, all the food comes out of the same hole it goes in, usually within the hour."

"Oh God, really?"

"If you repeat that, I'll deny it."

"What sets off your binges?" I asked.

"Guilt," he said earnestly. "Profound guilt . . . but also they have great food there."

"Guilt over what?"

"Only my priest will ever know that."

"What were you doing across the street just now?"

"Now?"

"Yeah, a few minutes ago, when you saw me. What were you doing there?"

"I just withdrew some money from the ATM on the corner."

"You don't still have the receipt, do you?"

He pulled off a glove and started rummaging through the pockets of his overcoat. Although I was suspicious of him, I was also curious to see how far I could push him before he'd tell me to fuck off. To my surprise he produced the ATM receipt. It was for a two hundred dollar withdrawal, timed about a minute before we met.

"Where were you last night?" I asked, figuring that had to be when the murderer had completed his bloody sculpture.

"On an airplane over the Atlantic, coming back from a shoot in Barcelona."

"What airline? And can you tell me the flight number?" I asked calmly.

"Wow!" he finally burst out laughing. "Am I really a suspect?"

"At this point everyone is," I replied, doing my best Jack Webb.

He smiled, took out his cell phone, and read off all the travel information I asked for while I busily scribbled it all down.

"Now it's my turn," he said. "What crime were you investigating?"

"There was a murder in that hotel you saw me leaving." I said, giving him the bare outline.

"I didn't even know it was a hotel."

A chirping sound indicated someone was trying to call him. Taking out his cell phone, he stepped toward the streetlight and told the caller exactly where he was. Now his face was brightly lit, I could see a faint scratch on his chin. It might have happened during his tussle with O'Ryan this morning—or maybe it had been inflicted by the victim? He chatted softly for a minute then flipped his phone closed.

"I know this sounds awful," he said, "but Crispin and Venezia are right around the corner, and we're supposed to go to the North Pole."

"Where's that?" I asked.

When he pointed uptown, I realized he was referring to *the* North Pole.

"I thought you were talking about some new dance club."

"It's a good name for one. I'll have to tell my club promoter friend."

"Why are you going there?"

"Advance publicity shots for *Fashion Dogs*."

"The North Pole?"

"Yeah, and then about half a dozen cities in Europe. I get back next Monday for a big pre-premiere party that the E.P. is throwing. Would you accompany me?"

"Aren't you dating Venezia Ramada?"

"Not really."

"I read you that two were a hot item."

"She'll be here in a moment," he said. "You can ask her yourself. Bear in mind that most of my life is little more than a publicity stunt. But here's a scoop"—he spoke very slowly as though to underscore that this was reality—"Movie star Noel Holden is asking you on a date."

"How very *Notting Hill*."

"Come on," he pleaded. "You can keep trying to figure out if I killed that lady."

"Who said the vic was a woman?"

"You got me!" he said, putting his wrists together as though I were going to cuff him, "And I'm glad you did, otherwise I never would've met you."

Two beautiful teenage girls who'd just walked past us suddenly stopped, conferred, then raced back to Noel, asking for a photo with him. One of them had a cellphone with a camera built into it—the first I had seen.

What made me finally relent and agree to see him again was the strange, admittedly remote notion that I might actually be talking to another in a growing group of celebrity killers. He had been in the area of the murder today; he might have had the opportunity, depending on how his flight details checked out, the time of death, and so on; and he seemed to have a fetishistic knowledge of serial murders.

It wasn't always that easy to verify a suspect's alibi; prints and DNA were much more reliable. Somehow I needed to get a sample of Noel's gorgeous hair and his fingerprints, or until we caught this guy I'd keep wondering if the matinee idol was our man.

"It's going to be a blast," he said, referring to the "pre-premiere" party he'd just invited me to.

"Okay, but I have to be in bed by eleven—alone."

"In that case I'll pick you up at seven."

"Fine."

A bright red Lincoln Town Sedan pulled up at the corner of Thirty-sixth and Ninth and started honking. We walked over to it. A smaller, uglier version of Noel was sitting in the back seat. Crispin Marachino.

"And there they are," Noel said. "Can we drop you off somewhere?"

"I'm already there," I said, pointing down the block. Abruptly a shaggy blond creature stuck her large bright head out the car window. Just as Noel had said, it was the shameless heiress Venezia Ramada.

"So where exactly do you live?" he asked, "Can I pick you up for the party?"

Instead of giving him my address, I said I'd meet him on the southwest corner of 16th Street and Sixth Avenue.

"You'll be picked up in one of these silly cars," he said pointing to the Lincoln.

"Who's the dominatrix?" asked the unattractive director from the back seat.

"This is Police Detective Gladyss. She's coming as my date to Miriam's party," Noel said.

"You're a stunner," Crispin shot back. "Want to be in my next film?"

"No, but I have a neighbor . . ."

"Where'd you get that get-up?" Venezia interrupted.

"I wear it for work."

"Shit, you're a real cop?"

"Have you ever had to draw your gun?" Crispin asked earnestly.

"No, but I sketched a knife once," I trotted out the old joke. He looked at me severely, so I gave him a smaller lie. "I just got assigned to homicide and I'm working on my first murder case."

"Who was murdered?" he asked.

"A hooker."

"She was murdered last night at a hotel on Forty-second," Noel pitched in. "Just a few blocks from here."

Crispin's eyes widened and his jaw dropped slightly. "Oh my God! I was just reading about two blonde hookers who were strangled around here over the past month."

"Where'd you read that?" It reminded me of my fear that the fake detective had in fact been a reporter.

"I forget which paper."

" I'll see you next week at Miriam's party," Noel said, trying to wrap things up.

"Wait, you're taking her to Miriam's investors party?" Venezia asked in a little girl voice.

"Unless you're still dating him?" I spoke up, since he'd said I could ask.

"Tell her it's only for appearances," Noel shot back to Venezia.

"I'm carrying his baby," the heiress instantly responded.

Crispin focused an expensive-looking camera on me and quickly snapped a flurry of photos. Noel finally got in the back of the car, said he was looking forward to our date next week, and the whole loony crew sailed away.

I had walked about ten steps when I saw Eddie O'Ryan standing in front of Midtown South, dressed in street clothes, staring at me.

"Did I mention that any man named Noel has got to be a fag?"

"Did you just see me with him?" I asked, happy that someone had witnessed it.

"I was waiting to tell you that I'm sorry," he said. I saw that he was holding a wilted rose.

"You should apologize to him."

"Actually I was talking about the whole New Year's Eve fiasco." It was the first time he had brought it up, but it was a month too late.

"I just don't know why you never called me back."

"Because I felt like an idiot, and I figured a little break wasn't so bad. I was trying to be cautious."

"Well, we still have time," I replied. He was a little awkward, it was true, and every cop I had ever gotten to know seemed to have serious intimacy issues—but O'Ryan was still hot compared to most of them.

"You're not really going on a date with him, are you?" he said, absently handing me the rose.

"Actually, I have reason to suspect he might be the murderer," I explained, as he walked with me toward the precinct.

"Give me a break," O'Ryan said, pausing at the door.

"CSI got prints and hair follicles from the first two crime scenes. I'll just collect some samples and run them. Make sure he wasn't there."

"You should clear it with command first."

"How do you know I haven't already?" I was tired of his authority crap.

He walked away without another word, so I went inside. There I vouchered the key to the hotel room, and the desk sergeant had me fill out an overtime form. Then I changed and headed to the last yoga class of the day.

I had first taken yoga in college and immediately got hooked. Though the practice was thousands of years old, and had been developed by holy men who could never have imagined my crazed existence on the other side of the world, it was perfectly designed to help with the stresses of modern life.

The studio I frequented now was a cozy little hole-in-the-wall place directly across the street from my house, which specialized in an ancient variety of yoga called Kundalini. I had chosen it because of its convenience, but I was a little skeptical about it at first. The guy who ran the place was more like a mystic—a strange, hairy, barefoot creature who looked like he'd escaped from the pages of a Maurice Sendak book. The first time I stepped into his tiny studio, I asked him what Kundalini meant.

"There is an immense reservoir of energy that lies dormant inside each of us," he said intensely. "Most people die without ever even knowing about it. We teach you techniques—exercise, breathing, mantras—to unleash and direct that untapped power."

"What kind of power?"

"The Kundalini is a snake of psychic energy that is coiled at the base of your spine, in your *Abadabado*. When awakened it soars up your body and into your crown chakra."

"So you become like a superman?"

"It's psychic power."

"What do you mean by psychic?" To me the word evoked fortune tellers and con men.

"I can introduce you to people who will gladly testify that after following our practice they've developed enhanced powers in everything from clairvoyance to telekinesis."

"But if I do your yoga, will I work up a good sweat?"

"Absolutely. And our first class is free."

"As long as it keeps me fit," I thought. And after the first, strenuous class, I got a discount for ten more sessions.

To the usual yoga poses and moves my new teacher added a whole regimen of stomach rolls, breathing moves, and strange sways that were intended to awaken my sleeping serpent. During the class, he also gave lengthy instructions on how to direct my consciousness. Since he frequently spoke in broken Sanskrit, I never knew exactly what he was talking about, but as long as I was staying fit I didn't mind.

The guy had some crazy-ass name I could never hope to pronounce, though it sounded like *Oogabooga*. Under a lot of long, twisted hair, he was actually a handsome guy in his late thirties who, I discovered, had one day given up his law practice and his family and devoted himself entirely to eating wilted celery stalks and teaching yoga. Since he truly seemed to have renounced all worldly belongings for the sake of inner peace, I simply thought of him as the Renunciate.

Over the following months, as others joined and left his classes, the Renunciate started focusing on me.

"I feel it," he finally said to me one day.

"Feel what?"

"Your cynicism, radiating like heat. If you chose to leave it at home just once and give us a chance, the Kundalini will be there waiting for you."

"Thanks, but I really just need the workout."

"Kundalini is arguably an evolutionary step for peoplekind. Using mental focus you can gradually learn to unleash the limitless powers of your chakras."

I asked him if he could explain this alleged power again. I never really got a straight answer before.

"You will become a better person in every sense of the word; More courageous, more attuned. You will have access to things that elude most people."

"What things?"

"You'll see people more clearly than they can see themselves."

But it was my neighbor Maggie who really sold it. One day soon afterward, she saw me carrying my sexy rolled-up mat to the little studio across the street and got excited. She said an old friend from acting school had studied Kundalini out in LA and it had really given her the edge in her career.

"What kind of edge?"

She speed-dialed a number on her cell and handed it to me. Like a living infomercial, her friend Jeanine told me how her life had been transformed since she started practicing. Her thoughts were clearer, her perception crisper.

"But it was more than that," she said. "It's as though I'm able to will things to happen."

Now she was getting work consistently. She'd been in a pilot for a sitcom called *Resplendent*, which she was just waiting to get picked up. She knew what casting directors wanted without them even having to ask.

"The real strength of Kundalini is in detecting hidden things," she said.

"I work with criminals who are habitual liars," I explained. "Do you think it could help me there?"

"Faith is always rewarded," she replied simply. "What have you got to lose?"

It still sounded flaky to me, but I figured that since I was paying for the classes anyway, what would it hurt if for once I left the cynicism at home?

After my next yoga class, I waited until everyone had left and asked the Renunciate what exactly I had to do to release my Kundalini.

"Focus on breathing and meditation."

Before my next class, though, I had an encounter with Maggie that undermined my faith in anything she and her loopy actress friend might recommend. She invited me over for some tea, and inevitably we wound up talking about the latest man in her life. When all the tea turned into pee, she ran off to the toilet. Alone at her dining table, I saw a half-written letter sitting off to the side. Glancing at it, I saw it was addressed to the film actor Viggo Mortensen, who'd recently starred in *Lord of the Rings*. Of course I had to read it.

> *Dear Viggo,*
> *Like you, I too am a thespian, so this isn't so much a fan letter as an epistolary salute from one colleague to another. When I first saw you in Indian Runner and later GI Jane, I felt an immediate connection . . ."*

Under it I discovered more letters, addressed to other box office stars, including Noel Holden.

By the time Maggie returned, I had put the letters back in place, but her slightly paranoid mind immediately grasped that I had read them.

"I kind of have a correspondence with Viggo," she said slowly and softly, "as well as several other actors I've met along the way."

"Do any of them ever write you back?"

"Not yet," she said. "But when everyone else forgets them, then they'll write me back."

After watching the crime scene all day, I let loose in class that night. I was trying to remain open to the mystical possibilities of Kundalini, but I was definitely getting a workout. Rolling my abs like a belly dancer I breathed deeply and audibly, sounding like an old vacuum cleaner. I went home bathed in sweat, showered, and prepared myself some dinner, tricolored bow ties in light pesto sauce, with a green salad. While I ate it, I watched a copumentary show called *Case File*, which I preferred to the usual TV cop shows because they covered actual cases.

Three deep low moans and one female gasp came through the wall Maggie's apartment shared with mine.

When I heard her door open a while later, I couldn't resist looking through my peephole at her latest lover. Some hottie I didn't recognize. It was a good sign—reality was slowly weaning her away from her Hollywood fantasy lovers. Ten minutes passed, during which I could envision Maggie washing, dressing, and reapplying makeup—then came her knock at my door.

"So how'd your . . . date go?" I asked, pretending not to have heard a thing. It was like she was getting laid enough for the both of us.

"I hope I wasn't . . . dating too loud." Her face had a post-coital glow.

"Not at all."

"That was Ricky."

I remembered the name. He was a chiseled actor she'd met on the catering circuit, an itinerant bartender. According to Maggie, he wanted to have a relationship with her, but she'd politely told him this went against two of her cardinal rules: She didn't date men who were younger than her, and she definitely didn't date actors—unless they were stars. Fortunately, she found a loophole in her rules: she skipped the dating and just started having sex with him.

"How was your day?" she asked, grabbing my salad fork and picking just the red bow ties off the side of my plate.

"Want some?" I tried to sound sarcastic.

"No, I'm off food for good. Change the subject quick." She kept downing my pasta.

"I guarded a murder scene today."

"Re-e-e-ally?"

The last time I had guarded something it was a public school gym that doubled as a polling station.

"I shouldn't tell you this, but the victim had her head lopped off, and her limbs were all taped together."

"Oh God!" Maggie finally put down the fork.

"And guess who I almost ticketed!"

"Conan O'Brien?"

"Noel Holden."

She froze in disbelief.

"And he was so sexy!"

"Please tell me it was for public urination!" She swore she once saw Richard Gere pee in public.

"Smoking inside DiCarlo's."

She asked me a zillion questions: What was he wearing? How tall was he? How much did he weigh? How did he smell?

"Was he with Venezia?"

"Later. She and Crispin Marachino picked him up."

After five minutes of frantic chitchat, Maggie suddenly checked her watch. She had to see her favorite rope-a-dope reality show—*A Most Singular Man*. I wished her good night and she was gone.

CHAPTER THREE

Early the next morning I awoke to the chirp of my cell phone.

"Tell me again why you think he's a murderer?" a sandpapery male voice asked.

For an instant I thought it was my brother, talking about Saddam. "Who is this?"

"It's Eddie," O'Ryan said. He sounded like he had been up all night.

"Oh, you were probably right." I said tiredly. "I just thought it was weird that he was standing across the street from the crime scene hours later. You know how murderers do that sometimes."

"Did you ask him what he was doing there?"

"Yeah. He said he'd just gone to an ATM machine, and he showed me the receipt."

"So why did it strike you that he could be the killer?"

I couldn't tell anyone about my possibly Kundalini-assisted intuition, so I said: "First I saw him that morning with you outside the restaurant. The body had only just been found a half block away, so he could've killed her just before. And he was having lunch at ten in the morning in an empty restaurant—that struck me as odd, particularly 'cause he mentioned later that he only ate when he felt guilty."

"And what would be his motive for killing the Jane Doe?"

"That I don't know yet. Maybe he's a thrill killer. When we spoke, he couldn't stop talking about the Green Tea murderer."

"The Green *River* murderer," he corrected me.

"Yeah, right. He was totally awestruck by the guy. I mean, he really seemed envious."

"How do you know it was envy? Maybe it was disgust."

"You had to be there. The body language, the tone of his voice . . .

He seemed particularly bewildered by the fact that the guy had simply been able to abruptly stop murdering."

"You mean, he stopped stabbing some girl in the middle of a murder?"

"No, he thought the killer had stopped just before he reached fifty victims."

"Maybe Holden just has a fixation on the guy. Maybe he has OCD."

"No, I'm the one with OCD. He's nuts."

"Did you ask him for an alibi?" O'Ryan said, apparently growing weary of the discussion.

"Actually I did," I replied. "He said he was on a flight back from Barcelona after a film shoot. I wrote down the information somewhere."

"What time do you have to report today?"

"Ten a.m., same as you. Why?"

"Maybe he is the killer," he said. "I mean that would definitely be a career boost."

"How would his being a killer boost his career?"

"No, *our* careers. Businesses will be open at nine, so we have an hour to go to the airline office and check if he was on the flight."

"Why don't we just do it over the phone?"

"Even with a subpoena it's difficult. But if we go to the airline in person, show our shields and use the right balance of charm and grit, we might get lucky."

I sensed he was doing this to get back in my good graces while casting Noel as a villain, but I was okay with that. I still had hopes for O'Ryan. And if displaying jealousy for the movie actor was the closest I could get to a show of affection from him, so be it.

Within an hour, I was showered, dressed and had my contacts in. O'Ryan rang my downstairs bell just as I was ready to go. I Starbucked a cup of chai, and roughly thirty minutes later we walked up to the counter of Iberian Airlines in Rockefeller Center just as they opened. O'Ryan's sanctimonious manner created a stronger impact, so I let him lead. He asked the clerk if they'd had reservations in the name of Noel Holden on an incoming flight from Barcelona a few days earlier. The clerk took us over to his supervisor. Again we showed our shields and O'Ryan explained our request.

The supervisor clicked his mouse for a moment until the right screen came up, then he said, "We have a first class reservation for a Noel Holden on a red eye flight from Madrid dated two days ago. And it says that he used the ticket."

"I thought you said Barcelona?" O'Ryan said. I shrugged.

"Do you know Mr. Holden?" I asked Mr. Rodriguez.

"The Hollywood actor?"

"Yes."

"I'm wondering if any staff member can confirm that they actually saw him on the plane or leaving the airport that morning?"

He sighed and said the home numbers of airline personnel were confidential.

"This is a murder investigation," O'Ryan said sternly.

"It would just take a simple phone call to ask one of the flight attendants if they remembered seeing him on the plane," I said delicately. "We don't want to have to bring anyone downtown for interrogation."

The supervisor ran his mouse around its black pad until a list of phone numbers appeared. He dialed a number, then listened a minute, hung up, and dialed a second number. I figured he was getting voicemails. After he dialed the third number, I heard him speak softly in Spanish, then he handed me the phone.

"Hola señora," I began in my awful high school Spanish.

"Alicia speaks fluent English," he assured me.

I introduced myself and asked if she remembered yesterday's red-eye from Madrid to New York.

"What about it?"

"Did you handle first class?"

"Yes. Why?"

"Do you remember Noel Holden being on the plane?"

"Who?"

"You know, the actor Noel Holden?"

"I don't really follow actors," she said softly.

"Who was the last celebrity you do remember serving?" I asked testing to see if she was deliberately withholding information.

"Officer, I've been up for forty hours over the last two days. I have to be ready in two hours to do a six-hour flight, so unless you have any questions that I *can* answer, I'd really like to get back to sleep."

I thanked her and handed the phone back to the supervisor. We thanked him and made it back to the precinct just in time for roll call.

As we patrolled the icy streets of upper Chelsea, we had an on-and-off conversation about the possibility of Noel Holden's guilt.

"Even though I think it's highly unlikely that he killed anyone, you can't eliminate him until you find a witness who puts him on that plane," O'Ryan said. "Perhaps you can call someone in Spain who was involved in the production."

"No," I replied. "We're already pushing it. If just one of those airline people calls the precinct, we'll both be in hot water. And I'll completely blow any chance of getting the homicide assignment."

"Do you know what the odds are you'll even get a thirty-day spot?" he said, needling me.

"I'm a tall blonde," I explained. "just like the three vics."

"Oh, right—and it would never occur to them to get a seasoned female detective and put a blonde wig on her."

"Yeah, but they don't have anyone who is already dating a decent suspect," I taunted him. O'Ryan nodded his head.

"There really is absolutely no reason he should be a suspect in this case," he said.

"I'm telling you he was *there*, right when I—" I had been about to reveal my Kundalini moment.

"What's his motive? Where is *anything* to tie him to the killing?" he said. "You're just like your idiot brother, you see only what you want to see."

"Don't talk about my brother that way!"

He apologized immediately, so after a moment I added, "How about the fact that Holden likes tall blondes, and that's the profile of all three victims?"

"What tall blondes does he like?"

"Me," I pointed out. "He asked me on a date."

"And that explains motive too," he added. "'Cause if all the victims were half as annoying as you—"

"Call me obsessive," I interrupted, "but I'm going to a party with Holden when he gets back to town. I'll get his prints and then we'll know for sure."

"What is this date anyhow?"

"A big investors party thrown by one of his producers."

"This all sounds really dumb."

"I'm doing it."

"The man definitely has a history of scumbaggery, and that director he hangs with, that Crispin character, is by all accounts even worse," O'Ryan said emphatically. "And you're doing it as part of an unofficial murder investigation, which means it's not only potentially dangerous, it's grounds for disciplinary action."

"Hey, you helped me, so you'd be up on charges too," I pointed out.

"And I was wrong to do it," he declared. "But it ends here."

"What?"

"Just suppose he *is* the murderer?"

"We'll know once I get his prints."

"Then I'll go with you as back-up."

"Back-up?" I asked. "I'm supposed to be his *date*. We're going to a party at his friend's house. And he knows what you look like. And he hates you."

"Just keep your cell phone on, and I'll be in a car downstairs. If there are any problems, I'll come up."

"No way!"

"Well I'm sorry, but I'm not letting you do this alone," he replied.

"You're not *letting* me?" I couldn't believe what I was hearing. "What exactly do you think you're going to do?"

"I'll report you. I'll call Farrell and tell him what you're doing." Typical macho control shit.

"I can't believe you'd even consider . . ." My anger paralyzed me, and I couldn't say another word.

"Look, I care about you, as your friend as well as your partner. You can date whoever you want. I fully respect your private life. But you're playing detective now, going undercover on a date with a murder suspect without back-up . . . If I did something like that, I like to think you'd care this much about me."

It was difficult to be angry with him when he put it that way.

"Tell you what," I compromised. "I'll call you before I go on the date, and then after I get home to let you know I'm okay. How's that?"

"You're not going to sleep with him for his DNA sample or something crazy like that?"

"Hell no! How can you ask me that?" He knew I was a virgin, and now he had the gall to imply I was a slut?

"Frankly, since New Year's I've realized I don't know you at all," he said coolly.

"I'll call you before and after," I said, which was more than he had done. "We'll let it go at that."

That evening, after my yoga class, I had intended to ask the Renunciate about my mini-Kundalini moment outside the hotel. I specifically wanted to know if wishing for something positive, something selfless, could actually facilitate realizing that thing. Then I realized I'd never even told him I was a cop, and that it could turn into a much longer, messier talk. I went home and at some point during the fifteen minutes that I listened to Maggie while she ate my salad, I idly asked her what she knew about Crispin Marachino.

"His real name is Chris Maron," she began and proceeded to download his bio from the web site in her brain: "He was a high school dropout who worked as a video store clerk by day and wrote scripts at night. When his mother, who was in the production department at Paramount Pictures, showed one of his scripts to an actor who was big in the 70s, the guy loved it. Marachino agreed to let it go for peanuts, provided he was allowed to direct it. *Crime Noir* was a big hit. Thirty million opening weekend. His second film, *Slim Jim*, broke even; his third film, *Killers In Love*, bombed. Noel Holden had small roles in all three films. Now he's starring in *Fashion Dogs*, which premieres in a few weeks."

"What do you know about Venezia Ramada?"

"Silicone D-cup bimbo. Born Vanessa Ramone. Granddaughter of Ronnie Ramone, the founder of the multinational candy manufacturer. She met Crispin at the Hollywood nightclub Vespers. He proposed to her on the dance floor and decided to make her his next big discovery. Then a month later, on the set of *Fashion Dogs,* she went crazy for Noel Holden."

"Which is probably why she was such a bitch to me."

"Oh God," she said. "You didn't fall in love with Noel, did you? Tell me you didn't!"

"I know this sounds bizarre, but considering O.J. Simpson and Robert Blake . . ."

"Neither of them were found guilty," she shot back before I could finish my thought. Maggie must've been the last kid in class who believed in Santa and the freakin' Easter Bunny. She swore Michael Jackson was repeatedly being framed.

"I'm supposed to go to some party with Noel."

"You what?"

"He invited me to the pre-premiere party."

"But he's dating Venezia!"

"It's all just show."

"He asked you on a date?"

Her right eyebrow twitched and her mouth dropped open, but nothing came out. Celebrity news came from dubious web sites or TV shows. Certainly not from the cynical virgin who lived next door.

"It's not what you think," I said, slightly fearful of her reaction. "I'm really not interested in him."

"Exactly which party are you going to . . . ?"

"Miriam someone is throwing it."

"Miriam Williams!"

"He said she was a producer or something."

"I've worked her parties before. She used to be the mistress of a big film producer. She got him to divorce his wife for her. When he died, she became the big producer. She's producing Crispin's latest project."

Catching herself, she added, "Be careful, Gladyss, these celebrities use little people like us, then toss us away like pistachio shells."

"I really am *not* interested in him," I said again.

"Then why are you going on a date with him?" She was indignant.

"I know what I'm going to say will sound weird, but, I think I had a Kundalini moment involving him."

"What does that have to do with . . ."

Since she knew so much about the superstar, I just asked her point blank: "I know it sounds weird, but do you think Noel Holden could kill someone?"

"What!"

"Twice in a twelve-hour period I saw him in the vicinity of a murder scene, on Forty-second. A crime scene that was not public knowledge at the time."

"Forty second Street is hardly the middle of nowhere, is it? And he's an actor. Just because he happens to be around there, that hardly makes him a murderer."

"I'm not picking on him because he's a big actor. I'm just checking his prints and alibi and that's the end of it. "

She sighed deeply, as if to keep from panicking, then she muttered, "My God, are you kidding? What did I do? What did I do!"

"What *did* you do?'"

"Don't you see? I did this! I wrote those letters to him and put all those messages out there."

"Out where?"

"Out there!" she pointed to the air around her. "And you must've been picking them up! Shit!"

"Look I just want to get his prints," I said, hoping to calm her. "Then I can eliminate him as a suspect."

"Once you get his prints you'll back off?"

"I swear."

"I'm better than I used to be," she said, showing that she was aware of her own flaky behavior. "I've stopped the letter writing . . ." She paused, because I guess she didn't want to lie, then amended, "Well, at least I've stopped mailing them."

I gave her a hug.

"Oh, look at the time," she said looking at my Elvis Presley wall clock. "I'm going to miss *A Most Singular Man*!" Before I could tell her that she was welcome to watch it on my TV, she was out the door.

CHAPTER FOUR

The next day at roll call, Sergeant McKenner informed me that my prayers had been answered, if only conservatively—my thirty-day reassignment to homicide had just come through.

"Thirty?" I replied. "It was supposed to be ninety." That was what I had put out into the universe à la Maggie.

"No problemo, I'll just tear this up."

I grabbed the reassignment order. It ended on the exact day I was scheduled to have my eye surgery. A coincidence? I thought not.

O'Ryan had a frozen smile on his face, hovering somewhere between jealousy and envy.

"If you like I'll buy you a blonde wig," I mocked him. He'd been so sure I wouldn't get the job. He called me a lucky stiff.

"If I get killed," I shot back. "I'll just be a stiff."

"Are you still going on your surreptitious date with the lady-killer?"

"Yeah, and I'll call you when I get home, just like I promised."

I cleared out my locker and headed over to Manhattan South Homicide, at Thirty-fifth Street near Ninth Avenue.

I checked in with the desk sergeant, who had me fill out a short stack of paperwork. Then I was directed up to Sergeant Farrell's squad room on the fourth floor. I felt like a child as he introduced me to the other two investigators assigned to the case; I'd seen them briefly at the murder scene two days before. Annabelle Barrera and Alexander Oldfield were both third-grade detectives. Annie, as she liked to be called, was an attractive middle-aged Latina; I would learn that she watched her diet and maintained an exercise routine as best as she could while fighting crime and raising two high school-age boys. Alex, who was African American and lived in Orange County, seemed intent on going the other way. As I witnessed throughout the first day, his large flabby body was constantly being fed from a bottomless drawer filled with extra large bags of cheese puffs. The one uncanny thing about them was that though they were of different races and sexes and had different body types, their faces were weirdly similar.

Hopping slowly around on his one good foot, Bernie led me into his small corner office, which had the name Herbert Q. Kelly painted on the glass door. It was his old partner's.

"Kelly?" I asked, "Herbert wasn't related to Ray?"

"He liked to be called Bert, and no, he was not related to our commissioner."

"Bert and Bernie?" The pair of them sounded a little *Sesame Street*.

"The reason you're here"—he was done with the chitchat—"is that yesterday we got a call from a downtown madam who said she had a john asking for a tall blonde."

"You're kidding."

"Annie pulled on a wig and we went in. The guy took one look at her and said she was too short, and too old."

"So you lost him." I only wished O'Ryan could hear this.

"No, we brought him in anyway, checked out his prints and his alibi for the three murders. So it wasn't a complete loss. But Annie agreed that we should find some sexy blond giraffe. So thank her for your assignment."

"I will."

"So here's the background. The first murder was reported a little over a year and a half ago, when a maid at the Olympian Arms on Fifty-third Street found the body of Mary Lynn MacArthur." He slid some gruesome photos over to me. "A few weeks later, a cleaning lady at the Spartan opened another door and discovered the grisly remains of Denise Giantonni." More horrific photos. Both women had been decapitated, like the one I'd seen at the Templeton, and large, crude numbers had been savagely carved into their limbs. "Both women were drugged," Bernie continued. "Mary bled to death while Denise was strangled and mutilated afterwards."

"I wonder why he only made this cut on the first vic," I said, pointing to a close-up picture that showed a long V-shaped scar running down MacArthur's right inner thigh.

"There are other differences, like Denise has a sock hanging from the toes of her left foot, but at this point we're focusing on the similarities between all three scenes."

I jotted down the dates of the first two murders so I could check and see if Noel Holden was around.

"Even though the killer was more brutal with the second vic, the crime scene was a lot messier with the first girl," Bernie said. "He probably strangled the second woman so there was less bleeding."

As Bernie flicked through the pages of his notebook, I took the opportunity to scan his dusty office. Above a stack of boxes was a wall full of commendations and pictures. At the center, I spotted a small picture frame holding a photo of a beautiful young Latina girl. Under it a caption read:

Juanita Lopez Kelly
Sleep with the Angels
(1968-1998)

It had to be a memorial card for his ex-partner's daughter. Apparently she had died just four years before her father.

Looking up from his notes, Bernie continued: "For some reason the killer cut what looked like a number seven in the carpet between the legs of victim number two, although considering all the knife marks it could've been accidental.

"The first two women were both naked, and their bodies were positioned beside the bed. The top of their bodies pointed north and their feet always point south. He also taped up the limbs in both cases.

"The main differences between the three murders are: one, the location, and two, the numbers he carved into their foreheads," he said, repeating what he'd told me at the crime scene.

"Are there any defensive wounds?"

"No, nor was there any epidermis under their nails. He drugged and strangled Mary Lynn MacArthur. Actually, first he stabbed her with a screwdriver."

"How'd he decapitate her?"

"The cuts indicate a knife, but I don't know why he didn't also use it as the murder weapon."

"Did they find prints, hair, fiber, anything like that?" I asked. I was hoping to match Noel's hair with something.

"Oh yeah, all that stuff. But the problem is, there are no matches between any of the three locations."

Bernie continued giving me background: Initially they had canvassed the area looking for witnesses and surveillance tapes from surrounding businesses. Nothing turned up. They had tracked down the escort services that handled the girls, and found that the killer had used stolen credit cards, never the same one. All three guys who'd had their cards stolen worked in midtown; other than that, no connections. The squad had spent the last few weeks going through the list of the victims' regulars. Again, no cross clients. They found johns with records, but nobody with anything serious. In short, the trail was cold.

A week ago, a profiler from Police Plaza, Barry Gilbert, had been assigned to the case. I remembered him from the academy, where he'd taught a class in forensic psychology: an intense guy with a shiny widow's peak.

"Barry thinks we're looking for a young white guy who is organized and modestly up on forensics," Bernie continued. "He probably has a history with hookers. He might have some priors for drugs, prostitution, and maybe credit card fraud, since he's used them for paying the ladies. Considering the hot-sheet dives he takes them to, I'm guessing he's broke. And he probably has sexual problems, seeing how he hasn't screwed any of the vics."

"Did Dr. Gilbert say anything about the taped-up limbs or the carved numbers?"

"He said considering the way the limbs were lassoed and the numbers looked branded on, we might be looking for a cowboy. I think he was kidding."

"It's so strange," I thought aloud, recalling my academy classes, "that one day, out of the blue, some john plans not just a murder, but the whole mutilation and post mortem numbering thing. In cases like this, isn't there usually an earlier version of the murder?"

"Crystal Hodges," Bernie responded. "Barry thinks I'm way off, particularly 'cause it was so long ago, but she was the only blonde hooker I could find whose murder could've been an early draft of the current ones."

"Was she tall?"

"Six foot and blonde. She was drugged and strangled, and her head was nearly hacked off. It all fits the M.O. But it was in the early Eighties."

"They never found the killer?"

"Everyone figured her pimp did it, because he was later arrested for killing another hooker, but he swore up and down he didn't, even though he confessed to the other murder."

"Shouldn't you interview him?"

"He died in jail in '87, so who the hell knows."

Bernie's phone rang. He said he needed a moment, so Annie took me into her office. She said their top priority today was finding out the identity of victim number three. They had taken her fingerprints and were waiting for her arrest record to turn up.

I said I was amazed they hadn't found more evidence at the scene.

"Her purse was missing, so there was no ID or anything. The killer must've took it," Annie said.

"Or the maid," Alex muttered.

"Maybe the killer dropped her lipstick. I found some on the staircase," I told her. "But it wasn't *in* the actual crime scene so Bernie chucked it."

"And Alex said Bernie was just looking for someone cute to work with . . . Then here you are finding lipstick."

"What kind of guy is Bernie?"

"Neither sleazy nor easy. He's actually a great cop who's going through a tough patch."

"He said his partner died?"

"Bert passed away late last year, yes."

"How did Bert's daughter pass away?"

"What daughter?"

"Juanita?" I asked.

"That was Bert's wife, his third wife," Alex interjected.

"He liked them young," Annie added.

"Where'd you hear about her?" Alex asked.

"I just saw the memorial card in Bernie's office."

"She died of AIDS about five years ago," Annie confided. "It'd be wise not to mention any of this to Bernie. One of the many things that will suddenly make him explode."

"He can be very moody, but he wasn't always that way," Alex said. "Things started going bad after the Towers came down."

"Both of them went down there. Bernie and Bert were pulling as much overtime as they could to boost their retirement package," Annie completed. "Then Bernie came back with a cough that wouldn't go away—"

"—And a firm decision *not* to resign," Alex tossed in.

"—But Bert just got sicker."

"You have to understand," Alex said, "Bert was more than the captain here—he really was a father to us all. He ran the show and we all loved him."

"He only just died," Annie replied.

The two of them really did finish each other sentences, it was kind of annoying.

"But he had been fighting cancer for years," she went on. "Thin as a rail. Always going in for more treatment."

"Actually I think it was the foot injury . . ." It was Alex's turn. "That's when Bernie started getting grouchy."

"He said it felt like a snake had bit him," Annie added.

"What happened to his foot?" I asked.

"Toward the end of the recovery period, Bernie fell through a hole at the Pile—that's what they called Ground Zero—and shattered his foot in a million places," Alex explained.

"It's been operated on like a half a dozen times."

"No sooner had he checked out of the hospital the last time, his foot still in a fucking cast, then Gayle moved out."

"So within three months he loses his partner and his wife files for separation. Now he's gasping for air, forced to stop smoking, and he's got a bum foot, no running around."

"He's barely able to walk. But what's worse is that he's as angry as a Tasmanian Devil on steroids."

"Someone said he had a nickname," I hinted.

"Burnout Farrell," Annie answered. "Don't ever say it in front of him."

"After Bernie had punched out a couple suspects and almost shot a young detective who was going to be his partner," Alex said, "the new captain put him on modified duty, hoping he'd get tired and quit with disability."

"Then these murders started popping up," Annie said.

"Bert was a truly great investigator, and this was their old turf," Alex concluded, "so the captain put Bernie back on the case."

As if sensing a disturbance in their vaudeville routine, both of them fell silent. Sure enough, the distant bumping quickly grew closer until Bernie limped in. He announced that he had spoken to the captain and got authorization for a one-week surveillance team on the two hot-sheet hotels in the area that still didn't have cameras in their lobbies.

Then he asked, "Do we have Jane Doe's name yet?"

"Still waiting," Annie replied without looking up.

"Get your coat," he said to me. "We're hitting the bricks."

"Where you going?" Annie asked as I wrapped my scarf back on.

"Back to the Blank," he said. "Shake some monkeys out of the tree."

Soon we were driving up Eighth Avenue in a dark blue Chevy Lumina. I spotted O'Ryan on patrol with old Lenny Lombardi, the cop who'd been first on the scene the other day. I suppressed the urge to flip Eddie off as we drove past.

The Blank was actually the Templeton Hotel. Bernie called it the Blank because the name had been pried from the rusty metal sign that hung over its entrance on Forty-second Street. Florescent red lettering still flashed the word HOTEL underneath a frame that now only held icicles.

It felt like ten degrees below when Bernie and I left the car and walked up the street. I thought the limp would slow him down, but the pain seemed to be a stimulant. We visited the neighboring shops, where Bernie showed his shield and our Jane Doe sketch to various clerks. None of them remembered her.

As we walked eastward, Bernie's exposed ears turned as red as brake lights. I wanted to tell him that most of our body heat escapes through our head and that he should wear a hat, but he was clearly the kind who didn't care for unsolicited advice. As we passed Holy Cross, his right index finger palsied out a slight up-down-right-left motion, the way a lapsed Catholic might from force of habit.

By the time we reached the old McGraw-Hill Building, I was

hoping we'd return to the car, but just then Bernie spotted something. A guy wearing a black vest over his old trench coat was passing out business cards to the V.I.P. Club on the corner of Fortieth and Eighth Avenue.

"These guys sometimes are good sources, 'cause they're stuck out here," Bernie said. Walking over, he showed the guy the sketch and asked if he remembered seeing her around.

"Sorry," he replied, handing Bernie a card advertising the nearby strip club.

"Already wanked today, thanks," Bernie replied. Turning to me he seemed to notice my casual attire for the first time and said, "Listen, we try to dress kind of officey. Dark, loose-fitting slacks and a conservative jacket should do the trick."

"Fine," I assured him.

Feeling acutely self-conscious, I caught our reflection in a store window as we walked past. I was wearing an off-white hat and a new suede jacket. Bernie, who was a little shorter and darker than me, was exhaling into his cupped palms to keep them warm. All I needed was a pair of cowboy boots and together we'd look like a tall, androgynous Jon Voight and an older Dustin Hoffman from *Midnight Cowboy*.

We turned right on Eighth Avenue and walked past the Port Authority. Since 9/11 it had been surrounded by a dozen big concrete planters to protect against possible car bombers. Wishful thinking, I thought. Over Bernie's head, I saw a billboard that the Patrolmen's Benevolent Association had recently put up: "NYC Cops Ranked #1 in fighting crime. Ranked #145 in Salary. It's Time to Fix the Injustice."

"See this?" Bernie said, pointing at the giant turquoise grill of the old bus depot. "When I first started working here, it was the newest, most modern building on the block, now it's the—"

"No! You're *not* supposed to eat sushi on a Sunday," some young cell-phone retard babbled as he walked beside us. "Cause the last catch is on Friday."

"It wasn't until cell phones were invented that I realized exactly how dumb most people are," Bernie declared.

"Yeah, we went out last night, but absolutely nothing happened!" the cellphoner either didn't hear or just ignored him.

"'Cause you're a fucking idiot!" Bernie yelled right in his face. The kid stopped dead on the sidewalk, allowing us to continue without his moronic accompaniment.

Along the east side of Eighth Avenue, from Forty-second down to Fortieth Street, almost all the buildings had either been torn down or were boarded up.

"Bert, my old partner, told me he once dreamed that somewhere on the north slope of Alaska there was a place where all the buildings that are torn down here miraculously reappear."

Did that include all the rats and roaches, and the riffraff?"

Bernie laughed. "Can you imagine, in the middle of some vast wasteland coming upon a frozen city consisting of all the old tenements and office buildings that this city has sloughed off over the years?" he asked. "The old Penn Station, the two former Madison Square Gardens. . ."

"I guess the Twin Towers would be there . . ."

"I wouldn't mind going there after I die," he said. "If you don't look carefully, I mean really look, you can miss how quickly this city shakes off its old skin. It's always growing another, taller, glistening new one. In a matter of months there'll be a row of shiny new office buildings there." Bernie pointed across the street. Word was, the New York Times was going to move its offices to somewhere along Eighth Avenue.

When we reached Forty-first Street, I noticed Bernie was staring dead ahead. Like a pitbull after a rat, he had caught a scent.

I tried to figure out who he was looking at, but before I could ask him, he pulled out an inhaler and gave it a hard shake, then pressed it three times while inhaling deeply.

"Would you mind looking behind me and tell me if you see a cop?"

"Why?" I asked as I turned, wondering if we needed back-up.

An older African American man in an army coat brushed by me, holding a pair of old shopping bags in each hand. Bernie whipped his arms up in a mock yawn, clocking the poor guy right on the jaw and sending him to the pavement.

"Hey! I don't see many faces from the old days," Farrell said, eagerly helping the poor man to his feet. The contents of his shopping bags—packaged bundles of new tube socks—three for ten dollars—were scattered along the icy ground.

"Please, I don't want no trouble," the guy said, searching for the black knit beanie that had fallen off his head. I wasn't sure what to do.

"Say hello to Youngblood Barnett," Farrell said to me. "Twenty years ago, he helped hookers off the mean streets of Brooklyn." Youngblood was no longer young.

"Officer," he replied, "I've been out for ten years and I don't do nothing no more."

"Hold on," Bernie grabbed him. "Last time we talked was in Queens Criminal Court."

"Yeah, and I didn't get out for twelve years." Youngblood replied.

"We still have to catch up about Lily," Bernie said, and he lunged forward, causing Barnett to jump back and smack his head into a bronze statue of Jackie Gleason's famed TV character, Ralph Kramden, which had been temporarily installed in front of the bus depot.

"You've got to be careful," Bernie said with a friendly grin.

"Look, I didn't know she worked for you, did I?" Youngblood winced, holding his scalp. "And why would I deliberately kill my best earner?"

"Let's see, that was around twenty years ago," Sergeant Bernie replied, "Lily would've been near forty now. She'd probably have two kids and a husband somewhere in Elmhurst."

"I'm not the only one here who wasted someone," Youngblood answered, loud enough for the few bystanders to hear.

Crazed, Sergeant Farrell pulled the guy backwards over his knee, knocking him to the ground again, then he bent his knee on the guy's chest. He leaned slowly on Youngblood's turkey gobbler with his other knee. A crowd started forming.

"Lily told me she wanted a little boy and girl, so that's two other people you killed." He smacked the old guy in the face. At that point I heard someone in the crowd mutter, "police brutality."

"Come on Bernie, we've got an audience," I nudged.

"Take a fucking look at a killer," Bernie yelled to me, but really to the surrounding crowd. "he used to beat up on innocent white girls for a living."

"The AIDS would've killed her by now anyway." Old Youngblood mumbled, squeezing out from under him and struggling to his feet. "It got them all in the end."

Bernie made a pained expression, then smacked the former pimp upside his skull, knocking a small flesh-colored wedge out of the old man's head.

"I know what you did in Bushwick," the ex-con squealed. "You wasted Tyrone saying it was a holdup, but we both know he never woulda drawn on you!"

When a pair of Port Authority cops came out of the bus station, I showed them my badge and explained that a drunk and disorderly situation had turned into resisting arrest. Bernie backed off, and the ex-con spat bloody saliva on the icy sidewalk. With the PA cops and the crowd watching, we couldn't just let the guy walk, so I pushed Youngblood against a wall and read him his rights.

As I cuffed him, I saw Bernie pick up the thing that had fallen out of Youngblood's head.

"Give it here," I said, before he could stomp on it. He tossed me a waxy hearing aid.

Somehow I sensed that I was now doing his old partner's job—reining Bernie in. After a minute, when most of the people had dispersed, I uncuffed Youngblood and handed him the hearing aid. The former pimp grabbed the one shopping bag that wasn't ripped apart and scooped up a handful of the bagged socks. Several packages had disappeared into the black slush in the gutter. Then he hurried off down the block.

"Isn't this the kind of shit that got you assigned to desk duty in the first place?" I said to Bernie.

He led us back to the car in silence. As we were heading downtown, his cell phone rang and he answered it, even though he was driving. I figured he was talking with his estranged wife. In a clear, somber tone, he started talking about his failures as a husband. I quickly pulled out my cell and called my brother.

Seeing my name on his display, without even letting me say hello, Carl began: "I know that sometimes I get a little manic, and you're always the first to warn me, but this time it's you. You went from one extreme to the other with this scorpion guy."

"Stop calling him that, asshole!" I shouted. Bernie looked over and abruptly ended his conversation.

"All right, I'm sorry," my brother replied. "I just worry about you. Are you still in that weird cult?"

When I'd told Carl about Kundalini and its alleged psychic properties, he insisted that it was dangerous and said I should stop attending immediately.

"It's just yoga," I said, and told him I had to go.

"Annie discovered our Jane Doe is one Nelly Linquist," Bernie said. Apparently it wasn't his wife but his fellow detective he'd been talking on the phone with. After establishing the vic's identity, Annie and Alex had called escort houses until they located the one our victim had worked for. Annie had just given him the address, so Bernie and I drove to a luxury high rise in Gramercy Park to break the news.

The madam was a big-breasted Southern magnolia with a head of stiff dyed red hair. When Bernie showed his badge at the door, she gasped.

"Relax," Bernie said, "We're homicide. We've found Nelly Linquist." He showed the sketch of her face.

"Damn! Nelly was such a special gal, you know?" she eulogized. "A lot of fellas will really miss her."

Using a rolled-up Kleenex, she dabbed her tears before they could erode the dried layers of mascara. It looked as if they had been plastered on her face one over the other for years.

Bernie cut to the chase." Who was Nelly's last customer?"

The poinsettia-haired office manager went to a little card catalog box, rummaged in it, and exclaimed, "Oh, yes! I remember now. This guy couldn't spell his own gosh darn name—Dhaka."

"Couldn't spell his own name?" Bernie echoed, glaring at her.

"Yeah, he had to do it a couple times till it came out right for the credit card."

"You're a fucking moron," Bernie spat ferociously. "I should arrest you as an accomplice."

She gave him a sour look.

"I don't care that you run a whorehouse, but at very least you should protect your girls! Which means if a guy calls up and can't spell his own fucking name, I'd expect you to be a little suspicious." I could see the madam looking puzzled.

"How would this guy have found out about your place?" I asked softly, since Bernie had immediately alienated her.

"We advertise on cable TV, and in the back pages of newspapers. We're trying to run a business."

"Why did you send Nelly?" Bernie asked.

"He asked for a big blonde."

Bernie reached into his pocket and located a photo of the crime scene, something he hadn't shown to anyone else because it was so disturbing and handed it to her. "First he strangled her slowly, then he cut her up like a piece of meat."

"I don't see her . . . face."

"That's because he chopped her head off," Bernie said bluntly. Pointing within the photo, he added, "See! That's where he stuck it."

She covered her mouth in horror then started weeping painfully. Bernie snatched the photo back.

"There's no possibility he saw any of your other girls?" I asked.

"I don't know. I don't know who he was," she said as she staggered into a seat.

"Do you recognize that?" Bernie asked, handing her a close-up photograph of Nelly's wrist that showed her blood splattered bracelet.

"No."

"No, it's not hers? Or no, you don't recognize it?" he pushed.

"I don't recognize it. It could be hers. I just don't know."

"And you didn't recognize the client's voice?"

"No, I don't remember anything unusual about it."

"Did he sound educated, foreign? Regional?" Bernie asked.

Looking grim, she stiffly nodded no.

Bernie handed her his business card, and said she should call him if anything relevant came to mind.

As we headed back to the car, Bernie called Annie who contacted VISA headquarters and tracked down one Mr. Ahmed Dhaka. Though he had used his credit card about a dozen times in the past week, the only place he'd used it recently, prior to paying for the vic, was at a porn arcade across from Penn Station. It turned out Mr. Dhaka worked for an investment firm on Times Square, Dunleavy Money Management. Bernie got the address: 3 Times Square. He thought it would be a good idea to pop in unannounced, just in case the guy really was a crazed murderer. Since our killer had already established a clear MO of stealing credit cards, he agreed this was a long shot. Still, Bernie pointed out that this was the first guy who hadn't bothered to report his card missing, and it seemed odd that the two sex-related expenses were back to back. The killer had never used a stolen card more than once.

We parked in a small police lot on Forty-second and headed to 3 Times Square, which turned out to be the new Reuters Building, an artsy-fartsy modern structure that curved every which way. It occupied the northeast corner between Forty-second and Forty-third. As we approached the entrance on Seventh Avenue, Bernie halted abruptly.

"What's up?" I asked, looking around nervously in case he had spotted another shady character from his angry past.

"I just need a moment," he said, going over to one of the many food carts that lined the curb. I watched him buy a cold can of Coke and reach into his shirt pocket. He took out a small pill, put it in his mouth, opened the Coke, took a sip to wash the capsule down, then tossed the remainder into the garbage can on the corner. Next he pulled out a cigarette, lit it, took one puff, then dropped it, crushed it underfoot, and walked past me into the building. When he looked up at the building index to check where we needed to go, I could see his forehead was covered in sweat.

Since 9/11, all modern buildings had installed security turnstiles, much like the subway, that everyone had to pass through to gain entrance. We showed our IDs, got sticker badges and went inside. As we took the elevator up to the 26th floor, I noticed Bern's jacket collar had flipped up so I reached over and folded it down.

"I don't mind you doing that when we're alone," he said, "but not when we're with anyone."

"I know."

When we stepped out in front of the firm's large, circular receptionist desk, Bernie flashed his badge. I belatedly took out mine as well. He asked for Ahmed Dhaka and we were redirected down to the sixth floor. During the elevator drop Bernie said, "When I show my shield, don't show yours."

"Why not?"

"Cause it makes us look like the fucking Bobbsey Twins."

The elevator door opened into a smaller reception area. Bernie asked for Mr. Dhaka.

"Who shall I say is asking for him?"

"Bernie Farrell," he said, without announcing he was a cop. He wanted to catch the guy off-guard.

As the receptionist buzzed Mr. Dhaka and repeated the name, I could see Bernie discreetly put his hand inside his jacket, checking his gun. A few minutes later a dark-skinned, heavy-set guy in a loose suit appeared in the doorway.

"Detective Farrell," Bernie introduced, discreetly showing his shield.

"Bloody hell," Dhaka said with a clear accent, "You're not with Homeland Security, are you?"

"No, why?"

"I'm just tired of being suspected of being a terrorist."

"Nothing like that," I reassured him.

"We can sit over here, he said, nodding toward a group of chairs in the corner of the reception area."

As he turned, I saw that the right sleeve of his jacket was sewn up, just below the shoulder. His arm was missing.

"With this new Patriot Act, I'm utterly terrified of being deported. Immigrants are totally unprotected now."

"Your credit card was just used in a murder that we're investigating," Bernie said.

Mr. Dhaka hunched tightly in his chair and lowered his voice nervously. "You're kidding."

"Can we talk about a purchase you made at Penn Video?"

"What? I mean . . ." he glanced nervously at the receptionist, who was busily typing into her word processor. "I never broke any laws in my life."

Bernie asked him where he was on the night that Nelly Linquist was murdered.

"At home in Jackson Heights, with my wife and two little girls."

"Mr. Dhaka," the receptionist said getting off the phone, "Hector Beck is waiting for you."

"Oh my God, my team supervisor is urgently expecting a progress report. All I'll need is ten minutes with him."

"You know the Starbucks across the street?" Bernie asked.

"On Forty-third?" he asked.

"Yeah."

"How about we meet there in fifteen minutes?"

"That would be bloody great!"

As we took the elevator back down, Bernie muttered something about being glad to be out of there.

"Why?"

"Sometimes interrogating someone successfully is as simple as finding a place where they feel comfortable," he replied. But I sensed it was more than that.

As we approached the coffee shop, I watched a group of men in Teamster jackets assembling a small platform on the traffic island across from the MTV window, while another group of contractors on the east side of Forty-third Street were dismantling a makeshift stage that featured the logo of the ABC morning show. The neighborhood that once epitomized crime and scum had been taken over and transformed into the glamorous showcase of corporate America.

No sooner had we reached the front of the line when Ahmed Dhaka came in the door. Bernie asked him if he would like a coffee.

He shook his head—"Stains my teeth"—and joined us at a table that had just opened up.

"According to our records," Bernie replied, staring at him, "Last week you paid twenty dollars for a tape at a video outlet near Penn Station."

I didn't correct him, but it was actually a DVD. The guy was clearly embarrassed, and unable to look up. Personally I did not think pornography necessarily led to violent behavior. If a man was able to release his tension, I was inclined to believe that it usually made him more manageable.

"Why didn't you call the card in as missing?"

Ahmed silently took his wallet out of his pocket and flipped through his credit cards. "Which one is it?"

"Your Bank of America VISA card."

To our surprise, Dhaka held up the card.

"Oh wait, " he said, nodding. "I remember now. The clerk couldn't slide it through his machine for some reason, and he had trouble reading the numbers, so I read it out to him."

"There you go," Bernie said to me. "Our boy was there."

Dhaka shrugged.

"You don't remember anyone standing nearby," I asked. "Maybe even writing it down?" After all, who could memorize a sixteen-digit number, along with an expiration date and a three-digit security code, all being spoken quickly aloud?

"I'm sorry, I honestly don't remember," he said. "And I don't want to be rude, but if I don't get back to work soon, Beck's going to notice my absence."

We both thanked him for his time and watched him cross the busy street, back to the giant wavy fish tank he worked in.

"I know this sounds disgusting," Bernie said with a grin, "but while I was talking to Mr. Dhaka, I had this awful image of the guy masturbating with his one remaining hand."

"Hey, physically challenged people get horny too," I replied.

"Physically challenged—that's what I love about you kids today, you're all so fair and sensitive."

I zoned him out as we walked down the north side of Forty-second, past the New Victory Theater and the American Airlines Theater across from Madame Tussauds and Ripley's Believe It or Not, then crossed at the newly established crosswalk between the two Avenues.

When we got back to the car I thought we'd head back to the precinct, but Bernie suddenly turned on Thirty-fourth and parked on the corner of Eighth, across from the New Yorker Hotel. Looking up, I realized we were idling in front of a porn arcade.

"This is where Dhaka had his credit card number taken. Come on. Maybe we can catch our boy in the act."

I couldn't help wondering if he was doing this just to toy with me. Half the establishment was crowded and the other half was empty. This was the amusing result of Giuliani's crusade to clean up Times Square. Current laws stated that only forty percent of any video store could be devoted to porn. To take advantage of this sticky loophole, sixty percent of these shops now stocked a cheap archive of dumb Kung Fu flicks or Bollywood musicals—films none of their customers wanted.

Even though the G-rated side of the place was unpopulated, I pushed into the smutty side of the store to show Bernie I wasn't timid. Apparently self-conscious in the presence of a female, many of the men discreetly vanished. Images of fucking and sucking were plastered on every box cover. The video tapes and DVDs were shelved by category: Anal, Oral, Group, Gangbang, Asians, Toys, and so on, but when I examined the dirty pictures on the wrapping, I realized how useless some of these divisions were. Asian women were clearly thinking outside the box, brazenly performing lesbian acts. Gangbangers could be seen multitasking, performing both oral and anal sex. Others used a wide array of plastic toys. Most the films seemed to be big sexual free for alls, though their titles, like *Pussy Lickers #43* and *Assgaper's Holiday*, indicated the intended themes.

"Cut it out," Bernie said softly as I began to slip misplaced boxes into their correct sections.

"We're checking on a credit card theft from last week," Bernie said inaccurately, showing his shield to the clerk. I knew he'd be pissed if I corrected him. "The victim was a one-armed Indian."

"Yeah, I remember him. I wasn't able to get a phone connection, so I took the number down and called it in later."

"Do you remember anyone standing nearby when he made his purchase?"

"No, and I was careful not to say it out loud."

Bernie nodded and took a step toward the door. I said, "So you wrote the guy's number down?"

"Yeah, he's been in a bunch of times, so he knows me. He pre-signed it and took the receipt."

"So our suspect might've waited around and then, after you were able to call it in, taken the number out of the trash when you weren't looking." I pointed to the can sitting right before me.

"What are you saying?"

"She's asking if you have a video camera focused on your cash register," Bernie asked, looking up for a lens.

"No we don't," he replied, then added, "Long as she's not suggesting it was my fault."

"Relax," I replied as we turned to leave.

"Hold on," Bernie suddenly stopped. "That's *exactly* what she's saying—and she's right, asshole!"

"Hey, don't call me—"

"You're a fucking moron who helped one guy get ripped off and assisted in the murder of a young girl," he yelled, compelling everyone to look over. "And the next time one of these pudpullers trust you with their credit card info, you should reward their patronage by tearing up the information before throwing it out."

I wanted to tell him that his outburst was counterproductive, but I knew he'd start yelling at me, so we returned in silence to the car and drove the few blocks back to the precinct.

"What were you doing with those porn boxes?" he asked.

My OCD had gotten the better of me. "Oh . . . I was just wondering if any of our vics had done any films." It was the only bullshit answer I could think of, and I didn't want to admit to my mild disorder.

As we pulled into the precinct's restricted parking area, Bernie spotted Annie getting into another car.

"Where are you going?" Bernie asked.

She said she had just located Nelly Linquist's apartment, in Bushwick, and she was going to look for information there that might enable us to contact her family.

"Gladyss will go with you."

As I was getting into her car, Bernie added, "I need to know if the killer is putting bracelets on these girls, or if it's their own stuff. Check out her jewelry box and see if she has any bracelets like the one she was wearing."

We drove down Broadway, over to Delancey, and then took the Williamsburg Bridge until we were driving under the Elevated J/M train trestle. We pulled up outside a rundown tenement off Myrtle Avenue. Annie got the super to give us access to Linquist's place. We found a tiny stash of pot, various pills, and a small bag that looked like heroin. She had a lot more drug paraphernalia—roach clips, bongs, syringes. I pushed through a drawer of cheap jewelry that looked like it had been picked up in endless thrift shops. It was an eclectic collection and gave us no clue as to whether the bracelet she was wearing was actually hers. Despite a thorough search, we couldn't find an address book, journal, or letters. The only items we found regarding her home life were a dozen or so sad old snapshots of her as a kid, smiling or playing with other kids, in what looked like a trailer park.

As we were pulling up the mattress and looking to see if she had anything taped under her drawers, Bernie called to ask if the bracelet was hers. I told him it could be, there was no way to know for sure. And we hadn't found anything that would enable us to contact her family.

"All right, get back over here. There's still a lot to do."

I hung up and told Annie that Bernie wanted us back, but she only searched harder without making eye contact. I sensed that over the years Annie had burnt out her tear glands on cases like this. All I could see was a faint gloss in her eyes. After a while longer, Annie finally gave up. And that was it. Now that Nelly's life was over, there seemed scant evidence that she had ever even existed.

"I don't care as much about the older ones or the high-priced girls, but the kids are just runaways," Annie said on the drive back over the bridge. "And we're their last chance to return their bodies to someone who might've loved them. After us, it's usually Potter's Field."

Back at the precinct, Bernie had us divvy up a comprehensive list of all Manhattan escort services. Stationed next to a phone, each of us worked our way down our part of the list. Speaking to the madam, or the manager, we explained that a serial murderer was on the loose. If any new johns asked for a tall, blonde-haired gal, we needed to be notified immediately, while the john was still waiting. Grateful that we weren't going after them, the purveyors of women were usually pleased to oblige.

"Bring some kind of sexy outfit with you on Monday," Bernie said to me as I was leaving for the weekend.

"Is that a joke?"

"That's why we got you, remember? Just keep the outfit in your locker, so if the killer calls you can throw it on."

As I was walking out of the building, looking forward to a seven o'clock yoga class, I heard, "So how's your big case coming?"

O'Ryan had just finished his shift as well. I told him we'd had no breakthroughs and asked how he was coping without me.

"They got me paired up with Lenny Lobotomy," he said as we walked south together. I didn't mention that I had seen them on patrol earlier.

"Are you getting along with him?"

"Oh yeah, he's great. He's offered to set me up on a date with his neighbor."

"You're kidding."

"No, but I am kind of seeing someone."

"Really? Who?"

"A girl." He obviously didn't want to be more specific. "But it's all still up in the air. Anyway what's up with your case?"

"Well," I said trying not to sound distressed, "We're setting some traps."

"That's right, you're blond pross bait," he said. "Nervous?"

"Not really." Then remembering my homework that night as we approached my building, I figured I might have another shot with O'Ryan. "Actually I have to find something sexy to wear for the stakeout."

"Sounds like fun."

"Wanna help?" I asked trying to sound seductive.

"How?"

I simply pointed into my apartment and opening the door, he followed me inside. As we headed up the stairs, I was shaking my ass in front of him, but instead of trying anything, he was busy recounting Bernard Kerik's meteoric rise to police commissioner.

"In 1994, he totally lucked out by getting posted to Giuliani's protective detail . . ." On and on he went. Little could O'Ryan guess at the time that in just a few short years, Kerik's stunning career would end with him being sentenced to four years in federal prison.

When we reached my landing, Maggie's door abruptly flew open. I could see her eyes widen instantly at the dimwitted hulk following me.

"Eddie, this is Maggie," I introduced them.

He nodded coolly. Maggie batted her long lashes and continued downstairs, probably to meet her non-boyfriend/bartender Rick. In a moment we were alone inside my place. I grabbed some clothes and dashed into the bathroom.

"So your neighbor's a little hottie," he said from the bedroom as I slipped into a corduroy miniskirt and skimpy halter top I'd bought but never had the nerve to wear.

"How does this look?" I asked, standing before him, revealing far more than I ever recalled doing before.

"Where are you going to hide your wire?"

"Thanks Eddie, you're a real confidence builder." The man was one frozen fish stick.

"Sorry," he said, then looked awkwardly to the floor. "I think you're beautiful. But my head's still on the job."

"Was your head on the job on New Year's Eve, 'cause you made me feel like crap then too."

"That was different," he said.

"Not to me."

"Can I make a confession?" he asked. "It might sound strange . . ."

As he usually was so guarded, I nervously nodded yes.

"That night something weird happened to me."

"What night?"

"You know. . . New Year's Eve."

"What happened?"

"Well . . . this is really embarrassing, so I don't want you to freak out or nothing."

"I won't freak."

"After you mentioned your . . . circumstances"—he was awkwardly referring to my virginity—"I was trying to go slow, and then your brother called."

"I remember."

"And I thought it was odd that you chose the call over me."

"I'm sorry, he hasn't been doing well lately . . ."

"No, that's okay. It when you showed me that photo of you and him, your twin . . ."

"Carl?"

"Yeah, it just kind of took the wind out of my sails, if you get my meaning."

"What took the wind out of your sails?"

"Seeing that photo of the two of you side by side . . ."

"What about it?"

"Well, first telling me you were a virgin sort of knocked me out, but then afterwards, when he called and you showed me that photo. How can I explain, it was like seeing you as a . . . as a man."

"What?"

"I'm sorry."

"What, are you . . ."—I wasn't even sure what to call it—"twinophobic?"

"No . . . I mean, if you had a twin sister it'd be hot."

"So you're homotwinphobic?"

"I don't think so. I have gay friends. I just didn't expect it. It kind of hit me out of left field."

"But I already told you I was a twin."

"I know you did. It was a spontaneous, visceral reaction and I'm truly sorry."

What could I say?

"The important thing is, I do really like you. I think you're hot and I want another shot."

"We'll see," I replied. What was I suppose to say—let's jump in the sack? Without asking for another date, he gave me a peck on the cheek and left, just like that.

I finally decided on my old high school shirt and skirt uniform, which I was now barely able to squeeze into, and packed it for work.

CHAPTER FIVE

"Steady breathing, steady pose," the Renunciate muttered to me when he saw me wobble in class as I recalled O'Ryan's twinly repugnance. Thanks to my teacher's constant guidance, I was gaining greater strength and flexibility than I'd ever had before. But during final relaxation, as hard as I tried to achieve that divine vacancy of thought—I found I was unable do so. And it wasn't the usual petty distractions that prevented me from emptying my mind. It started out as a kind of shimmering light. Slowly, though, a vision emerged. It was a figure—a tall svelte female, no Lady of Guadalupe, posing proudly. She seemed to be naked. Her arms were stretched out majestically, but her hands seemed to be clenched. Then I realized she wasn't making fists, she was holding something. From the position of her right elbow, it had to be a bow and arrow. but why would such an image enter my head? Instinctively, to get a better look at her, I opened my eyes, and poof! She was gone. When I closed them again I couldn't get her back. A moment later the Renunciate had us all doing final chants and it was over.

As the class was leaving I lagged behind. He spotted me and said he thought I was really coming along.

"Has anyone ever had visions in class?" I asked.

"All the time," he said calmly.

Before I could be more specific, another student came up and asked him about ashrams, so I waved goodbye and left. I reached my front door just as Maggie arrived.

"Where's that gorgeous hunk you were with earlier?" she asked as we went upstairs together.

"Eddie had to run," I said, without adding that he had lost interest because I had a twin brother who looked freakishly like a male version of me.

"Let me ask you a hypothetical," she asked. "If I ever saw you with Noel Holden, would you introduce us?"

"Geez, I've only met the man once myself," I replied, somewhat pissed.

She giggled in embarrassment and dashed inside her apartment like a chipmunk.

On Monday morning, Bernie reported for work late. He was wearing a baseball cap and sunglasses as he limped into his office. When Annie followed him in, I heard a gasp.

As I stepped inside too, Bernie released a cascade of wet, nonproductive coughs, then explained, "I was at a bar over on Twenty-sixth Street, had a few drinks, so I went back to my car to sleep it off. When I wake up—boom." He removed his cap to reveal a walnut-sized purple lump.

"Looks like it could use a few stitches," I observed, looking at the jagged gash along its swollen center.

"What happened?" Alex said, coming in late.

"Some cocksucker walloped me over the head and took my cash."

"Holy shit! You didn't get a look?"

"I was passed out. I just woke up the next morning with a hell of a headache and blood all over my freakin dashboard. The thing is, I got this awful feeling it was a Maglite I was hit with."

"He didn't get your gun, though?" Alex asked.

"No, I learned long ago to stash my gun if I'm going drinking." He smiled and said, "Fuck! Two hundred bucks—gone."

"But he left the wallet?"

"He musta seen my shield," Bernie said. "That would've been a disaster. I'd have had to tell the captain."

"Thank God for that."

"Yeah. Well, I'm staking out my car for the next few nights in case the fucker comes back. I'm thinking he followed me from the bar, so maybe I'll go back there and act like I'm loaded."

"Bern, be careful. Go to Robbery. If you think he's still working the area, let them do the stakeout."

"I just can't fucking believe I got hit. I thought the city was supposed to be safe now."

We convinced Bernie to go to the hospital, but before he left he ordered the three of us to spend the entire morning on the computer working on the Blonde Hooker case, breaking down the various components of the crimes. We typed them into the NYSPIN system, trying to put together a broad list of possible suspects.

Between the solicitation and murders of Mary Lynn MacArthur, Denise Giantonni, and Nelly Linquist, our killer could've had priors for anything from credit card fraud, robbery, and possession of narcotics to abduction, assaulting prostitutes, and post-mortem mutilation. Bernie told us to focus broadly on those who had been convicted or even faced accusations of attacking women. The fact that our killer hadn't sexually violated any of his victims made it difficult for sex crimes to place him.

Soon after Bernie returned with a big bandage on his head, he got a call from an old informant at Riker's who gave him the name of someone he'd heard had recently killed a hooker. He sent Alex to check it out, but he returned an hour later, saying it was all bogus.

By early afternoon we had a list of forty ex-cons whose priors related to our killer in some way. Bernie took it to the captain, to show him we needed help, and he assigned three more pairs of detectives to our case for the week. Bernie split the list between the five teams.

The next six days were a gradual process of elimination: Pairs of investigators systematically went out and interviewed the forty suspects, checking their alibis, then crossing them off the list.

By Friday not a single escort house we'd notified had called in any of their johns—and no new victims had turned up either. In case there was a connection, Bernie had me work with Robbery and check out a guy who, a day before the last murder, had brazenly robbed two pharmacies around Penn Station, grabbing handfuls of prescription sleeping pills. It turned out the criminal was just a run-of-the-mill speed freak on his way back to Long Island.

Bernie and I teamed up the next day and he led me out into the freezing cold without giving any idea of where we were going. And when he finally started talking I couldn't understand what he was saying. I heard the phrase, "thousands of delicate bones"; it seemed like he was talking about a fish skeleton. I had to move in close to catch mumbled terms like "fractured metatarsals," "torn ligaments," "irreparable nerve damage."

It took me a while to realize he was talking about his own foot. I smelled whiskey on his breath, and wondered if he had mixed it with pills. He rambled on while we soldiered through the dirty snow. His right foot had gone under the knife repeatedly, he said, but the operations had led to neither a reduction in pain nor increased mobility.

"Where exactly are we going?" I finally interrupted him. He said we were hunting some "ex-cockroaches" who were on the suspect list. When we finally located one of them, Edgar Martinez, in a public housing project in the East Village, I saw how Bernie was able to put his suffering to good use. When Martinez grew reticent under his interrogation, Bernie shoved the guy against a wall and terrified him into talking. Later, another, more cooperative suspect who worked in the food stamp office on Fourteenth Street made the mistake of shrugging at one of Bernie's questions. Bernie pulled him out of his chair and tossed him against the wall of his office in front of his co-workers. When he found a third suspect sitting in a McDonalds on Sixth Avenue, Bernie ordered him to freeze. The fella, a swarthy middle-aged ex-con, fell to the floor of the fast-food dive where he held a perfect downward facing dog.

"I didn't say hit the deck!" Bernie barked. "Back up here!"

"What kind of yoga do you practice?" I asked the man as Bernie patted him down.

"Prison yoga," he answered politely. "It drains off all the tweaks and twitches."

Bernie gave me a nasty look. You weren't supposed to fraternize with the enemy.

That afternoon, we walked into a rundown SRO and tracked down one geriatric suspect who genuinely did belong in a small cage. According to his record, he had viciously murdered three different women over a period of sixty odd years; each time he'd gone to prison only to serve his sentence and then be given another chance. Somehow he had been paroled a third time. At eighty-five the ex-con was barely able to cough out a "fuck off," but Bernie was just as tough on him, waving his hand in his face as he questioned him, inches from hitting the old bird. The entire time the wrinkled prick just scowled at me.

"Maybe I resemble his last cellmate," I kidded as we left his hovel.

"After a lifetime in prison," Bernie said, "he's learned to hate anyone he thinks is weaker than him. And fear anyone stronger than him."

Over the course of the following week, I wondered if Bernie's life lessons weren't much different. At the precinct, he was always trading on his presumed power. He would only let me see parts of a file, like an M.E's autopsy report, if I joined him for lunch. He'd let me read some useless witness statements only after I brought him a cup of coffee.

I finally lost it. "Tell you what! I'll toss you a donut if you tell me why the maid at the Templeton said she saw you with the victim *before* she was murdered."

"Wow," he responded. "I'm impressed that you sat on that for this long. Let's see, it's probably because I interviewed Nelly Linquist at the hotel a few weeks earlier. I knew I'd seen that fucking maid somewhere."

"Shit, you interviewed the victim?"

"For another case, yeah. Crime is a small world filled with the same cast of sad characters. A witness to one murder advances to being a victim in another. It's a strange promotion in this miserable career, you'll see."

"Why didn't you mention this before?"

"Who the hell are you? Some fucking shoofly?" That was a cop who worked in Internal Affairs, investigating other cops.

"Look, I'm just trying to learn how this job is done. And you won't even let me see autopsy photos. If you think you're protecting me . . ."

"It's not you I'm protecting," he said and let loose a sigh. "Seeing dead bodies never bothered me till I worked down at World Trade. When someone found someone in the rubble, everyone wanted a look. After so many years in homicide . . . I don't know, I just felt like this was the last courtesy I could afford them."

"But how am I expected to ever solve a case if..."

"You're not gonna solve shit!" he shouted. "You're just a blonde kid who flirted with me so I picked you as bait for a killer. Is that clear enough for you?"

"Fuck you!" I yelled back and stormed off.

I worked with Annie for the rest of the day, while Alex, who was fairly thick-skinned, teamed up with Bernie. Annie assured me that Bernie had always been a gentleman in the past. His lashing out was a recent development. Privately, though, I felt like maybe Bernie was right. What right did I have to expect anything? I was a giant blonde virgin freak who couldn't even get Eddie O'Ryan in the sack. Being with Annie for the next few days slowly restored my ailing self-confidence. Once I spotted a cardboard box in the top drawer of her desk. When I asked her what it was, she handed it to me. Inside I saw the long piece of plastic I recognized instantly.

"You've got Hermione's wand!" I said. waving it like the character does.

"Oh my God, *you're* a Harry Potter fan too?"

We started laughing, comparing notes. She confessed it was her kids who got her into it. She told me how she had stood on line for three hours when the last book was published. Trying not to blush, I told her I had bought it on the second day. We were two of the three million people who bought a book written for children on the very first weekend it had come out.

Annie could be as tough as Bernie, but without being an asshole about it. When one ex-con we stopped thought he could screw with us, two defenseless chicks, she knocked him against a wall, kicked his feet apart and warned him that if she got stuck by a needle while patting him down, he'd spend the rest of his life pissing through a tube.

"There's one in my back pocket," he warned her. "But I just got it from the Exchange. Please don't toss it."

She let him remove the syringe and place it carefully on the ground. He was instantly grateful.

By the week's end, we had nearly exhausted the entire list of suspects. Most of them had either vanished, were dead, or were back in jail doing hard time. The rest had solid alibis. That Friday I was just too cold and exhausted to go to yoga. Even though I needed to unwind, I dragged my skinny butt home to bed, where I lay on my back and stared at the small square of wall I shared with Maggie until it seemed to be staring back. At least it was quiet. She wasn't home. I had started to drift off when my cell chimed.

"I just heard Burnout got mugged," O'Ryan said.

"Yeah, last Monday."

"Poor guy. Must be embarrassing," O'Ryan said, his voice shading into sarcasm.

"Try saying that with a little humility," I shot back.

"What are you talking about?" he asked playing dumb. "I was being sincere."

"What do you want, Ed?"

"Actually it's almost Valentine Day, so I was wondering if you wanted to grab some chow and finally have that big romantic night we were supposed to have."

I remembered how the last time I saw him I had invited him up. I'd changed into a skimpy miniskirt, but instead of making a move he'd confessed he was dating someone else and that he'd lost his New Year's Eve hard-on once he saw a picture of me and my twin brother.

Despite all that, I was about to say yes when I suddenly remembered. "Oh shit! Tonight is the night!"

"What night?"

"I'm supposed to meet him."

"Meet who?"

"The great Noel Holden. Tonight is when he's finally returning home from the North Pole for a pre-premiere party."

"Are you fucking kidding me?" he blurted. "You're rejecting me for that big fruit?"

"I'm not rejecting you for anything," I explained. "It's work, remember?"

"Do us both a favor," he said lowering his voice. "Believe me when I say he's not the killer and let's have some fun."

"We'll have some fun tomorrow night. I'm just going to get his prints and that's it."

"Is he coming to your house?" Eddie asked as though planning a stakeout.

"He's suppose to pick me up on the corner in a private car," I said, "and I'm being driven to the party."

"Where?"

"I don't know where." I was glad that I couldn't tell him.

"You bringing your 9?"

"Where would I put it?" Nothing was bulkier than a handgun.

"Be very careful. Don't drink. Don't go anywhere alone with him."

"Relax," I said again.

"If I don't hear from you by ten I'm calling in an APB."

"Make it two. You're worse than my brother."

"I thought this was a murder investigation."

"But it's supposed to be a date."

"Do you plan to kiss him?" he ventured.

"I'll call you later," I said, unwilling to talk about my personal life with the one and only guy who had decided to proceed cautiously when I was finally ready to go all the way.

Without proper time to doll myself up, I quickly pulled on a dress and heels, touched up my face, took out my contacts, which were irritating me, spritzed on some perfume, grabbed my glasses, and dashed out the door. There on the corner, as though carjacked from a high school prom, was a white stretch limo. Tiredly I opened the door and hopped in. I found myself sitting next to a sweet little old lady puffing on a cigarette.

"Who the fuck are you?" she asked.

"Sorry, wrong limo!" I got out as the light changed, and her car sped off up Sixth Avenue.

"*Pardonnez-moi, Mademoiselle*," I heard a baritone voice behind me. A stocky, middle-aged man in an dark suit approached. "Monsieur Holden asked that I pick up someone fitting your stunning description."

He led me halfway down the block to a dark blue sedan and opened the back door.

On the leather seat was a small wrapped package with a beautiful silver bow. Next to it was a single rose. A small card from Tiffany's jewelry said: "To my favorite law enforcer. Here's some added protection from your loving culprit, Noel."

I unwrapped the package. Inside was a silver derringer that looked like it was from the 1930s. When I pulled the trigger, a little blue flame shot out the muzzle – it was a cigarette lighter. As we drove, I wondered if there was any way I could get the actor to give O'Ryan some lessons in charm.

CHAPTER SIX

Noel's chariot sped me north through the glossy blur of a crisp New York night. In what seemed like a few seconds we stopped in front of an older, figurative-style high-rise apartment building on Central Park West. A doorman dressed like an admiral opened the front door and, without my asking, directed me to the elevator to the penthouse. The polished brass elevator had a throne-like chair in it, which I only mustered the courage to sit on when we were almost there. A valet waiting in the hallway took my shabby jacket, and I could hear a lively party raging. As though by invisible radar, Noel intercepted me at the door. He wore a tuxedo and held an empty champagne glass. I realized that I was embarrassingly underdressed for the occasion.

"You should have told me this was formal," I reproached him.

"Nonsense, you look great," he replied. As a waitress passed with champagne, Noel handed over his empty flute and took two fresh glasses, handing me one.

It was hardly the classic eight-room apartment. In fact this place was unlike any residence I'd ever seen in the five boroughs. House music played from a large and distant room. Noel led us toward the tasteful sounds. Soon we were in a space entirely enclosed in glass, lit by a fuzzy, white sheen from the rising moon. Everyone but me seemed to be wearing clothes designed by Edith Head. It was as if we were all on a 1940s film noir set. According to Noel, the massive living room was domed with a series of glass panels, operated by cranks and levers and resembling a miniature version of England's historic Crystal Palace. At least half the space was convertible, he explained. During the warm months the top was opened, so the apartment became al fresco.

I quickly downed the expensive bubbly and Noel lifted two more glasses from yet another roving tray.

I gulped down my second glass and asked, "So who lives here anyway?"

"Miriam Williams, the producer."

I remembered now, and Maggie had been impressed by the name. As I looked around the room, I spotted quite a few celebrities, including the latest rap sensation, Slimdonk, and WB's hottest teenage star, Ji. Floating above the crowd in long delicate steps, she looked like a vertebra that had been dipped in tanned flesh-colored paint, then slithered into a strapless silk stocking. As she levitated around the room, I could only wonder where she kept her vital organs.

Everybody knew Noel Holden, and he introduced me to everyone. Between countless air kisses and tiny hummingbird hand waves, Noel explained that most of the beautiful faces were actors or models, while most of the "real-looking people" were behind-the-scenes types.

"What scenes are they behind?" I asked. After all, this wasn't Hollywood.

"Here's the face to ask," Noel said as a middle-aged man with oily skin approached.

"Gladyss, this is my all-seeing, all-knowing agent, Igor Moore. Gladyss wants to know what I do for money."

The agent grinned impishly, as though he might not utter a single word without a commission, but then he spoke. "In addition to playing constantly challenging roles that plumb the crisis of human existence, Noel Holden is in great demand as himself. Every luxurious product needs a trusted celebrity spokesmodel to assure its usefulness to the discriminating and sophisticated masses. Noel Holden's glorious form is under contract to several major clothing designers. Furthermore, his voice is licensed to a world-class car manufacturer as well as to a highly reliable maker of double-A batteries."

"Speaking of which, where the fuck is that indigo Dino?" Noel interrupted. Igor said he was talking to a member of the press and pointed across the room. Dino turned out to be Noel's press agent, an African American.

"It's only a fortnight till fashion week," the agent shouted as we moved off. That was when Noel was doing his publicity walk for *Fashion Dogs*. "Party! Party! Party!' he chanted at us.

"What was all that about?" I asked.

"Igor's always pushing me to get out there more. Get my face on magazine covers and my name in columns. Frankly, that's the part of this job that I hate." Noel seized two more glasses from a passing tray and handed one to me. "Constantly hustling for endless endorsements . . . I mean, what the hell happened to the art?"

"Oh my God!" A tray-toting caterer suddenly screeched. Behind her false eyelashes I recognized my neighbor, Maggie.

"Noel Holden, this is my dear friend and neighbor Maggie Bernardo," I introduced.

He delicately kissed the knuckles of her forefingers. Although I suspected that Maggie had moved heaven and earth to get the gig, and intrude on my date, I was still glad to see her there.

"*Enchanté*," he greeted her.

"*Enchanté* back," she echoed awkwardly, apparently paralyzed by his presence.

I explained that Maggie was an actress struggling to get a break. Noel listened sympathetically.

Perhaps because of the bubbliness of the champagne, I'd forgotten for a moment that this party consisted of other movie stars too. Jodie Foster scurried past; Madonna was just leaving; someone who looked a lot like Tom Cruise seemed to zip right between everyone's legs like a soccer ball with great hair. The Lilliputian mafia seemed to run Hollywood and, clannishly, they seemed to pick their own stubby stars.

"What's good here?" Noel asked Maggie, looking at her tray of appetizers.

"Good here?" she asked as though he was asking about her.

"Yeah, you know, foodwise?"

Before she could respond, a goateed food handler came up from behind and said to Maggie, "They're asking for you in the kitchen."

"Oh shit," she awakened to the moment. "I'm going to get fired!"

She dashed off. Now I realized why just a few days earlier she had asked me if I would introduce her to Noel should the occasion ever arise. She must've already known she'd be working this little soirée.

"This is Seymour Phelps," Noel abruptly introduced me to a middle-aged man with pores as big as a sponge. He explained that

Phelps had just produced *Screwed Bigtime!* an over-touted reality show featuring Venezia Ramada and some other rich kid celebrity.

As the producer babbled on, it occurred to me that movie stars were little more than children wandering around in a playground of filmic possibilities: inside were hypothetical swing sets and topical seesaws that these people assembled and disassembled as quickly as the Army Corp of Engineers. Each one had a sandbox filled with agents, lawyers and financial consultants, in which these eternal juveniles tried to divine which of the little projects had a jungle gym that offered them a climb to the top.

"So what exactly is it that you do?" Phelps finally turned the spotlight away from himself.

"I'm a big game hunter," I kidded slightly drunk, "but to pay for the bullets I work as a cop."

When the producer politely chuckled, Noel perked up. "She's not kidding, show him your pistol."

I took out the silver derringer-cigarette lighter that Noel had just given me.

"Oh, you got my gift!" Noel exclaimed clapping his hands together. "I hope you like it."

"It's wonderful." I pecked his cheek without thinking. After a little more cajoling, since I left my gun at home, Noel had me flash my shiny badge.

"I hope I'm not out of line in saying that not since Angie Dickinson have I seen such a beguiling and clever police lady." Seymour Phelps addressed this remark more to Noel than to me.

"That's exactly how I'd typecast her," Noel said, with talk-show suavity.

"You wouldn't be interested in auditioning for an upcoming show I'm putting together, would you?" the producer asked me.

"What is it?" Noel asked.

"*Fatigues Conceptual,* my latest reality TV show. I'm going out with it next week. Fatigues are the clothes that soldiers wear."

"I know," I said, "but you know who'd be perfect for it?" I scanned the mobile mosaic of moving faces until I spotted her, chatting with the cute goateed waiter, and waved.

"Since September 11th," Seymour explained, "public sympathy toward first responders has gone through the roof."

"I'm not an actor," I said. As Maggie struggled to make her way toward us, hungry carnivores picked at her fresh tray like piranhas going after a deer fording an equatorial stream. "But I have a friend who's a very talented actress . . ."

"I got actors popping out of my ass like hemorrhoids. I'm trying to find someone real . . ."

" . . . Maggie," I said, "she's more real than real."

"What's going on?" Maggie popped up, balancing a tray that had been packed with skewers of marinated squab.

"Oh, perfect," Seymour said, relieving her of her last remaining sticks. "I'm famished."

At just that moment the entire crowd seemed to hold its collective breath. Flashes popped as Crispin Marachino and Venezia Ramada entered, then the talking resumed and grew louder. The heiress's hair was overly teased, and her make-up was nineteenth-century goth. Her decolletage barely hangared her saline-filled zeppelins. A feathery outfit that looked spot welded to her belly, thighs, and nipples flowed down to her feet where it seemed to be hemmed with bubble-wrap. It was as if she were perpetually stepping out of the frothy ocean.

"I'm a little confused as to which of you dated Venezia first."

"Dating is such a harsh word," he replied.

"So neither of you is jealous of the other?"

"Jealous of her, no. But in fairness, I started dating Venezia as payback, so I guess he was dating her first."

"Payback for what?"

"When Crispin and I first started hanging out ten years ago, he had just done his first feature. He was the hot young director, whereas my star was still rising. I was dating Rima Bergman at the time."

"Was she in *Pals*?" It was a TV show that didn't outlive its third season.

"Yeah. Anyway Crispin took me aside one day and claimed she was giving him serious vibes. I said I thought that was highly doubtful, so he asked if I wanted him to test her loyalty."

"What does that mean?"

"He offered to wait till he was alone with her, and then make a move."

"What kind of a move?"

"The usual: say he might have a role for her, then see what happened. I mean, he made a persuasive argument. He said if she cheated on me with him, she could cheat on me with anyone."

"And you agreed to that?"

"Well, look at him. He's not very good looking and—call me old-fashioned, but I really thought Rima loved me. She was a star and I figured she wouldn't be taken in by some goofy-ass director. I mean, she was higher up on the acting pyramid than either of us. Also I didn't think he was serious, so I said something like, I'd like to see you try."

"He took her on a date?"

"All I know is he called me the following week and told me, shall we say, intimate details of her anatomy and proclivities. Things that painfully indicated intimacy."

"You're kidding!"

"Wish I was. I wept like a baby."

"Don't you think you at least owed her the chance to explain?"

"Oh I did. She confessed to all of it."

"So you turned around and did the same thing to him."

"Not at all. What happened was, we were on a film set years later, and he asked if I was still pissed about his doing Rima. I said it was long forgotten. He told me that if he were in a similar situation, he'd want a friend to do the same for him. So when I found myself alone with his fiancée, and she was fawning all over me. I just sort of let it happen."

"And you don't think he's pissed about you sleeping with Venezia?"

"Look at them. Do they look broken up? The man's impervious to jealousy. Sex to him is kind of a long, wet handshake, nothing more."

"So you all secretly hate each other?" I asked softly, just as they approached.

"What a beautiful couple you two make," the director greeted us. He and his swollen blond accessory looked tipsy already.

"Now Vanessa"—Noel spoke slowly to her as though talking to a child—"You remember Officer Chronou from the other day, don't you?"

"When you said you were inviting her to this, I thought you were kidding," Venezia responded. Then she floated away to the bar, as if to get away from me.

"Any new developments in your big murder case?" Crispin asked.

"No."

"I've played a cop in four films," Noel said, "so I always feel like such a phony when I meet a real one."

"Actually," Crispin kidded, "I need to shoot a female cop soon."

"Maybe *she* should shoot *you*," Noel replied.

"For my next movie. You remember, a cop gets killed."

"Oh, cut it out."

"I'm absolutely serious. It's called *Times Squared*." He ran his eyes over my body and added, "You'd be great."

"And casting her would piss Venezia off no end," Noel uttered.

"If someone saw me getting killed as a cop in a movie, I'd be up on disciplinary charges so fast . . . Luckily though, I have a gorgeous neighbor who happens to be here at this very party." I called out her name, and Maggie suddenly popped up like a cork right beside me.

"Why would I want to use your goddamn *neighbor*, when I can get a *real* cop?" Crispin whined. Maggie sighed, and Crispin looked at her and added, "But maybe I can use you somewhere."

"Thanks!"

Pointing at my glasses, he asked, "Are those prescription?"

"Unfortunately they are," I said. "My contacts start to irritate my eyes when I wear them too long."

"I find eyeglasses so sexy," Noel said. "So intellectual."

"Yeah," Crispin said. "Lawyers are always throwing them on murderers they're defending when they're about to go in for sentencing."

"I'm scheduled for Lasik eye surgery, so I'll be free of them soon."

When Maggie reappeared carrying a fresh tray of sushi hors d'oeuvres, I gave her a proper introduction to the director.

"Nice to eat you," he said, grabbing a handful of inside-out rolls.

"I've seen all of your films," she replied eagerly.

"Well I hope you'll check out *Fashion Dogs*, which is opening very soon," he said, rubbing a roll into a bulge of wasabi.

"Absolutely."

"'Cause if it doesn't hit at least thirty million on that first weekend he's never making another film again," Noel added.

"So," Crispin inquired. "What are the chances that you'd be catering at a big celebrity party that your neighbor is attending. That's one for the books, huh?"

"Well coincidences do happen," she replied sweetly. They kept talking as Noel steered me across the beautiful tiled floor toward an attractive, elegantly dressed woman in her mid-forties. "Gladyss, this is Miriam, our hostess. Miriam, this is the friend I told you about, Police Officer Gladyss Chronou."

Miriam was a tall, angular Waspy woman with silver streaks in her short, straight hair. She wore a shimmering evening gown. If she'd had a tiara and a torch, she could've passed for a size two Lady Liberty.

"Officer Chronou!" the hostess shrieked, as though I were a celebrity. "I'm so glad to meet you!"

"Why?" I asked before I could catch myself.

"Because you are one of New York's Finest," Noel began. "And Miriam has a mystery for you to solve."

"What mystery is that?" I assumed he was just kidding.

"One that can wait until the party is over," she said, focusing on a commotion at the door. A lanky man who looked like Jim Carrey had just entered and launched into comic capers.

"What's this mystery?" I asked Noel.

"It's some nutty internet thing."

"Miriam looks familiar."

"She tries for that Marilyn Monroe look. Only she's tall and skinny, so it doesn't really work."

"Then why does she try for it?"

"Her first big project was a Marilyn biopic that she wrote and directed. Strictly made for TV. But she fell in love with Marilyn. She even started one of the first fan web sites for her."

On three occasions people asked either for Noel's autograph or for a photo with him. He always consented. It was exhilarating just being with him. Strangers were kind. Servants were eager. Everyone wanted his love and approval. And he seemed only to want mine. For the first time, life seemed to be the way I had always thought it would be when I was a child. I was particularly proud that I had displayed some self-restraint, only downing three glasses of champagne. I couldn't remember the last time I'd had so much fun. Soon Noel and I were dancing up a storm, until a large wrinkly hand reached out of the noisy crowd and tapped me in mid-hop.

It was a butler. Noel leaned in and we heard him say, "Ms.

Williams asked if you and Mr. Holden could join her immediately in the study. It's a matter of some urgency."

I followed Noel as he followed the butler through a series of ever-unfolding rooms to the other side of her museum-like home. Eventually we entered a study that was bigger than my entire apartment.

Miriam was nervously puffing on a fancy-looking cigarette and staring out of a huge bay window with an intimate view of Central Park. From here it looked like her own private garden. When she saw me, she tensely rubbed out her cigarette and apologized for the hasty summons.

"I'm sorry, I wasn't planning on bothering you until after the affair, but my personal assistant just called me and I saw it."

"Saw what?"

On her desk was a huge flat screen hooked up to a tiny, shiny laptop. She clicked the Internet icon and in a moment we were on her Marilyn Monroe web site.

"Did Noel tell you anything?"

"He mentioned you managed a web site."

"Yes. Well, just in the past few days I've been getting these poetically threatening emails."

"Poetically threatening?" The phrase sounded oxymoronic.

"I can't think of another way to describe them, really. So I called Noel, only because he played a police detective so convincingly."

"So someone is threatening you?"

"Actually they were addressed to Marilyn."

"Okay," I said with a slight grin. Since Marilyn Monroe had been dead for over forty years, the whole thing sounded ludicrous. I tried to think of some consoling response.

"The thing is, the threat seems to be escalating. My assistant just found these awful pictures. That's why I pulled you out of the party."

"Violent pictures?"

"Well that's the thing, I'm not sure if they're real or if they're pranks. Knowing how far special effects have evolved, I fear this whole thing might just be some macabre joke. And I certainly don't want to waste the police's time." She smiled awkwardly.

"You're such a dear," I said, expecting to see a couple of jpegs that some pimple-faced geek probably downloaded from an internet F/X magazine web site.

In a few seconds the first picture appeared on the screen: it showed a woman with curly blonde hair lying on her back—alive, but drowsy looking. She wore bright red lipstick and little else. In the second picture, I could just make out a pair of gloved hands around her neck. The woman's eyes were focused in terror and her mouth was wide open. gasping. In the third photo, her eyelids were semi-closed, her mouth hung loose, drool was visible. She appeared to be dead. In the fourth photo, the gloved hands were shoving a long fish knife into her right breast. In the fifth, they were cutting off her left breast, severing it from the body. By the sixth photo I could feel my heart beating: both breasts had been cleanly amputated. I let out a gasp when I saw the next picture. The woman's limbs had clearly been taped together and pointed upward. It was definitely our guy. The final photo was a close-up: the pointy tip of his long knife was carving a line into one of the vic's soft white limbs—it was the number 1.

"I think the girl is supposed to be Marilyn Monroe," Miriam broke the silence.

"God." I felt nauseous and sucked in a deep breath. The long day had finally caught up with me. "Show me those email threats you got."

Miriam explained that they weren't quite threats. They had been posted on her web site's "poetry page" over a period of days. Each of the poems was more violent and weirder than the last. She was about to show them to me, but before she could start typing, I stopped her and asked if there was any danger of deleting anything.

"No," she said: the images were saved both to her hard drive and a zip disk. As she typed some commands into her computer, she explained, "It started a week ago. And though I really didn't care for their tone, I'm not a control freak. But then as they started getting uglier I removed them from the site, I saved copies in a separate file, though. Then my assistant, Bryce, saw that we had just received these awful pictures, and they came from the same email address.

"When did Bryce discover these latest pictures?" I asked.

"About twenty minutes ago."

"And what's the sender's email address?"

"Cathy something. I didn't recognize it."

"Have you ever gotten into a fight with a Cathy about Marilyn?"

She immediately started shaking her head no, so I kept adding on questions, "Is there anyone you can think of who knows you and is nuts, or violent, or perhaps just an ex-con?"

"The only felons I know are tax cheats," she said just as the first poem popped up on the screen:

> *Eminem thinks he's got ma grief,*
> *least his stinkin ma didn't cut & leave,*
> *Marmalyn claimed I was a spleenectomy,*
> *yet her suicide*
> > *was a wreck to me,*
> *Now it's my turn to cleave,*
> *& yours to be bereaved.*

"What do you think this spleenectomy refers to?" I asked Miriam. A slim, sandy haired lad was standing behind her, the aforementioned personal assistant Bryce.

"Marilyn had a spleenectomy," she replied. "Actually a jpeg came with that poem too." She pressed some keys and an image was displayed.

When it did, I gasped. It was the mug shot photo of Denise Giantonni—victim number two. It was the photo that had run in the papers when she died, but the image had been defaced. Colored markers had been used on the black-and white photo to give her big red lips and turn her short curly hair yellow. She had been Marilynized.

"Do you know her?" Miriam asked.

"She was one of our victims," I answered curtly. With Noel behind me, I didn't even want to talk about the case.

Underneath the photo was another poem:

> *GLAD IT'S US*
> *Marmalyn, you left me to die,*
> *Just like she did you,*
> *Why oh why?*
> *Boo hoo! Boo hoo!*
> *Cruel world, bye, bye.*

Underneath was the email address: *CathyofAlexandria@Eureka.com.*

I felt a chill crawl down my spine as I read the title: Gladyss was my name, after all. As if sensing my fear, Miriam hastily said, "Marilyn Monroe's mother's name was Gladys—she was psychotic, and died some time in the 1980s."

"I'm relieved to hear it."

"Here's the first poem that actually suggested violence," Miriam remarked, scrolling downward:

On this e-altar, this cyber tomb,
I leave my sacrifices
to your cold womb,
There might be no pardoning for what I do,
but who will, or ever can, forgive you?

It was also from CathyofAlexandria.

"The whole thing might be a hoax," repeated Miriam.

I had my doubts. The mug shot of victim number two, Denise Giantonni, was definitely real, and the latest photo of the blonde-haired vic with the dissected chest was more than enough.

Even though he was probably passed out at some bar, I called Bernie on his cell. The phone rang six times then went to his voice mail. I called a second and then a third time before he finally picked up with the salutation: "What the fuck now?"

"Did I wake you?"

"No," he grumbled, "I didn't want to pick up 'cause I'm driving to a crime scene in midtown. Our boy struck again."

"Are the vic's breasts severed but her head's still attached?"

"How the fuck did you know that!"

"I'm at a party just off the park. The hostess has a web site and somebody posted the photos on it. They're of the murder as it was happening."

"Then that's part of the crime scene. Your job is to protect it till we get there."

"It's a web site on the internet," I explained. "But she said she'd backed it up onto her hard drive."

"Just stay with that computer until I get some uniforms there to take it to the precinct. Write out a precise description of the item and give her a voucher. Tell her we're going to need it for the investigation."

"Will do."

"Also, if she can print up whatever pictures and stuff you got and bring it in, that'll help."

"Gotcha."

"And tell the hostess she can't use the site with any computer until the techies have checked it out. We don't want any contamination."

"Okeydoke."

"In fact when the uniforms get there, join me at the new crime scene."

"Where?"

"The Ticonderoga." He gave me the address.

"So he finally made his move," I said, "and it wasn't at either of the two hotels you staked out."

"Rub it in, why don't ya. The good news is, it looks like we finally have his fucking face on tape. The Ticonderoga has a surveillance camera in the lobby."

When I hung up, I explained to Miriam that another murder had just been reported and it looked like the victim might be the girl in her photos.

"You mean this is *real!*"

"Afraid so."

She was stunned. I added that unfortunately we were going to have to take her computer as evidence. She pursed her lips tensely and said she understood, but asked if she could copy some files from it first. She swore they weren't related to the site; they were for her upcoming trip to Europe. I told her that was fine. When she was done, she was about to unplug the laptop when I asked her if she could first print up the poems and pictures she had shown me.

Using her color printer, she made a hard copy of everything and slipped it into a manila envelope for me. She then went to a nearby closet and retrieved the box the computer had come in, along with the Styrofoam packing.

"The password to the web site is 'Jean Norma'," she said as she unplugged various cables from the laptop and carefully loaded it into the manufacturer's box. "It's the reverse of Marilyn's real name, Norma Jean."

"You understand that you mustn't access the web site until one of our technicians has checked it out and given you the all clear," I clarified.

"Of course."

I wrote down my name and the extension of the homicide squad handling this case. "If you need anything . . ."

"If you have any questions for me," she replied, "please call me in the next two days. I'm leaving for the Florence Film Festival on Thursday."

I thanked her, and she returned to her fabulous party. Assuming he might be worried about me, I called O'Ryan on her phone.

"You're home early." He sounded bored. His TV was on in the background.

"I'm still at the party, but there's been another murder."

"Which means I was right. It isn't Noel Holden."

"Well, I'm still going to check him out."

Before we could talk any further, one of the butlers escorted a pair of uniformed cops into the study. I pointed to the packed box, which they picked up. I wanted to grab a ride with them, but I'd lost Noel in the crowd and didn't feel right leaving without saying goodbye, so I told the uniforms to go ahead. No sooner had they gone then Noel reappeared.

"There's been another murder."

"No!"

"Yeah, I have to leave immediately." I said. Noel walked me through the party, into the elevator, and down to the lobby, where he had the doorman hail a cab that he put me in.

"If it's still early when you're done, give me a call."

I told him I would and thanked him for a great time. He gave me a peck on the cheek and the cab sped downtown.

CHAPTER SEVEN

As I headed to the crime scene I couldn't stop thinking that this was just too much of a coincidence. Some vast and mystical force must have shepherded me to Miriam Williams' party to receive these photos of the murder via her web site. Was it the power of the Kundalini that the Renunciate had been helping me channel? I started to breathe deeply, inviting its endless possibilities.

At Fortieth Street, still four blocks shy of my destination, traffic slowed to a halt. Though it was cold out, I paid the meter and walked down Lexington the rest of the way. The Ticonderoga Hotel was across from the Soldiers' and Sailors' Club, and down from a church soup kitchen. This place was outside our killer's usual hunting ground. The hotel was also of better quality than his prior dives.

There were so many cops around that unless you were showing a badge you couldn't even get on the block. Two TV vans were already parked across the street, with their microwave dish antennas and film crews setting up outside. A huge Irish cop named Matt Pattingly stood like a superhero in the lobby. All he needed was a cape. The clerk on duty was a woman with a beehive hairdo and tortoiseshell glasses on a chain around her neck. She was being interviewed by Annie.

While I was looking for Bernie, I spotted one of the elderly residents sitting in the lobby. His hair was dyed shoe-polish brown in front, while the back of his head, presumably not visible in his bathroom mirror, was downy white. He was talking to one of the investigators, a young man with a peach-fuzz mustache.

"Getting anything interesting?" I asked, sidling up to him.

"I've got things covered here," he said, not even looking at me.

I grabbed the little shit's left wrist and twisted it behind his back, then tossed him against a column. He missed it and fell to the floor. Everyone in the place looked over at me. I started reading him his rights.

"What's up?" one uniform asked as I tightened the handcuffs on the kid's bony wrists, then began to search his pockets. As I saw Bernie slowly limping over, I said, "Meet the reporter who photographed your last crime scene. And he's still posing as a cop."

"Where's his shield?"

I handed it to him. Bernie led the cuffed reporter past everyone else to the front door; I stayed within earshot. Bernie reached into the kid's front pocket and pulled out his wallet. He flipped it open and took out his press card.

"You know what I really hate," he began. "I hate it when some fucking asshole thinks he's smarter than everyone else. 'Cause then I got to deal with his stupidity, but also with the insult that he actually thought I was dumber than him."

The reporter ignored this and asked, "Don't you think the public deserves to know when a serial murderer is hunting them?"

"Shut the fuck up, you moron!" Bern shouted. His nostrils flared and his eyes glazed over. The guy began to look nervous as he realized Bernie was clearly unsound and might lose control. I stepped closer in case things started going south. Perhaps my sudden proximity made him aware of his temper, because the old cop suddenly threw his hands up and said, "I went through this whole freedom of the press bullshit with this guy's editor ten years ago. Some things just don't change."

"Come on, we're on the same side," the reporter made the mistake of saying.

"You used a fake ID to gain access to *my murder scene,* then you published vital information about an active investigation," Bernie responded, visibly restraining himself. "We got someone much crazier than me who is butchering women limb from limb. And you've given out details that only the killer would know, blowing several ways we might've tracked him . . ."

"I was just trying to warn the public . . ."

"Guess what?" I said to him as Bernie limped over to Officer Pattingly. "*We* do that. We're a full service police force."

The huge patrolman returned with Bernie, who told the reporter, "You're under arrest for obstruction of justice. This officer will take care of you."

Pattingly recited him his rights a second time as he walked him out to his patrol car. Bernie and I went over to the elevator.

"You're a little overdressed, aren't you?" he noticed.

"Like I told you, I just came from a party. What are you going to do with the kid?"

"I'll cut him loose soon enough," Bernie said as we stepped onto the elevator. "But first he's gonna get a little time-out."

"You're putting him in the back of a patrol car," I deduced.

"Thirty minutes cuffed in the backseat and he'll always remember the night his balls froze solid."

"Just arrest him," I said. After all, the guy had given our killer a peephole into our investigation.

"It's better this way. No paperwork."

The elevator opened at the sixth floor and Bernie led me to the room. From the wild swing followed by a gentle release he took with each step, I could see his foot was acting up. Between the crime scene people scouring the bloody carpet and the other technicians taking photos and otherwise documenting the scene, it was difficult to even see the vic—which was fine with me, because the killer had really done a number on her. Bernie made a couple of observations about the double mastectomy then hopped back into the hall. I was glad to follow. When someone pushed open a large metal door leading to the stairwell, Bernie caught it and led me into the solitude of the brightly lit landing.

"So where are these computerized pictures?" he asked, slowly sitting on a step. I gave him Miriam's manila envelope.

"Wow," he said. "This is a new one for me."

"What is?"

"Did you see the body just now?" he asked.

"Yeah, so?"

"Did she look like this?" He held up the last of the death scene photos for me.

"I guess so," I replied tiredly. With all the commotion and the blood, I hadn't actually retained much.

"You guess so?" he grinned. He had barely had time to glance at the scene himself, so I found his question typically patronizing.

Silently I pushed open the stairway door, crossed the hall, and went back to the crime scene. I stepped past the techies and stared at the poor woman, still profanely exposed, taking in all the gory details. Sure enough, she looked different now than in the pictures. The killer had washed her down. She had a slim wish bracelet around her left wrist and a glossy credit card in her right hand, but there wasn't a trace of the red lipstick. And her blonde hair was a wig—it had popped off the crown of her skull like a shaggy yellow rag. When I left and pushed open the door to the stairwell, a pungent stink slapped me across the face.

"Jesus, it smells like she was killed in here." I pinched my nostrils.

Bernie had removed the shoe from his aching foot, releasing a truly evil odor.

"Sorry," he muttered, rubbing the circulation back into his extremity, which was black, blue, and swollen. Fresh scars crisscrossed it.

I remained silent as he delicately pulled his sock on and tenderly inserted his foot back into his shoe.

"The last podiatrist I showed it to recommended I have it chopped off," he commented.

"There's got to be someone who can help you," I said.

As he loosely knotted the shoelace and slowly struggled to his feet, I reported what I had just seen and added, "If this is our killer he's broken out of his old hunting ground."

"That's obvious. I want you to try to focus on what's not obvious, like the fact that this girl looks different than his other victims."

"Physically she's shorter and rounder," I said.

"Again, that's obvious. What would've impressed me is if you'd pointed out that she has a different look. She's cleaner. Takes better care of herself. Has a style. Big colorful tattoos. More of a downtown type."

"So she's a downtown hooker," I said.

"Annie just told me that the clerk at the desk didn't remember her coming in blonde. She was a brunette, which means she put the wig on in front of him."

"Or maybe he put it on her. And that would be a big departure for him."

"Maybe. And instead of chopping her head off, he gave her a double mass," I added.

"We'll get a lot more done if you stop stating the obvious," he chided.

"I guess it would be obvious that this is the first time he's photographed a vic and posted it on the internet prior to the discovery."

He ignored me and just stared at the photo with the bright lipstick smeared on the mouth of our latest victim. I remembered the lipstick I had found on the corner of the Blank Hotel.

"I wonder if he took lipstick from the last victim and put it on this one."

"No," Bernie said simply. "What we have here is an entirely different killer."

"But there's so many similarities with the other murders," I said. "Maybe something happened that made him change what he does."

"I hope you're right," he said. "It's difficult enough finding one serial murderer; two is going to be a bitch."

"At least we have a picture of the knife," I said, pointing to the computer printout. "At least, the knife handle."

"Tell me again about this porn site."

"It's a *fan* site, devoted to Marilyn Monroe."

"Maybe he's sent the pictures to other Marilyn sites too. We'll have to check."

"He's also sent poetry about Marilyn being his mother."

"A killer who writes poetry?" he said, raising his eyebrows. "We don't get a lot of verse in this business."

"It's in the envelope too."

He slid it out and I saw his lips moving as he silently read it.

"Who the fuck is CathyofAlexandria?" he asked, seeing the email address.

"No clue."

"Check her out, will you?"

"Okay," I said, scribbling it into my notebook.

"Did Marilyn Monroe ever have a child?"

"I don't think so," I replied and asked back, "Do they know exactly when this girl was murdered?"

"The desk clerk said she got here at six, and her body was found around eight."

It was at about six that I got picked up by the Lincoln Town Car, which prompted me to remember that Noel *wasn't* in it.

Alex suddenly appeared and announced: "They just took the surveillance video to the tech van out front."

The NYPD's answer to the space shuttle, a state of the art technical support van had landed. A Pakistani-American techie who introduced himself as Winston had been looking at the footage from the lobby in a high-tech video machine.

When Bernie asked Winston how the tape looked, he simply pushed a button, and the reason for his reticence became obvious. People looked like ghosts; they were only slightly more discernible if they were large and dressed in dark colors. Bernie got the techie to fast-forward the tape till the time stamp in the bottom left corner showed just before six. After a couple of minutes we saw two dark fuzzy figures who had to be Jane Doe, our call girl, and her killer. They went to the front desk, where she signed in, then they turned and vanished at the elevator bank. Most of the time the suspect had his back to the camera.

"Shit! He must've known the camera was there," Bernie said, "which means he'd probably scoped the place out earlier."

For a brief second, though, the suspect turned to the right in a well lit spot, so that he was staring directly into the camera. But it didn't matter: all his details—race, age, even height—were washed out. He was little more than an outline, a terrifying specter.

"I see this shit all the time," Winston moaned. "Instead of dropping a couple bucks each year on a new tape, they use the same one over and over. Just rewinding and pushing record every eight hours until the fucking thing loses all its magnetic properties."

To the tech's credit he had been working at enhancing and enlarging the image, but he hadn't gotten very far. Our suspect was probably a Caucasian male. Maybe a little younger than the figure in the earlier "Unabomber" sketch.

"Bad news is the clerk remembered the girl, not the guy," said Bernie.

Suddenly the door of the van opened and Alex entered. He put his large hand on Bernie's shoulder and announced, "Good news, everybody—we caught our killer."

"Just tell me," Bernie said, in no mood for clowning.

"It's you, pal."

"What's me?"

Alex held up a credit card in a plastic evidence bag.

"Plucked from the cold fingers of the vic's right hand."

He also handed me a credit card receipt for the room rental. I felt a chill as I read, under cardholder's name, "Bernard P. Farrell."

"We're waiting for your credit card company to get back to us, but it looks like he also paid for the girl with it."

Bernie inspected the receipt carefully. He pulled out his wallet and went through it, looking for the card. "I didn't even notice it missing. It must've been the night I got mugged! Fuck!"

"How could the killer know you were on his case?" Alex asked.

"Bernie was mentioned in the papers," I reminded him.

"Where is that fucking kid!" Bernie shouted. Suddenly he broke into a coughing fit.

"He's playing us," Alex said.

"He's playing *one* of us, anyway," I muttered, looking at Bernie.

"He targeted your fucking *friend*, asshole," Bernie shot back angrily. "Maybe he's targeting *you*."

"All right, calm down," Alex said.

"Who is this Marilyn nut anyway?" Bernie asked me.

"What Marilyn nut?"

"The one who runs this Marilyn computer thing? Why does she do that?"

"Miriam Williams. She produced a Marilyn biopic a few years back and became a huge fan. And I met her through a friend."

"Hell of a coincidence, that you happen to have a friend who knows her," Bernie said.

"Maybe the killer knows Gladyss," Alex said.

"Miriam's rich," I pointed out. "Didn't Barry profile our killer as some poor guy?"

Staring at me suspiciously, Bernie asked, "How exactly did you happen to meet this rich woman who runs this web site?"

"She's a friend of a friend. I only met her a few hours ago," I said simply, not wanting to open up the whole can of worms involving Noel Holden.

"It's one fuck of a coincidence," Bernie said, giving me a fish eye.

I had a growing belief that my Kundalini studies had played a role in this "coincidence," but knowing that Bernie was such a philistine, I didn't dare mention it.

"Maybe *she* did it," Alex said, grinning at me.

I recalled something that had come to me on the cab ride down from Miriam's house. "You know, the first names of the first victim—Mary Lynn MacArthur—are very similar to Marilyn."

"I'm more impressed that you just happened to stumble across this lady with the spider web site." Bernie was not quite comfortable with the latest computer terms; I made a mental note to set him straight the next time we were on our own.

"She's leaving town in a few days so we have to question her soon."

"Did you take advantage of the occasion by asking her if she had any idea who it could be?" he asked with his usual surliness.

"Actually I did," I snapped back.

"What'd you say?"

"I asked her if she knew any Marilyn-obsessed fans who were nuts, or violent, or previously incarcerated," I replied.

"And did she?"

"She said the only ex-cons she knew were tax cheats."

"Good for you." He sounded earnest this time. "I don't mean to be an asshole, but I just don't have the energy to break in any more rookies."

"Is there anything else I can do here?" I asked, tired of his shit.

"No, Alex and Annie are interviewing everyone here. You've had a long day. Go home, get some sleep. I'm going to need you fresh in the morning."

With the wind chill it was about twenty degrees outside. As I walked past Matt's patrol car, I could see the cuffed reporter hunched forward in the backseat shivering his ass off.

I was about to grab a cab home, but I was still wide awake. Flipping open my cell phone I called Noel.

"This isn't my missing press agent, is it?" he answered.

"No it's last night's date. I was just leaving my latest crime scene and thought I'd . . ."

"Need a ride home?"

"I can just cab it," I said, since he sounded slightly intoxicated. "I just wanted to tell you I had a great time and wish you a good night."

"I'm literally getting into my car now," he said. "Where are you?"

"Thirty-seventh and Lex, northeast corner." Most of the emergency vehicles had gone, and traffic was flowing downtown again.

"You were a big hit," Noel said. "Miriam loved you."

"I didn't do anything."

"She loved the whole act."

"What act?"

"The whole police thing."

"It's not an act! Although, frankly, I'm a little new at it myself," I confessed. "I don't know all the cool jargon, and my partner keeps saying that all my insights are obvious."

"Nonsense, you're Oscar caliber," he replied. "Listen, I've got an important cameo in the upcoming Julia Roberts film, *Pretending To Speak French*. It's premiering in about a week. Would you join me as my date?"

"I've been working a lot in the evenings," I said, trying to spare his feelings.

"You sure? Cause I can send another car to your corner on that night, around seven."

Before I could reply, his car pulled up in front of me. He got out and gave me a hug, then held the door as I climbed in. I wiped my cell phone against my jacket sleeve and dropped it beside me on the seat. As he drove, Noel's hand slid up my arm and he idly caressed my bare shoulder. We chatted about the delightful party, and then the grim crime scene.

"Usually girls I date either fawn all over me, or they act like Venezia—total prima donnas," he concluded. "But you and I make a great team. I mean, I really enjoyed myself."

"I enjoyed yourself too."

"Then why don't we go on a second date?"

His car pulled up in front of my building. I open my door and stepped out, but before closing it I leaned back in.

"I'm kind of seeing someone right now."

"Ah."

"Sorry . . . Oh, I dropped my cell."

Noel snapped it up from the seat and handed it back, looking up at me as he said, "Well, you have my number if things don't go well."

I took the phone by its short stubby antenna, slipped it back into my bag, and thanked him again for a marvelous time.

When I arrived upstairs, I dropped the cell phone into a baggie. I called O'Ryan on my home phone, just to let him know that I had just got home unmurdered. The call went straight to his voicemail. So much for him having my back.

As I readied myself for bed I thought of Maggie, who was probably still gathering up half-finished plates and glasses, then cleaning up at Ms. Williams's mansion-apartment. Considering all the times I'd waved her over to me at the party, only to have people simply pick food off her platter and make annoying remarks, it must have seemed like I was deliberately trying to embarrass her.

I lay in bed awake for a while, half-hoping to catch her when she came home, so I could explain my honorable intentions. Eventually though, I was just too tired and sleep overtook me.

Some time later I awoke with a start. The door of the adjacent apartment had slammed shut—Maggie had finally returned. I listened for her TV; it was her habit to flip it on as soon as she came in, day or night. Instead I heard a garbled male voice, quickly followed by the frantic rhythms of fucking. She must've got lucky again with non-boyfriend/bartender, Rick.

Unable to return to sleep, I finally turned on my old Dell and Googled "Marilyn Monroe." I wanted to read up on Marilyn, but I also wanted to check out other Marilyn fan sites, to see if the killer had posted his murder jpegs and psycho poems there too. Eighty-two pages of Marilyn references came up, offering everything from her alleged stag film (accessible with a credit card payment) to Slavic language chat rooms devoted to her.

Though the platinum bombshell had other fan sites, I didn't see options for uploading pictures or poems on any of them. What I did see was how the internet fragmented Marilyn's life like a shattered mirror. Her abused childhood was rarely mentioned, and if it was, then only briefly, while her adult life—the years of her celebrity—was redundantly cross-referenced. For an hour I sifted through the lurid gossip surrounding her brief existence: chatter about sexual favors she possibly performed in exchange for film roles; details of her failed marriages to Joe DiMaggio and Arthur Miller as well as her flings with other celebrities, which allegedly included every bad boy of the day from Brando through Elvis and the glamorous Kennedys to a young Rip Torn.

As I read one article that described the constant flow of pills and alcohol she had consumed, not to mention the leaning tower of fame built upon her emotionally unstable childhood, I realized it was a miracle that she had lasted as long as she did.

As an afterthought I remembered that Bernie wanted me to check out the name, CathyofAlexandria, the email address attached to all the homicidal documentation. It turned out Catherine of Alexandria was a saint who had been tortured to death by a pagan Roman emperor rather than renounce her Christianity. Eventually the emperor had her beheaded—which seemed ironic, since this latest victim was the first our killer *hadn't* beheaded.

CHAPTER EIGHT

Early the next morning, I was awakened by a phone call. It was my brother.

"Turn on the TV, quick!"

"Hold on!"

Assuming it had something to do with my murder case, which he knew I was assigned to, I put on my glasses and flipped it on.

"What happened?" I asked him groggily, nervous that the killer had struck yet again while I slept. But onscreen I saw Colin Powell, the Secretary of State, speaking in a large auditorium filled with suits.

"What the hell is this?"

"Powell is at the UN, making a case for war so that we'll invade Iraq."

"Carl, I was sleeping!"

"We're being pushed into a war for absolutely no reason. Doesn't that bother you?"

"There's no draft, Carl," I said, turning the TV off. "It's not like Vietnam. No one's going to be forced to fight if they don't want to."

"How about the Iraqi people?" he shouted.

"I gotta go," I said, not caring to debate this bullshit any further.

"Do you mind if I ask you a personal question?" he said.

"I'm still a virgin, okay?" I said.

"How's the OCD?"

"All cleared up," I said and hung up. I lay back down. This was why I was glad Carl was no longer living in the city. He'd be breathing down my neck every second, trying to control my life. But I was always worried about him.

I closed my eyes, breathed steadily and tried to push all concerns out of my head The only thing that stuck in my mind was the vision

I'd had in yoga the other day—a tall, slim, shimmering woman holding a bow and arrow. After a while I showered, dressed, and went off to work. When I arrived, Bernie was sitting at his old partner's desk, resting his head against a cardboard box in front of him.

I peeked to make sure that his shoe was still on, then approached him. "You didn't call One PP about the Marilyn web site, did you?"

"Yep," he said, without making eye contact.

I didn't need the crisp morning light to see that Bernie needed a shave and a change of clothes. He looked haggard. Finally he sat up in his chair, swallowed down whatever bile had risen in his throat and said, "Last night after the credit card theft, I figured that this guy might be targeting me. So I've spent the last eight hours going through all my cases over the last fifteen years." He hit his head against the cardboard box. There were several more on the floor behind the desk.

"Those are all your cases?"

"Decades of pulling rats out of glue traps and putting them into tiny cages upstate. But I came up with nothing."

"So what now?"

"The problem with this business isn't running out of ideas, it's having too many of them. Bert used to say that."

"What ideas?"

He opened the file in front of him. It was our case. Aside from various reports, I saw a stack of crime photos. Close ups of severed heads. Detailed pictures of wrists and ankles splattered with blood and taped together. Single digit numbers carved painfully into soft flesh.

"I'm sure you noticed that all the numbers cut into the vic's limbs correspond with the numbers cut into prior vics . . ." I again made the mistake of stating the obvious.

"Yeah, yeah. The way the bodies are positioned, the numbering on the limbs, the crap he shoves into their hands—all that shit. If you can figure out what it means, I'll give you ten bucks. Otherwise . . ." He made a zipper gesture over his mouth. All these dead ends were evidently driving him nuts.

"The thing I find most interesting is the actual taping," Bernie finally said. "It must be really hard to get their limbs like that and balance them all to stay upright."

"Maybe the guy worked for Mailboxes Etc."

"And why is this the only victim he didn't decapitate?"

"Yet he still did the numbering and taping," I pointed out.

When I looked at the Polaroids of our latest Jane Doe, I gasped. The killer had been so violent that even her implants were sliced apart. Also, unlike the other girls, she had a tattoo on her back—a coiled and sleeping dragon.

"What now?" I asked.

"I'm going to shave, change my shirt, and get a coffee. Then we'll go back to the list."

I used the recess to dash to the lab, where I gave my baggied cell-phone to a techie and asked him to lift Noel's prints from it, then run them through the file to see if they matched any we had found at the other crime scenes. He told me the CSI techies had found two new fingerprints at last night's crime scene that they were pretty certain belonged to the killer.

As I got back to the squad room, Alex and Annie arrived, both at the same time. Just when I began to wonder if they were sleeping together, Bernie explained that they had gone out to Brooklyn to check up on some possible leads regarding the latest victim. A wonderful way to spend a Saturday morning, considering they both had families.

"Find out anything?"

"Her real name was Jane Hansen, nickname Minty," Annie said, reading from her notepad. "She lived in Greenpoint with her cat Angus. Went to NYU film school, and was still paying off her student loans. She's the first vic who doesn't seem connected to any escort service, though I guess she might be a freelancer."

"But she might not be a hooker at all," Alex added.

"Why do you say that?" Bernie asked.

"She has no record, and we haven't found anything tying her to the sex industry," Annie said, almost happily. I remembered how bad she'd felt when we found so little at the last vic's house.

"Did the receptionist at the Ticonderoga ever see her before?"

"Nope," Annie replied. "And she has no priors of any kind."

"Do me a favor," Bernie said to Alex, handing him a piece of paper with a phone number scribbled on it. "I've called them twice already. This is tech support. Can you stay on them to get us a computer geek? I need someone to look at Gladyss's friend's laptop, check out this, uh, web site, and help determine if our guy is targeting this lady." I wasn't sure why they would need to look at her laptop, but I didn't say anything as Alex took the paper.

With the help of last week's expanded task force, we had whittled our list of suspects down to roughly two dozen names consisting of those we couldn't find or hadn't interviewed yet and three men we had interviewed who were deemed persons of interest, worth interviewing again.

Using details from the Ticonderoga Hotel case, Bernie was now able to cut the list down further, bringing our suspects down to a baker's dozen. They consisted of eight whites, two light-skinned blacks and three Latinos, all of whom could've matched the poor-contrast image of the suspect on the washed-out Ticonderoga tape. All were relatively thin and had a history of theft, or frequenting prostitutes, and/or violence against women.

"If we can hit these guys," he suggested. "a series of quick field interrogations should give us some idea if any of them is our boy."

I didn't share in his optimism about detecting instant guilt. To me it was more like a big, chilly fishing expedition. Again I was teamed with Bernie. I didn't know if he took painkillers or simply wore a more comfortable shoe, but he seemed a little less angry this time. As we headed out to his car, I asked him what the plan of attack was.

"You want to know the plan of—" he caught himself. I knew he was about to say something nasty. "Okay, unless they're complete psychos—zero affect—these guys are usually right on the edge. Ready to pop. You don't have to press that hard. If they start coming apart, you lock 'em up, sweat them, run their prints, and check their alibis for the night of the murders."

When I asked him if he could remember his first murder case, he said it involved a drug dealer back, when he was "a ghetto cop in the Bushwhack." It sounded like an old *Kojak* rerun.

"The difference is provincialism," he said as we drove up Eighth Avenue. "Out there, you knew your characters and what they were up to. Manhattan is different. Everyone's just blowing through," he said just as an arctic gust blasted down the avenue, tagging any flesh left exposed by poorly wrapped scarves and the bright pink earlobes of those who didn't pull their hats down tight enough.

106

"Was Youngblood just blowing through?" I inquired, remembering the geriatric tube sock hustler. Since Bernie seemed in a relatively good mood, I thought maybe he would open up a bit. But he didn't hear me.

"I was just too young to know any better," he muttered.

"What should you have known?"

"A cute young teenager gets into drugs. The boyfriend who got her hooked leaves her. Her dealer moves up to being her pimp. To avoid going away for her third conviction, she becomes your own private ghost. I was a lonely kid—not much older than you—who made the mistake of getting too close to a beautiful, damaged girl. Same as Bert, only at his age he should've known a lot better."

"Bert, your old partner?"

"Yeah, except he married his snitch. Mine was found in the bottom of a filthy air shaft out in the Red Hook." He paused a moment, and I could see by the way he chewed his inner lip that he was reliving the moment. "I've had to spend the last twenty years knowing it was my stupidity that put her down there."

Bernie's cell rang; it was Alex to say that tech support at One Police Plaza was a little backed up, but someone would definitely look into the web site by tomorrow.

Of the six remaining suspects Bernie and I were checking, we knew we'd be lucky if we got to the three most promising ones today. All had been in prison within the past five years. Two of them, Joseph Donnelly and Nessun O'Flaherty, had done time for assaulting hookers, but the last and best suspect was a pimp named Howard Sprag who went by the moniker "Hozec." Bernie explained that this nickname was a shortening of either Whore Executive or Whore Executioner—Sprag was rumored to wring the necks of his bottom earners. Bernie seemed to have a particularly vengeful place in his heart for pimps who killed their hookers.

What's more, Sprag had also been arrested a few years ago on a murder charge involving ligature strangulation —a girl named Sally DiNasio was found with a telephone cord wrapped around her neck. She was a Garden State runaway who he'd probably recruited at Port Authority. Although the case went to trial, he got off due to insufficient evidence. He was later arrested for drug possession and did the majority of his twelve-year sentence, though he shortened it somewhat by informing on another inmate.

According to his parole officer, Sprag worked for a few months for the Forty Second Street Partnership, a halfway house for early releases. He was one of those guys who wear a white jumpsuit and sweep the streets around Times Square. Then one day he stopped showing up for work and coming to meetings. The parole officer explained, "I have a warrant out on his ass, but haven't had time to hunt him down."

Sprag's last known address was a transient hotel, the Lathem, at Twenty-eighth and Tenth. As we parked in front of the place, Bernie said he had interviewed another suspect here just last week during the initial dragnet. The desk clerk, a tall Indian gentleman named Lionel, recognized Bernie as he entered.

"How can I be of service, Detective?"

When Bernie asked him if Howard Sprag still lived here, Lionel paused, sighed, and responded in a watered-down British accent, "About two months ago Mr. Sprag called down to the desk saying there was a dead body in his room. I went upstairs and saw him standing in the hall smoking a cigarette. When I asked about said body, he just nodded inside his room. I went in, looked around, peeked under the bed, and told him I didn't see any dead body. 'It's out the window,' he replied. I figured he was pulling my leg, you know. So I went back downstairs. By the time I reached the lobby someone out front was screaming. Apparently Mr. Sprag finished his fag and jumped out of the window."

"Rest in peace, Hozec," I muttered.

"Why doesn't his PO know this shit?" Bernie asked no one in particular.

"You're the first person who's come around asking about him," Lionel replied.

Bernie asked when this had happened exactly, and Lionel's answer told us Sprag had been dead before the last two murders were committed.

Joe Donnelly was next up. He had briefly been a member of the infamous Irish gang the Westies, but reportedly they tossed him out when it became clear he had a greater loyalty to heroin. More recently Donnelly had been living in and out of his mother's place in the Penn South Housing Projects, Section Eight Assistance, along Twenty-fourth and Eighth Avenue. Bernie recalled arresting him for something once before. Maybe extortion.

"So maybe he has it in for you," I pointed out, referring to his stolen credit card.

"Maybe," he replied.

We parked in front of the building, got in the front door without ringing, went up the stairs, and knocked on his mother's door. Bernie was a big believer in the surprise drop-in.

"In here, pronto," a deep, hoarse voice hollered. The place was a mess, and smelled of sardines and boiled eggs. A bloated Raggedy Anne from hell seemed to be permanently parked inches in front of a loud and angry TV set; a half empty 40 of Coors and a box of saltines on a table beside her chair.

"You're not Meals on Wheels," she growled.

"And you're not Vanessa Del Rio doing Desire Cousteau," he replied. I had no idea who he was talking about.

"The TV is *not* loud, so don't tell me it is!" she said defiantly when we identified ourselves.

"We're not here for that," Bernie shot back and turned it off. "We're looking for that evil shit that you let loose upon the world."

"Ain't here."

Bernie pulled out his pistol and kicked open her closet and bathroom doors, checking for himself.

"Joey's a good kid," she replied. "What's he done now?"

"Killed some girls."

"Huh?"

"Dead girls," I repeated to her.

"When's he s'posed to have killed 'em?" she asked.

"Where the fuck is he?" Bernie shouted.

"My kidneys are killing me," she complained. "I need dialysis."

"Where the fuck is your kid?"

"That's what I'm trying to tell yous. He's been in Riker's for six months now—shoplifting."

Bernie used his cell to call the prison and confirm it. Two down.

"Now can I watch the rest of my shows?" she asked, turning the TV back on.

"It's too loud," I said, turning it down.

"I can't hear it like that."

"Get a hearing aid," I shouted.

As soon as we stepped into the hallway, the volume shot back up. At least I'd given her a little exercise—she'd had to lift the remote again.

When we returned to the car, Bernie looked at the info sheet for suspect number three and saw that he was still on parole.

"Christ it's dark," I said, amazed that it was already pitch black even though it was only late afternoon. I was fired up about interrogating the other suspects but by now Bernie's foot was clearly agitating the hell out of him.

"Let's call it a night and try to reach his parole officer tomorrow," I suggested. That was the state parole office on Fortieth Street.

"All right," he said.

We returned to the precinct where Bernie suddenly realized he was way behind on the paperwork needed for a court case tomorrow morning. He took a Valium to handle the pain, but as soon as he sat down, he passed out with his head on his desk.

My phone rang: the lab tech with the test results I'd asked for. Noel's prints didn't match any of those found at the various crime scenes. So much for my theory.

It wasn't the end of my shift yet, so I grabbed Bernie's pen and spent the next hour and a half trying to extract vital information from him so I could finish his paperwork. Otherwise a homicide charge would get dropped the next day.

"Is this the squad that investigates Hollywood stud muffins?"

O'Ryan popped his head round the door. He told me he'd just finished logging in a box of stolen iPods in the property room downstairs. Even though Bernie was snoring away on the couch I walked out into the hall to talk with Eddie.

"My cell phone died, I'm really sorry," he said referring to my date night with Noel. Then he asked if the actor's fingerprints had matched anything.

"No," I replied. "But you still could've called me the next morning to see how I was doing."

"I heard that you roughed up some boy reporter at the Ticonderoga Hotel, so I figured you were doing fine," he replied.

Before he could get around to asking if I wanted to go to dinner, his temporary partner, Lenny, suddenly appeared and the two had to run. I headed to yoga, leaving Bernie sleeping in his office.

CHAPTER NINE

When I arrived at the precinct the following morning, Bernie was already there. I couldn't tell if he'd stayed there all night. He told me he had just gotten off the phone with Dan Rasdale, O'Flaherty's parole officer.

"He said he's been missing a couple of his boys 'cause of their work hours, and he was hoping to sneak up on them this Sunday."

"I just hope he's better than Hozec's P.O.," I said. "Did he tell you anything about O'Flaherty?"

Bernie read what he had wrote down: "Nessun O'Flaherty, 57 years old. Twenty-two years ago, when he was thirty-five, O'Flaherty graduated from Queens Law. But before he could take the bar exam, his wife accused him of statutory rape. He'd apparently been screwing his underage stepdaughter. He was a drunk, and during the arrest he popped a police officer, which earned him a couple of years inside. He passed the bar in jail."

"Christ!" I said, "with a first-time statutory rape he probably would've got off with probation."

"It gets worse. In prison he gets into a fight with another inmate and kills the guy. He gets another ten years added to his sentence, and after a series of fights and other charges, he doesn't get out until a year and a half ago. He's got fifteen months left on his parole."

"Amazing he's managed to stay clean."

Bernie went on: "O'Flaherty stopped showing up at his AA meetings about a year back. Roughly nine months ago, he got picked up for jostling in Times Square." This meant he was bumping into passersby then picking their pocket while they were distracted. "The plaintiff vanished before they could have him swear out a complaint. Then, about six months ago, he got picked up by the pussy posse during a big hooker sting in the area. He was charged with a 230-02, but that's only a class B misdemeanor, not enough to put him back in jail. He also got picked up for slapping a female tourist. Again the parole officer tried to put him back in, but the fucking tourist refused to fill out a complaint."

"Where is he now?"

"An SRO on Fortieth and Eighth, across from Port Authority."

We double-parked in front of O'Flaherty's dump, which turned out to be across the street from where Bernie had clobbered Youngblood, on Eighth Avenue between Fortieth and Forty-first. Every other building on its side of the block had been pulled down as part of New York's latest nip and tuck. Engraved in the filthy stone over the doorway I could just make out the building's name, The Centurion, one of those many urban details no one notices any longer. Inside we saw it was clearly a place where neglected seniors slowly ran out their clocks.

Bernie recognized the desk clerk, a retired cop named Hal. He asked him if he knew O'Flaherty.

"Sure, he's a regular hero around these parts." The clerk explained that the ex-con had been instrumental in getting a stay of execution for the old hotel. He had managed to unify the remaining tenants in the dilapidated building and lobby local politicians, and somehow convinced the court to grant a six-month injunction against knocking down this final, teetering domino at the end of the dying block.

"Have you ever seen O'Flaherty with any prosses, or smacking anyone around?" Bernie asked.

"Nessun? No, he's harmless. Why, what did he do?"

"We got some dead girls in the area. Is he upstairs?"

"I doubt it. Every morning, he's out early. He goes to the OTB on Forty-fourth and Seventh. He loves the ponies. Spends the day out."

"At the OTB?"

"He used to hang out at the Cupcake Cafe over on Ninth, but from what I heard, he would complain that the holes were too big in their donuts, so they eighty-sixed him. Try the Starbucks at Thirty-eighth and Eighth." He gave us a brief description of O'Flaherty.

As we walked over there, Bernie said he wanted to try a little test. Once we'd located our suspect, I was to watch O'Flaherty closely as Bernie walked past him. It was my job to determine whether O'Flaherty recognized Bernie. If he did, he was probably the one who'd mugged Bernie, since Bernie had never previously met him.

Three-quarters homeless shelter, one-quarter corporate refueling depot, the Starbucks was an amusing blender of social classes. Sleeping junkies, turned-out shut-ins, and misguided tourists were interspersed among the usual laptop jockeys, who I liked to believe were struggling writers. But it was the steady flow of busy yuppies who popped in, bought their sugary hot fuel, and dashed back out, that bankrolled the franchise. In the back, settled in a cozy armchair which he probably shared with endless microscopic parasites, was our lapsed sex offender. He was a balding, jaundiced man with dark, deeply inset eyes. A gray trench coat insulated him in the poorly heated establishment, and an old fedora with clipped-on waterproofing rested on the coffee table. When we got closer I could see his ruddy, pockmarked cheeks. Matching the stereotype, every capillary in his nose had been ruptured by booze. If I hadn't known he was in his late fifties, I'd have guessed he was at least ten years older. To his credit, the ex-con was deeply engrossed in an old leatherback.

Outside, Bernie had taken off his coat, scarf, and jacket, rolled them into a ball, and handed them to me. With a discarded section of the *New York Times* folded under his arm, he now lumbered by the old ne'er-do-weller and plunked himself down in a chair across from him. I watched diligently as O'Flaherty glanced up at Bernie. He seemed to genuinely take note of him, but there was no display of guilt, or any indication of twitchiness.

"Excuse me," I finally approached. Bernie took back his coat.

"If it's locked, it's occupied," O'Flaherty muttered without looking up. He thought I was inquiring about the bathroom. Its door was right there, a foul odor emanating from behind it.

"Nessun?" Bernie asked.

"Officer." He looked up with a pleasant smile. Either he had great instincts or he was Bernie's mugger —and our killer. Then looking at me, he joked, "What's this, Take Your Daughter to Work Day?"

"Actually it's Take Your Convict to Jail Day," Bernie countered. "Parole violation."

O'Flaherty closed his book. It was a weather-beaten copy of *Bullfinch's Mythology.* He gulped down the dregs of his small coffee, grabbed his hat, and labored to his feet. I could see him grimace as he shuffled along.

"What's with the leg?" Bernie asked, perhaps wondering if he was being mocked.

" Hip replacement in my right leg two years ago, and the cartilage in my right knee is shot." O'Flaherty explained. "An old prison injury that just gets worse and worse." We let him walk the few blocks in silence before directing him to the Lumina.

"You're not carrying anything?" Bernie asked before opening the car door. "Drugs or weapons?"

"No."

"I better not hit a needle," Bernie said as he patted him down, then cuffed him. I opened the back door and helped O'Flaherty inside, Bernie slid in next to him. For the first time with him, I got to drive.

"Christ it's a freezer in here," O'Flaherty said, as Bernie started going through his pockets. "What's this—a shakedown?"

"Got any ID?"

"Library card, voter's registration," he replied as Bernie pulled out his wallet.

"You went to Sacred Heart?" Bernie asked, seeing something.

"Oh yeah, you too?"

"For two years."

"You know Sister Mary Ellen?"

"Oh God, did she fill her habit." Bernie replied. "You knew Father Bill?"

"Shit, don't get me started. That poofter tried to finger my holy ghost every chance he got."

"He almost caught me in the boy's room once. I never ran so fast."

"Oh, I miss the old days. Cardinal Spellman mighta sucked off an altar boy or two, but we had style and power back then."

The two of them made the Roman Catholic Church sound like the golden days of the mafia.

I parked in the rear of the precinct on Thirty-sixth. Bernie tried to suppress his own limp as he led O'Flaherty upstairs to an interrogation room. Before our suspect could sit down, Bernie had him take off his coat and told him to roll up his sleeve. When O'Flaherty did so, I watched Bernie looking carefully at him. I thought he was looking for possible track marks, but when he made him undress to reveal his chest, back, and neck, I realized he was hoping to find a defensive wound, a possible scratch or bruise on his arms inflicted by poor Jane. None were apparent.

"So what are you doing for money these days?" Bernie asked.

"Disability," he said. "This isn't just about a parole violation, is it? What am I suspected of, exactly?"

"You tell us."

"Oh wait! You're her, aren't you, officer?" he asked, suddenly turning to me.

"What are you talking about?"

"I saw the photos, read about those killings. Tall, sexy, and blonde, and here you are."

"Do I look like one of the victims?"

"You look like all of them, which is why you're the bait," he replied. "But here's my question: how do you know he didn't kill all those girls just hoping the NYPD would eventually sacrifice *you*?"

"What are you talking about?"

"He's saying, he killed all the blonde hookers so that he'd eventually find a blonde cop posing as a hooker," Bernie said, amused.

"Not me, and not quite," Nessun replied, staring at me. "I'm saying those hookers were the bait; the killer was just waiting for the NYPD to toss you into the bear trap."

"And now that you know I'm the bait, you wouldn't come on to me?"

"That's right," he said with a smile.

"How about that guy you pickpocketed at the Starbucks a few months back," I replied. "What was the matter—he didn't have a credit card?"

"An innocent mistake. I thought it was my coat. That's why the good man dropped the charges."

"Did you think it was your wife when you got stung with the hooker?" Bernie asked.

"In enlightened countries prostitution is legal."

"See a lot of hookers, do you?" I asked.

"The last one I saw was just some curly haired runaway, followed me home from the bus depot across the street."

"And that's when you choked her?" I asked, approaching him.

"Hey, I've had hundreds of bus depot runaways in my place and I never touched the one of them."

"Tell us about the last one," Bernie said.

"She laid back on my bed and I could see right up her skirt. Damned if that wasn't the day her knickers were in the wash. So young, she hardly had any hair down there." Narrowing his eyes right at me, he smiled and in a throaty tone, added, "Damned if she didn't look just like you."

I just meant to scare him. but accidentally I dropped my clunky Motorola police radio right on his bum knee.

"Fuck!" he screamed, clutching it painfully.

"It just slipped out of my hands," I said to Bernie, who smiled, probably thinking I was finally toughening up.

"Accidents happen," Bernie said philosophically.

As O'Flaherty clenched his knee, tears flowed down his cheek. I honestly felt bad for him, but I knew I couldn't let on. When he struggled to stand up on his one good leg I pushed him back into his chair.

"Let's start again. The last girl you were with?"

"I don't remember. Honest to God . . . Christ!" He spoke between gasps, still squeezing out the pain. He claimed he had to get something from his coat pocket. Bernie checked the pocket and found some loose pills.

"Looky here," he showed me. "Possession of narcotics, a class C felony. That's a ticket back upstate."

"They're Advil, just over-the-counter painkillers."

"We won't know that for a couple days, until we get the lab reports back."

"I don't think I can walk," O'Flaherty groaned.

Bernie gave him two pills. He swallowed them then looked fearfully at me.

"You want out, start talking."

"I spent the last fifteen years in jail because one night I got into a fight with my bitchy teenage stepdaughter, and she gets back at me by telling my wife that I'm screwing her."

"You went to jail 'cause you hit a cop."

"He hit me first."

117

"Then you killed an inmate."

"Fucker grabbed my Thanksgiving turkey right off my plate—the best meal of the year. But his neck looked just as juicy, so my fork went right into his jugular."

"Sure, a piece of turkey for ten years of your life," said Bernie, as if it seemed like a fair trade to him.

"Would you believe me if I told you I had ten grand in Microsoft stock in 1982? It would've been worth a couple million today, if I'd just left it there."

"In Microsoft?"

"No one believes me, but an aunt left me the cash, and someone in law school gave me the tip, so I bought the stock. But I sold it the day after I got arrested to pay for a lawyer. The ambulance chaser turned out to be worthless. I shoulda defended myself."

"We each create our own life," I said, "and everything that comes with it." The Renunciate had said that during his last class.

"Sick . . . alone . . . broke. I'm the youngest resident in a hotel of dying old losers."

"And in six months you're all going to be evicted anyway," Bernie added blithely.

"My family owned a brownstone on Forty-fifth between Tenth and Eleventh, right across from Shamrock Stables. It was taken by the city in '89 for nonpayment of taxes. All I got now is what you see."

"You like tall blondes, don't you?" Bernie asked.

"Please, I can barely walk, let alone whack off anymore."

"Just give us someone who saw you on these three particular days," Bernie said, flipping through his notepad. He read out the dates and times of the four murders, including Jane Hansen's death two days ago.

Two days ago was still fresh in his head. He told us he was hanging in the lobby with Hal, the retired cop, and a half a dozen geriatrics.

"Call and confirm it!" he said eagerly. "We have a fixed routine on Fridays. We eat hot sandwiches and watch the replays of the races at Belmont and Aqueduct."

When Bernie pressed him about the other murder dates, O'Flaherty said he wasn't sure about anything beyond a week ago. But he was definitely watching the races with Hal and others on any given Friday. He never missed one.

Bernie put the old guy in lockup, then he called the retired cop. Hal said they didn't meet every single Friday, but most weeks they did. As luck would have it, Mary Lynn MacArthur's body was discovered on Friday, but that wasn't enough to rule him out.

"Is there another clerk who might've seen O'Flaherty?"

"No, Rubin leaves the TV off. Keeps his own counsel."

Bernie thanked him and hung up. Just to be on the safe side, Bernie said we should check O'Flaherty's room.

"Do we have enough to get a warrant?"

"All we need is his parole officer. Bernie called Danny Rasdale and explained that we wanted to search his ex-con's room. He had to reassure Rasdale: "No, no forensic people at this stage, we'll go in on our own first and just look around. If we find anything suspicious, I'll call them after . . . When's your lunch break? . . . Okay, we'll drop by your office and pick you up at noon, then."

Bernie hung up. Apparently he'd been stood up by parole officers before, and learned the best way to get them to the suspect's residence was to take them there himself.

Now Bernie took a sheet of paper and walked over to the holding cage where O'Flaherty was sitting.

"Make you a deal," he said to the prisoner, "Let us search your room and we'll cut you loose."

"You like playing tiddlywinks, don't you?" O'Flaherty smiled. "We both know that since I'm a predicate felon, you don't need my permission. All you have to do is get my PO to join you."

Bernie turned around and stormed into the hallway.

I followed him out there. "What's the matter?"

"He's on to us."

"What do you mean?"

"He might be bullshitting, but if he knows we can toss his room, the odds of us catching something in there are pretty damn long."

We had to try it, though. With O'Flaherty sitting in lockup, at noon Bernie and I headed over to the parole office on Fortieth, where we found ourselves standing in the packed waiting area with all the sad and misbegotten types waiting for Rasdale, who was running late, just as Bernie had predicted.

When he finally came out twenty minutes later, Rasdale turned out to be a walking beer belly. But he moved surprisingly quickly.

In about five minutes we were in O'Flaherty's squalid lobby just around the corner. Hal gave us a passkey and together we went up in an incredibly slow elevator to his room on the top floor. His private bathroom looked like it had never been cleaned, but his room was spotless. His clothes were all on hangers or folded in a cardboard box. His bookcase was stuffed full but neat. Even his bed was made.

The only unsavory thing about the room was a faint odor of horse shit. Rasdale explained that O'Flaherty liked to visit the stables over on Forty-fifth Street. Apparently he was friends with one of the buggy drivers.

There was little by way of display: a couple of library books (overdue, I checked) stacked next to his bed, some disability insurance documents taped to the back of his door, and over his bed he had stuck up a postcard. I moved closer to look at it and gasped. It was the vision I'd had in class during final relaxation a few days ago. The postcard showed a gleaming golden woman, standing on a pedestal, holding a bow and arrow.

"The place is too fucking clean for a sleazebucket like him," Bernie was saying to the PO. "He was definitely expecting us."

"O'Flaherty is really a sad case," Rasdale said. "He's sharp as a rusty razor. I mean, he's one of my few cons who sounds uptown all the way, but he has this major fucking chip on his shoulder, and it'll always keep him in the gutter."

"What is it?"

"He believes he was cheated out of his true destiny."

"He's not dead yet," I said. "Why can't he reach his destiny now?"

"It's a lot easier to be bitter than to try and succeed," Bernie said.

"Actually, this isn't even about his life really, it's more about this area," Rasdale said. "He obsesses about the developers destroying his old neighborhood."

"When your best days are behind you, it's difficult not to live in the past," Bernie responded dolefully.

"I tried telling him that he should be a tour guide—he can point to any corner within a ten-block radius of here and tell you who lived where, and what stores and shops came and went over the past forty years."

"Good for him," Bernie said. "Almost no one has a clue about this city's past. Hell, we might as well be an overpopulated Provo, Utah."

"Do you think he's capable of killing and decapitating four women?" I tried to cut to the chase.

"I got a dozen other guys who I'd suggest first, but you never know."

"He did it," Bernie said simply.

"Just because he keeps a clean room?" Rasdale asked.

"Our killer is a DNA wiper. Just like this guy."

"He's got a solid alibi for the evening of Jane Hansen's murder," I reminded Bernie.

"Yeah and that was the one fucking murder that was different from the others, wasn't it?"

"It wasn't that different," I said, lifting the untaped bottom of the postcard, so I could read the title: *Augustus Saint-Gaudens, Diana, [Greek Goddess of the Hunt]*.

"What the hell are you looking at?" Bernie asked, coming toward me. I didn't want to talk about it because I knew he'd think I was crazy if I told him I'd seen the image in a vision.

"Just a postcard."

He looked at it for a moment and said, "I met her."

"You met a Greek goddess, did you?"

"Actually, that was a common fallacy."

"What was?"

Bernie sighed. "Let me try this again. Ever heard of Evelyn Nesbit?"

"Nope."

"She was this *It* girl about a hundred years ago, and a lot of people think she posed for that statue, because of the way the story's told in that novel *Ragtime*. The statue used to be on top of the old Madison Square Garden, and Evelyn Nesbit was the lover of Stanford White, the architect who designed it. But she wasn't the model for that"— he pointed to the postcard—"she was only a child when the statue was made.

"And you met her?"

"Yeah, once, in the early 1960s. I was a kid and she was an old lady."

"And who exactly was she?" I asked.

"A model, and a chorus girl. You know what? Just rent the movie *Ragtime*." He paused, then added, "Only remember, she didn't actually pose for that statue."

Rasdale cut in. "So what do you think?"

"I think this is our guy," Bernie said flatly.

"What exactly is it that tells you it's him?" I asked, intrigued by his rock-hard confidence.

"Intuition," he replied. "Bert used to say that was the most valuable tool a detective had."

"He's right," Rasdale added. "I can feel it in my gut when one of my boys has gone off the reservation."

While they were chatting, I took a couple steps away, closed my eyes, and tried to push out all external thoughts. Nothing came to me. I took some shallow hyperbreaths and focused on the striking image of the hunter goddess. Then I realized all was oddly silent around me. When I opened my eyes, Bernie and Dan were just staring at me.

"So are you calling CSU or not?" Danny asked Bernie. "Because I got a roomful of ex-cons waiting for me back at the office."

"No, they won't find anything," Bernie said.

I looked over the contents of O'Flaherty's bookcase. It was mostly histories of New York City. There were also a handful of books on horse racing; the guy sure loved his ponies. An old tourist book of the city dating back to the '50s had little yellow post-its leafing along the top. And there were three large old picture books showing Times Square over a century ago. There were a couple of general history books, flipping through them, I didn't see any references to Catherine of Alexandria in their indexes.

We walked Rasdale back to the State Parole Office, where we thanked him for his help and watched him hustle up the steps.

"What the hell was going on back there?" Bernie asked me as he pulled out a cigarette.

"What?" I thought he was referring to the postcard of Diana again.

"You, with the closed eyes and deep breathing."

"Oh, I thought I was getting a migraine," I lied. If I told Bernie about the whole Kundalini thing, I know he'd transfer me straight back to NSU.

He struck a match, lit his cigarette, and immediately started coughing. I silently nodded.

"Hey, I've smoked for thirty-five years without so much as having to clear my throat," he said. "This fucking cough is from inhaling two hundred stories of glass, plaster, and everything else that was in those goddamn towers."

"At the time you were working on the excavation, you couldn't tell the air was toxic?"

"I was wheezing at the time, but the goddamn EPA and every other government agency said it was all fine, just a little dust and smoke—fucking Christine Todd Whitman!"

By the time we got back to the precinct, O'Flaherty had been hauled off to Central Booking. It would take the night to get a court date for skipping out on his parole appointments. Unless he had any other outstanding warrants, he'd be released tomorrow.

At five o'clock, we all conferred on our progress. Of the seven names Alex and Annie were supposed to check out, they had cleared five—two suspects were in prison, two had solid alibis for most if not all of the murders, and the last one had turned up in Potter's Field.

We had five more to go. Though Bernie couldn't shake the feeling that O'Flaherty was the one, the rest of us were doubtful, and felt disappointed that we were running out of suspects. The confidence I'd gained from my Kundalini experience, that vision of Diana, was fading.

While I was on-line, I Googled Diana, Goddess of the Hunt, and was startled to find I had some things in common with her. Diana was said to have been a tall blonde—like me. Also, like me, she had a twin, the god Apollo. Okay, my brother Carl was hardly a god, but we were close to one another, like Diana and Apollo apparently were. Then it got even more personal: I read that Diana had remained a virgin, even if it was for different reasons than mine. She supposedly prayed to Zeus not be distracted by the confusion of sexual desire so she could stay focused on her sacred mission, which was the protection of childbirth. So she was the goddess of hunting, but she was also a sworn defender of women. Which was kind of my role in life, too. All that gave me something to think about.

After the humiliation of being stared at in O'Flaherty's hotel room, I decided to skip the beginner's class, which was mainly stretches, and try the master class later that night. The Renunciate hadn't arrived when I got there. For the other members of the class, it seemed to be Off-White Pajama Day: two heavy, older men with long scraggly

123

beards bookended two emaciated older women. They all wore turbans. They all had their hands folded, their eyelids closed, and seemed to be on some higher plane of consciousness. I feared that once they opened their eyes and saw I had sneaked in, they'd toss me the hell out for not being in uniform. After a moment though, hoping that maybe I might gain some guidance from these learned elders, I took a deep gulp of their air and spoke softly to the nearest lady, "How did you know when you first released your Kundalini?"

Their eyes all popped open and for a moment I thought they were going to laugh.

"There is nothing subtle about it," she said. I lost myself completely, then I spent the night weeping in supreme ecstasy."

"I breathed through waves of heat," the other woman chimed in. "That's how I knew it was happening."

"That's your chakras running full throttle," replied the barely younger old man.

"My *Sahasrara* was spinning so fast," the older woman added.

"As were my *Anahata* and *Vishudda*," the older old man whispered. I had a feeling these terms might be Sanskrit for the gall bladder and the spleen.

"Have any of you ever *seen* anything unusual while this was happening?"

"I think I know what you're getting at," said the older woman. "It must be scary if you don't know what you're seeing. You're seeing a person's aura."

"What's that?"

"Usually a color radiating from them," the other woman replied, and the first one nodded.

"Have any of you ever seen anything like an image of a statue?" I asked, tiring of the new age bullshit.

"A statue?" one repeated, while the others shook their heads. "That sounds more like a Christian thing. There are no statues here."

At this point, the Renunciate entered, and we all closed our eyes and mouths. He took his place at the mat in the front of the class. Closing his eyes, he began his ancient chants, as though summoning up the spirits. The breathing and the poses all started out the same as in the other classes, but here he slowly led us to positions that were far more challenging. Unlike the easier classes, he gave no explanations or advice. He simply did the moves and his students silently followed. Aside from their strength and flexibility, I strangely admired their shameless ability to fart without apology. They seemed to unfold and contort their late middle-aged bodies in ways that only the purest of heart could venture. The Renunciate finally got to the inversions. I was proud that I could hold a handstand, but looking around I realized the other yogis were actually balanced on their turbans, their arms against their sides. During final relaxation, I lay flat; this time, instead of seeing anything, I closed my eyes and wondered if the vision I'd had of the statue of Diana earlier was the sign that some divine force was telling me, per that picture on his postcard, that Nessun was our killer.

On the short walk home, the cold air gripped my hot skin like the frosted hand of God. I decided to skip dinner and, after a hot shower, barely made it to bed.

"No! Please!"

I awoke with a start. From the rhythmic thumps against the common wall, I knew Maggie was getting seriously banged. When I first became friends with her, I was going to ask her to move her bed, but I came to see the occasional rapping as a reminder that I had to start my own sex life.

"Stop it, I'm begging you!"

I sat up and wondered if I should intervene. Grabbing a glass, I pressed it against the wall to try and determine if she was okay.

"Say it!"

I clearly heard the male command and recognized the voice from somewhere. I could barely hear her reply.

"She'll never go for it."

"Just say it, if you want me to stop," he said in a calmer tone.

"All right! I'll do it! Stop!"

After a few more minutes I heard Maggie moaning steadily until finally it sounded like she was climaxing. Then, when I heard the man groaning, I realized who he was.

About a half an hour later, when the clock said six, I heard her door open. I was able to confirm my suspicions by looking through the peephole. The gnarled face of Crispin Marachino flashed by as he left.

By Monday afternoon we had checked out the remaining five suspects on Bernie's list. Two had gotten permission to move out of state. Two more were keeping their noses clean, according to their parole officers' accounts, and had good alibis. Only one was a fugitive. According to his ex-wife he'd last been spotted in the state of Delaware.

At the end of the day, when we realized our suspect list was a bust, Annie said the good news was that the computer tech from One PP was finally on his way over. The Marilyn web site connection was now our best hope for moving forward. Only then did I remember that Miriam Williams had flown to Europe yesterday.

The tech support guy turned out to be Indian-American, but from his Westernized demeanor I knew he'd never practiced any form of yoga. Raj said he had done some work on the case already at Police Plaza. He had discovered that the horrific images of Jane had been sent from a computer in the Midtown Manhattan Library on Fifth Avenue at Fortieth Street, which had been open until 11 p.m. that night. He inspected Miriam's' laptop, which we had kept in Bernie's office.

"What exactly is the deal with using the library computers?" Bernie asked.

"They allow you to use them for fifteen-minutes at a time, but you have to sign in first."

"It's probably the closest library for O'Flaherty," I pointed out.

"Let's take a walk," Bernie said, rising slowly onto his tricky foot and grabbing his coat.

"Are you sure you're up for this?" I asked. He had been wincing all day. But as if it were possessed, his bum foot seemed to lead him right out the door.

Halfway into our little walk, Bernie started gasping for air. When he seemed to get dizzy, I feared he was having a heart attack. On the northeast corner of Thirty-ninth and Seventh Avenue, he parked himself on a short metal platform that held a steel sculpture of an old Jewish man sitting at a sewing machine.

"Let's go back to the precinct," I suggested.

Bernie looked up at the garment district statue he was sitting under and said: "There was a lot more jerking off around here than sewing. If they're going to put up a memorial, it should be to all

126

the lonely guys who whacked off in the porn arcades around Times Square."

He pulled his inhaler from his coat and took a deep suck from it, then rose to his feet and resumed walking, throwing his foot out before him like an anvil. When we got to the library, we found a dozen old PCs side by side. We carefully inspected the sign-in sheet, looking for the names of people who had used the computer at 7:45 p.m., roughly the time the jpegs had been sent in to Miriam. It proved to be useless: most of the names were illegible, and of course there were no closed-circuit cameras. Before Bernie could even begin to describe O'Flaherty, the librarian was shaking her head. Apparently she never saw anybody, ever.

"We know O'Flaherty uses the library," I said to Bernie. "Why don't we check his withdrawal records to establish if he was here that day, and see if there's a match with the times the jpegs were uploaded."

Bernie barely nodded. He never gave anyone any credit.

After an hour of going through various bureaucratic channels, we discovered that O'Flaherty's most recent withdrawals were all made at the Donnell branch up on Fifty-third and Fifth. I was going to suggest walking up there and checking their sign-in sheet to see if he might've logged in for any cyber-hijinks up there as well, but I didn't have the heart to put Bernie through another lengthy walk.

Not long after I got home that evening, I heard Maggie's delicate Morse code knocks at my door. We hadn't seen each other since the celebrity party at Miriam's house.

As soon as I opened the door, Maggie handed me a frosty bottle of Grey Goose vodka – I didn't know why, nor did I care. I took out two tall thin-stemmed aperitif glasses and poured us each a shot.

"I know you have a big crush on Noel Holden," I said. "I wish I could just wrap him up and give him to you." I was trying to give Maggie the opportunity to mention her fling with Crispin.

"Don't you want him?" Maggie asked instead.

"Maggie, he spends most of his time out in LA, and he has a million adoring fans. Even if he did sleep with me, it would only be a matter of time before he'd toss me aside for the next coat-check girl."

"If you really feel that way, why are you seeing him?" she asked.

"I'm not. It's over." I didn't want to explain the whole fingerprints thing.

"So you wouldn't be angry if he . . . if I . . ."

"If you what?"

"Well, if one day a miracle should occur and I got together with him."

I stood there a moment wondering if she was insane.

"Go for it, girl," I finally said. I shouldn't've been surprised by her reluctance to talk about Crispin. After all, this was where her crazy flag flapped out of control.

We clinked glasses and knocked back our vodka. After another drink, Maggie dashed back to her apartment—probably to watch the same dumbass TV shows as I did on the opposite side of the same wall—all alone.

CHAPTER TEN

A few days later it finally happened. At four in the afternoon Annie took a call from the "office manager" of College Girl Escorts. The madam told her a guy had just requested a "Kim Novak-sweetheart type." He was waiting in a classy midtown hotel.

"Kim Novak was a big blonde, right?" Annie asked.

"Who knows?" Alex replied.

The suspect had said he just wanted to "sit with a girl for a while, and share a smile." When the office manager asked for his credit card number, he offered to pay in cash. When she told him, according to the instructions we had given all the agencies, that they preferred a credit card, he gave up his number. She checked and found that the card had been canceled, but it hadn't been reported missing.

Annie instructed her to say that his Kim Novak was on her way, but he had to negotiate with the girl directly.

The office manager gave Annie his room number at the Grand Hyatt at Forty-second and Lexington, only a few blocks from the Ticonderoga, the last murder site. We had maybe twenty minutes to get across town if we were to have any hope of catching him. I said I'd change into the schoolgirl outfit I had left in my locker as quickly as I could.

"Put it on in the car," Bernie yelled, desperate not to lose our one and only suspect. We ran outside, Annie and Alex joining us for back up.

As we barreled up to Forty-second, siren blaring, snaking over the double gold lines and in and out of opposing lanes, I frantically pulled off my clothes and squeezed into my schoolgirl outfit while rolling around in the shotgun seat.

"Pull up your shirt," Annie said from the back. When I did so she taped a transmission wire and microbattery pack to my ribs. For the first time I was wondering what the hell I was doing here. Instead of quietly ticketing cars with O'Ryan, I was about to get intimate with a possible serial murderer. The only problem with my little girl costume was there was no where to tuck my gun and shield. Annie held on to them.

"Now listen up." Bernie went through the drill. "The only way you're going to get hurt is if you try pulling some kind of heroics, understand? But this guy has brutally butchered at least four women. He's not stupid and he's not compassionate."

"I'm aware of that."

"So you have to have *him* solicit *you*. That means even if we can't get arrest him for the murders, we'll have him for prostitution. And we can hold him while we check his alibis."

"I understand."

"The good news is," Alex half-joked, "he hasn't shot or stabbed anyone."

"Yeah," I replied. "He only drugs, strangles, and mutilates."

"Just don't drink anything," Annie said.

"But if anything at all happens, we'll be in there in a matter of seconds," Bernie insisted.

"I know," I said, trying not to sound terrified.

"We're going to be right outside the door," he said emphatically. "So if we suddenly don't hear *anything*, we're coming in."

"I know, it'll be quick," I assured him, cracking my knuckles tensely.

"What exactly are you going after?" he tested.

"Verbal contract: blow job for fifty bucks."

"That's all you're charging?" Bernie said, as if he was about to take me up on the offer. "A BJ through an escort service has got to be at least a couple hundred nowadays."

"Whatever," I said tensely.

"It's important, you have to sound credible. Ask him for one fifty," he said, like a true pimp.

When we got to the lobby of the hotel, Bernie got me to go ahead of the rest of them, just in case the suspect was scoping out the lobby. As I walked toward the elevators, Bernie identified himself to the manager at the front desk and got a passcard to the suspect's room. By the time we took separate elevators up to the eleventh floor, the suspect had been waiting for almost thirty minutes.

Bernie had me test my transmitter one final time. As one of the hotel occupants was exiting an adjacent room, Alex flashed his shield and we all crammed inside for an instant, just in case the suspect peeked out into the hallway when I knocked on his door. Apparently this had happened to Bernie and his old partner once.

When I was ready, I finally tapped on the suspect's door. A soothing male voice called, "Come in."

A small, well-dressed man who looked at least seventy was sitting in an armchair next to the draped windows. He didn't look anything like the image on the overexposed video footage or in the rough sketch, but that was hardly conclusive.

He looked so benign that I had to reject the urge to relax and remind myself that despite his appearance, this guy might be a crazed killer.

"All right sweetheart," I began. "What can I do for you?"

"Oh, I'm Thad," He introduced and extended his hand. "Pleased to make your acquaintance."

"Okay." I tried to hide the fact that my hand was trembling. On the bed was a paper bag from Genovese Drugs. I couldn't help but think those pharmaceuticals might be meant for me. No drinks were in view, though, nor anything that might be a weapon.

"I thought maybe we could just talk." He had some kind of backwoods dialect and spoke very gently.

"You want to talk while I'm sucking your cock?" I asked, hoping to get things moving.

"Gosh, no. I was hoping that maybe we could just catch up on old times."

I watched as his large hands fluttered nervously in and out of his jacket pockets.

"Sure. But I need to know what we're going to catch?" He had to say *Blowjob for one fifty* in order for us to make an arrest.

"Did the lady at the service tell you—"

"She didn't tell me a thing," I interrupted. "She just sent me here. I'm not one of the house girls. I make my own deals and take cash, so . . ."

"I understand," he said tensely. He slowly took out his wallet and politely said, "Allow me to make a small donation toward your education." He counted out seven twenties. That was progress—he had offered me money. But I still needed to hear some reference to sex.

"Look," I said, "I'll go out with you, but you got to tell me exactly what you want."

"I just want to talk about good times."

"Then you want a blow job? 'Cause I give great, sloppy blow jobs."

"No, I just . . ."

"You want your balls licked?"

"Please, stop!"

"Hold it!" I held up my hands in frustration. "Do you know what I do for a living? I'm a working girl."

"Of course," he replied, holding out the twenties. I didn't touch them.

"We're not communicating here," I said, grabbing his sleeve. "Repeat after me: *Put my dick in your* . . ."

"Let go of me!"

When he pushed me away. I should've just let him go, but the longer he kept me there, the more likely it seemed that he was the killer and I was being lured into some kind of trap. I could feel the sweat trickling down my back. I was afraid the adhesive holding my wire in place was going to fail and it would slip off.

"Just say you want sexual gratification," I stated, which was clear entrapment. When he stood up, I was so full of fear that I seized his arm. Nervously he tried to push me from him.

"Relax," I said tensely, still holding on. But he panicked and pulled away, inadvertently smacking my cheek and squealing, "LET GO OF ME!"

"Fuck!" I yelled in shock. He shrieked.

Suddenly we were in hyperspace. The door flew open and Alex and Annie had the old guy on the bed, face down, his hands cuffed behind his back. Bernie read him his rights, then looked through the guy's wallet. I guess he was looking for the stolen credit card, but he only found one card, which he held up.

"Thaddeus J. Tinkerman," Bernie read, adding, "You know your credit card is invalid."

"I was going to pay in cash. I swear it!" Tinkerman said, as though they were working for Mastercard or Visa.

Bernie inspected his other ID and announced: "Our friend here is a veterinarian from Buffalo Mop, Texas."

The old guy didn't respond. He just sat there looking sincerely ashamed.

"You okay?" Annie asked me quietly. I didn't mention the slap.

"Yeah," I whispered. "Actually, he was the one who yelled."

"What happened?" Alex asked.

Still whispering, I confessed, "I got nervous and pushed him too hard."

I took Bernie aside and asked him what he was going to do.

"We'll check him for warrants and prints. If he comes up blank, we'll just write him a summons."

On our way out Bernie thanked the hotel manager and returned the passcard. We squeezed the old gent him into the backseat and headed back to the station.

"So you got a thing for Kim Novak, do you?" Bernie yelled over the blaring siren. Mr. Tinkerman didn't utter a word.

"She was the Scarlett Johansson of his day," Annie said, and they both chuckled. I looked in the rear view and saw Tinkerman staring despondently out the window.

We returned to the precinct where he was interrogated. It wasn't until he was alone with Bernie that the old guy opened up. Evidently he was embarrassed to talk in front of the gentler sex. I watched through the one-way as he explained that he no longer had sexual urges. Fifty-six years ago he had married a young girl. Her parents annulled the marriage and took her away, and soon after she died of pneumonia. But even though she'd been dead for over half a century and he had remarried more than forty years ago, he still needed to speak to her from time to time.

"One's first love is always the strongest," he said. And unfortunately for him, she happened to be a big blonde.

Apparently when the ache to see her got too bad, the old veterinarian would reincarnate her for a few minutes in the form of a hooker. He had no priors. He had only arrived in town that morning to attend a convention.

When I finally finished filling out a half a dozen forms and reports,

I found myself walking out of the precinct at the same exact time as our geriatric john.

"Mr. Tinkerman," I began awkwardly. "I'm sorry for the inconvenience, but we have a killer who's going after the type of girl that you asked for."

He didn't reply.

"I just want you to rest assured that no one will know about this." I was referring to his wife.

"Wait until you reach my age, my dear, when young surrogates like yourself are the closest you can get to those you lost so long ago, leaving so much unfinished."

"Nothing personal, but if I ever reach that point, I'll use my pistol to make my own happy ending."

I knew it wasn't kind, but the man had freaked me out. I had been expecting him to jab a syringe into my neck at any moment. And even though the suspense was over, I kept replaying the anxiety of those few minutes as I walked home. I kept thinking about how I had panicked and grabbed his wrist— to keep his hands off of my throat.

By the time I reached Twenty-third Street, I found myself breathing deeply. I finally reached my front door at the same time as a lady who looked quite a lot like Maggie, except this woman had canary yellow hair and wore tight black spandex.

"What the hell is this?" I said, when I realized it was in fact my crazy neighbor.

"I just landed this three-week role on the soap opera *Siblings and Spouses*. I play an arty bisexual type, and since it might be my last big shot, I figured I'd try to become the character in advance."

In the elevator, I couldn't get a word in edgewise. She rambled on electrically about her first work day, and told me that tomorrow she was scheduled to do a big on-air kiss with another woman.

When I opened my door, she followed me inside uninvited. While I was putting down my things, I realized my cell phone had been turned off the whole day. Since Maggie was rambling on, looking this way and that, I headed into the kitchen and listened to my three messages.

They were all from Noel Holden. The first was asking me where I was for our second date, apparently forgetting that I had already turned him down. "I'm outside your place," he said, "and I'm trying to remember the last time I got stood up."

"Oh fuck!" I exclaimed, reducing Maggie to silence.

In the second message he was calling from the premiere: "Gladyss, I wanted to introduce you to Julia Roberts. She's such a sweetheart." I could hear a bunch of people squawking in the background.

"What's the matter?" Maggie asked.

Absentmindedly I told her that I had missed a date with Noel Holden.

"You're kidding! Where is he?"

I focused on the third message, which had only just been recorded. "At a party at the Cavalier Club, wherever the hell that is."

"You should go!"

"Really?"

"Absolutely. It's early. You can still make it."

After the pointless hotel sting that day, and feeling so knotted and tense I couldn't even face yoga, the idea of being out with a movie star at a glamorous party suddenly sounded wonderful.

"What the hell," I said, and called his cell. It went straight to voice mail.

"Just go there," Maggie prompted.

"I don't even know where it is."

"The Cavalier Club is near Fulton. On the South Street Seaport," Maggie said. She made it her business to know the location of every major club as well as all the premiere and post-screening parties in New York City. It was as if her fabulous life was always elsewhere but had forgotten to invite her along.

When she left, I exchanged my sweaty shirt for a newer, nicer one, perfumed myself, then dashed downstairs and hopped a cab down to the South Street Seaport.

A 'roid-abusing doorman wearing a black velvet sports jacket over a white cotton tee stretched out by bulging muscles, blocked my entrance. When I explained that I had a date with Noel Holden, the four-hundred-pound ape shook his head. "Unless you have an invite, you ain't going in." So I opened my wallet and flashed my shield, which he showed to another doorman before he let me pass.

The Cavalier Club was designed in a shiny hi-tech style. Everything was new and glossy. A large cardboard standee showed Julia Roberts in a cute beret holding a crepe suzette in front of the Eiffel Tower. At the bottom was the tag line, *If you're pretending to speak French, you'd better not slip...*

Most of the glamorous guests and the paparazzi crud were gone. Busboys were clearing the buffet tables. But one last gasp of partygoers had rallied at the end of the bar, where they were still drinking and laughing it up.

"Darling!" a voice shot out.

It was as though a spotlight were focused on Noel Holden's extremely angular face. For the first time he truly looked magnetic, made of steel. He raced through all the little people and gave me a big hug.

"I can't believe you actually made it! I just realized I forgot to mention where the club was."

"Maggie told me."

"I waited for you. It broke my heart that you weren't there."

"How'd it go?"

"Oh, same old crap. Tell me about your day."

"Well, we finally made an arrest . . . but it turned out to be the wrong guy."

"No one got shot or anything?"

"Actually I got slapped, but I'm fine."

"Oh God! Where?"

I pointed to my cheek. Noel looked closely at it, then planted a sharp yet delicate kiss on the injury. At that moment, I wished I had pointed to my lips.

"What are you drinking?"

I looked up and saw the dog-faced director.

"A light beer would be great."

When Crispin turned to wave toward the bartender, Noel told me he'd got some good news. His agent had just messengered a script to him. He pulled it out of his pocket and handed it to me. It was entitled, *Flat on My Back.*

"It's a romantic comedy with Angelina Jolie—and it's not awful."

"That's wonderful."

"What's wonderful is the two million dollar paycheck."

Instead of thinking that he was being paid more for one film that might take two months of his time than I would earn in my entire working life, all I could think—despite myself—was that Angelina Jolie was gorgeous—and single.

Crispin handed me a tall, frosted pint of beer and a Bushmills chaser.

"We're having a chugging contest," he said, dropping the short glass into the frosty mug and sending beer splashing over the sides. "Officer, if you can down this in one go, I'll confess to any crime you want."

"Crispin! What does she look like, some fat frat boy?" Noel rebuked him.

"Just to show that a woman can hold her own with the men," I answered, bringing the tall glass to my lips. I had to use yogic breath control to chug the beer down to its frothy depths, but I did it. Then I let out a long, unladylike belch. Crispin and a group of male spectators applauded and pounded on the oak bar.

"Another!" one of them called out.

"Another! Another! Another!" the guys at the bar all joined in.

Before I could reply, Noel grabbed my arm and led me outside. As we climbed into his waiting Lincoln, Noel told the driver we'd be heading first to my apartment and then to his. Perhaps because of his stated itinerary– which precluded even the possibility of seduction— I felt a little bolder than usual. As the car pulled out, I mentioned to Noel that the river view was romantic this time of year.

"Driver," he called out. "Let's go south along the FDR and up around the West Side Highway. We need to see the river."

Wordlessly, the driver complied.

After several back and forth moves, I found Noel Holden holding, kissing, and caressing me. In what seemed like seconds, the car halted in front of my house. We continued kissing, while the driver just sat silently, staring dead ahead.

"God, you're good," I said, finally coming up for air.

"You're not half bad yourself."

For the first time I felt I was looking at him through Maggie's eyes. Without even knowing it I asked, "Would you like to come up?"

"Not tonight," he replied with a sigh.

Why the hell did he bother with all this if he didn't want to follow through?

"Fine."

I opened the door and jumped out. Before I could slam it in his face, he said, "I'm going back to LA soon, Gladyss, and I really am not the Casanova they all make me out to be. I need to move at my own pace."

At least we weren't naked and he hadn't suddenly seen a photo of my twin.

"All right," I said, doing my damnedest to swallow my fears of rejection. "We'll take it nice and slow, I guess."

"I'd like that," he said with a smile. The car sped off to the economic sanctity of his uptown palace.

I didn't know how drunk I was until I took the few wobbly steps into my apartment building. The elevator seemed to be spiraling upward. I tried closing my apartment door gently, so as not to alert my nosy neighbor, but of course Maggie came dashing over immediately. She was holding a large, black hardcover book in her hand.

"You're alone," she said almost gleefully, as she dumped her heavy book on the cabinet across from my sofa.

"What are you reading?"

"The Bible. I need it for my scene tomorrow." She spoke with a slight slur that made me realize I wasn't the only one who had been drinking.

"You're rehearsing now?" I asked, feeling wobbly from the beer and whiskey.

"Sure," she said, then eagerly asked, "So tell me about the big date."

"Well . . . for the first time, I found myself really turned on by him."

"You're kidding!"

"No, but . . ."

"What happened?"

"We started kissing on the drive back here, then the next thing I know he's wishing me a good night."

"When?"

"Just now."

Maggie thought for a moment. "I don't mean to be presumptuous, but it might be that you're not using the right technique."

"What kind of technique should I be using?"

She got up, went to my pantry, and took out the bottle of vodka she had given me earlier that evening, along with two old wine glasses.

"Over the years, I've collected quite a few tools in the art of seduction." She plunked down on my couch and flipped on a lamp.

"Like what?"

"Trust me," she said, patting the cushion next to her. When I took a seat, she poured a shot of vodka for each of us.

"First, let's toast to losing your virginity to the most eligible bachelor in the world." We clicked glasses and down the hatch.

"Now let's see how you smooch," she said.

"Am I suppose to kiss the air?"

"No, kiss me."

"Uh, I don't think so."

"Why? What's the big deal?"

"Maggie, I never suspected you were a dyke."

"Weren't you the one weeping to me for weeks after your cop buddy rejected you?" she asked.

"That's low!"

"I'm just saying, this is the second sexy guy you had on the hook who wriggled free. Now if you like, I can show you how to reel them in."

"I know why you're really doing this," I suddenly realized. "You want practice for your lezzie soap kiss tomorrow."

"You caught me," she chuckled, and poured us both a second shot. We knocked them back in unison. "Okay, now come on and pucker up!"

I started giggling.

"Look, I'm an actress, not a lesbian." Pinching her arm, she said, "This is just a big pink instrument that I've spent years learning how to use in order to get specific reactions. If you don't want me to share the secrets of my craft, that's fine, but I'm telling you—a good kiss is your gateway to love . . ."

Just to shut her up, I closed my eyes, aimed my head toward her, and nervously pursed my lips.

Delicately she put her lips over mine. Then, withdrawing just a bit, more tenderly than I'd ever experienced it, she grazed the tip of her lips over the bulbous edge of mine.

When I opened my lips to inhale, she plunged her hot tongue into my mouth. Instinctively, I tried to back away. She reached around and embraced me tightly. Soon I felt my heart going pitter-patter as she held me and playfully flicked her tongue back and forth. Then she brushed her fingertips down my bare arms, and along my chest, until I felt paralyzed by the tenderness.

"Come on!" she suddenly broke off.

"What?"

"This is a rehearsal, remember? I'm supposed to be one of the handsomest men in the world."

"So?"

"I've seen more responsive corpses!"

I took a deep breath. "I'm just not used to being . . . the assertive one."

"There's your problem!" she said. "Modern guys are a lot softer than they used to be. They'll just melt away like marshmallows if you don't take charge."

"What should I do?"

"You took some acting classes in college, didn't you?"

"Yeah, one. Why?"

She poured us both another shot of the Grey Goose. "Pretend you're the man. I'll be the chick. *You* kiss *me*."

"I'm the man?"

"Yeah, you're a little tomboyish already. It shouldn't be that hard."

"How?"

"Think of some specific guy you find manly and be him."

I closed my eyes and considered some of the macho men I knew. For a moment, O'Ryan crossed my mind, but after his reluctance to ask me on a second date, he seemed more like a wuss. What other attractive, intriguing men did I know? Surprisingly, Detective Farrell popped into my head. Even with his wheezy remarks and decomposing foot, he struck me as a decent, courageous man and a straight shooter.

Leaning forward, I fixed on the thought that I was Bernie, and Maggie my little coquette. Matter-of-factly, I put my mouth around hers and slipped my tongue between her soft lips. I felt her swoon, and the warm, wet tightness of her vodka-flushed mouth. Moving my hand up her back, I held her firmly and pulled her in. Just as she had done to me, I started caressing her large, firm breasts.

Stop!" Maggie said, pushing me back. "I just can't."

"Can't what?" I asked, thoroughly lightheaded.

"I mean . . . Good! That's a good start." She got up, blushing, and grabbed her Bible off the chest of drawers.

"So that's it?" I asked. I was hoping there was something more she could impart.

"If you showed him you can be submissive and he doesn't bite, try that."

"I guess I can try."

Glancing at my wall clock, she said it was time for Letterman and Leno and dashed back to her place. It was her habit to sit, remote in hand, and ping pong between the two, making them into one single, blurry talk show. TV really was the center of her celebrity-driven existence.

My brother called before I went to sleep. He was unusually mellow, even sort of sad. I figured he was on his meds. Usually it was hard for me to get a word in, so I took the opportunity to mention that I had met a new guy, a movie star, and we'd actually made out.

"Who?" he asked, clearly not impressed.

"Noel Holden," I said, expecting him to ask what life was like in the fast lane – or at least not the slow lane.

But he answered, "Then things are over with you and the scorpion."

"Yes, but Eddie's a good guy. Please stop calling him that."

"Goodnight," he said, and hung up before I could tell him anything more.

I had a mini-hangover the next day, but I took off my sunglasses as soon as I walked into the precinct. I didn't want anyone to sense something was wrong. In the squad room, Bernie was reaching for his coat as I was taking mine off.

"Leave it on," he said. "We got a new one." Clearly he meant a victim.

"It gets worse," he said as we started down the stairs. "Remember your cheap date, Tinkerman?"

"What about him?" I asked, thinking, *Could he be the killer after all?*

"He went back to his hotel room last night, called his wife, told her he loved her, then hung himself."

"Oh no!" I froze mid-step, recalling that I had essentially told a desperate, old man that it was time to kill himself if he couldn't handle his loneliness.

"She told me he was battling cancer."

"Shit!"

"Come on," he said. "Feel bad on the way to the scene."

"Where is it?"

"That's the kicker. You remember the two hotsheets we had under surveillance?"

"Are you kidding?"

It was the Hotel Fabio, one of the two remaining establishments he'd said did not have closed circuit cameras. After Jane Hansen's body was found at the Ticonderoga, the captain decided to pull the surveillance teams, which were needed elsewhere, since the killer was evidently now working outside his original territory.

As we drove to the hotel, Bernie called Raj to see if pictures of this new crime had turned up on the Marilyn web site. More importantly, if the killer did upload the photos, could Raj again trace their point of origin?

I could tell Raj's response by the disappointment in Bernie's voice. No new pictures had come in.

It didn't really matter. All I could think about was Tinkerman. I kept remembering his sad little shriek when he thought I was trying to rape him. I might not have murdered the poor old guy, but inadvertently I had been an accomplice in his death.

We doubleparked at Thirty-eighth and Ninth and went up to the fifth floor of the Fabio, where uniforms had already locked the scene down. O'Ryan and Lenny were stationed outside. Eddie said hi to me as I walked past.

The techs had widened the perimeter of the crime scene this time, and were combing the entire stairway. We snapped on our rubber gloves and overshoes and I followed close behind Bernie.

The killer had returned to all his original rituals. A tall blonde had been drugged and strangled: Her limbs were taped up. Her head had been brutally cut off. The same numbers were carved on the same corresponding limbs, just like the first three vics.

"See, this isn't like the Jane Hansen murder," Bernie said. "This is Coke Classic—like Mary Lynn, Denise, and Nelly."

In addition, a long V-shaped incision had been made up and down her inner right thigh, as with the first victim. And, again like Mary Lynn, a sock had inexplicably been left dangling from the tip of her left foot. The number 8 had been gouged into her forehead. A paneled bracelet, set with what looked like jasper, was dangling from her left wrist, and wedged in her right hand was a business card for this rat hole hotel.

Another fallacy I had picked up watching movies was that you could run your hand over the eyelids of the deceased and gently close them. But however much I tried to close her sad eyes, they remained fixed in an upward gaze, as though she were longing to be reconnected with her detached body.

Bernie looked closely at the point where her head had been severed. Judging by the corkscrew twist of the top of her spinal column and the way a piece of the esophagus trailed below the head like a little tail, it looked as though the fucker had literally twisted her skull off.

"Did he ever *twist* off a head before?" I asked Bernie.

"He had to cut the muscles before he did the twisting, but no." Then he added. "This is one pissed response."

"To what?"

"He's got to be one of the cocksuckers we interviewed. This is his fuck-you to us."

"Why did he go back to West Side fleabags?" I asked. "Do you really think—"

"—The same reason he went back to decapitations and forehead numbers and single socks . . . Who the fuck knows?"

After I interviewed the witless desk clerk, who apparently had noticed absolutely nothing, Annie and I spent an hour knocking on all the other doors in that house of horrors. Next we canvassed other residents of the block looking for possible witnesses, and checked for any outside surveillance cameras—no luck. Bernie had me keep pushing Missing Persons, whose job it had been to take the dead girl's prints and try to make an ID. By three o'clock we got a hit. Her name was Tabetha Sayers.

Bernie had Alex attend the big news conference the commissioner was holding in time for the six o'clock news. The commissioner had decided it was time to reveal more details about the murders of Tabetha and her four predecessors. If we couldn't catch the son of a bitch, he wanted to make sure that any blonde hookers who were tricking around midtown knew what was awaiting them.

CHAPTER ELEVEN

After work, late that night, feeling unbelievably crappy but fearing that unless I tuckered myself out, I was going to do something foolish like get drunk and kiss my neighbor again, I caught the final yoga class of the day. Again I encountered the turbaned gang of four.

I took a deep breath and unrolled my mat. This time, the pajama-clad elders had been conversing when I entered. I discreetly listened to their strange Engskrit chatter: "When he wished me a happy birthday, my *Buddhibuddheh* latched onto my *Anaditvam* with his own *Abhinivesa* . . ."

During a pause I asked one of the older women, "Do you think Kundalini can be used to combat injustice?"

"Absolutely," the other woman spoke up. "After all, it was originated by the warrior class."

"Is there anything I can do to develop this skill more quickly?"

"One is always one's own greatest hindrance," one of the males said. I couldn't tell which.

"How do you mean?"

"The ego is always an obstacle," said the Renunciate axiomatically. He had entered the room without me noticing.

It must've just been a meditation class, because the next sixty minutes were mainly taken up with mantras and hyper shallow breaths. Nevertheless, when we chanted our three final Oms, I was so exhausted and covered in sweat I just lay there trembling and twitching like a freshly hooked fish. The others thanked the Renunciate and left, but he remained seated as I finally peeled my mat off the floor.

"On one hand, I wish you could find peace with where you are instead of only focusing on where you want to be. On the other hand, it's so rare to see such enthusiasm from a weekend practitioner."

"Thanks," I said uncertainly.

"What you want is called *Shaktipat*—it's the transmission of power from one person to another."

"You can pass along Kundalini?"

"Some say it can be transmitted in a breath, others say with a flower, but in your case Grinlik has offered his inspired services."

"Is he a Sikh?"

"They all are. But he's also a swami, and from time to time he has performed Shaktipat." A swami sounded to me like the equivalent of a captain in the yogi police, and a Shaktipat sounded like a good exorcism.

"Let's do it."

"The thing you should know is that it is probably going to seem a little disappointing. It's not that dramatic, and it doesn't always take."

"We can only try."

"You'll be working alone with Grinlik. Are you comfortable with that?"

"Does Grinlik have any priors?"

He misunderstood. "Oh yes, he's done this many times."

"Fine."

The Renunciate stepped out and a moment later the oldest male yogi in the group, the great Grinlik, entered. He'd been in tonight's class; his tight turban looked like a brain tourniquet.

"So does this mean. . ."

"Shhh."

Over the next twenty minutes or so, he instructed me to perform fire breaths—deep and intense inhalations—with my eyes closed. When I finally thought I was going to collapse, I felt his cool hand on my sweaty back. Slowly he pushed me back and forth, swaying me in my seated position, like a buoy, and directing me to take short shallow breaths. After about ten minutes, when I was about to pass out, he gently smacked me across the face.

I didn't feel any different.

"Try it again," I whispered with my eyes still closed. "A little harder."

After a long, suspenseful minute, I opened my eyes to discover I was all alone in the darkened room. When I rolled up my mat and went out, I could hear the Renunciate talking with the others, but I didn't want to bother him. Either I had been Kundalinied or I hadn't.

I staggered home and opened my front door just as my phone rang.

"Hi," Noel said. "I just wanted to say goodbye before leaving. I'm going to LA tomorrow."

"I wish I could run off with you. I'm having a hell of a time here."

"Why?"

I explained that another victim had just been found and her head had literally been twisted off.

"Yuck," he said softly. "And yesterday you got assaulted by some guy."

"That was nothing much. A veterinarian from Texas was just looking for a little human companionship." I paused and added, "He went back to his hotel afterward and hung himself."

"You know, I played a police captain in an episode of *Law and Order* who was suspected of abusing perps. It turned out my character was suffering from post-traumatic stress due to a shooting."

"I never heard of a captain having to draw a weapon, except in movies. They're usually administrators."

"I'm only saying it sounds like you might be suffering from it."

I didn't answer. I was depressed enough that I thought his diagnosis might actually be right.

"I'm sending a car to pick you up," he said.

I told him I'd come in on my own, but I couldn't stay long. I showered, put on a sexy dress, then touched on some make-up and perfume. I grabbed a cab to his apartment, which was at Seventy-sixth and Central Park West, ten blocks north of Miriam's mansion.

Noel greeted me at the door wearing a burgundy satin robe that revealed a chestful of curly black hair. He handed me a dirty martini and gave me a tour. It was one of those prewar luxury apartments with spacious rooms and unobstructed views to all four points of the compass. If I wasn't already drawn to him by his celebrated good looks, I could now worship him just for his place. It was the kind of apartment that middle-class characters in the movies live in.

When he led me out to his balcony, I looked westward over Jersey. He offered me a cigarette. Though I feared cancer, my greater concern right then was of possibly losing the romantic momentum, so I snatched it. He lit it with the derringer cigarette lighter he had given me earlier. I must've left it at Miriam Williams house.

Soon we were seated on his divan. Without any prompting he started telling me how one time when he was a kid he had wound rubber bands around a cat's front paws.

"I really didn't mean to hurt it. I swear, it belonged to my neighbor. I was just teasing it, watching it trying to shake them off. Well next thing I knew the cat ran off. I don't know what I was thinking. I was a dumb kid. A few weeks later, my mother told me the neighbor's cat had to have its front paws amputated."

"Why are you telling me this?" I asked.

"Guilt," he said. "To this day I feel awful about that poor kitty cat."

If that was the worst thing he had done in his life, he was still better than most.

His voice grew fainter, as his touch became more substantial. His fingers stroked along my arm and shoulder. My heart fluttered as he kissed his way up my neck. When his sharp but delicate lips reached my jawline, he backed off. I remembered what Maggie had told me. He was hooked, but I still had to reel him in—and this was usually where I lost them. Before he could yawn or say it was late, I leaned forward and kissed him.

Just like I had practiced with Maggie, I pretended I was some he-man and he was a shy little schoolgirl I had just picked up. A moment later I had him backed up against the armrest and was darting my predatory tongue into his scared little mouth. The next moment, I grabbed his thick shock of hair and led his angular face down to my non-cleavage.

Taking the cue, he unbuttoned my shirt, popped open my bra and proceeded to lick and nibble my eraser tips. Then, closing my eyes and taking a deep breath, I pushed away all my instincts as I lowered my panties.

He gently pushed me back on his over-upholstered sofa, parted my legs and took charge. Unlike O'Ryan, he knew his way through the untamed forest. Gradually, I found myself rushing down a stream of licks. By the time I collapsed over the frothy falls, I had enjoyed my first orgasm ever administered by someone other than myself.

"My God!" I said, leaning down to kiss his slick face. It was hard to believe: one of the hottest actors alive had just gotten me off.

Although I was nervous, I decided now was not the time to retreat, and reached down to reciprocate. He took out his cock and began to move his hips toward my exposed position.

"Why don't we just . . ."

I desperately wanted to lose my virginity, but I suddenly decided I didn't want it to be like this, a hit and run followed by him dashing off to LA. I delicately took his bowed flesh in hand and said, "Let's wait till you get back."

"Oh," Noel groaned, and in an amusingly agonized voice sang the opening lines of "Don't Leave Me This Way."

I lowered myself and slowly tried to take him in my mouth, but found myself choking. I closed my eyes and heard the Renunciate's voice instructing me how to achieve self-control through breathing. As he rocked back and forth, I was able then to suppress my gag reflex and service him until, after several minutes, he reached liquid nirvana.

CHAPTER TWELVE

After our erratic, erotic episode of oral gratification and role swapping, Noel drove me home. In his car, I drifted in and out of sleep as he rambled on about being back in town in a couple days for the Rocmarni Fashion Show, at which time we could "finalize things."

"Sure, great," I said dreamily. As he kissed me, his car screeched to a halt. I wished him *bon voyage* on his flight and he sped away. I floated up the stairs to my apartment and jumped into bed, where I fought to get him out of my head.

Early the next morning my phone woke me up. I would've let the call go, but I knew it had to be Noel calling from LA to say he couldn't wait to be back in New York.

It was Bernie. He was with the rest of the squad at the latest crime scene. Victim number six was resting in pieces at the King's Court Hotel, a decent, upscale place on Forty-fifth and Eighth. This was on the outer rim of the killer's original hunting ground.

"How the hell did he pay for the place?"

"He didn't," Bernie said. It turned out that the killer had again changed his MO. He managed to find an empty room after the maid had cleaned it and he took the vic there. Just an hour ago, a family from Wichita had opened the door and discovered the mutilated corpse.

"Should I meet you there?"

"We're just wrapping things up. Meet us back at the precinct."

Showering, dressing, and grabbing a cab, I walked into the squad room just as they were returning from the scene.

"Big meeting in a half hour," Bernie said before I could ask anything. "The captain and Chief of Detectives are going to be there. I'd appreciate everyone keeping quiet about my getting mugged."

150

"'Course." He didn't even need to ask.

"Why is the chief coming here?" I asked.

"These murders have put our com stat rates through the roof," Bernie said, referring to the weekly meetings, which the mayor is known to attend, where the top brass discuss crime levels throughout the city.

"I don't want to blame the victim," Alex said, "but why the fuck would even the dumbest blonde hooker in Midtown go out with a john hours after the Police Commissioner issued a warning?"

"Prostituting isn't a career choice," Annie said. "They're usually hooked and just trying to pay for their habit."

"Whatever," Bernie said.

"Did Raj trace where the photos were sent from?" Alex asked.

"A laundromat on West Thirty-eighth Street that sold five minutes of internet access for a buck. No surveillance cameras, and the attendant is an illegal who don't remember nothing."

"He sent pictures again this time?" I asked. "To the Marilyn web site?"

"Oh right," Bernie said. "Yeah."

"So that brings us to six," Annie said.

"Mary Lynn MacArthur, Denise Giantonni, Nelly Linquist, Jane Hansen, Tabetha Sayers"—Alex intoned the roll call of the dead—"and now . . ."

"We don't have the name of number six yet," Annie said.

"This is getting ridiculous," I said.

"Hey, this is nothing," Bernie said. "Ten years ago, Bert and I did some of the post mortem investigation on the Joel the Ripper case. Rifkin killed three times as many, and no one even suspected there was a murderer at work. Hell, the moron only got caught when a state trooper smelled a decomposing corpse in the back of his pick-up."

"This guy is deliberately doing it like this just to embarrass us," Alex said.

"Yeah," Annie added, "Why can't he just quietly dump the bodies in the river like everyone else, then we'll leave him alone."

Instead of showing me the new jpegs, Bernie pointed to a pile of new paperwork he had saved for me. It swallowed up time until I realized everyone else had vanished. They had gone to the big meeting without even telling me.

I sneaked into the big conference room and quietly took a seat next to Annie at the round table along with Bernie, Alex, our profiler Barry Gilbert, and a couple of suits I didn't know. They were all listening to a lieutenant I didn't recognize, who was saying the cost of this investigation had now topped a hundred thousand dollars. He started itemizing the number of man-hours that had already been spent on the case, in addition to all the lab work and other expenses.

"It would've been cheaper just to pay all blonde hookers to stay home this month," Bernie said when the lieutenant finished his tally.

On the adjacent wall one of the team had pinned up photos of the latest crime scene as well as what must be printouts of the computer images of victim number six being drugged, strangled, and mutilated. Like Jane Hansen, number six was wearing a curly blonde wig; she wasn't really blonde either. Underneath the photos was another freaky poem the killer had posted on Miriam's web site:

They always cry:
    "Why am I being strangled!
And I reply,
    "'cause I too was mangled."
Why the knife
    to my tender breasts?
'Cause my heart too
    was plucked from chest,
Don't blame me
    if you're slashed and torn!
I never wanted . . .
    always hated being born!

I stared for a while at the poem trying to make sense of it. Then I looked at the jpegs and listened as Alex, Annie, Barry—in fact, everyone but Bernie—bounced theories against the facts of the latest murder to construct possible scenarios while they waited for the captain and the chief of detectives to arrive.

It turned out they had first learned of the homicide the previous night, when the pictures were uploaded to Miriam's web site at 9:38

p.m. The email address this time was *MarshalBoucicaut.@wonder-link.com*. Annie had looked up the name on Wikipedia. Apparently this Marshal was a medieval French knight who founded a chivalrous order—the Order of the Green Shield with the White Lady—devoted to protecting the honor of womankind. My guess is he was never married.

"This guy's on some kind of historical purity kick," Alex said, recalling the earlier reference to Catherine of Alexandria, the patron saint of virginity.

Suddenly in came a short, fat man with a walrus mustache, wearing a tight, plaid suit. He mumbled his name and announced that the chief was unable to attend; he was there in his place. I confirmed later that none of us heard his name and no one dared ask him to repeat it. All I could focus on was the fact that his multiple chins bulged so low over his striped shirt collar that they completely hid the knot of his crassly colored tie. It seemed that the poorer their fashion sense, the higher up the ranks the department seemed to hoist them.

"So now he's killing at the rate of one per day." He finally spoke to the entire group.

Our latest victim was a short, curvy brunette, another departure from the usual tall young blondes. Since I no longer fit the victim profile, I was a little concerned that I might be taken off the case. But inasmuch as the crime scene last night was even more gruesome than number five from the day before, the focus was elsewhere right now. Instead of stabbing the latest victim from a downward angle, like he'd done yesterday night, the killer ran his knife cleanly around her breasts until he sliced them right off, like in the Jane Hansen murder. Also, unlike Tabetha with the twist-top neck, this girl's head was still attached. The most troublesome departure from the pattern in this case was that this was the first victim who, according to the ME, had just *had* sex. It wasn't clear if she had been raped. There were no signs of a struggle, nor was any sperm present. Since Hansen's murder at the Ticonderoga Hotel, Bernie had said he suspected there was a second killer at work, but to everyone else that just seemed too unlikely. In addition to the particulars that all six murders had in common— tall blonde prostitutes who had been drugged, strangled, mutilated in the same bizarre way but not sexually violated—serial murders simply weren't that common. Nevertheless, this case was just getting weirder.

"Any thoughts, Bern?" Annie finally asked. We were all a bit surprised by his silence.

"Yeah," he finally said. "It's a contest."

"What's a contest?"

"This whole thing . . . I mean, we had a murderer and he was doing these crazy-ass murders. Mary Lynn, Denise, then Nelly—all clearly hookers. There was something genuine about them. A little artsy with the body stacking and carved numbers—but original, real. Then suddenly the murders are getting all this press coverage and bam! These new murders start happening."

"You mean the last three?" Alex asked.

"Not number five, Tabetha. That's the first guy again, responding to the Jane Hansen killer. But Jane and this new one, yeah, and you know what they are? They're bad imitations trying to pass themselves off as real, but they don't wash with me. The first group are genuine New York murders, your usual streetwalker whores in the last of the bona fide Times Square dives. That killer knows this landscape and its characters. But these new ones, no way. The guy is a fucking tourist posing as a native, loading down peglegs,"—he meant uploading jpegs—"putting makeup on the girls, overcompensating for his ignorance. He's trying to compete with the other guy."

"You might be right, but if so, how can we use that to help us?" asked the walrus in the tacky suit.

"Frankly, I just wish we could keep this under wraps until we figure it out," Bernie said.

"Bernie, you know we are obligated to warn all possible vics," the lieutenant said.

If I'd had the courage to speak right then, I would've said that maybe we should be looking for a pair of ex-cons who had previously worked together. But the more I thought about it the more I realized that after spending the past week running down a whole list of suspects, we would've caught this by now.

"Not to discourage your theory, Bern," said Barry, "but let's get back to this latest vic a minute. I'm still intrigued by the fact that he had sex with her . . ."

"There were no defensive wounds."

"Maybe she was unconscious."

"Or maybe it was consensual," Alex said.

"With the murderer? You think number six knew him? This late in the series?" Annie shot him down.

"Maybe six was coming from another room and was just leaving," Bernie said. "No one even saw her come into the hotel."

"Why do you think he sometimes removes their heads and other times their breasts?" the second to the chief of detectives asked as he stared at one of the more gruesome photos.

"Well, there might be some kind of mother fixation involved," Barry stated.

"The two girls who he's double mastectomied had relatively large breasts," Alex pointed out.

"If it *is* the same killer," Bernie said, stepping away from his hypothesis a minute, "It takes a lot of work to remove a head. It ain't like popping a champagne cork. He might be getting lazy."

"And if he didn't even rent the room this last time," Annie added. "he didn't know how long he might have before someone would just walk in."

"What did CSU find?" the lieutenant asked, flipping through the forensic reports.

"Four clear prints and two partials, along with some hairs and fibers—but as before, nothing connects to any of the previous murder scenes," Annie said, "We suspect that most if not all of what they gathered is from prior residents of each hotel."

"And no signs of a struggle?" the chief's man asked.

"He drugs them all first," Alex replied. "That's the way he works."

"The tox screen hasn't come back, but the ME said he didn't think this one was drugged," Annie said.

Bernie started coughing and though he tried to suppress it, it soon grew violent.

"You really got the World Trade hack," the visiting detective said. "This kind of respiratory crap is getting to more and more of the cops who worked down there."

"It's really just a cold," Bernie said.

The door opened and the captain stepped inside.

"Well, if you need more cops, more anything, just tell your captain," said the assistant to the Chief, overriding all the lieutenant's concerns about limited resources. "We got to get this solved fast."

He thanked Bernie and the rest of us and was led out by the captain and the lieutenant. We walked back to the squad room, where Annie immediately got on the phone and Alex retreated to his desk.

"Do you think that went well?" I asked Bernie, since it was the first time I'd ever witnessed an inspection from the brass.

"Yeah, they just want to make sure we're not missing anything."

"So we have to get an ID on the latest girl?" I asked.

"Funny you should say that," Bernie said limping to his office. In the short time since I had been assigned here, I saw what a mess it had become. Boxes, bags of clothes, all kinds of clutter. Lying on the few square inches of clear desk space was a new-looking membership card for Rectangle Video, which was apparently in Union City, New Jersey. It had an ID number written on it but no name.

"It looks like the asshole grabbed her purse but dropped this at the scene." Handing it to me, he said, "See what you can find out." His phone rang and he took the call.

All the other squad room desks were occupied, so I plugged in a phone at Bernie's now vacant desk in the bullpen. Crime scene photos of all the victims were taped to the glass frame bordering the hallway. Before I could make my call, Alex came over with a magnifying glass and started inspecting the photos closely.

I was about to ask what he was looking for when he turned and volunteered, "They found some kind of adhesive on vic six's face." He had just gotten the preliminary report.

"What would he—"

"That's what I'm trying to figure out," he said, still staring into a large photo of the vic's pale white face.

I got on the phone to Rectangle Video and explained that I was an NYPD officer working on a case. Based on the membership card number I wanted to get the identity as well as the home address and phone number of the holder.

"Her name is Caty Duffy," he said after I read him the membership number. Then he gave me her home number and address in Union City.

"Any other names on the account?"

"Yeah, one. Frank Duffy."

"And when exactly was the account opened?" I asked, wondering if it had taken Caty a few years to fall from suburban grace to urban prostitution.

"About three months ago. The last film borrowed was *The Two Towers*, just a few days ago. It's still out."

When I thanked him, he suddenly grew suspicious and said, "You sound pretty young to be a police officer. Do you have proof of who you are?"

I considered telling him to call me back at Manhattan South Homicide, but hung up instead.

"If this is her Rectangle Video card, our vic is Caty Duffy," I told Bernie. "She lives in Union City. I got her address and phone number too. Should we head out there?"

"Hell, no. Give the info to the Union City PD," he said. "Have the morgue send them a photo of her and ask them to go to her house. See if anyone's there who can confirm her identity. Let them break it to the family. If it is her, we'll take it from there."

As I followed his instructions, calling the morgue to fax the photo and then notifying the Jersey police, I was relieved that I wouldn't have to give her family the awful news. The Jersey detective asked for some details in case there might be a connection between our crimes and any of their recent unsolved murders. Then he asked me where to send the next of kin to ID the body. I gave him the morgue's number. He thanked me and said they'd send a car to the house.

Roughly forty minutes passed before a civilian call from Union City was directed to me. Figuring it was almost certainly our latest victim's next of, I asked Bernie if he would take it.

"You called the Jersey police?"

"Yeah."

"So the worst is over," he said. "Just confirm whatever the Jersey cops said and see if the next of kin works in the city. Save us a trip across the river."

"What if he asks about her murder?"

"You don't know shit and the detectives are out detecting."

He never failed to make me feel like a receptionist. "Just get his contact info and tell him we'll pay him a visit and answer his questions as soon as we can."

"Okay," I said and took a deep breath as I picked up the phone.

"My name is Frank Duffy," a frantic male voice said. "She's been missing for the past twenty four hours and a Union City officer just came to my door and . . . and told me my wife Caty was . . .

157

murdered." He started to weep just as Bernie began coughing in the background.

"I'm so sorry, Mr. Duffy," I said as delicately as I could. "We would've notified you ourselves but since you live in Jersey . . ."

Over the phone I heard convulsive gasps, the sort of primal cries you imagine someone would make when their heart is ripped out of their chest. After a few minutes of groaning, he regained a modicum of composure.

"How did it happen?"

"I'm sorry, sir, I don't know. The lead detective and his team are out investigating."

"What's his name?"

"Farrell, Detective Sergeant Bernie Farrell," I said. Then I asked, "Do you work in the city? I'll have him call you and arrange to come see you."

"Was she raped?"

"We don't have any details yet, sir. We're waiting for the medical examiner's report."

"Did she suffer? I mean, she had a low tolerance for pain. She would cry over a paper cut."

"I'm sure it was quick," I heard myself saying.

"What the hell am I going to tell our boy?" He started weeping again. I waited a bit before asking, "Should I tell Detective Farrell to come out to your house in New Jersey?"

"No, I work in Times Square." He gave me the address. "I stayed home today because..."

"Do you have any idea why your wife was in Manhattan?" I asked softly, since I could hardly ask if she was a drug-addicted hooker.

"We both work in the city and commute."

"So she didn't come home last night?"

"Yeah, but that happens sometimes," he said. "There's a sofa in her office. But she always calls if she's not coming home, so I knew something was wrong."

"Where exactly did she work?"

"The Condé Nast Building on Times Square—she works for a law firm, Shades, Holts and Pierce."

"A law firm?" I said surprised.

"Yeah, they do corporate work."

"What did she do there?"

"She's a senior paralegal. She's been there for twelve years."

"Mr. Duffy, could you give me the phone number of her office, so we can speak to whoever saw her last?"

He gave me a name, work address, and phone number with an extension.

"When is the soonest the detective can call me?" he asked.

I assured him that Detective Farrell would call him back as soon as he returned. Mr. Duffy took my name and number and said he'd call again if he could think of anything that might be helpful. I repeated my condolences and hung up, then tried not to think of the unbelievable anguish the poor man had to be experiencing.

"Remember when Alex asked why any blonde hooker would turn a trick after the Commissioner issued a warning of a serial murderer."

"Go on," he said, rolling his hand impatiently.

"Caty might be our first non-hooker."

"No way."

"Not according to her husband."

He smiled and in a mocking tone, he said, "I got news for you. Some hookers are married."

"She's got a kid."

"If all the prostitutes who had kids joined the PTA they could rename it the PPTA."

"Her husband says she's been working for the past twelve years as a paralegal in a corporate law firm in midtown."

"Did you get her work number?" He was testing me more than asking me.

"Yeah, and her supervisor's name," I said holding up the info. "Should I call her?"

"What do you think this is, Domino's Pizza? We have to put on our coats, go out and interview her."

"Can't we give Caty the benefit of the doubt that maybe she's not a prostitute?"

"I'm not being sexist," he said. "Serial killers usually have a strict victim profile. If she was simply abducted off the street then we are seriously fucked, 'cause it means the killer is suddenly fishing from a much wider victim pool."

Then he asked me to call "my friend" Miriam Williams to see if she had returned to the States yet. I got her assistant Bryce, who said that she'd be back in town in four days.

When I checked my voicemail, I found my optometrist had left a message reminding me that my eye surgery was coming up that Friday—which was also the last day of my homicide assignment. I also needed to come in on Thursday to get my eyes measured before the procedure. I called back to confirm and the receptionist told me I should arrange for someone to pick me up after the surgery and take me home, because I wouldn't be able to see straight for a while.

I spent the rest of the morning filling out a backlog of forms and reports dealing with the last two homicides. At one o'clock Bernie stopped at my desk and announced that we were going to lunch.

I grabbed my jacket and he took me to a nearby diner that was probably a real find twenty-five years earlier, when cops first started going there. Since then it had evidently degenerated into a health code nightmare. We each grabbed pathogenic plastic trays and slid them along a steamed-up glass case, conjuring up scary parochial school lunches of years gone by. Throwing all nutritional wisdom to the wind, Bernie selected a high-carb pasta dish. I moved down the line to the refrigerated area, where I selected a severely wilted arugula salad.

"Hi Glad!"

I looked up to see O'Ryan standing before me in uniform. He looked more handsome each time I saw him.

"Eddie!" It was actually nice seeing him. Since I'd started seeing Noel, I realized that simply having sex was not nearly as easy as it sounded. Pornography and even TV shows made hooking up sound so effortless, but finding someone you could feel comfortable with—and trust—took a lot of work and sheer luck.

O'Ryan gave me a warm hug followed by a surprising peck on the cheek. It made me think he had to be with some new lover.

"Who's this?" Bernie said, suddenly showing up with his tray of baked ziti.

"Eddie O'Ryan," I said "This is Detective Bernie Farrell."

"How's it going there?" Bernie asked without making eye contact.

"Yeah," Eddie replied, absently staring at a wall. An awkward pause followed, as is common in the cop world when a female is present.

" I guess I'll see you later then," Eddie finally said before leaving.

Bernie led us to a booth that had just opened in the rear. Sitting down he said, "Sorry if I seemed a little grumpy back at the precinct."

"Is your foot hurting?"

"Usually that's what it is, but this time I'm just worried about our guy. I mean, if it is one guy, and if he really is just grabbing any women now, and not even trying to sedate them, just strangling them—not to mention raping them—then we're in serious trouble."

Bernie snared a forkful of ziti, shoved it into his mouth, and added, "And what the hell did he put on Caty's face, I wonder."

"Maybe a Santa Claus beard," I tried to joke, since it still felt cold enough to be Christmas.

I chewed on a couple of rubbery leaves and shriveled stalks before abandoning the wilted bowl of greens. In another moment, Bernie had gobbled down all his pasta and cheese and we were out the door.

As we walked, I was about to remind him that my homicide assignment was set to expire on Friday, when a college-age kid with a clipboard stepped into our path. His wore a visored cap that read GREENPEACE.

As he started talking about saving the planet, Bernie interrupted him, "Sorry son, it's too late for that. Have as much fun as you can, 'cause it's only going to get worse from here."

"That's simply not true," the kid replied.

Bernie took out a dollar and said, "I'll give this to you if you don't say another word."

The kid took the buck.

"Hold on," I said. I took out a five and donated it. He tried to get me to fill out some form, but Bernie wouldn't stop, so I wished him good luck and caught up.

"I happen to think there's still hope."

"Sure there is," Bernie replied. "Everyone's going to finally wise up about global warming. Any day now they'll replace their SUVs with bikes. And politicians will tell the corporate lobbyists who bankroll their campaigns to fuck off, and they'll quit with the partisan bullshit and work together to fix the problems that are killing the planet and melting the polar caps. And all the pollution that's been building up since the dawn of the Industrial Age will miraculously evaporate."

When we reached a corner, Bernie looked up at one of the city's latest innovations—a dark blue street sign with illuminated numbers. Rummaging through his pockets for the info sheet, he asked, "So where exactly is Caty Duffy's firm?"

"Three Times Square."

We walked north toward the coven of glossy new high-rises that now encircled Times Square. Soon we were back in front of the wavy new Reuters Building where we had recently interviewed the one-armed immigrant with the stolen credit card number.

"What the fuck is that?" he asked, pointing at a strange, flat object projecting from the top of the building like the edge of a giant surfboard.

"I think it's some kind of architectural homage to the marquees that once lined the Great White Way."

Bernie looked at the area as if seeing it for the first time. When a member of the Forty-second Street Security Team passed, he asked him which building was Three Times Square.

Instead of answering, the guard started turning clockwise and rattling off the addresses of each skyscraper in turn, "That's number one, then four, seven, five, and three—"

"The whole point of addresses is to make the location easy to find," Bernie interrupted. "If you're just going to throw numbers on buildings in no particular order, you're missing the point."

"Hey, they don't pay *me* to number the damn buildings." the security guard shot back before walking off.

For a moment I checked out the new Condé Nast Building. It had curvy sides and unusual surfaces that made me wonder if the architect was drunk when he designed it. It rose nearly fifty stories high. Just below a giant hypodermic-like antenna were four black squares paralleling each of the building's sides.

"There's a reason they stopped grouping battleships together after Pearl Harbor," Bernie muttered.

"What?"

"Putting all these skyscrapers so close together makes them all such easy targets."

As we crossed over to the northeast corner, I asked Bernie if he knew the purpose of the four mysterious black squares on the top of the Condé Nast Building.

"Giant fly swatters . . . in case any planes come too close."

The awning in front of the Condé Nast building looked like the shiny scoop from a monster garbage truck, ready to claw unsuspecting tourists into its lobby, which was funnel-shaped like a giant meat grinder. We entered the bright marble lobby and walked toward the wooden security desk as employees ran their magnetized ID cards over a reader before entering through a turnstile. We showed our badges to the guard on duty, who gave us adhesive labels to put over our shirt pockets and let us through a metal gate.

"The last time I was at this spot," Bernie said. "It was 1472 Broadway—the Longacre Building. Ten spacious stories filled with waterbugs and Joe Franklin."

I guessed Franklin was an old-time gangster.

Abruptly Bernie paused as we approached the first bank of elevators. "You didn't happen to catch today's safety color, did you?"

I thought he was kidding. Roughly a month ago, the newly formed Department of Homeland Security had begun issuing threat levels based on a five-color scale. I happened to remember that the most recent warning was amber, but I couldn't remember exactly what degree of menace that color was meant to indicate.

I watched Bernie fumble through his pockets and finally pull out a orange pill container.

"Never in my fucking life did I think twice before entering a building," he said. "It never even occurred to me that they could collapse. But after digging through layers of rubble, finding fragments of bone and pulped human flesh, it's hard for me to ever see these buildings the same way."

"How else can you see them?"

"Like giant Cuisinarts just waiting to slice and dice us."

From the sweat on his brow I could see he wasn't kidding.

"If you want to wait here," I said. "I can go up and talk to the supervisor. It's safe. I'll come right back down and no one will be any the wiser." Frankly, I was tired of dealing with him and I knew nothing dangerous would happen in this giant parked spaceship.

"I know I haven't been very patient with you," he said. "But you're a good partner, Gladyss."

It was the kindest thing he'd ever said to me. He slipped the pills back in his pocket, patted me on the shoulder, and led the way into the elevator as though walking to his death.

CHAPTER THIRTEEN

Bernie calmed down as we entered the law firm's reception area on the thirty-seventh floor, where we were greeted by Caty Duffy's supervisor, Yolanda Bellow, an attractive African-American woman. Before Bernie could break the bad news, she said that Frank had already informed everyone of Caty's untimely passing. Bernie must've sensed something was not quite right, because he immediately went to work on her, asking endless questions about the victim: the type of clothes she wore, conversations she'd had that day. Did she take any mysterious breaks? A lot of sick days? How did she look? Did she wear sleeveless shirts? Drink a lot of cranberry juice? Any unusual pills? Any indication of a secret life? I knew he was still hopeful that the poor woman was a weekend junkie, and a closet hooker.

Finally Bernie asked if he could check out Caty's desk.

Yolanda led us to Caty's work station. After she left, a red haired woman seated nearby watched intently as Bernie went through Caty's desk drawers. Ketchup packs, Kleenex, lip gloss, cinnamon-flavored gum, nothing out of the ordinary. When he took out the drawers and inspected their undersides, I walked over to the redhead.

"What's he looking for?"

"Anything that might help us solve her murder."

"I just can't believe this happened," she said, sipping a cup of coffee.

"Were you friends with Caty?"

"Not really friends, but friendly."

"Do you know anyone who was close with Caty?"

She looked around. "Vince Reynolds in accounting," she said in a low tone, then picked up a sheet of paper and walked away.

By now Bernie had finished searching Caty's work station, so I reported my conversation to him and we went back to reception and asked for Mr. Reynolds in accounting.

"Accounting is down on fifteen."

We took the elevator to the fifteenth floor, where the doors opened almost on top of the receptionist's desk. Bernie asked for Vince Reynolds.

"Have a seat," the receptionist said, indicating a waiting area then picking up the phone.

"Do me a favor and let me talk to him alone," Bernie said to me.

"Why?"

"'Cause if he was having an affair with Caty, he'd probably be more inclined to open up with another guy."

About five minutes passed before a dashing type in a nice suit emerged. He was probably forty, but could pass for ten years younger.

"Vince?" Bernie rose and took a couple of steps away from me. I heard them talking quietly back and forth for a while.

I watched Vince closely as he was talking to Bernie. I could see him twisting his lips and contracting his face. as if trying to knot up his tear ducts. Bernie whispered into his ear. He answered most of the questions simply with a nod. Bernie thanked him and, after staring at the carpet for a moment, his hands sunk in his pockets, Vince returned to his cubicle in the back.

"Yep," he said when we were back in the elevator.

"Yep what?"

"Twice a week after work at the King's Court Hotel."

"Twice a week!" I realized what he was talking about. "Wow! Who paid?" The place wasn't cheap.

"The room was on a corporate account and they used it when it was available," Bernie said. "He said the husband didn't know, which leads me to wonder if he didn't find out and O.J. her himself."

"So I guess she stayed in the hotel after Vinny left that day," I said.

"Vince said he had to leave to meet his wife, and Caty would routinely take a shower while waiting until it was time to catch the bus to Union City."

"Maybe Vin's wife did it."

"Sure, maybe we have an imitator imitating the imitator," Bernie kidded, apparently mocking his earlier theory that two of the killings were by a different murderer.

As we reached the street and started walking among the crowds, I asked, "So do you think the killer knew either of them?"

"No," he said. "I think he found an empty room in the hotel he could gain access to, then he waited for the first shapely woman who passed by and that just happened to be Caty."

"He never did that before."

"You know, I'm beginning to think it's all the work of one killer after all. But whoever it is, he probably heard the news conference like everyone else and just figured, hey, if no blonde hookers are available I'll just grab anyone," Bernie hypothesized. "Most of these guys have a victim profile, but they can also be incredible opportunists."

As we were heading toward Eighth Avenue on Forty-first, we spotted a guy in a bright red day-glo vest who was touching a pencil-like object to each lamppost he passed.

"Excuse me," Bernie said, flashing his badge, "but what the fuck are you doing?"

"This is an AC locater," the man said, holding up the small wand. "I work for Con Ed, and we're checking for live lampposts 'cause of that woman who just died downtown."

A graduate student had recently been electrocuted along with her dog by a live junction box in the East Village. I remembered that her dog had been electrocuted first; she died trying to rescue him.

"Were you around here two days ago?" Bernie asked.

"I've been checking all the lampposts in this whole area the past two days."

Bernie took out a photo of Caty Duffy's face, taken at the morgue, and showed it to the guy. "You don't remember seeing her?"

"Are you kidding," the worker replied with a grin.

"She might've been fighting with someone," I added. "She might've screamed."

"If I saw that, I would've helped her," he said.

"How about this guy?" Bernie asked, taking out a mug shot of Nessun O'Flaherty.

"You know what," said the worker. "I actually do remember this clown. He was pissing against a lamppost on Ninth Avenue as I was trying to get a reading."

"You're sure it was him?"

"Yeah, and when I told him the post could be live, he said that'd be the only buzz he could get without paying a hooker."

"He actually said hooker?"

"Yeah."

It hardly seemed like much to go on, but Bernie pointed out that O'Flaherty's SRO was only a few blocks from the crime scene and suggested we pay him a surprise visit.

"And charge him with public urination?"

Bernie didn't reply.

I asked him, "Where'd you get that photo of Caty?" I didn't know he had visited the morgue that day.

"Another great weapon Bert left me, in addition to his collection of bow ties, was the simple Boy Scout slogan: Be prepared."

"You really miss him, don't you?"

"It was kinda like having your mother for a partner. Nothing was ever good enough. But, in fairness, he would've had this case closed by now."

It was freezing cold inside O'Flaherty's fleabag hotel. Before he got to the clerk's little office, I stopped Bernie and asked him what we were doing there.

"Call it intuition." He used that secret word. "I just feel like something's up."

"Based on what?" I asked. "We have no new evidence. We were up here already with his PO, when we could've tossed his room and you didn't want to. So isn't this just a waste of time? Don't we need to talk to Frank Duffy?"

Bernie stared at me. "Last I checked, I'm in charge."

He stepped up and asked Hal, the ex-cop clerk, if he had seen the convicted sex offender early last night, around the time of Caty's murder.

"Nope. He's on a binge right now, so he might've been in his room."

"A drinking binge?"

"Yeah. I saw him with a gallon-size plastic bottle of scotch yesterday morning."

"When did this binge start?"

"Probably yesterday, but who knows?"

"Is he up there now?"

"No, I saw him leave about ten minutes ago."

"What's up with the heat?" I asked shivering. It was even colder in the building than outside. "Is the boiler broken?"

"No, it's just a little slow in warming up." Inside Hal's little booth a small space heater was churning at his feet.

"I want to grab him where he feels the most vulnerable. Let the little roach feel like he has nowhere to crawl," Bernie explained to me. Turning to Hal, he asked, "Mind if we wait in the hallway in front of his room?"

"Tell you what," said the clerk, reaching behind him. "This is the key to the room right before his. It's a little warmer in there."

"Great, thanks," Bernie said taking it.

We'd just missed the elevator, which was as slow as the geriatrics who used it, so we took the stairs. As we climbed, I suggested that if Caty was killed last night and O'Flaherty was drunk all yesterday, there was no way he would've been physically able to commit the murder, especially if he didn't drug her first.

"Trust me," Bernie responded, "alcohol affects different people differently. Most get horny and lazy, but there are a few who get angry and energized."

When we reached the top floor, Bernie listened outside O'Flaherty's door for a minute, then he knocked. No answer. He tried the door and it opened. He looked inside briefly, then closed it again quickly.

"I'm not going to blow this on some technicality," he said, and we went down the hall to the room Hal had offered us. Inside was a stripped, stained mattress on a heavy metal frame. An old end table held a clunky intercom phone. It didn't feel any warmer in the room than it did in the hallway.

As we sat there, I realized that if some mystical revelation were ever to occur, this had to be the time and place for it. I focused on my breathing and tried to evict my ego from the random thoughts that buzzed through my head. Soon only one image remained: the postcard of the Diana statue on O'Flaherty's wall. I didn't know why I had envisioned the image, but why had he taped the postcard up in the first place? What Nessun had suggested to me at the station— and it struck me as incredibly odd—was the notion that the killer had targeted a certain kind of victim entirely with the hope of luring me out. It made me wonder if he hadn't fashioned this clue just for me. Being a cop, I'm kind of a warrior, I guess, but how could he have known what else I had in common with Diana?

"Hey!" I suddenly heard, "You sound like a pug with a head cold!"

"Sorry." I guess my *Pranayama,* my breath of fire, had gotten too loud and intense. I closed my eyes, breathed through my mouth, and stopped wondering about O'Flaherty and the goddess Diana, and myself.

"When they built the Towers," Bernie broke in, "they also put up all these medium-size buildings around them, so there was some architectural transition between the colossal skyscrapers and the rest of the neighborhood," Bernie said. "Now that the Towers are gone, those transitional buildings make no damn sense."

Looking out the window, I saw what had sparked his comment. Looking eastward over the snow-encrusted lots whose buildings had recently been leveled, behind a turn-of-the-century theater that was being retrofitted as a multiplex, above the Disney store and Madame Tussaud's wax museum, there was a clear view of some of the skyscrapers that made up the new Times Square complex.

"Bernie, I wanted to tell you that my assignment's almost over and—"

"What was the address of Caty's office building again?" he interrupted, staring transfixed at the new high-rises.

"Three Times Square."

"And that was on the northeast corner, right?"

"Yeah, the one with the flyswatter roof," I recycled his joke.

"What did that security guard say?" he asked urgently. "How were those buildings addressed?"

"Christ! I think Number One is the Times Tower, the old skyscraper with the Zipper. The Reuter's Building on the northwest corner is Number Three. Number Four on the northeast corner is the Condé Nast Building. I think Number Five is southwest. Number Seven is the southeast one."

"What about Number Two?" he asked with a slight twitch of his right eye.

"I think he said that was a couple of blocks further up."

Bernie dug into his coat pocket, pulled out his notebook and flipped through the pages, then asked, "What about numbers Eight and Nine?"

170

"I don't know about those."

"Fuck!" Bernie said, and started quickly scribbling something into his book. When he was done, he looked at what he had written and gasped: "That's why he cuts their heads off! 'Cause Number One was below the shoulders and Two is a few blocks up."

"What are you talking about?"

"The bodies are on their backs facing north. On the vic's right shoulder is always the number three. On the left is the number four, on the right leg is five, on the left is six."

"You're saying the numbers correspond to the addresses of the *buildings?*"

"Yes! It's got to be O'Flaherty. Those new buildings signify the destruction of his old neighborhood. They represent everything he hates."

"That's a bit of a stretch."

"Want to know what's a stretch? Those clunky bracelets he puts on their left wrists? They're meant to resemble those flyswatters on the top of the Condé Nast Building," he pointed out the window. "And the cards and crap he sticks in their right hand is that surfboard thing on the Reuters Building."

"Still, even if the killer is mimicking Times Square, that still doesn't prove O'Flaherty did it. Most of the suspects lived around here."

Bernie simply planted himself at the window and stared eerily out. I folded my arms together, sat in silence, and watched as the afternoon sky darkened.

"There were seven buildings in the World Trade Center complex too," he finally said, clearly still obsessed by his months of cleanup at Ground Zero.

"O'Flaherty might not even come back until tomorrow." I rubbed my freezing hands together.

Bernie opened his cellphone and punched in a speed-dial number.

"Alex," he said. "Listen, we're waiting for O'Flaherty at his SRO," Pause. "Grab a pen." Pause. "On my desk is Nessun O'Flaherty's file. He was originally arrested way back on some kind of statutory rape charge. Call his tail—"

"Danny Rasdale," I prompted.

"Right, call Rasdale and find out who O'Flaherty's original vic was—who he raped twenty years ago. In fact, check if she still lives

171

here and, if so, bring her in for an interview." He paused while Alex was speaking, but then yelled impatiently. "Call right the fuck now! 'Cause I think we caught a break here, but we have to move quick. Find out where she is. Pronto. I'll be there with him soon."

Bernie flipped off his phone and sat on the bed, leaning against the wall while I stared out the window. Exhaling on the cold, filthy glass, I wrote the name Gladyss Holden on it. As I wiped it off, I noticed movement below. In the adjacent lot, I saw a big, hairy rat slowly make its way across the hardened crust of snow toward some distant crack. I had a sudden realization that I hadn't seen rats in a while. The city really had made progress in eliminating undesirables. For a moment, I was nostalgic for the urban wilderness. The rat seemed vaguely bucolic, more like an evicted squirrel or an endangered groundhog.

When a large truck sped up Eighth Avenue, we could feel the old building shake.

"If there's an earthquake, you're supposed to stand in a doorway, right?" Bernie tried for some small talk.

"I guess, but I'm more worried about freezing to death."

"I can't stop wondering what it must've been like for them," he said quietly. "Those poor bastards didn't even have time to . . . If this building started to collapse, I'd jump out the window."

"You wouldn't survive the fall."

"But at least they'd have my corpse to bury. When I think of the rotting crap we found." He nodded sadly. "Without a lab test we couldn't be sure if they were someone's remains or their lunch. And poor Bert, having to go through that in his condition."

"You mean with cancer."

"It wasn't cancer," he said softly. "And everyone knew it wasn't cancer."

Bernie didn't say what it was, but I'd figured it out when I was told his young wife Juanita had died of AIDS.

I breathed into my cupped palms, trying to warm them up. A view of Times Square from a distant window hardly seemed like a smoking gun, even if the carved numbers did line up. As the icy minutes grew colder, I warmed myself with thoughts of Noel, wondering if he might be thinking of me while he was in sunny LA.

When I was awakened from my daydream by Bernie's snoring, I realized I was shivering uncontrollably. I suddenly felt bad for the cub reporter Bernie had stuck in the back of the patrol car. It wasn't even five o'clock and the sky was black as charcoal.

"I'm fucking freezing." I said, rising to my numb feet. "There's a deli on the next block. Want a coffee?"

"Light and sweet," he mumbled without opening his eyes.

I peeked out the door. An old lady was standing there in a nightgown like a frozen ghost. As I walked past her, I realized she was leaning against the radiator, which emitted a faint hiss as if letting out its dying breath.

"You should call the Heat Hotline and complain," I suggested, though I don't think she heard me. "You can call 311 and they'll put you through."

I took the stairs down, dashed through the lobby and out to the well-heated corner deli, where I got on the end of a long line. I was grateful that it moved slowly enough for me to get my core temperature back up. When it was my turn I ordered two cups of coffee, and in another minute I was back in the meat-locker lobby holding the burning hot brown bag. Seniors were standing around and the clerk was watching his portable TV as I raced through.

When the dented elevator door opened, I patiently waited as the frozen lady who had been holding onto the radiator slowly exited. Suddenly a violent force slammed into me, throwing me forward. As I fell to the floor, I whacked my forehead against the back wall of the elevator. The hot coffee, crushed under my chest, scalded me from my belly to my neck. As I struggled to get up, my assailant jumped on my back. Grabbing my hair he tried to slam my head against the floor. The elevator doors slid shut with him on top of me.

My first instinct was to go for my pistol, but with his weight on top of me I was unable to grab it.

"My fucking knee hasn't been the same since you hit me, you bitch!"

A sharp punch to my right kidney was followed by a succession of blows. I shoved my hand down and grabbed my piece from its holster.

Sensing what I was doing, O'Flaherty flopped forward, his chest pressed down on my back. His hands reached under my arms just as my elbow was pulling it up. Feeling his hands dig in under me, I shoved my piece down below my waist, so it was out of his reach.

Pissed that he couldn't snatch the grip, he shoved his hands further down into my underwear.

"You motherfucker!"

"Fuck you, cunt!" he screamed back. Unable to reach any farther, his cracked yellow claws dug into my belly like a wild animal's. Finally he grabbed my hips and started dry-humping my ass.

"You fucking cocksucker!" I shouted as I reached down and found the top of my Glock. As he frantically ground his loins into my buttocks, I slowly worked the gun up between my flattened body and the filthy, wet elevator floor.

Just as I pulled it up, he grabbed hold of it and tried to yank it from my hand. Just as he succeeded, I pushed the release lever, popping the ammo clip out of the bottom. But there was still one bullet left in the chamber.

Breathing deeply and conjuring up what had to be Kundalini strength, I hoisted his bucking ass up in the air just as he squeezed the trigger. My head slammed against the floor as the shot went off. Feeling the burning sensation, I feared I had been hit.

"Fuck!" he cursed as he collapsed on top of me. Angrily he shoved the hot muzzle of my pistol hard into the back of my skull and pulled the trigger again. *Click.* I lost bladder control.

"*Cocksucker!*"

I frantically twisted to my side and finally knocked him off me. As we rolled around on the coffee-drenched floor, he cursed at me nonstop. Suddenly a blow hit me across the mouth. Another, sharper one across my nose brought him closer to me. I used everything I had to grab his wrists and yank him forward, taking away his space to wind up and punch me. But now his saggy, bristly face was just above mine, and he tried to shove his rotting tongue into my mouth. I clenched my jaws shut and dug my fingers into his side until he rolled over. Then we struggled until the elevator door finally slid open.

As soon as it did, Bernie reached in and grabbed O'Flaherty by his hair, peeling him away from me, and threw him backwards onto the hallway floor.

"'Are you shot?"

"No," I managed to say.

Without any sign of his foot problems, Bernie raced down the hall, catching up with O'Flaherty just before he could slam the door of his room behind him. I grabbed my bullet clip and slipped it back into my gun, then rose on wobbly legs, fell to my knees, and rose again. As I was pulling my pants up, I suddenly vomited. Straightening up, I gingerly felt my head. The flash from the gun blast had singed my hair; there was pain, but no blood.

Slowly I stumbled down the hallway after my partner. When I reached O'Flaherty's room, I saw that Bernie had cuffed him and was dragging him screaming into his disgusting bathroom.

"Close that door," he yelled. As I did, I saw him kicking O'Flaherty repeatedly in the crotch and belly. His bum foot seemed to have miraculously recovered.

"Don't do this," I said to Bernie, struggling to catch my breath. "You're going to blow the arrest."

"Stay out!" he shouted, closing the bathroom door. I could hear O'Flaherty screaming for help, but I felt nauseous and frail. The struggle had left me covered in sweat and utterly exhausted. Having my own pistol grabbed from me and pointed at my skull was as close to death as I had ever come.

As the adrenaline in my system ebbed, it took all my strength just to stay seated on the bed and stop myself from trembling and crying. My ribs and back throbbed with pain where I'd been punched. When I pulled up my shirt and looked at my stomach, it was burning bright red from the hot coffee. Three purplish-red gashes ran down the center of my belly into my pubic hair.

"You fucking *dare* shoot at a cop!"

I looked inside the bathroom and saw that Bernie had O'Flaherty on the floor. He was kneeling on his ass, while yanking him back by the collar of his cheap trenchcoat, pulling his neck back so far I thought it would snap.

"She kneecapped me!" O'Flaherty gagged.

"Let me fix that for you, you fucking—" Bernie shifted his weight onto O'Flaherty's bum knee. The man howled in agony.

"Bernie, stop it!" I said.

"He got me too, goddamn it. Didn't you, pal!" Bernie shouted.

"What are you talking about?" I asked.

"He was the one who whacked me over the head while I was sleeping in my car!" Bernie said, yanking O'Flaherty's neck back farther. Pushing the cuffed man forward, he shoved his face right into his black-stained toilet. When I made an effort to stop him, he shoved me out of the room and closed the door. My muscles and nerves throbbed and twitched with pain. I was too shaken up to stand any longer. This had to be what they meant by being in shock.

"Bernie," I said, kicking the door. "Remember Diallo! Abner Louima! You wanna drag this department through that shit all over again?"

"Take a look at yourself in the mirror," he yelled. "Then tell me Amadou Diallo!"

Catching sight of myself in a small oval wall mirror, I jumped. My upper lip was split and blood was streaming out of both my nostrils. My nose didn't seem to be broken, but several cuts and bruises were rising on my cheek and forehead.

The crackling of the police radio over O'Flaherty's gurgling broke my exhausted trance. I heard official policespeak, although it sounded like a foreign language. The bathroom door popped open, revealing Bernie calmly holding his radio in one hand as he requested an ambulance and backup. With his other hand he was still plunging O'Flaherty's face deep into his filthy toilet bowl, as if cleaning it with a johnny stick.

I opened the window and gasped involuntarily. As the cold air filled my lungs, I looked again at the postcard of the Goddess of the Hunt statue that was taped to O'Flaherty's wall. I grabbed it and stared at it for a moment as a very palpable force rose out of me. I tried to regain composure, steadily breathing the freezing air. Suddenly I felt I was being pulled forward. I dropped the postcard and grasped the ancient wooden window frames with both hands to keep from tumbling downward. With my head entirely outside the room, I saw that there was an adjacent window between this room and the next that looked like it had been bricked up decades ago. Something small, dark, and compact hung in it like a pendant, barely visible in the darkness.

I reached back for one of O'Flaherty's t-shirts and, using the tips of my fingers, tried pulling at the object, which was stubbornly wedged in a crack where the concrete had eroded, between the old bricks. Soon there was a bit of play. What I was holding was a wooden handle. In another moment I was able to pry it from the cement crevice. It was a large, thick knife.

Back inside the room, I turned on the bedside lamp. I could make out a rinse of dried blood, not only on the blade, but all along the wooden handle as well.

"Got him," I whispered. Then shoving my way into the bathroom, I yelled to Bernie, "We've got him!"

Bernie was still drowning O'Flaherty, and cursing at him all the while.

"Stop it before you blow the case! I've got it!"

"What do you got?"

"The murder weapon!" I held it up.

In order to inspect the knife, Bernie released O'Flaherty, who rolled onto his side on the bathroom floor. He was coughing up toilet water, gasping for air. His swollen, purple hands were still cuffed tightly behind his back. The detective carefully took the t-shirt in which I held the knife. Putting on his reading glasses, he held the weapon up to the lamplight in the bedroom and carefully studied the thick layers of blood that had coagulated and dried on the blade and along the handle. Far from cleaning the knife the way he had cleaned every other aspect of the crime scene, O'Flaherty was evidently proud of the caked strata, a sensual talisman of his savagery.

Bernie returned to the bathroom and shoved the blade toward O'Flaherty's dripping face. "I don't even need luminol to check this. It's all right there, fuckface. All your little blood sacrifices."

"Brutality . . . unlawful . . . search . . . civil suit," O'Flaherty gasped, still hyperventilating.

"Ass rape . . . slapped around by monsters . . . lethal . . . injection," Bernie mimicked his gasps.

"I was the victim! . . . They . . . ripped me off . . ." he continued as Bernie handed me back the weapon and called Crime Scene.

I couldn't look at O'Flaherty again, so I waited in the hallway. To think I'd ever wanted to be in homicide. Bernie must've sensed my doubts, because he opened the door and said, "If you were a male cop, instead of punching you out he would've just executed you as soon as he got you in the elevator."

"Have you ever been attacked?"

"Two weeks ago, remember?" he said, gently rubbing his crown. "Anyone can get blitzed from behind."

"If you hadn't come when you did . . ." I couldn't talk any more. We heard sirens outside and Bernie quickly recapitulated what had happened, leaving out his little water torture. We had to get our stories straight to protect each other. In another moment, the first cops, including Sergeant McKenner, raced up the stairs.

"You okay, Gladyss?" he said inspecting my cuts and bruises.

"A little banged up, but—"

"When are you due back in NSU?"

"In a few days."

"Thank God for that."

A moment later the elevator opened and the supporting cast of technicians and EMS workers came flooding out. The uniforms took O'Flaherty downstairs, while the paramedics checked me out and treated me for cuts and trauma. When I showed them the burn marks on my stomach, one large medic with thick black hair pointed to the scratches trailing down my belly and below my belt. "Did he do that?"

"Yeah."

"Would you mind opening your pants?" he asked. No one else was around, so I unbuckled my pants and pulled them down, along with my underwear, to the top of my pubes to show where the scratch marks ended.

"Did he penetrate you?" he asked, looking up at me.

"Christ, no!"

Any kind of penetration legally constituted a rape. If his fingers had been longer, or my torso any shorter, technically I would've been violated. He delicately swabbed a yellowish-brown liquid on the eight-inch scrapes and that was it.

"He mainly just hit me on the back and ribs," I said sternly.

"They'll take care of you at the hospital."

The rank and file started pouring in, then sergeants, lieutenants, and the ADA.

"Why's he wet?" the lieutenant in charge asked Bernie. "He's claiming you stuck his head in the toilet."

Bernie calmly relayed how he'd heard the gunshot in the elevator, then how he pulled O'Flaherty off of me. "The prick raced back into his room with me in pursuit. We struggled at the door. He hit me a few times, then managed to make it into the bathroom. We struggled some more, and when I finally was able to grab him I knocked him into the toilet, that's all. I mean, it's a small fucking room."

"Where exactly was your partner during all this?" the lieutenant asked.

"Still near the elevator. She'd been beaten and burnt, almost shot. This guy was moving pretty quick."

"Then what?"

"Then I was alone, fighting for my life. I mean, you know I'm not in the best of health. I've had this goddamn lung thing since the World Trade Center."

"So why don't I see a mark on you, while he's all bruised up?"

"I was alone and the man had just shot my partner. I mean, I was fighting for my life here."

"He's claiming you cuffed him and tortured him."

"With all due respect, after he fired at Chronou in the elevator, if I'd wanted to, you know I coulda just shot him, and been entirely within my rights."

"What are you saying, we should be glad he's not dead?" asked the captain, who had quietly entered and been listening in.

"Captain, you know me. I mean, you've accused me of getting rough over the years, so for me I'd call this exercising self-restraint." One of the other cops chuckled.

"Okay, so you're fighting with him in the bathroom, then what?"

"Only when I finally got him on the floor was I able to cuff him. And only after I got the cuffs on him could I radio for help."

"So you weren't drowning him in the shitter with his hands cuffed behind his back?"

"Hell no! I knocked him in there while we were fighting, but once I got him cuffed it was over."

The story was loosely as we had rehearsed it.

"Exactly what time did you hear the shot in the elevator?" asked the captain.

"Give me a break. You know how fast this shit goes down."

The captain turned to me. "You had gone down to the corner deli for a coffee?"

"Yes, sir. I was in the store a while 'cause there was a line."

"Still, the clerk should be able to give us an idea of what time you left there," the lieutenant said.

"They probably have a surveillance camera, maybe it's time-stamped," the captain added.

"I suppose so," I replied.

As the lieutenant was about to ask me more questions the black-haired paramedic came to the rescue, pushing in a wheelchair and saying I really had to go to the hospital now.

He wanted to strap me in, but I insisted I could walk down to the ambulance. As soon as I rose to my feet, I found myself shaking. I walked along the hall and watched as the crime photographer began snapping photos of the filthy elevator floor: it was a dark interplay of piss, blood, coffee, and vomit—all mine.

Before I could give it any more thought, the paramedic returned with the wheelchair and we were going down in the freight elevator, packed with black garbage bags. Soon I was being lifted into the damn ambulance like some strange piece of living furniture. Just before they closed the back doors, Eddie O'Ryan appeared out of nowhere and jumped inside.

"I just heard you were shot!" he said, grabbing my hand.

"It wasn't that bad."

"They got him?" he asked.

"Yeah, and I found the murder weapon."

Lowering his voice, he said, "He didn't . . . You weren't . . . raped?"

"No."

"You're sure?" He looked at me funny.

"I'd fucking *know* if I'd been raped, wouldn't I!"

The paramedic who was sitting with us looked nervously away.

At St. Vincent's Hospital on Twelfth and Seventh, I was given priority treatment. I told Eddie I really needed to be alone, so he gave me a pat on the back and told me to call if I needed absolutely anything.

The paramedic must've mentioned my scratches because an older female lieutenant I didn't know, from Sex Crimes, sat down and delicately interviewed me. She carefully filled out a detailed report while an aide snapped Polaroids for evidence: unflattering photos of my face, my ribs, my lower back and forehead, the first and second degree burns on my chest and stomach. And the humiliating scratches across my belly, of course. I got a band-aid for the cut on my forehead and even a dab of ointment for the singe at the back of my scalp. The doctor gave me prescriptions for a burn ointment for my stomach, some antibiotics, and a mild painkiller – none of which I intended to take. A member of the PBA showed up and said I was entitled to so many sick days and counseling, then asked if I needed a representative or anything else. I told him no thanks. By the time the doctor offered me a sedative, I already felt steadier and didn't want to go back to being groggy. He asked me if I had someone to look after me.

"My boyfriend's waiting for me at home," I lied to comfort him. A patrolman drove me to my door and waited until I closed it before he sped off.

CHAPTER FOURTEEN

As soon as I'd locked my apartment door, I found myself trembling uncontrollably. *I wasn't alone!* I pulled out my gun and checked my apartment thoroughly. It was empty. Still wearing my overcoat, I sat down and just felt profoundly stupid and guilty. Why the hell did I ever choose to descend into that miserable underworld and put myself in such a clearly awful situation. What the fuck was I thinking!

I punched myself in the thigh and, before I could do anything worse to myself, went into my kitchen and started cleaning the shelves. I started with the canned and bottled items, wiping them off then washing down the shelves and putting them back in place. Then I worked my way through the seasonings rack, cleaning as I went. Finally I dusted and reorganized the pots, pans, plates, and silverware.

I basically had this OCD thing under control except for mild flare-ups now and then. On New Years Day. after things had gone poorly with O'Ryan, I'd spent three hours reorganizing all the soaps, sprays, lotions, and pharmaceuticals in my bathroom, feeling better even as I did it.

This time it was different. As I cleaned, I kept remembering the moment when O'Flaherty had shoved his claws down my pants. It literally felt as if he had inserted some awful part of himself inside me. I shattered a crystal champagne glass my grandmother had brought here from the old country. That was enough. I carefully swept up the shattered pieces and ran a bath.

I sat in it and had a long cry. Then, just as I was beginning to drift off, I saw O'Flaherty's bony fists coming down on my face, his broken claws scratching along my belly. Bolting upright, I sent a splash of water over the sides of the tub and onto the floor. After I'd dried off, I lay down and dozed for a while.

When I awoke and thought about the afternoon's events, I realized with a start that after the attack in the elevator, when I was exhausted from the beating—and perhaps liberated from self-consciousness—I must've finally had some kind of mystical experience. How else to explain the way I was drawn to O'Flaherty's window where I spotted the tip of what turned out to be his knife? It truly felt as though the spirit of Diana had shoved my head out of there to show me the bloody weapon. I was too tired even to be excited by this, so I took a sleeping pill and slept right through until early the next morning.

When I turned on my computer, there were various local news stories with headlines like NYPD POLICEWOMAN NARROWLY ESCAPES DEATH CAPTURING KILLER! and a vague but sensationalized description of what had happened last night, along with my official NYPD photo.

As I thought about Nessun O'Flaherty and the postcard of Diana in his room, I wondered if, consciously or unconsciously, he was giving us a clue to what he'd done. I went back to a web site about Greek myths, intending to read more about Diana, but ended up finding something even more interesting. Because his name was so similar to our suspect's, I was drawn to the story of Nessus. He was a centaur—half-man, half-horse, who abducted Deianera, the wife of Hercules. But before he could get away with her, Hercules shot him with an arrow. While the lecherous Nessus was dying, he told his would-be victim that his blood would ensure that her husband remained faithful to her. Later, when she feared Hercules was losing affection for her, she spread this blood on her beloved's shirt—it ended up killing him.

I'd been ordered to rest, but I felt too restless, so I went downstairs to the yoga studio across the street. It was just before noon, and several students were rolling out their mats. The Renunciate waved me in.

He looked at the bruises on my face. "What happened?"

"An accident," I said dismissively.

"I have to teach a class, but—"

"I was wondering if you could give me a little advice," I said awkwardly.

"Sure."

"I'm feeling a little . . ." I spun my hand and let out a deep breath.

"Uprooted?" The room was filling up.

"Yeah. I was wondering if there was something I could do for that . . ."

He thought a moment then calmly said, "Wear red. It will comfort you."

"Red?"

"Yes, it's the color of the root chakra. Visualize it around you."

I just stared at him, thinking I could've just left last night's blood on my face.

He closed his eyes peacefully. The room was full of seated women who seemed as calm as purring cats. His Oms were a signal for me to back out of the sacred space.

Since I couldn't do a workout, and felt too tense to stay at home, I decided I might as well go see if O'Flaherty had confessed.

By the time I got to the precinct, the capture of the Blonde Hooker Killer had gone viral. News vans lined the sidewalk, waiting for the latest briefing. Apparently O'Flaherty had refused to say a word last night until he had been taken to the hospital, where a doctor insisted that he be sedated and allowed to sleep. So it wasn't until a couple hours ago that they finally were able to start interrogating him.

The bruises on my face must've bloomed into a colorful bouquet, as everyone did a double take. Because I'd been dumb enough to get sacked from behind and almost killed, the sergeant and others treated me like a hero.

"What the hell are you doing here?" Bernie asked when I got to Homicide. "You were injured in the line of duty. Go home!"

I said I wouldn't have any peace of mind until I knew my pain had earned us a confession, and asked, "Did he lawyer up?"

"He declined a lawyer because he *is* one," Annie said. "We're pretty pissed he got a good night's sleep, though. We should've had his statement by now."

She and Bernie led me into the surveillance room, where we could watch the interrogation from behind a one-way mirror.

Because Bernie had nearly drowned O'Flaherty in his own crapper, he had to leave the interrogation to others. Alex, Barry, and the ADA who'd been appointed to the case were taking turns questioning him.

On the wall behind them, Annie had taped up large photos of the carnage he had wrought—the butchered bodies of Mary Lynn MacArthur, Denise Giantonni, Nelly Linquist, and the others.

"It's a simple question." We listened as Alex spoke softly. "Why did you kill them?"

"You're worried about a couple of two-bit hookers while an entire *city* is being murdered. How about going after the real criminals!" O'Flaherty hissed.

"And who would that be?" the ADA asked.

"These entitled fucking rich kids who have invaded New York because their own homes are sterile shells. And what's the first thing they do? They destroy *our* city and replace it with the kind of boring, suburban shit that made the rest of this country so meaningless."

Annie silently offered me an ice cube wrapped in a napkin, which I pressed in turn to my cheek, nose, and lips. Like me, O'Flaherty was flamboyantly cut up and bruised. He was babbling on about how his community had been systematically decimated by the invading army of Yuppie ants, whose money was manipulating the police, politicians, and developers, and how all he was doing was trying to defend it.

After a half hour of this, it was clear that the interrogation was stalled. He simply wouldn't own up to the killings. Fortunately, we probably didn't need a confession—the fact that we had the weapon pretty much sealed the case—so Bernie received permission from the captain to see if he could get a result.

Before going inside though, Bernie rummaged through the communal refrigerator and grabbed a dried-out American cheese sandwich that had been unclaimed for a week now. He tipped out the pens and pencils from the mug on his desk and filled it with the burnt dregs from our coffee pot and added some skim milk long past its expiration date.

O'Flaherty flinched as his tormentor from last night entered the room and placed the offerings on the table before him.

"From one lapsed Catholic to another, here's my little act of contrition," Bernie said, taking a seat across from him. "When you shot at my partner, some poor young girl, I'da been well within my rights to splatter your brains on the elevator wall. But I didn't, did I?"

O'Flaherty began wolfing down the moldy sandwich. In between swallows, he told Bernie he was sorry for what he had done to me. He glanced at the one-way glass, and I knew he was looking for me.

"Look, Nessun," Bernie began. We've got you on this. It's an open-and-shut case. You're staring six murder one charges in the face. In other words, lethal injection. If you confess, maybe you can plead diminished responsibility and escape the death penalty."

"That's not the way I see it," O'Flaherty said. "The way I see it, you got me for assaulting that Amazonian kneecapper, but that's it." He took an authoritative sip of the burnt coffee.

"We got the murder weapon from your room, with various blood samples and your prints all over it."

"That'll be thrown out of court! It was an illegal search. You had no warrant!"

"You're not stupid," the ADA said, "so let's not play games."

"Maybe so," O'Flaherty replied calmly. "But as you well know, I have alibis for some of those killings."

"So what are you saying?" Bernie asked.

"Voluntary manslaughter. Murder two, tops. Twenty years with a parole option."

The ADA responded that if O'Flaherty worked with them, providing iron-clad alibis for the times of the murders he said he didn't commit and confessing to the murders he did, then he'd take it to the DA and see if he could get him a deal.

"I only killed two girls," O'Flaherty said bluntly. "and I only did them in self-defense."

"Sure," Bernie replied. "They attacked you while they were unconscious, so you chopped their heads off."

"All the butchery was *after* they'd died. They didn't feel any of it."

"Okay, so what did you do to them while they were still alive?" the ADA asked.

"I had a little routine, really nothing more than a harmless chat. Verbal foreplay. In fact, I never even had sex with any of them—it was all just talk. Been doing it that way for years."

"Years?"

"Suffice to say, I've been with a lot of girls. If you ask some of the regulars they'll tell you I was always a gentleman."

"So why did you 'butcher' two of them, as you put it?" Bernie asked.

"What you need to know is: Number one, I had no premeditation. It was a crime of passion, so to speak."

"If it wasn't premeditated," began the ADA. "then how do you explain using sleeping pills—"

Bernie raised his hand to silence him.

"Number two, they went calmly to sleep, without any fear or suffering. And number three, all the messy stuff took place *after* their spirits had left their bodies."

"Just walk us through it," Bernie said. "Who was first?"

"Mary Lynn was the first."

"Why'd you kill her?"

"She tried to run off with my disability check so I . . ." His voice trailed off.

"Where'd you meet her?" Bernie asked.

"Some sordid agency I found in the back of one of those disreputable newspapers. I asked for a tall blonde and they sent her."

"Where'd you get the credit card?"

"From some yuphole at Starbucks."

"I don't understand," Alex spoke up. "So you had the girl come up and give you a blow job, then you killed her?"

"Please!" O'Flaherty groaned in disgust. "They're all infected with HIV. I don't want to get AIDS. I don't even shake their diseased hands. I just talk to them."

"So what did you do, pray together?" Bernie asked.

"Freud said that the female libido is essentially masochistic while the male libido is sadistic, and this dynamic has always intrigued me. I start by asking them about their past, what drives them to degrade themselves with strange men."

"Does this little routine ever involve Marilyn Monroe?" Barry spoke up for the first time.

"Is that some kind of joke? Are you mocking me?"

"Not at all," Barry said earnestly. Although O'Flaherty had evidently read about the additional murders, we had managed to keep the Marilyn Monroe details out of the press.

"So Mary Lynn tried to rip you off and you fought back?" Bernie said, returning to the narrative.

"That's right."

"You killed her."

"Yes."

"And which one was Nelly?" Bernie said looking at the gruesome pictures behind him.

"She was the one with the tear drop marks near her eyes," O'Flaherty pointed to the photo of her. "Crappy prison tats. That tipped me off immediately that she was no good."

"And Denise . . ."

"Yeah."

"And Tabetha," Bern said as almost an afterthought.

"Who?" O'Flaherty said.

"You cocksucker, you twisted that girl's head right off her fucking shoulders and you're gonna sit there and say who?"

"I just didn't hear her name, goddamn it!"

"The one at the Fabio." Bernie leaned forward so he was right in the man's face. "You twisted that poor kid's head off and you're gonna tell me why."

"Why?"

"Yeah, why? What the fuck did she do to you?"

"Nothing, she was dead. I just got tired of cutting their heads off. Takes a lot of work to butcher a body."

"That would explain these two, Jane and Caty," Bernie tapped at the other photos. "Their heads were still attached."

"See, this is the kind of shit that pisses me off!" O'Flaherty hissed. "I'm being straightforward with you and then you start throwing in every whore in the city who winds up dead."

"Fine, let's just talk about your gang of four," Bernie pointed to their photos. "Because it's four killings you've now confessed to, not two. You expect us to believe they all mugged you, or what?"

"I'd perform a little test. I'd leave my wallet out, go to the bathroom."

"Sounds like entrapment," Bernie said.

"Yeah, that's what I thought when the NYPD did it to me. But then when it held up in court, I figured, what's good for the goose . . ."

"Okay, so if your cash was missing when you came back, what then?" Bernie asked.

"Did any of the prostitutes *not* take your wallet?" Barry asked delicately.

"Yeah, some didn't."

"If we could get their names," Barry continued, "it might help your case."

"I didn't exactly stay in touch."

"Getting back to those four, the ones you say ripped you off," continued Bernie.

"With them, I'd . . . get justice."

"By cutting their heads off?" Alex asked.

"No! I told you I never hurt anyone. I'd simply offer them a bottle of beer laced with sleeping pills—if they didn't drink the beer, that would be the end of it, because I don't believe in violence. But guess what? They always drank it." he said with a snicker. "Then I'd just talk until they passed out."

"And then you'd strangle them?" the ADA asked.

"They had ripped me off. I was merely defending myself and my property."

"Fair enough, but what was the purpose of this gruesome display?" Barry pointed to the post-mortem tableaus on the wall.

"After someone's dead, what does it matter?"

"Well, years from now criminologists are going to be debating the significance of the numbers you carved into their limbs, as well as the fact that you always arranged the body in the same exact position," Barry said, elevating O'Flaherty's crimes to legendary status.

"Call it late Abstract Expressionism," O'Flaherty said, refusing to be drawn.

"From your window I could see the new Times Square complex," Bernie said tiredly. "You must've hated watching those damn buildings going up."

"So you figured it out," O'Flaherty replied. "Bully for you."

"And you're a lying piece of shit," Bernie said, leaning into him again. "You didn't kill those girls because of your empty wallet. You

189

did it because you're a fucking faggot who hates women."

"Our SRO was purchased by a developer three years ago," he replied. "We stopped them demolishing it for a while, but now we've only got a couple months left, then we're all out on our asses. Do you know, some of the residents have been living in that neighborhood as far back as the 1920s? Anna Hurley in room 306 was in Times Square when they announced the end of World War Two. Just 'cause rents are going up shouldn't mean you can just roll up the past and chuck us all into homeless shelters in Queens!"

"What the hell does all this have to do with you butchering hookers?" Alex asked.

"High crime rates kept the property values down for years," O'Flaherty replied.

"Boy, Jane Jacobs woulda given you a handjob out of sheer gratitude," Bernie said straight-faced. "You're a political fucking prisoner, fighting to preserve the integrity of old New York."

"You're goddamn right I am!"

"There are just a couple small problems . . ."

"Like what?"

"For starters, the very first hooker you killed," Bernie said.

"What?"

"Crystal was murdered back in the early '80s, when the neighborhood was still a big stinking shitpile."

"What the hell are you talking about?"

"Crystal Hodges. And don't tell me you don't know her. I checked her records and she lived in your shitty, rat-infested tenement on Forty-fifth Street before you even went to jail."

"I don't know who you're talking about."

"They didn't have DNA testing then, but guess what, Crystal had sperm in her and we still have that stored, so when we test your DNA against that sample . . ."

"Even if what you're saying were true, any specimen would've undoubtedly been corrupted by now. But it was a good bluff. Kudos to you, Junior."

"We're getting a warrant to take a DNA sample from you," the ADA fired back.

"Her pimp killed her."

"Oh, look at this! Suddenly he remembers a twenty-five-year-old case," Bernie commented. "They charged her pimp, it's true, but he went to jail for another murder. And three months later you got sent away for what turned out to be twenty years. Tell me there is no God."

"The murder rate in this city was through the roof back then," O'Flaherty responded. "Good luck proving I killed some hooker trash all those years ago."

"You've confessed to four murders," Bernie said. "And I bet we can convince the jury of the last three murders."

"You want to accuse me of seven murders," O'Flaherty said with a grin, "Be my guest. When my buddies line up to say I was with them on most of those dates, it'll be a lot easier to beat all the charges."

At that moment, I realized we had a photo of the knife that was used in the Jane Hansen murder—one of the two killings Bernie had suspected were done by someone else. It was visible in one of the jpegs that had been sent to Miriam's web site. I went to Bernie's desk and flipped through the file until I located the hard copy. The knife handle in the photo didn't look anything like O'Flaherty's weapon.

But I shouldn't have been disappointed. Bernie had been saying for a long time now that two killers were involved. Still, we'd hoped that it was all over.

Annie was taking a call at a neighboring desk. When she hung up, I told her what I'd discovered. She said she had just got a phone call from the desk sergeant. O'Flaherty's first official victim, his step-daughter Daisy Leary, whose statutory rape had got him jailed over twenty years ago, was waiting downstairs. We called Bernie out of the interrogation room to tell him, and he instructed Annie and me to try to extract any useful information from her.

As soon as I saw the stepdaughter, sitting blankly over a can of Diet Coke, one big mystery was solved. She was a tall blonde, now heavyset and middle-aged, with deep, dark circles under her bright blue eyes. And because she was a tall blonde, all the victims were as well—which in turn was why I had gotten this assignment.

Annie thanked Daisy for coming in, and introduced me as one of the investigators on the case.

"What happened to you?" Daisy asked as we walked, looking at my bruises.

"Your stepfather," I said.

"Nessun did that to you?" she asked nervously as Annie dashed before us looking for an available conference room. They were all occupied.

"You're not charging Nessun with those midtown murders, are you?" Daisy asked. To my surprise, she seemed to have some sympathy for her former rapist.

"We know he did them," I said.

"Oh my God . . . What do you want from me?"

"It was your case that led to his initial arrest."

"But he was never violent to me. Not once. He probably would've gotten off if he didn't hit that cop. That was what got him jail time. He always had problems with authority."

"So he didn't forcibly rape you?" I asked.

"Come on," Annie said, spotting Bernie's office as the only empty room that offered some privacy. "Let's go in here."

"He didn't actually rape me," she said, taking a seat. "What happened was, he started dating my mother. I was 16, stupid and lonely, and we ended up getting involved."

Apparently the details of the case had gotten screwed up in the retelling. I had gotten the impression she was only thirteen at the time.

"So you started a consensual relationship with him?"

"It's complicated." She looked to the floor.

"Well you must've had sex with him if he was charged with statutory rape."

"Let's just say he took advantage," she said simply.

"How did he take advantage?" Annie pushed.

"He used to watch me."

"Watch you undress?"

"Yes, but . . ." she paused, "See, I knew he was watching me, and I kept doing it. Then he'd give me a few bucks here and there. He was a peeper, which was probably why he lived near Forty-second Street." Before the Internet, Times Square was the closest you could get to a 24-hour supply of porn.

"Look, if he went to jail on false charges . . ."

"They weren't entirely false," Daisy said.

"Maybe you should just tell us what happened. That'll save us all time."

"I was young and dumb, and the ADA kind of pressured me, so if you want me to say more, I'm gonna need some immunity," she said directly.

Annie excused herself while she made a call to the ADA upstairs. When she came back, she said he'd checked O'Flaherty's file and discovered the statutory rape charge initially brought against him years ago had ultimately been dropped due to insufficient evidence. Daisy never even testified, so there was no question of her being prosecuted for perjury.

Annie resumed questioning her: "According to your mom's statement, she found several thousand dollars in your drawer that she said O'Flaherty had paid you."

"That was a lie. I mean, it wasn't from sex."

"You made all that money from his peeping?"

"Sure."

She was being too protective of the sleazebag, I thought. She had to be hiding something herself.

"You helped him, didn't you?" I asked.

She flinched, then recovered. "Helped him with what?"

"He told us everything about the girls," I replied playing up what I knew. During our first meeting with O'Flaherty he had all but said that he collected runaways, probably from trawling the Port Authority Bus Depot right down the block from his house.

"So he did a little chickenhawking now and then," she said. "Big deal." The fact that she knew the lingo made me realize how sleazy she really was.

"He was a pimp?"

"No, but he'd . . . find girls for pimps."

"How many girls are we talking about?" Annie asked.

"Who remembers?"

Suddenly her eyes widened and her jaw dropped. She looked like she'd seen a ghost. Following her sight line, I saw that she was staring at the little wooden framed picture of Juanita Lopez Kelly, Bert's young wife from whom he'd contracted HIV.

"You remember her?" I asked.

"Yeah," she said softly, and reflected for a moment. Then, without prompting, she continued, "We were heading into the bus depot one night just as she was leaving. She had this little knapsack on her back. She was trying to cross the street when she fell right into this huge puddle. The drain was stopped up so it was more like a fucking lake. And it was cold out. Nessun went right in after her. He was a real gentleman that way. She was sopping wet. She said she had just got off the bus and didn't know anyone here. I mean, she might as well have been wearing a bulls eye. Nessun invited her to come home with us to dry off."

"Then what happened?"

"She had no job, nowhere to go, and she was just a kid, like me. Ness would let the girls stay in an empty room in the basement and I'd hang out with them for a few weeks. Become friends. And after a while he'd bring pimps by."

"So how exactly did it work? Were they raped or drugged?"

"Hell no, it was all on the level! The girls were given a tour. The guys were like, 'Look what I'm doing for my ladies.' Pimps would drive them around and say shit like, 'This is the sweet life. I love them and they love me back.' Easy money. Nice clothes. Coke and clubs. If they went with the pimp, Nessun would get a quick grand and he'd throw me a couple hundred."

"How do you live with yourself?" I asked.

"It wasn't like I was pulling any triggers. I just went along with it and got some cash. We never forced anyone to do anything they didn't want to, and that's the truth!"

"So how'd your mother catch you?" Annie asked.

"I thought Nessun had shortchanged me over one girl. I was sure we was alone so I was cursing and yelling at him when suddenly my mother walks in. I hushed up, but it was too late. She asked me if I was fucking Nessun and I said no, which was true. But she took me to a doctor who examined me and saw that I wasn't a virgin."

"But it wasn't Nessun?"

"No, I had a boyfriend by then. Still, my mother asked if Ness had raped me, and I thought I'd be helping him if I said I had consented. She went nuts. I swore he hadn't fucked me, but it was too late. She was the one who said I had to claim it was statutory rape. Between losing my mother and sacrificing Nessun . . . Well, I didn't think he'd go to jail. But I sure as shit didn't expect him to do what he did then."

"Which was?" Annie asked.

"Some smartass rookie cop started pushing him around, so

Nessun waited until the officer was talking to my mom and then he jumped on him, knocked him to the ground."

It sounded familiar.

"He didn't hit the guy hard, just knocked him over, really. But when they dropped the rape charge, some other detective who was there said that he'd seen Ness hanging out at Port Authority and knew he was up to no good. He was the one who pushed for the assault charge on Ness."

Looking at the file Annie was reading from, I saw her finger pointing at the name. Kelly, Bernie's old partner, who was working in Vice at the time, was the detective.

"Did Nessun ever make any attempts to get ahold of you over the years?" Annie asked.

"At first he did. For the first year or so, while we were still living in the neighborhood, he sent threatening letters from jail. So Mom moved us out of the city down to Asbury Park, in Jersey. That was over twenty years ago, and I never heard from him again after that. I moved back up here a few years ago when my second marriage ended."

Annie had me stay with Daisy Leary while she went to discuss what we'd discovered with the ADA. When she came back she told Daisy the statute of limitations had run out on any possible charges against her for involvement in Nessun's chickenhawking activities, and she was free to leave.

Daisy stood up and looked at each of us in turn. "For the record, Ness was never mean to me. He never forced me or any of the others to do anything, and that's God's honest truth."

After she left, Annie said, "You did a great job with the interview, Gladyss, but I want you to do me a favor. Don't mention any of this to Bernie."

"Why?"

"I can see him putting two and two together, figuring out it was Nessun who turned Bert's wife into a hooker. And then going on to blame him for Bert's death, with all the aggravation that will bring. But Bert already knew Juanita was a hooker when he met her."

Just the similarity of their unusual names should've cued me into it earlier, but it wasn't until Annie made that remark that it all started to fit together. The discovery that it was Nessun O'Flaherty who had led Detective's Kelly's wife into prostitution had an odd parallel to the Greek myth I'd had just read, the story of the Shirt of Nessus. The fact that Juanita Kelly had contracted AIDS and passed it along to Bert was reminiscent of the strange way in which Nessus's blood had ended up killing Hercules long after the centaur himself had died. But how could O'Flaherty have retro-plotted such a complex revenge? He knew his Greek mythology—he'd been reading Bulfinch the other day in Starbucks when I first met him—but back then, how could he have known that one particular runaway of the many he had carefully inducted into the whirlwind life of whoring would contract AIDS and subsequently marry a cop who had been instrumental in getting him sent to prison, and that almost twenty years later the virus would end up killing Detective Kelly? It sounded like the plot of a tacky sci-fi novel.

"I'm still blown away that it was Bert Kelly who was behind Nessun's arrest," was all I could say. Just to explain the parallel myth would require more energy than I had.

I stayed in Bernie's office until he'd finished interrogating O'Flaherty so I could break the news that the knife used in the Jane Hansen murder was a different one. While I was waiting, I picked up the Duffy file and looked closely at the autopsy photos. I tiredly compared them to the dolled-up jpegs that had been uploaded to Miriam's web site. That was when I figured out why there were traces of adhesive on Caty's face.

"Bernie, the knife in the jpeg photo of the Hansen murder is not the one we found at O'Flaherty's place. It has a completely different kind of handle."

He sighed.

"Also: it's a poor man's facelift."

"What is?"

"The adhesive residue on Caty's Duffy's face."

I showed him the emailed image. "See, she looks younger in the jpeg than in the autopsy photos. That's 'cause he taped her face back." I held up the two photos for him to compare."

"Holy shit! But why?"

I felt slightly vindicated, since he had spotted (and I had initially missed) the differences between the jpegs we'd been sent of Jane Hansen's murder scene and the crime scene as we found it. I had no answer for his question. Solving the other killings would have to wait for another day.

I wished him a good night, put on my hat, scarf, and coat, and walked outside. A crowd of reporters and cameramen filled the street like a hostile surprise party, starving for any further news on the Blonde Hooker Killer. I retreated back in and went out the rear exit and walked east to Eighth Avenue. I was still too frazzled to deal with yoga and meditation. As I walked down street after street, I couldn't turn off that perpetual loop of film in my head, reliving being beaten and terrorized in that filthy fucking elevator.

I kept recalling the sensation of O'Flaherty's knobbly hand shoving its way down the front of my pants and his grimy fingernails ripping into my crotch. The only memory that could push it out was that of the moment when I felt my gun's muzzle pressed to my skull and that bladder-releasing click that I was sure would be the last sound I'd ever hear.

A van turned sharply in front of me, nearly running over my toes. I punched the side of it and screamed, "FUCK YOU, ASSHOLE!" If the driver had stopped to argue, I'm sure I would've pulled my Glock. When I reached the next corner I stopped and took some deep, steady breaths, telling myself, *You are above this.*

When I arrived home, I started surfing the Internet looking for more stuff about Greek mythology, something that might explain the co-incidences I'd spotted between the Nessus/Hercules myth and what I'd just learned about Nessun O'Flaherty and Bert Kelly. The closest I could come up with was something about a theory of archetypes developed by the psychoanalyst Carl Jung. Apparently he believed that different types of personality recurred through the ages, and he used certain myths to categorize these character types. But none of them really shed much light on my concerns.

As I was reading further, I heard rapping on the wall and Maggie shouting, "Gladyss! Turn to Channel Two!" When I turned the TV on, Leeza Gibbons of *Entertainment Tonight* was beginning her news piece:

"A scandal of epic Hollywood proportions spilled onto the red carpet today during the premiere of *Fashion Dogs*. It had begun earlier this week when movie starlet and disinherited heiress Venezia Ramada turned up in a sex video that has gone viral on the Internet. But scandal turned to scuffle when her co-star Noel Holden and her fiancé, the film's director Crispin Marachino, exchanged blows when the two met at the grand opening."

The onscreen footage showed a reporter approaching some young starlet who was strutting between velvet ropes. The garbled sound of two men yelling could be heard in the background. The camera swung around and slowly focused on Crispin, who was squaring off against Noel. The taller, more muscular leading man gave his director a poke in the belly, which sent him to the ground. Others raced over to separate the celebrity pugilists.

"Oh shit!" Maggie said, entering my apartment and seeing my checkered face. "What the fuck happened to you?"

"Shush!" I said, swept up in the story.

"Although neither party explained why punches were thrown, rumors flew back and forth about whether Venezia's unidentified partner in the sex video was either Noel Holden or Crispin Marachino. However, such reports were quickly denied by spokesmen for both camps. After the premiere, a red-eyed Venezia was seen getting into Holden's limo." As Leeza said this, they showed footage of Noel and Venezia kissing passionately in the back of a shiny white vehicle.

As the show headed to commercial, Maggie asked again, "So who the hell hit you?"

"I got into a fight with the murderer."

"Wow, are you okay?"

"Yeah, but that's the least of it," I began.

Before I could say another word, she ran to my desk and sat at my laptop. "Let's see which one's nailing Venezia." She was Googling the sex tape.

"They've both dated her," I replied, closing the lid. "So why does it matter?"

"Crispin would've told me if he'd done it," she said.

I remembered being woken up a few nights ago and hearing the director's grating voice accompanied by her shouts coming through her wall. Since this was the first time she had confessed to their being together, I asked, "So when did you two start seeing each other?"

"After that party at Miriam's house, he escorted me home. We've dated a couple of times since."

Though the guy struck me as kind of sleazy, I really didn't mind. But I was pissed at myself for feeling jealous at the sight of Noel kissing Venezia. I'd only agreed to see him in the first place because I thought he might be the murderer, and it was clearly dumb of me to have gotten involved any deeper. Oddly, it was all because of Tinkerman. If the old animal doctor hadn't hung himself, leaving me feeling guilty and vulnerable on that particular night, I would never have let my defenses down and gone to Noel's apartment. Right then and there, I decided to end things with the flaky movie star.

Maggie said she had to see the Venezia tape for herself and went back to her apartment.

The effect of the painkillers I'd been given at the hospital the previous night had thinned out sufficiently that my facial bruises were starting to throb. Stupidly I hadn't bothered to fill the scripts the doctor had given me, and I couldn't face going out again tonight. I took a big swig of vodka and lay down in bed. But the alcohol only sped up my system and made me flush. Unable to watch TV, or call Noel, the asshole, I broke down and got my laptop. Unable to resist, I found a web site offering Venezia's pornographic performance, and after paying with my VISA card, I watched the brief, poorly lit footage of a faceless male having frantic sex with the brainless starlet. It might've been Noel but I couldn't be sure.

CHAPTER FIFTEEN

"You are legally required to take a few days off."

I got up the next morning to find Bernie had left a message on my voice mail. It went on: "You're listed as injured. If O'Flaherty finds out you were back at work the next morning, he can use it in court to argue that he never really assaulted you."

He was right. I needed to calm down and heal. Recalling the Renunciate's advice, I went through my wardrobe in search of red clothing. My root chakra desperately needed grounding. Before I'd located more than a pair of crimson socks, my cell chimed. It was the great star of stage, screen and credit-card-accessible Internet, calling from an eastbound plane to ask if I'd heard about the runway fiasco at the premiere of *Fashion Dogs*.

"Yeah," I said trying not to sound like I cared too much. "So whose prick is starring in the Venezia video?"

"Oh, you don't think—"

"I'm just asking. I mean, I saw you get into a fistfight with Crispin."

"It was totally bogus," he said in a whisper. "The son of a bitch orchestrated the whole thing."

"What do you mean?"

"You don't think it's a coincidence that the sex tape happened to hit the Internet just before the film premiered, do you? It was all a publicity stunt."

"You're kidding."

"What I don't know is whether Venezia's career will survive this. If anything, she was the injured party. I mean, I found the whole thing vulgar. But she's always so out of it, she doesn't seem to know or care."

"So you didn't sleep with her?"

"Of course I slept with her. I told you about it."

"But you weren't in the video?"

"Hell no."

"Did you sleep with her this weekend?"

"Absolutely not."

"I don't understand how getting into a fight with your director makes good publicity."

"Well *you* heard about it. It got top billing in all the tabloids. And after all, the plot of *Fashion Dogs* is about a love triangle between the three of us. It's all about trying to make people believe that whatever happens up on the screen is really happening on the street."

"Why did you have to make out with Venezia in the car?" That had looked incredibly genuine to me.

"We didn't make out. She was crying and I was consoling her. I told you, we still have to appear to be together for the movie. Remember?"

Of course I remembered, but I was still jealous.

"But I also have to show that I'm still best buddies with Crispin tonight, when we're all at this ridiculous fashion thing, the Rocmarni show. Both Venezia and I will be on the catwalk. Why don't you come by? We can hook up afterwards."

"I don't know if you'd want to be seen with me. I got a little bruised up yesterday," I said.

"What happened?"

"If you'd flipped from the gossip page you would've read that we caught the Blonde Hooker Killer two days ago."

"I didn't have time to read anything. Tell me what happened."

"We were on a stakeout. The place was freezing so I went out to get coffee and as I was coming back the asshole jumped me from behind."

"You're kidding me!"

"He knocked me down just as the elevator door closed. I was stuck fighting him alone in there for like ten minutes, and—"

"Oh my God! Are you okay?"

"I got punched a couple times and scalded with coffee, and then he put my pistol to my head and pulled the trigger."

"You are fucking kidding!"

"He missed, but the long and short of it is, I don't think I'm ready for any public appearances."

"Come on, you *have* to be there." He really sounded as though he wanted to see me. "Maggie will help you, won't she."

"Maggie?"

"Yeah, Crispin said he invited her."

I sighed. "What time is the show?"

"Eight o'clock." It's at Bryant Park. I'll make sure there's a ticket waiting for you at the door." Even as I wrote down the details, I wondered what the hell I was doing.

I spent the entire morning sitting at home, trying to relax. Shallow breaths, calm visualizations, soothing teas, red (well, off-red) clothing—nothing was helping. When I wasn't reliving my near execution, or fingernail rape, I found myself obsessing about whether Noel had actually cheated on me with that silicone-upholstered tramp.

At 2 p.m. I got dressed and again went to the precinct. When I walked into Bernie's office he was talking to Barry.

"Are you deaf, girl! Bernie shouted. "I told you, *you have the fucking day off!* Get the hell out of here!" He started coughing.

"Relax, no one will know. I'm going batty just sitting at home."

"Shit!" He took a hit from his Ventolin inhaler. He needed a break much more than I did. The stakeout that night in O'Flaherty's meat-locker must've given him pneumonia.

"Okay, you're here cause you left something at work," Bernie said, giving me an instant alibi. "But think of something specific just in case he finds out, 'cause I guarantee he'll ask you that in court."

With that technicality covered, Bernie confirmed what we already knew. The prelims had come back, and although we had no fiber, hair, or prints that connected him to any of the crime scenes, the blood on his knife was enough to pin four of the six murders on him. As I expected, neither Jane's nor Caty's DNA was on the blade. What's more, O'Flaherty had solid alibis for the nights of those two murders.

Bernie took yet another squirt from his inhaler, then continued. "O'Flaherty claimed that when he first realized someone else was mimicking his M.O., he tried to quit his little murder spree and let the new guy take the fall. Ultimately though, he just couldn't stop himself. They never can."

"That's probably why he started binge drinking," Barry threw in.

"The thing that's weird is that our new killer has put his own spin on the murders," Bernie said. "He's taping up their arms and legs, and carving the old numbers on them, but he's getting girls with bigger boobies, he's taking them to more upscale hotels, and he's leaving their heads *on* while slicing their tits *off*."

"And he's posting pictures of what he's doing," I added.

"Yeah. See, that's what I was talking about. O'Flaherty is old school, he wouldn't do any bullshit like that."

"So the new guy is not quite copycatting, is he?" said Barry. "The big question is, why."

"And his latest vic isn't even a hooker," I pointed out. "We don't know that Jane Hansen was, either. He could start killing anyone now."

"That's the first thing we got to figure out," Bernie said. "We need to find out why he killed Caty Duffy."

"Well, you established a possible motive for her death," I reminded him.

"That's right!" he remembered almost happily. "The bitch was cheating on him with Mr. Reynolds in accounting. Get me the husband's number."

Since Caty was clearly not one of O'Flaherty's victims, we definitely needed to talk to her husband. Bernie called the widower and asked if he could pay him a visit. After he hung up he said Mr. Duffy told him he was at work because it was too painful to stay at home alone. I could identify with that, but Bernie found it suspicious.

As we were walking out the rear door of the precinct to the Lumina, Bernie had another of his sudden coughing fits. After he finally spat out a disgusting gob of green phlegm he said, "This guy tries to blitz me, it'll be your turn to shove his head in the toilet."

While we were driving up to Duffy's publicity firm on Madison Avenue, I asked Bernie if he really thought we could get anything from the widower.

"Considering the fact that she was seriously cheating on him, we'd be pathetic if we couldn't," he replied. "Spouses are always offing each other. Jealousy, betrayal, shared property—custody problems if they got kids, and the Duffys do. That shit turns love into a minefield."

Hearing the bitterness in his voice, I couldn't help thinking that poor Bernie was reviewing his own recently failed marriage.

"You know, I can see him killing his wife and trying to make it blend into the serial killings, but do you really think Frank Duffy killed Jane Hansen first to cover his future tracks, and *then* killed his own wife?"

"No, Hansen's husband probably killed *her*," he kidded, adding more seriously, "We have to do a face to face just to be sure."

"Are you really going to tell him his dead wife was having an affair with another man?"

"Hell no. I want to see if he suspected anything."

We parked in a loading zone and went up to Duffy's office. Bouquets of flowers and condolence cards littered his room. Frank Duffy was a small man with graying sideburns. He looked permanently drained of happiness. If he had killed his wife, or for that matter if he knew she was cheating on him, he was doing a great job at covering it up.

Before he even closed his door he asked us a rush of raw questions—How was she killed? Was she raped? Did we have any suspects? Bernie threw him a curve ball, claiming that we had a suspect in custody. He was either trying to throw the widower off-guard, or he was holding back until Duffy could be completely cleared. Then he delicately mentioned Caty's mutilation and poor Mr. Duffy broke down, nearly collapsing onto the carpet. Bernie helped him back into his swivel chair while I went to get him a cup of water. When Frank regained his composure, Bernie asked him about his marriage.

"We used to meet at her office, and commute home together, but they had her working later and later at night. Whenever she was alone, Caty would walk west on the north side of Forty-second to Port Authority, where she'd grab the bus to Union City."

"Do you know if anyone at work ever walked her to the bus?" he asked.

"Maybe her lover," Frank said casually. "She was having an affair."

"How do you know that?" I asked.

"She told me," he said. "It wasn't her first."

"How long have you been married?" Bernie changed his tone.

"Just over ten years . . . She told me she had met some young hotshot at work."

"Did she tell you anything else?"

"She said he was married with a kid, too. Neither of them wanted to leave their families."

"Didn't that piss you off?" Bernie asked.

"Officer, please, we're realists."

"Really?" Bernie said, leaning forward, "so being at home, changing your kid's shitty diapers, and picturing some guy banging your wife—that realistically didn't bug you?"

"I cheated on her a couple of times and never even told her about it. Do you think it would've bothered her?"

"Guys tend to be a little more possessive," Bernie said.

"What can I say? We loved each other but, however much we wanted to be, we just weren't intimate anymore, so we had affairs. We agreed to be discreet about it."

"Do you think there's any chance the other guy killed her?" Bernie asked. "Maybe he actually did want her to leave you and run off with him."

"Guys usually don't want their mistresses to leave their husbands, only the mistresses want that. No, he had exactly what he wanted: a wife, a kid, and an afternoon lover."

"I gotta tell you, all this would just burn the shit out of me," Bernie confessed.

Duffy sighed. "I wish the kind of passion and loyalty I felt toward Caty would've lasted forever. We were together for over fifteen years. For ten of those years she was my wife as well as my lover, but gradually the sex came to a halt. We tried to fix it, we really did, but we finally decided that at least we could be honest with each other. We amended our vows and agreed we would stay together and try to hold on to what we had. You can always find another lover, but a best friend and a loving mom for your child, those are a lot harder to find."

The *New York Times* on Duffy's desk was open to a full-page advertisement for *Fashion Dogs*. As Bernie asked a few final questions, just formalities really, it occurred to me that it was only after my evening with Noel at his apartment—specifically after I had told him details of O'Flaherty's crimes—that the two copycat murders had occurred. Bernie thanked Mr. Duffy and said he'd be in touch when there was any news.

When we returned to the precinct, I was able to look at the evidence logs forensics had compiled for the Hansen and Duffy crime scenes. Among the dozen or so new prints, fibers, and other microscopic details that had been painstakingly lifted from the two scenes was a size eleven shoe print—Noel's size.

Caty Duffy had been killed earlier the same evening that Noel saw me, just before his big trip to L.A. For someone so in control and in a weird way asexual, Noel was oddly virile that night. It was after I'd heard that Tinkerman had killed himself that he called and insisted he had to help me deal with my guilt, as though he had a lot of personal experience coping with it. Then I remembered that he had painfully recounted that weird incident in which, as a child, he had unintentionally maimed a cat. Strangely the victim who would die the following morning was named Caty. I'd been taught at the academy that murderers were always leaving subconscious traces of their guilt behind. Could removing her breasts be some kind of parallel for his amputation of the cats' paws?

But why? Why would he do this? Other than the fact that he was fascinated with murderers—which was probably true of most Americans—Noel never displayed any violent tendencies.

I couldn't fully dismiss him as a suspect, and yet I was supposed to meet him tomorrow for his publicity stunt on the catwalk. What had I gotten myself into?

CHAPTER SIXTEEN

Back then, Fashion Week was held in Bryant Park, just east of Times Square, at the top end of the Garment District. Twice a year, the park was occupied by four huge white tents, in which the new spring and fall fashions were trumpeted. As usual, the entrance was lined with white French doors, and a pair of cops had been assigned to those doors. Of the thirty thousand or so police in New York City, of course it was Officer Eddie O'Ryan and his partner who'd drawn those short straws.

"Holy shit! Look at you!" O'Ryan said, inspecting my face and forehead, which were still visibly bruised despite the layers of concealing and foundation I'd applied. "I hear Burnout is putting you in for a commendation."

"I didn't hear that."

"Well you deserve it, after what you've been through."

"Give me a break."

"Aside from the beating you took, you found the murder weapon! Because of you they'll be able to put away the cocksucker who butchered those women. That's amazing."

"I appreciate that."

"Listen, Gladyss, you trust me, right?" he asked softly.

"Why?"

"I know that I can be difficult, but I do care about you."

"And I care about you too, Eddie."

"I heard a rumor that Internal Affairs is going to call you in."

"Me?"

"That's what I heard. I don't know what it's about," he said, looking down Sixth Avenue toward his partner Lombardi who was stationed by the doors at the southern end of the park. "If you want to grab a bite, I'm going on break soon and—"

"Eddie," I said awkwardly. "I'm off duty. I'm here to see the Rocmarni show with Noel Holden."

"You're kidding! I thought you were done with that clown."

"He turned out to be a nice guy." I said, not entirely truthfully, given my wild speculations of the previous evening.

He smiled politely, and I said I had to run. "Thanks for the heads up about IA."

Within the tents, four venues operated simultaneously all day long. Each show lasted only about fifteen minutes, but the load-in and load-out took nearly an hour. The Rocmarni show was taking place in the largest tent, the one in the front that could hold over a thousand people. I had arrived unfashionably early. The previous show was just ending, so most of those present were just staffers. Picture IDs dangled from bright ribbons around everyone's necks. I was directed to a hip-looking woman with a earpiece and a glass clipboard, who checked my ID, gave me a temporary badge, a seat ticket, and a catalog. She let me inside.

I headed to the back of the heated tent, past the long narrow runway. Glancing into an adjacent tent, I saw that another show was still in progress there. The catwalk was bordered by row after row of rising seats. I hadn't thought it was possible that there were many women bonier and taller than I was, but a succession of them emerged, scantily clad, one after the next through a narrow space between two brightly lit flats in the rear. Among the bars of swirling colored lights, through the pounding music, they strutted in rapid sequence to the very end of the catwalk. Each one paused there in front of a firing squad of flashes, then turned about face, and hip-snapped her way back to the narrow exit. All I could think was how grateful I was that the heating system pumped out such an abundance of warmth. It was freezing out there.

I heard a commotion, then spotted a crowd of people at the back of the room. Noel, wearing clearly borrowed finery, was busily signing autographs. When he saw me, he excused himself, a sun bursting out of its own little solar system. He dashed over and casually gave me a big hug, as though endless cameras weren't documenting his every move. Despite an acute ache from my recently pummeled kidneys it felt wonderful. When he finally let me go, a shooting sensation radiated up and down my back that momentarily made me light-headed.

"I don't suppose you saw today's *Variety*?" he asked modestly. "*Fashion Dogs* topped forty-two mill this weekend."

I had barely made it through that month's issue of the PBA newsletter.

"Great," I said tiredly.

"Here I am bragging about my weekend box, and look at you," Noel said, closely inspecting my face.

"I'm okay."

"I meant to pick up something for you in LA," he said, "but it was crazy. This is a small way of saying I'm sorry." He handed me the gift basket that Rocmarni was giving all their invitees. In addition to samples of their latest skin cream and perfumes, and CDs by hip hop bands I had never heard of, there were gift coupons for luxury items—but these weren't exactly free. One coupon offered fifty percent off at an ice spa near the Arctic Circle. Finally, at the very bottom of the cloth bag, I found the only useful item inside, a miniature bottle of designer vodka.

"Perfect," I said unscrewing the little top. "My back is killing me."

The throng of guests had not entered the vast showroom yet. Noel took advantage of this to rummage through several other gift baskets placed on nearby seats, harvesting three more small bottles of vodka, which he discreetly slipped into my bag.

Noel parked me in a front row seat. "We'll talk afterwards," he promised and dashed.

Spectators entered over the next twenty minutes, filling the seats, as I discreetly sucked down one little vodka bottle after the next and felt the ache in my jaw and forehead replaced by warm giddiness. Eventually after most of the seats were filled, I felt someone gently touch my back.

I turned to see Maggie. I didn't know if it was my breath or the gloss to my eyes, but she immediately asked, "Are you drunk?"

"Just a couple of minis." I held up the last empty bottle. "To dull the pain."

"How are you feeling?"

"A little bruised and battered, but fine."

"You and Crispin could be twins," she said. "he got attacked too."

"My favorite ladies born in the Eighties," Crispin rhymed,

appearing out of nowhere. Sure enough, he had a shiny black eye.

"I was just telling her about your attack," Maggie said.

"Oh yeah. Some guy walloped me over the head."

"What happened?" I thought she was referring to his highly publicized fight with Noel.

"I'm staying at the Hyatt and I decided to go for a walk early this morning. So I'm walking to the corner and this guy clobbers me over the head, takes my wallet."

"Where was this?"

"Forty-third and Eighth."

"Maybe crime is finally making a comeback," I said.

"Christ, Venezia looks out of it," Maggie commented as the big blonde stumbled out from behind the scrim. One of her massive boobs suddenly made an unscheduled appearance, breaking free of its strap. The double-sided tape that presumably epoxied it into the low-cut satin gown prevented full exposure.

"We got a loose beach ball in aisle three," Crispin muttered as though into a PA system.

One of the behind-the-scenes underlings dashed forward and grabbed her as she began nodding forward. Like a human tugboat, he delicately steered the barge-size model back behind the curtain.

"Since that porn tape came out, she's been Oxying herself through the floor," Crispin explained. Then he spotted the famed designer talking to Noel and headed over to them.

As they chatted with Antonio Rocmarni, I told Maggie the odd coincidences I had noted while reading up on Greek mythology. I told her about Nessus the centaur and his clever way of murdering Hercules in the future, then explained how this had strangely been re-enacted in the deaths of Detective Kelly and his ex-hooker wife.

"How the hell did you happen to be studying Greek myths?"

"You're not going to believe this," I said, "but during my final relaxation at the end of my yoga class, I had this vision of a statue who turned out to be the goddess Diana, Diana of the Hunt, and since I hunt killers . . ."

"Until recently you were just hunting parking violators," she pointed out.

"My Diana identification only began after I got this homicide assignment."

"What identification? You had a vision in yoga?"

"There have been other similarities." Like the fact that I'm a virgin, and I've always seen myself as a protector of woman, I thought, but didn't say out loud.

"Tell me one other thing you and the goddess Diana have in common," she said.

"We're both twins," I said.

She chuckled at that and said, "Wow, and I thought I was supposed to be the flaky one."

Suddenly the music swelled and it became difficult to talk. The unesteemed members of the fashionista brigade, buyers for major outlets, critics and the like, as well as endless minor deities in the fashion pantheon had taken their reserved seats in or near the front rows. Members of the press set up their cameras. Some celebrities made much-heralded entrances and waved at Crispin, who was sitting just behind me. While I was trying to identify faces on the far side of the catwalk, I heard him mutter, "Christ, the girl just doesn't quit!"

In a slight gap between the outer edge of the scrim and the rear curtain, where few eyes paused, the disinherited heiress was bending mindlessly over a small table. Barely able to keep her eyes open, she fumbled through her tiny wristlet. We watched as she unthinkingly tapped out a small pile of magic powder and used her temporary ID card to cut it into wobbly lines.

"I can't believe I'm seeing this," Crispin said, barely restraining a chuckle. "I mean, the Internet tape showed that she's a slut, but does she have to demonstrate that she's also an addict?"

Venezia put a thumb over one nostril and snorted with the other. The only problem was, she had forgotten to lean into the powder. She was still two feet above her tiny pile. With closed eyes, and still without closing the gap, she snorted the empty space again. Finally her pinky reached down slowly until she touched the powder from the table and rubbed it along her gums.

Maggie chuckled as Crispin started using his cell phone. "Who're you calling, darling?"

"Noel, he's the only one who knows how to handle her."

"Really?" I said while yawning.

"Yeah, after the premiere, when her sex tape had come out, she went on a real bender. She pulled her clothes off, trying to fuck him right there in the limo. He straightened her out quickly."

"I'll bet he straightened her out," Maggie kidded.

At that moment, I decided to call it a night.

"Where are you off to?" Maggie asked as I rose to leave.

"I'm tired of waiting for this goddamned show."

"It's going to begin any second," Crispin said.

"I'm just not feeling well."

He handed me a green bottle that I presumed he had pulled from his gift bag. "Have some peppermint schnapps."

"I really should go home."

"Have a drink and relax," Crispin said politely. "Noel really needs your support tonight."

"Please don't go," Maggie pleaded. "Diana wouldn't abandon a wood nymph in need, would she?"

"If you still want to go in a few minutes, I'll take you home myself," Crispin said.

Still feeling too sober to deal with the jealousy Venezia aroused in me, I took his little bottle, twisted off the top, and downed it in two gulps. I'd knocked back the vodkas without much effect, but this one peppermint drink really gave me a jolt. I realized I had to pee badly, and rose slowly to my feet.

"Are you okay?" Crispin's voice was like tiny fingers in my fuzzy consciousness.

"No . . . I mean, Yes, just . . ." All I knew for sure was that I wanted out of this shiny vortex. I breathed deeply, trying to regain lucidity. Time seemed to be propelling us forward, then stopping abruptly, then speeding up again, like existence was being driven by a bad cabby.

When the lights started to dim, I found myself giggling. The show was finally about to start, and it suddenly seemed very dark. Everything was slowing down. Models were going around this way. Photographers were shooting that way. All in straight lines.

Elaborately dressed crowds of latter-day shamans and sorcerers were casting silent spells. The young models had to be sacrificed to the gods of celebrity. Maggie and I sat perched on the shadowy rim of this event with all the other lesser beings.

Again we watched as some thankless production assistant went over and tried to guide bovine Venezia back into her stall. Snapping awake, Venezia saw the pile of magic dust still on the table and swatted the soap-bubble assailant away. Slowly she began the whole pathetic process once more, but this time she had a coiled hundred dollar bill. She lowered her dinosaur head, dropping it down slowly in front of her, then placed the tip of the bill in the pile and snorted deeply.

At first I simply wanted to be rid of this annoying spectacle. I just wanted to leave this kaleidoscopic chamber and slither back to the warm obscurity from which I had arisen. But as I stepped forth, a thought hit me like a thunderbolt: If gamelegged Bernie Farrell were here, in the same way as he'd shoved O'Flaherty's face down into his shitter, he'd walk right up and arrest Venezia, because *you can't fucking snort drugs in public!*

The crazy ape thing wasn't really my style, but due to my disdain for Venezia, I figured I'd give my own lite version of it.

When I got up, I'd heard someone say, "Sit down." As I marched over, I heard, "Where's she going." When I reached Venezia, I simply said, "Stop it or I'm going to have to arrest you."

"Fuck off," she replied without even looking at me.

"You fucked him, didn't you?"

"Fuck off, slag,"

"You have to remain silent," I said screwing up the policeman's mantra. "If you give up the right . . ." I reached forward and grabbed one of her breadstick wrists and yanked it behind her back. Reaching for my cuffs, I realized of course that I didn't have them, so I just held her arm tightly.

"Fuck off of me, you ugly freak!"

"You have the right to be quiet," I slurred to the silicone implants under a blonde wig. "If you give up that rife, everything you can say, everything will be . . ." I couldn't remember how the Miranda warning ended.

"What the hell is going on!" Noel said, racing up to us before the show could officially commence.

"Your ugly tranny asked me if I fucked you!" Venezia hollered, still trying to break free. "Now she won't let me go!"

As if from a giant spider web, Crispin slithered down from above and said, "This is fan-fucking-tastic! It'll be all over the news!"

"GET HER OFF OF ME!" Venezia shrieked, trying to yank her arm free.

"I told her to cease using narcotics," I said formally. "She declined.

I've read her her rights and now I'm arresting her."

"This has got to stop right now," Noel whispered urgently.

I just held on to Venezia's wrist.

"Please! Look behind you."

When I turned I saw that the entire pantheon, all the beautiful witches and warlocks were focused on me—a thousand daggers aimed right at my heart. The moment seemed to hang there, unable to proceed. Something was terribly wrong. I attempted to regain composure with deep breaths, but pulsing waves made up of a thousand tiny flashes were slice-dicing the moment into a zillion luminous lines as it was all parceled out like heroin into little glassine flashes.

"Get this fucking drag king off of me!" Venezia yelled, trying to shake me off.

"Hon, trust me, please," Maggie whispered out of nowhere. "This is a really bad idea."

"The girl is an addict and she's going to kill herself," I tried to argue. "Do you want that, Noel?"

"That's not the point," he said. "You're clearly drunk and everyone knows it."

"Get the cops!" someone shouted.

"I am the cops," I said tiredly. I still wasn't thinking about what I was going to do next.

Walking in front of me, so that we were eye to eye, Noel said, "Look, you're right. This *is* between us. Why don't you go home and I'll be there after this is all over."

It wasn't what he said, it was his look. At that moment I knew I had him, and he knew it. And I knew he knew I knew he knew. I felt myself go limp as Venezia limped away.

Some of the other models who had been watching quietly started to applaud. Noel had defeated the Goliath NYPD. I heard some Queer-Eye-For-the-Straight-Guy shout out, "Check the police state at the front door, sweetie!"

A chorus of laughter, boos, and hisses followed me as I was led out of the large white tent. I could barely keep my eyes open as I was handed off from one person to another.

"Can you put her in a cab?"

"Yeah, I'll take it from here."

CHAPTER SEVENTEEN

What seemed like a moment later, I felt a stiff object being thrust into me, compelling me to punch O'Flaherty and roll backward. When I looked around, all I could see were white bolts of sunlight blinding me.

A voice said, "I'm really sorry!"

It took me a moment to get my bearings. I was apparently naked in bed with Noel. He was also naked, and he had an erection. He was holding his jaw where I had just socked him.

"What is *wrong* with you?" I asked through a blinding headache. It wasn't a moment later, it was the next morning. And Noel was here with a hard-on.

"Me? It was you—you rubbed up against me, in the nude!"

"I don't even know how I got here."

"SUUUEEEE WEEEE!" I heard in the distance. A few seconds later, I heard the cry a second time, and then a third.

"What the hell—"

"SUEEEE WEEEE!" Noel suddenly squealed back.

"Ow! Stop that!"

I had passed out without taking out my contacts and my eyes were dry and irritated.

"Sorry," he replied, getting out of bed. "he wouldn't stop until I did that."

"Did what?"

"It's something I did in *Frat Trap* twenty years ago."

I dimly remembered the movie—a bad hybrid between *Animal House* and *Porky's*. I stumbled out of bed, holding my pounding cranium.

"I can't believe you didn't even have the courtesy to wake me up before you . . ."

"I thought you *were* awake."

"Well, I woke up when you shoved your dick into me!"

"You're making it sound like I raped you," he said, pulling his boxers on.

"Technically you did."

"Look, I drank too much too, so . . . I'm sorry if I misunderstood." He put on his shirt.

It was all a blur, so I couldn't really argue with him. And since I had never actually told him I was a virgin, I would've felt like a fool mentioning it now.

"SUEEEWEEE!" we heard again through the wall.

"Who the fuck *is* that?"

"Crispin the evil clown. He stayed over with Maggie after the show." Noel explained, filling a glass with water from the sink. "And I told you I'd come by, remember?"

"How'd you get in?" I asked.

"Maggie has your key."

"I don't remember a thing," I said, trying to flip on my brain.

"You got totally shitfaced at the Rocmarni show and caused a huge scene with Venezia—"

"Oh shit, did any photographers.—"

"Yeah. I tried stopping you, but . . ."

"Then you brought me home?"

"No, I still had to do the show, I came here afterwards."

I felt like a total fool. "I just can't believe..."

"I'm sorry, sweetheart. I really am," he said earnestly.

When I got to the bathroom, I confirmed that I had officially lost my virginity, but I had no reason to celebrate. I was sore and my breasts felt raw as hell. When I looked at myself in the mirror, I saw bright red bruises around my nipples.

"Did you do this?" I asked opening the bathroom door.

He asked what I was talking about.

"These marks," I pointed to the red welts around my breasts.

"You can barely see them."

"I can sure feel them," I said, cupping them in my hands.

"I don't recall being that hard . . . Gladyss, I'm really sorry."

When I closed the bathroom door I could also see the bruises along my lower back and belly in the mirror, still healing from O'Flaherty's attack. I started the shower and brushed and gargled while it was running hot. As I gently soaped up, I tried to wash away the humiliating memories of last night, which were unfortunately coming back to me. After I'd drunk all those tiny bottles and made a complete ass of myself with Venezia, I remembered being escorted out of the fashion show. I also vaguely recalled being brought home by someone and then passing out.

When I tried toweling off, I almost lost my balance. All my muscles were trembling and my head was spinning. Noel stood next to the window, where his cell phone got the best reception, talking plans and deals. Slowly I set about making coffee, but had to dash back into the bathroom to puke.

I couldn't stop wondering what the hell Noel thought he was doing. It had replaced the O'Flaherty attack as my number one anxiety. The whole thing was so strange because he was here, and I liked him, and more than anything else I had wanted to have sex with him. And to his credit, he had held back the first time when I'd invited him in. But now he'd done this creepy thing, entering me when I was asleep. And I felt guilty, as though I had brought this on myself. I was also having difficulty understanding why I'd been so out of it—usually I could tolerate more alcohol than the contents of a few mini bottles.

I flushed and washed my face, then as I exited the bathroom Noel dashed into it. After he'd showered, he came out nude and glistening, as though he had bathed in oil.

I would've rushed to get him a spare towel, and make coffee, but it took all my concentration just to down two aspirins.

"Are you okay?" Noel said with a look of concern.

"I don't know, was I?"

"What?"

"I just would've liked being conscious for our first time."

"I'm really sorry," he said timidly. "You were rubbing up against me and you were naked, so I thought—"

"I can't believe I got so plastered." I placed my sweaty face flat on the cool Formica tabletop. "Oh God! I made a complete ass of myself in front of all those people!"

"Venezia has a three-hundred-dollar-a-day habit, and in all the time I've known her, you're the only person who's ever tried to stop her," he replied. "You should be commended. Hell, I'm sorry for preventing you, it was just awkward with the press and all those people watching. Poor Antonio. He had invested so much money in the show, and he was freaking out."

"I'm sorry for embarrassing you," I said earnestly.

"Being embarrassed in this profession is like being shy in a porn film," he replied and kissed me gently between my bruises. "Maybe you should call in sick today."

"I'm already on the sick list," I mumbled. Maybe it was part of my OCD, but I just couldn't stay still.

When I struggled to rise, Noel helped me over to my closet. As I slowly dressed, he kept trying to convince me to stay home in bed, but I was propelled by the humiliation of last night. Noel hailed us a cab and deposited me in front of my precinct. Only after I'd staggered up the stairs did I realize exactly how feeble I was.

"Aren't you supposed to be at home recuperating?" Annie said as I reached the squad room.

"Yes, I know," I replied. "But now that I'm here I feel too weak to leave." She laughed as though I were kidding.

Bernie and I must've been born under the same sign, because he called in saying that he too was sick and would be late. I dozed for about an hour with my head on my desk until I could hear his wheezing. He staggered into his office, slamming his door behind him. Apparently I wasn't the only one who had gotten blasted last night.

Alex told me we had a variety of interviews lined up for today, tracking down anyone and everyone who knew Jane Hansen or Caty Duffy, the two victims of the unresolved Marilyn murders, as they were now being called.

"If I'm not mistaken, William Holden died of an alcohol-related injury," I heard Annie saying from afar.

"So who's this guy? His son?" I heard Bernie ask. I figured they were talking about me.

"Well no, they just happen to share a last name," Annie clarified.

"Christ, you're dating Noel Holden?" Alex asked me.

I got up, and shuffled into Bernie's office, where I was immediately greeted by his decomposing foot, which he had propped up on a box in front of him. Swollen and purple, shading to a yellowish green around the heel, it looked like a rotting piece of exotic fruit and smelled like Limburger cheese. I plunked myself down on his couch and said, "If you don't mind, my private life is my own business."

"Not when it's on page six of the *New York Post.*"

Bernie held up the morning edition. "If IAD wasn't overwhelmed by real cases, they'd be tearing you a new one right now."

I didn't tell him that according to O'Ryan they were already after me.

"What the hell did you *do* to Venezia Ramada?" Annie asked out of nowhere.

"Hundreds of people were just sitting, watching her snort a mountain of coke, so I tried to stop her," I said, as Bernie gingerly wedged his swollen foot back into his shoe.

"Then why the fuck didn't you arrest her?" he asked, before launching into a coughing fit that compelled Annie to scoot.

"What's the name of this woman who has the Marilyn Monroe web site?" he asked when he could finally talk again.

"Miriam Williams."

"And she's friends with this Noel character?"

"Correct."

"He introduced you to her?"

"Correct."

"How'd you meet this Noel clown?"

"I threatened to give him a summons for smoking in a restaurant."

"When was this?"

"That day when I met you at the Templeton. Earlier that day."

"While you were in uniform?"

It seemed like an opportune time to explain that I was initially interested in Noel because I thought he was a possible suspect in the Blonde Hooker murders.

"You thought he was a suspect for *that* case?"

"Well, he was a half a block away from the Nelly Linquist murder scene that morning. And when I left the hotel that night after I'd sealed the room, hours later, I spotted him across the street as though he had been watching all day. Then I talked with him afterwards. He seemed to have a weird fascination with serial murderers."

"Did he pick you up while you were in uniform?"

"I agreed to go to a party with him while I was in my blues, yeah."

"See, when you're wearing a uniform, you cease to be a woman, understand? You're a New York City police officer, and you abused that position."

"Male cops hit on girls all the time," I pointed out.

"It's still abuse. And you know what, once they're done fucking the uniform, and they see the slob underneath, they always dump them. Always."

"Well considering *he's* a big celebrity, maybe I'm abusing *his* uniform."

Bernie rolled his eyes.

"Look," I said. "I did suspect him at first, which was why I became friendly, so I was able to get his prints. For that matter, I even checked his alibi with another cop."

"With someone in homicide?" Annie asked from the doorway. Apparently she had been eavesdropping.

"No, when I was still in NSU."

"Let me get this straight." Bernie was growing more pissed by the minute. "Without consulting me, you checked out his alibi and prints. And once you were convinced he was innocent, you started fucking him?"

After what seemed like minutes of angry silence, I told Bernie I had an unbelievable headache.

"Go home!" he roared. "You're still on sick leave. And be grateful—if you weren't all bruised up, I'd start disciplinary action against you myself," he said as I headed out of the squad room.

I cabbed it back home and made it to my bed by noon, kicking my shoes off and dropping my clothes on the floor. Just as I hit the bed my phone rang.

It was my brother, calling to tell me he'd had a really bad twenty-four hours. It was hard to imagine his day could be any worse than mine, but in an effort to be supportive, I asked him what was up. He said he'd been hearing voices nonstop.

"Let me guess, you're off your meds?"

"They're making me feel so weird. I just tried to reduce the dosage a little."

"Carl, that's how you have an episode!"

"I know, I know. I was just wondering, do you never hear anything weird?"

"And by weird you mean . . ."

"In your head, I guess."

"I *saw* something weird," I said tiredly, then wished I hadn't.

"Yeah? What?"

"I'm sure it was just because I was finishing a yoga class, so I was sweaty and overheated."

"Well what did you see?"

"While I was relaxing, with my eyes closed, I had a vision of this figure. It turned out to be Diana, the goddess of the hunt."

"You're kidding!"

"No, but it was no big deal," I replied. "What did you hear?"

"It was about 9/11?"

I groaned inwardly. "Yeah?"

"Well, I had this vision . . . And then I did some research, and . . . See, this is where things get weird, because I found a link between reality and what I heard in my head."

"What link?"

"You're going to shit yourself, but Osama Bin Laden selected Bloomberg to be the new mayor of New York.

"See?" I said exhaustedly. "This is why we need to take our meds."

"He didn't launch the attack on 9/11 because those numbers, 9-1-1, also signify an emergency—he did it 'cause it was the primary!"

"*What* was the primary?"

"The Democratic primary for mayor of New York! It was scheduled for September 11th. Remember, they postponed it. Mark Green ended up winning the nomination. He was the Democratic candidate in a city where Democrats outnumber Republicans five to one, while Bloomberg was little more than a blip on the radar, no one took him seriously. He'd always been a Democrat and only switched to the Republicans to avoid the primary. A billionaire with no political experience was the candidate for a party that no one would've voted for after eight years of Rudy. Then the planes hit the towers, and suddenly everything goes topsy-turvy. Giuliani becomes insanely popular, because everyone loves Daddy during a crisis. And he throws the mantle to this little guy who's out in right field . . . What you have is one billionaire in the Middle East helping another billionaire, one Arab, the other Jewish, but it doesn't matter because money is the greater identity . . ."

I was woken by the sound of Maggie's door closing. It was dark. I had slept for twelve solid hours, after dropping off with the cell phone against my ear. I threw on a bathrobe and knocked on Maggie's door.

"I just wanted to apologize about last night," I said when she peeked out. I was still embarrassed by my attempted arrest of Venezia.

"I warned you that these assholes use up people like us," she said softly, looking at the ground.

"Well, I finally lost my virginity, which was all I really wanted."

"Gladyss, you were drunk off your ass. Isn't that called date rape where you work?"

Her response surprised me. She thought Noel had taken advantage of me, and since she didn't know how deeply I had fallen for him, I guess it must've seemed that way.

"I kind of consented beforehand," I equivocated.

"Really?"

"What can I say, Maggie? Feelings have a way of just creeping up on you. I mean, I didn't even know I felt like that about him until I saw him in the news with that bitch. I mean, if I didn't get drunk last night . . . But I feel like such an idiot. I can't believe I tried to arrest her in front of all those people."

"Gladyss, last night was *not* a good thing."

"Don't you think I know that?"

Lowering her voice, she said, "Look what they've turned us into!" She was still seeing Crispin but obviously didn't care for the way he was treating her. I sympathized with her, but I didn't feel the same way about Noel.

"Whatever it is we've turned into, we did it on our own," I said. "We have to take responsibility for our actions."

She looked almost ashamed. I wanted to say that she never should've insinuated herself in my goddamn life in the first place, but she was now my friend as well as my neighbor, so instead I said, "Maybe you should stop seeing Crispin."

"I'm going to, but . . ." She was struggling with something.

"What?"

"Well," she lowered her voice again, "when I initially asked you about Noel, you said you didn't particularly care . . ."

"Care about what?"

"You said you wouldn't mind me . . . dating Noel."

"*Dating* Noel?"

"Sleeping with him," she clarified.

I remembered I had said that, but that was when *I* wasn't involved with him. Now it was a very different story. I was so aghast at Maggie mentioning the idea of sleeping with the man I was beginning to think of as my boyfriend that I was unable to respond. Her star obsession had clearly supernovaed, but I was still too exhausted to get into a messy fight. Afraid to talk, in case I lost my temper, I just nodded my head tiredly.

She nodded her head back. After a minute or so I retreated to my apartment and closed the door.

I was determined to return to work on Thursday morning. As soon as I walked in, Annie told me that Miriam Williams had arrived back in the country and agreed to come in for an interview at noon. She said Bernie had called a meeting for 11:30 to recap everything we had on the Marilyn murders and try to work up a new profile of our copycat.

I entered the conference room just after Barry, the forensic psychologist. Taped evenly to the wall of our squad room were crime scene photos of our two unsolved cases: Jane Hansen and Caty Duffy. Below them were the photos the killer had emailed of the murders *while* they were being committed. Using a magnifying glass, Barry inspected them carefully.

"We should have realized these were two separate cases from the start," the psychologist began. "The make-up and platinum wigs, for one thing. Not to mention the fact that he signed the photos with these arcane references before uploading them to this Marilyn Monroe web site. He was clearly someone other than Nessun O'Flaherty."

"But in taping up the arms and legs, he really did make an effort to copy him," Bernie said emphatically.

"This second killer might not be as prolific but he's more sophisticated, what with the jpegs and the fact that he's mimicking," Annie said.

"If he is a copycat, what will he do now that we've caught the guy he's copying?" I asked.

"That's a good question," Alex said. "One thing's for sure, he won't stop."

"We do have one potential clue," Barry said to Bernie. "The killer mugged you and used your credit card."

"Yeah."

"How long have you been on the force?"

"Almost a quarter century," Bernie said tiredly, taking another hit from his inhaler.

"And presumably you considered that this guy might be someone you had once put away?"

"First thing I did was spend a night going through my last ten years of cases."

"Anything?"

"The smartest and angriest of them are either in prison or dead."

"Why do you think this second guy chops off the breasts instead of the head?" Alex asked.

"He wrote several poems in which he verbally abuses his mother." Bernie reminded him. "He referred to her as Marmalyn."

"Sounds like mammaries. The breasts are classic symbols of motherhood. I wouldn't be surprised if our man has an awful relationship with his mother," Barry had a knack for stating the obvious.

"Maybe it was something about O'Flaherty's murders that triggered this guy," Annie suggested.

"Well obviously he's fixated on O'Flaherty's murders, but I don't see how that would trigger him."

"And why would anyone repeatedly act out killing Marilyn Monroe?" Annie asked.

"What does Marilyn represent? Glamour? Vulnerability? Promiscuity?" Bernie asked.

"Did a new book or documentary about her just come out?" Barry asked.

"That would be a good question to ask this Miriam woman," Bernie said, looking strangely at me.

"What else are you planning on asking her?" Annie asked.

"Well, the killer is posting the murders on her web site as a kind of performance piece," Barry said. "He even wipes them clean when he's done, almost like he's doing it just for her."

"See, this is what I figure," Bernie said. "He *is* doing it for her! So she must know the killer. I bet she got into some big discussion or fight with him about Marilyn. And these murders are his response."

"What's the connection between you and Miriam, exactly?" Barry asked me almost accusingly.

"She's a friend of Noel Holden's, and she seems to like me."

"And how does he know her?"

"She produced a film he was in."

"So maybe that's the tie-in," Bernie said.

"What is?" Annie asked.

"The killer wants to fuck Miriam, but she's got the hots for our young friend here." Bernie pointed to me. "Maybe he's attracted to this William Holden wannabe as well."

"Noel does not want to be William Holden," I said defensively.

"That might make sense," Barry said. "How else could he compete with a hot young cop and a movie star?"

"That's the point of the murders," Bernie said. "He's responding to his powerlessness."

"Let's size up our suspect," the profiler concluded. "He's white, and in his thirties, possibly his forties—"

"You don't think he's older, with his Marilyn fixation?" Alex asked.

"Unlikely, 'cause he's computer literate. The poems and references to obscure historical figures like Catherine of Alexandria suggest that he probably went to college. Maybe he even has a graduate degree. Considering all the Mama-Marilyn stuff, he may well be adopted, or has a screwed-up relationship with his mother. Like O'Flaherty, he may even be impotent—it was her lover Caty Duffy had sex with shortly before she died, not her murderer. In fact, given the costuming and make-up, I haven't ruled out that he might be a repressed homosexual, maybe a crossdresser. Unlike O'Flaherty, he may not have a criminal record. Because he's computer-savvy, he may have an account on eBay, or Amazon. Regarding his Marilyn Monroe fixation, he might belong to some fan club or attend conventions, something like that."

Barry paused a moment then asked, "Anyone want to add anything?"

"I was looking at the photos," Annie said, staring at the display wall. "If you think about the composition and the lighting, he doesn't seem particularly skilled at photography."

"I thought about that, too," Barry said. "In fact, they suggest a distinct *lack* of skill. And when we consider how thorough he has been in cleaning up his crime scenes—just like O'Flaherty—it seems inconsistent. So he might be bad at taking photographs, or he might deliberately be making them appear amateurish to hide his skill."

"It's a good point," Bernie said. "The guy has a clear visual excitation. Hell, he might even *be* a photographer."

A moment later Barry's cell phone beeped. He answered and hung up quickly. "I'm due on the stand. I've got twenty minutes to get down to Centre Street." With that he was out the door. Almost immediately we got a call from the desk sergeant saying that Miriam Williams had arrived.

"Since she likes you," Bernie said to me. "You take the lead on this."

I went downstairs and walked her up, telling her how much I'd enjoyed her party and her fabulous apartment. I introduced her to Bernie and the others, and together we led her into the conference room.

"I'm sorry about being away so long," she began. "I'm trying to get some European backers for my latest project, and I ended up going to sixteen different cities in two weeks. It was exhausting."

"You told Officer Chronou in advance that you were leaving town," Bernie replied. "We should have got to you before you left."

"I just hope that my little web site didn't somehow encourage this nut."

"I don't want to alarm you," I started out, "but we're currently operating under the assumption that the killer knows you or might even be targeting you with these pictures."

"Oh my God! Really?"

"I'm afraid so. What we need to do is come up with a list of possible suspects based on who you know. A good place to start might be with someone who for some reason has very negative feelings about Marilyn Monroe."

"Gee . . ." She thought about the question.

"He's probably white and in his thirties or forties," I parroted Barry's line. "He may have an odd relationship with women, and difficulties with his mother. He might even be adopted. And he might be a computer person, or possibly a photographer."

"Well," Miriam exhaled. "There have certainly been people I knew who didn't *like* Norma Jean, but none of them really fits that bill."

"Maybe just focus on anyone who didn't like her," Bernie said, as if I weren't there.

"Okay." Miriam stared up at the blank wall from which the crime scene photos had just been taken down. "Let's see . . ." she mulled it over for a minute. "Linda Sanders once said that she thought Marilyn acted the same way in all her movies . . ."

Bernie pulled his chair closer. "Do you know any guys between twenty and fifty who hated the actress?"

"Well," Miriam replied, "there *is* Roddy Potter's son, Blair. What a young cad! During a dinner party he said he found Marilyn annoyingly cloying in *Asphalt Jungle*. But that was a small role. And yes, come to think of it, I clearly remember him saying that he found her ditsy in *Diamonds Are a Girl's Best Friend*."

"Ditsy?" Bernie seemed amused.

"I believe so." Miriam said very correctly.

"I don't suppose you know anyone with violent tendencies?" I asked, hoping to trim the fat.

"Oh, of course!" Miriam snapped her fingers. "Sammy Wochenskil! Why didn't I think of him before. He despised Marilyn Monroe like no one else alive."

"Who is Sammy Wochenskil?" I asked.

"You know, the fashion designer," she replied as though he were the president of the United States.

"Is he gay?"

"Heavens to Betsy, yes. Actually he retired a number of years ago. I don't know what became of him, but I remember he just detested Marilyn."

"You sure it wasn't Marilyn Manson that this Sammy guy detested?" Bernie asked. I thought he was kidding, but apparently he was serious.

"No, it was definitely Marilyn Monroe. When she was still alive he used to call her Miserable Marilyn."

"You never heard him refer to her as Marmalyn, did you?" Annie asked.

"No," she replied with a chuckle. Then she asked if she could use the bathroom.

After I'd given her directions, Bernie explained that murderers usually selected their victims within their own groups—straights usually hunted straights, and gays usually hunted gays. Still, he said, this might explain why our second killer dresses them up, almost like drag queens, and doesn't have sex with them. He asked me to dig up anything I could find on Sammy Wochenskil, then got on the phone. I was about to go online and Google the guy when it occurred to me that Crispin Marachino knew Miriam well. And, being a director, he certainly had some kind of background in photography. He was part of the whole Hollywood world, too. He seemed a weak suspect, but we had virtually no one else in our sights right now. I grabbed a second phone and called Noel's private cell phone.

"Yellow?" he answered.

In my most official tone, I asked him for Crispin's cell phone number.

"He doesn't have a cell phone."

"How does he not have a cell phone?"

"Actually, someone else has it. Crispin got mugged."

"Oh, right." I suddenly remembered his black eye.

"He flew back to LA today to recuperate. He's coming back to New York in a few days. I'm sure he'll have a new phone by then."

"Did he file a police report about the mugging?"

"He was too embarrassed."

"I need to speak to him when he gets back."

"Why?"

"Police business."

"You don't trust me?"

"After the other morning, I'm not sure I even know who you are."

"Look, I am really sorry about that. Will you meet me tomorrow night and I'll try and make it up to you. Miriam's throwing a dinner."

"She's here right now. We're in the middle of an interview."

"You're kidding."

"The killer used her web site."

"Oh right," he remembered. "Well, she apparently discovered some hot, young European *auteur* and brought him back with her. The dinner tomorrow is part of her attempt to woo him into directing her latest project. Please join me."

Though I now felt I wanted to end whatever relationship I had with him, I just couldn't say no to the guy. He told me he'd pick me up outside my house at seven. Before he ran off, I asked him if he had ever heard of Sammy Wochenskil.

"Sure, Sammy is a living legend."

"So he's definitely still alive?"

"Yeah, I'm pretty sure. But he's old."

Since our killer drugged his victims, physical strength wasn't a major issue, so being old didn't automatically rule him out. And no one would think twice about trusting him.

"He lives in Chelsea somewhere," Noel added.

Not that far where most of the murders had occurred.

"Did you know anything about him and Marilyn Monroe?" I asked.

"Oh," Noel suddenly woke up. "Actually, yes. There was some story that he once attacked her."

"He attacked her physically?" I asked in disbelief.

"Yeah. Something like that. At a party."

When I got off the phone, Bernie was just finishing up too. He told me he'd confirmed that Sammy Wochenskil was still alive. What's more, he'd once had an assault charge filed against him, though it was dismissed for lack of evidence.

"You're not going to believe what I just heard," I responded.

He didn't immediately ask so I told him. "I just heard that this guy once assaulted Marilyn Monroe!"

"Shit! He's *got* to be our man," Bernie said, sounding excited for the first time.

"He must be freaking old."

"*I'm* freaking old. But killers are ageless."

When Miriam returned, Bernie took her over to the couch and turned on the charm. The two were nearly the same age, and they seemed almost playful. The chip that I'd always seen on Bernie's shoulder seemed to vanish completely. As he flirted with her, I got some idea of what he must've been like when he was young. I couldn't stop smiling. He was so much more of a guy than any of the younger men I knew.

After a half hour of back-and-forth memory-jogging, Miriam came up with eight more names—all oddballs, most of them seniors—who at one time or another had expressed antagonism, or at least annoyance, with the blonde bombshell.

When we were done, I walked her downstairs, and as I saw her into a cab I told her that Noel had invited me as his guest to a dinner at her house tomorrow night.

"That's wonderful," she replied. Then she pointed to my cheek. "You have some bruises . . ."

"I'll use a lot of foundation," I said, instead of explaining what had happened.

"It's not a formal affair, so please dress casually. And please don't mention anything about today. Some investors are going to be there and I don't want to scare them off."

She closed the door of the cab and it sped north to where the wealthy went.

Back upstairs, Annie had located the address of the only Sammy Wochenskil listed—in an apartment building on West 16th Street. Bernie told me to come with him. As we drove west toward the river, Bernie radioed for backup. If this was our killer, particularly if he was old, he might not want to be taken alive. We parked underneath the old train trestle and waited for the patrol cars to arrive.

"Is that one of the old El lines?" I asked him, pointing at the overhead track. I had heard that trains used to run on elevated tracks up and down some of Manhattan's avenues, as recently as the 1950s.

"That's the old High Line," Bernie answered. "It was for moving freight, when they had warehouses along the river here." Spotting some middle-aged tranny hooker skulking underneath it, he added, "I just read they're planning to turn the whole thing into some kind of park."

"How do you turn an old train trestle into a park?"

"Maybe it'll be a big roller coaster ride, who knows?"

Suddenly two cop cars from the West Side Highway zoomed up behind them, sirens wailing. Bernie quickly got out of the car and waved at them to kill their sirens. We didn't want to give the killer any warning. The building had art galleries on the ground floor; the area was turning into the new SoHo. We rang the buzzer of one of the galleries to get inside. While talking to one of the gallery staff, we located a fire escape at the rear that ran up outside Wochenskil's window. Two of the uniforms were instructed to climb up there and stay out of view until we radioed them.

In the elevator, Bernie reached discreetly into his jacket. I knew he was checking his gun. He was eager to believe this could be our guy. For the first time we finally had someone who seemed to have an inkling of a motive and opportunity.

We got off at the eighth floor. We waited for the backup to radio that they were just below his window before we knocked on the door. As soon as it started to open just a crack, Bernie rammed his way in, shoving a handsome, strapping blond guy against the hallway wall.

"Please don't kill me!" he said in a shrill voice. The young man was terrified.

"NYPD." Bernie held up his badge while I searched him for a weapon.

"Are you Sam Wochenskil?" I asked as Bernie cuffed his hands behind him.

"No! Heavens, no. Sammy can't get out of bed. I'm her nurse."

Bernie pushed the man forward, and we followed him, guns drawn, into a spacious apartment.

In the bedroom watching daytime TV, wearing eyeliner and a badly balanced toupee, was a living skeleton of a man. Outside the window, the two patrolmen peeked in from the fire escape, looking bewildered.

"Pardon us," I said, as Bernie unlocked the window to let them in.

"Dear God! What the hell is going on?" Wochenskil asked, putting a hand over his heart.

It was clear that the only thing this old boy could hope to assault these days was an aluminum potty. The two uniforms climbed in through the window and quickly exited by the front door.

Bernie was unable to repress an embarrassed smile as he asked the bedridden man, "Did you by chance ever assault Marilyn Monroe?"

"The actress?"

Bernie nodded yes. Looking over at his attendant, Wochenskil rolled his eyes and the two of them snickered a little nervously. Bernie uncuffed the young man.

"Actually, we shouldn't laugh," the old man said. "I did once have an altercation with the late Miss Baker DiMaggio Miller Kennedy."

"You physically assaulted her?" I asked.

"Oh yes. About fifty years ago, at a party thrown by that pint-size monster Truman Capote. Before he did his big white-on-white bashes. She made some insipid remark about one of my fashions, don't you know. So I flicked a pimento at her when she wasn't looking. It landed in the top of her bouffant do. Everyone laughed."

"Is it true that you assaulted another lady?" Bernie asked sternly, trying to retain a sense of purpose to our visit.

"That was no lady," Sam replied. "That she-devil was my sister. We got into a vicious fight after my mother died. The bitch was talking trash, don't you know. Well, next thing I know she slaps me, so let me tell you, I slapped her right back. And she filed charges." Looking slyly over at his attendant, he ran his knuckles over his fingertips like an emery board and said, "I only filed my nails."

"The woman had a different last name than yours," Bernie said, reading from his notepad.

"It's her . . . mar . . ." Suddenly he started gasping. "It's her marr . . . married name." He continued gasping. The attendant, who turned out to be a licensed nurse, moved quickly and gave him an injection via a central IV line.

Bernie looked up at me. It was obvious we were interrogating a dying man. I apologized for the intrusion and we left.

"My last murder," he said almost fondly as we were waiting for the elevator, "some guy rips off his buddy, so the dude, who he'd known since high school, grabs a lead pipe and clobbers him three times over the head. Four people see the whole thing and two of them squealed. No overtime, no techies, no labs, no profiler. Not even a trial. Just sentencing. The whole event was wrapped up by lunchtime."

"Maybe the NYPD should give incentives to blunt trauma murderers with witnesses."

"They do. They call them plea bargains."

The elevator doors popped open and we stepped inside.

"What's worse is that we got seven more of these nutcases to track down—and this guy was our best shot."

It was five o'clock when we arrived back at the precinct. After a good laugh over the story of our geriatric suspect, we split the other seven names Miriam had given us with Alex and Annie, and planned to check them out the next day.

CHAPTER EIGHTEEN

That morning Bernie showed up with a five-o'clock shadow and another of his thousand yard stares. It turned out his wife had finally served him divorce papers. Alex tried to convince him to take the day off and relax, but Bernie said that all he really wanted was to catch this cocksucker before he sliced and diced another girl. Annie said it would be a relatively easy day, since our next task was to check out Miriam's uptown suspects.

"No way," Bernie said tiredly. "Her list is a fucking joke. It's only been a few days since Caty's death. so I want to go back to the King's Court and see if we can find any witnesses."

"We already canvassed the hotel," Annie pointed out. "And we looked at all the surveillance footage."

"Somebody must've seen something," he insisted.

"Why don't you two go ahead and do that," Annie said. "Alex and I can finish up the Williams list ourselves."

Bernie and I spent the day interviewing staff and tracking down the guests who were still occupying rooms on the floor where Caty stayed, but it was all a big bust.

As we were walking down a street back to the precinct, I caught Bernie staring at an older homeless man sitting in a doorway.

"The older you get the less desirable, more avoidable you become," he announced. All the little systems in your life start breaking down like you're an old appliance—the emotions, the love, the ability to socialize . . . And don't get me started on the failures of the body."

"Hey, they've got drugs for all those things." I tried to lighten his mood. At that moment, a sexy girl walked by and the comment assumed a connotation I hadn't intended.

"Sex went from being ten times a day to maybe once a year, if I begged my wife enough. But even that one night made me feel like a million bucks," he said as he eyed her. "All gone forever."

I gave him a sympathetic smile, then headed to yoga class to process my own stress. Much to my chagrin, the Renunciate was away on some Buddhist retreat in the Catskills. even though his life seemed like one big vacation to me. A wide-eyed yogarexic named Penrose conducted the class. Apparently she was not fluent in Sanskrit, because she used boring animal names for the old positions—pigeon pose, crow pose, camel pose, dolphin pose. Although I worked up a good sweat, I sort of felt spiritually cheated by her American narrative.

Before going home, I stopped at the Rite Aid to pick up some more concealer, so I could cover my bruises before Miriam's party that night.

When I entered my place, on the floor I found the same page from the *Post* that Bernie had waved at me. Maggie must've slipped it under my door. The headline read COPS OUT ON SEX SOCIALITE. The quarter-page article loosely described my near-arrest of Venezia at the Rocmarni show. I didn't so much mind the unflattering photo of me trying to keep Venezia's slippery arm pinned behind her fat back. What pissed me off most was that we were described as rivals for Noel Holden's affections. I guess at least I hadn't received any visits from Internal Affairs.

I tried to push it all out of my head as I showered, tended to my face, squirted on perfume, Visined my eyes, and changed into affordable elegance. I made it downstairs just as Noel got tired of waiting in his car out front and was about to ring my doorbell. He kissed me on the lips instead.

"I missed you, dear," he said as he helped me into the back seat.

"I miss you too."

"How's the crazy neighbor?" he asked as we drove away.

"I'm more than a little pissed at her."

"Why?"

"Do you know what she said to me the other day? She asked me if I would mind if she slept with you."

His eyes widened and for a moment he was dumbstruck. "I told Crispin she was a starfucker from the very start," he finally said as we arrived in front of Miriam's urban chateau.

The guest of honor at tonight's dinner, Noel told me, was Martinique Doll, the French writer/director Miriam had brought back with her from Cannes. He had just won the prestigious Palme d'Or for his latest flick, *The Doppelganger*, which was about two nearly identical women who coincidentally are in love with the same man. People from his production company, and other figures from the worlds of finance, film, and fashion were already there when we walked in, hobnobbing and knocking back drinks.

Initially all the talk was focused on the young filmmaker; I spent most of the time trying not to think about whether Noel would attempt to bed me again tonight, and how I would respond if he did. Several skimpy courses were eventually served and guiltily nibbled on. after which conversation broke into small, swirling groups. I was sticking to ginger ale, intent on staying sober as the evening progressed. If we did have sex again, I wanted to remember every detail.

I listened attentively, but I only participated in the conversation when I had something to add, which was seldom. At one point, though, I overheard someone refer to one dapper blond youth as Zeus. I discovered the young man was an aristocrat from some duchy in northern Europe, and when his conversation companion moved on, I asked him, "Is your name really Zeus?"

"That's me, king of the gods," he kidded.

"What do you know about Hercules?"

"Well, I know he wasn't actually a god."

"Do you know anything about his death?"

"I know that his wife unwittingly caused his demise."

"Anything else?"

"And she felt so bad about it that she subsequently killed herself."

Detective Kelly's wife had died before him, so that detail didn't fit into my pattern.

"But why are you asking me this, please?"

"Would you believe me if I told you I was the goddess Diana."

"I thought you looked familiar," he said with a grin.

"I'm joking, but I did actually see a divine sign." When Zeus looked at me pityingly, I added, "but maybe it was just something I ate."

"You shouldn't shortchange signs," he said. "Some great events in history only happened because of signs."

"Like what?"

"The one that comes to mind involved the Roman Emperor Constantine. As he was about to go into battle, he supposedly looked up and saw a cross of light above the sun, and because of this sign, he wound up converting the Roman Empire and subsequently the Western world to Christianity."

Suddenly Zeus' entourage. who seemed to have been scattered throughout the party, all converged on him; they were bored and wanted to go to yet another fabulous party. He bade me farewell, said he'd see me on Mount Olympus, and was gone.

I sidled up to Noel, who was putting a lot of effort into charming another flamboyant young director, who in turn was trying to interest Miriam in producing a biopic of Montgomery Clift. Noel was clearly laying the groundwork for an exciting audition.

Not wanting to interfere with his business, I stood by quietly and listened in. As their talk progressed, though, it became increasingly obvious that the filmmaker had neither money nor connections—nor, for that matter, did he have a script. He was just another bullshitter in the land of bullshit. When Noel realized the silliness of it all, he politely extricated himself from the conversation and the guy grabbed his coat and left.

All the gourmet food had long been eaten, so the other posers and frauds began defecting as well. And the VIPs were long gone. Soon Noel, Miriam and I found ourselves alone. When Noel asked Miriam whether she had succeeded in snaring the young French director for her latest project, she said she didn't know. He was in demand, however briefly, and fielding other big offers. After an interval of silence, she seemed to suddenly awaken, saying she had just read that I had been attacked while arresting a serial murderer.

"It was nothing," I didn't want to go into it.

"Nothing!" Noel replied. "He nearly blew her brains out!"

"Really!" Miriam replied. "How modest."

"It's sounds a lot worse than it was," I replied.

"Show her your bruises!" Noel said excitedly.

"They're really nothing."

As if I were a life-size doll, Noel and Miriam proceeded to pull up my shirt and spun me around so they could see the welts on my stomach and the bright scratches along my belly, as well as the colorful bruises on my back.

"Oh, Gladyss!" Noel impulsively changed the subject. "Because of you, Crispin and I are doing another fashion show."

"Me?" I asked, rearranging my clothes.

"Yep. The Venezia incident got us even more press than the runway fist fight. Another designer called Crispin's agent and asked if we would strut our sexy stuff on *his* runway."

"Who is this?" Miriam asked.

"Loot. He's a gangsta rap producer but he has a hot new winter line. He's premiering it on the last day of Fashion Week."

"You're kidding!"

"Not only am I not kidding, *you've* got to come too. Everyone will want to see the fashion policewoman who keeps the drugged-up models in line."

I thought about telling him I was awaiting possible disciplinary action over the incident, I simply moaned.

"We can go to his party at Cithaeron's afterward," Noel added, namedropping the latest hot downtown club.

Miriam asked the question that was upper most on my mind. "Is Venezia going to be there?"

"She's gone into hiding. The sex video was bad enough, but the negative publicity from almost being arrested for drug abuse on the runway . . . Well, her family are really pissed. Her grandfather has threatened to re-inherit her just so he can disinherit her again."

"Poor kid," she said with a sneer.

"Did you see the sex tape?" Noel asked me.

I shook my head as Miriam asked, "So when's this rap fashion show?"

"Thursday at five. It's going to be big."

"And he's doing it to publicize *Fashion Dogs*?"

"Kind of. It's called Fashion Dogs on the Catwalk," he repeated. "In addition to showing his debut line, Loot is having us walk actual dogs down the runway."

"Is he getting any other stars out there?"

"Oh yeah, he's paying Beneathra twenty-five grand to sit in the front row, to help him gain visibility for his clothes."

"Wow, I'd sit there for twenty-five bucks," Miriam joked.

Noel turned to me. "You really *have* to be there."

"Actually, my boss ordered me to break up with you."

Miriam laughed.

"I'm not kidding!"

"He can't do that," Noel said.

"Technically, he can. Apparently sleeping with you is unethical."

He started laughing.

"I'm serious, you're a s—"

Instead of saying suspect, I said "star."

"It's unethical to date a star?"

"That's economic discrimination!" Miriam said.

It occurred to me that my thirty-day stint in homicide was effectively coming to an end on the very day of this show. I had an appointment to get my eyes measured that day, then on the Friday I was having the Lasik surgery, and the following Monday I'd be back in uniform with O'Ryan, the emotional snowman. "Look, I don't even have a dress."

"The girl definitely needs a dress," Miriam said, "Last year some big actress was turned away for looking too grungy."

"What's your size?"

"I'm a four."

"Perfect," Noel said. "I happen to have an incredible Roberto Cavalli in a size four, just waiting for you."

"You're kidding!" I'd never heard of a boyfriend getting his girl a great dress.

"I hope you two aren't running off," Miriam fretted, apparently fearful of being alone except for the servants.

"Oh no, we'll stay till dawn," Noel soothed her. "There's nothing like watching the sun come up over Central Park. The entire gorge just fills with copper light!"

"It's true," Miriam said to me. "Because of the surrounding high rises, Central Park resembles the Grand Canyon at that hour. We'll have breakfast and watch."

Miriam led us into her study, where Noel flopped onto her antique divan, and after a brief spell of conversation passed out. After a little while, Miriam excused herself, presumably to go to bed. So much for the dramatic breakfast. Softly I whispered to my date that I had to go home.

"Back to him, huh?" he said, his eyes still closed, half-intoxicated.

"Who?"

"The cop." He sat up.

"What cop?"

"You know, that handsome brute who knocked me down when I first met you. Maggie said you two were dating."

"I can't believe Maggie told you that," I said, pissed. "We went on one date and it didn't go well."

"Why not?" He asked earnestly, making me aware that I hadn't revealed the two big secrets that had sunk my big night with Eddie—that I was a twin, and that I'd been a virgin.

"I'm still not sure," I answered.

"So you were lovers?"

"Actually, we weren't."

"You can admit it, I don't care."

"It's just not true! In fact . . ." I stopped just short of telling him.

"In fact what?" he pushed.

"Until you and I did it, I was a virgin," I finally confessed.

His mouth fell open.

"It's no big deal, I was glad to lose it."

"Are you religious?"

"I sure am, and now you'll have to marry me."

He froze for a minute. When I broke out laughing, he didn't join in.

"You know what," he said looking at his wristwatch. "It's late and I probably should get you home."

"But I thought—"

"You're not the only one that has to get up tomorrow. Hell, I'm not even going to sleep, I have a packed bag in the back of the car and I'm going straight to the airport. We're doing a couple of days of preliminary shooting for a new film in Florida tomorrow morning."

Noel hadn't mentioned this before, and I didn't believe him now, but I kept it together. He called the car, which was out front in a flash. The silence thickened as we went downstairs and the car sped south.

"I'm really sorry," he finally spoke as we pulled up outside my building.

"For what?"

"I didn't mean to sound cavalier. A lot has happened recently, with Venezia and all, and . . . I didn't know you were a virgin." I went limp as he hugged me and murmured, "That's why you stopped me the first time, isn't it?"

"Look," I said, "you didn't do anything wrong, and I'm not expecting anything from you."

"Well maybe you should. You deserve someone a lot better than me."

"Is this your gentle way of dumping me?"

"Only if you're not joining me on Loot's catwalk," he said with a smile. "I'm getting you a really nice dress."

"Why is everyone so freaked out about my virginity?"

"The truth is, I'm pissed at myself."

"Why?"

"It's just that . . . Well, call me sentimental, but to me there's something sacred about the first time. I mean, all the other times in life are just other times, but the first time should be special. And frankly I was kind of shitfaced and I guess initiating sex with a woman who was technically unconscious isn't very thoughtful."

"Technically it's illegal."

"I just wish you'd told me up front that you were a virgin. I would've made sure and done it right."

I assured him there was no need to feel guilty. Hell, he had done me a favor. He looked away, and I realized he was actually ashamed. I really didn't understand the man at all. He got out of the car, saw me to my door, and kissed me tenderly on the cheek.

Even if I did see him at the rap fashion show, I had a sinking feeling that we were over. I watched him get back in his clean, rented car, and then he was gone. Feeling isolated, I called Carl to see how he was doing. As though he had eavesdropped on me, he immediately asked: "You don't really think you're the goddess of the hunt, do you?"

"Why would you ask me that?"

"I just spoke about it to my shrink, and he said he's had clients who believed they were figures from history and mythology."

"Yeah?"

"Yeah—and he says it's always a sign of some kind of psychosis."

"I just meant that I'd found some weird similarities between me and Diana—fact-based stuff."

"Like what?"

"Well, we're both tall blondes, both twins, and . . ."—I was about to tell him about my lost virginity, but I couldn't face it—"both guardians of females, in different ways."

"Everything I told you about Bloomberg getting elected due to the 9/11 attacks was based in fact too, but you hung up on me."

"Actually, I didn't. I fell asleep."

"Gladyss, I'm only saying that hallucinations, delusions . . . I mean, I've been diagnosed with schizophrenia, and those things are classic early warning signs."

"If I experience any more of it, I'll seriously consider getting help, but"— my voice took on a severe tone—"if you start nagging me about this, and that's what you usually do, your calls will go straight to voicemail and your messages will get deleted."

"Okay," he conceded.

When I arrived at work the next morning, Bernie hadn't come in.

Annie tried to reach him on the phone, but he didn't pick up. Alex said he probably needed some alone time, so the three of us started working through Miriam's oddball list of people who'd talked trash about Marilyn.

Without even leaving the office, we discovered that three of the eight suspects had died of old age. Two more might as well have been dead, insofar as they couldn't possibly have committed the killings— one was suffering from second-stage Alzheimer's, and the other had been an invalid for some years. A further suspect had moved to Montenegro twenty years ago, which left us with only two. The first fellow was a man named Glen Mueller, who according to Miriam was still in his seventies. As with Sam Wochenskil, we located him via the phone book. It felt kind of pointless, but Annie and I headed over to Mueller's place while Alex remained at the precinct, tracking down the whereabouts of the last suspect on Miriam's list.

Mueller lived in an Upper East Side walk-up. He was a semi-retired sports reporter. He opened the door wearing a loosely cinched terry cloth robe and filthy flip flops. He had a small cigar in his yellowish mouth and he seemed to have a speck in his left eye, which he kept tightly shut.

"I just got out of the shower," he said, gingerly touching a towel to his thinning gray hair. "Come on in." He turned away from us and walked to his medicine cabinet. A moment later he spun back to face us with both eyes wide open.

"Sorry ladies," he said, pointing to his left eye, "I always take it out in the shower—it's glass. So how can I help you?"

In his living room I saw that he had turned TV trays into his primary furnishing. Two televisions were on, both tuned to sports channels and muted. He didn't turn them off, but he didn't look at them either.

"We're investigating a murder," Annie began, "do you know a Mrs. Miriam Williams?"

"Miriam Williams?" he said, flipping through the Rolodex of his memory. "Oh yeah, I was married to a woman in the early Seventies who was a friend of hers. Was she killed or something?"

"No, she's fine. Do you remember the last time you saw Miriam?"

"It had to be a while ago, because I remember meeting Jackie Onassis at her place." Mueller took a seat in an old, over-upholstered leather chair and flipped off one of the TVs with a very small remote.

"Mr. Mueller, can you tell us where you were on the evening of February 23rd this year?"

He sighed. "Look, if I have to get up and find out what the hell I was doing on February 23rd, I'd at least like to know why?"

"That's the date of a murder we're investigating," Annie said. It was the day on which Jane Hansen had been butchered.

"Good enough." He went over to his desk, rubbed out his miniature cigar, and flipped through an appointment book.

"I was staying with my kid brother Louie and his wife, along with their three kids and their families, on Martha's Vineyard from the 20th until the 27th," he replied. "We sat around the fireplace, drank cognac and watched TV. If you want, I can give you his number."

"That should do fine," Annie said.

On the ride back to the precinct, Annie commented that ninety percent of this job consisted of colorful interviews that led to dead ends.

"Officer Chronou?" I heard as we stepped into the office.

I turned to see a pair of heavy-set, dark-suited men; they looked like pallbearers for a mafia funeral.

"I'm Lieutenant Lucas, this is Detective Paste, Internal Affairs," he showed his shield. "You got a minute?"

Annie gave a tense smile. Silently they led me down a corridor into an empty interrogation room. O'Ryan had warned me that this day would come. And more than once, Bernie had told me to drop

Noel Holden. The Page Six item must've been the last straw.

Three chairs were arranged around a small table, but I was the only one who sat down. Thoughts were racing through my head, and quickly a mitigating mea culpa came together: I'd met Noel Holden while on the job. Initially I considered him a suspect, but once I cleared him, I realized I liked him. Of course, I couldn't say any of that. I wondered if I could bargain with them: Let me just go back to NSU and I'll write parking tickets till I die.

"Officer Chronou, you've kind of become Detective Farrell's partner over the last few weeks," Paste began.

"Huh?"

"Since Bert Kelly died, you've probably been partnered with him more than anyone else."

"Okay . . ."

"We've been getting a steady stream of complaints about him, allegations of abuse." Lucas said. He seemed to be the lead.

"If you're talking about O'Flaherty, the man had just tried to rape and kill me, so—"

"We *are* talking about O'Flaherty, yes," Lucas interrupted. "Considering what he did to you, we're prepared to let that one pass. But unfortunately there are half a dozen other complaints, too, apparently without any such mitigating factors. And they seem to keep on coming."

"Like who?"

"For one, an entrepreneur from Brooklyn named Charles Barnett."

Paste pulled out a Polaroid photo of a man with a black eye and a split lip. It was Youngblood, who Bernie had beaten up outside Port Authority.

"He just filed a law suit against the NYPD for half a million dollars."

"Give me a break," I said, trying to act like it was all utterly ridiculous.

"Look, we know you're not going to turn him in," said Paste. "And hopefully he still hasn't done anything that he could lose his shield for. But when the time comes that he seriously hurts someone and is facing jail time, and loss of pension, not to mention a civil suit that takes whatever assets he has, you should remember this moment when we came to you and asked you to help your partner."

"Bernie's rough, but he's not corrupt or anything. And there's no way I'm going against him," I said, feeling like a thousand cliché characters in a thousand crime films.

"We just need you to swear to a lesser charge, enough to get him off the street."

"You want me to help you force him to *retire*?"

"You know what's worse than living off your pension? Not living off of it." Lucas said.

"And even worse than that," said Paste, "Is spending your golden years in an eight by ten cell, surrounded by vengeful guys competing with each other to take out the cop."

"Is that it?" I said, rising to my feet.

"Look," Lucas said quietly. "Bernie has been around since the bad old days when this place was hell. No one wants to hurt him. But he's sick. Physically and in other ways, we both know that. You might think we're the bad guys, but we really want what's best for the guy."

I had nothing to say, so I walked out. My thirty-day assignment ended tomorrow, then this would be someone else's nightmare. I returned to my desk and checked the voicemail on my cell. Surprisingly, I had seven messages. The first message was a tense one from Eddie O'Ryan asking me to call him back; no doubt he wanted to warn me yet again about the IAD interview, which hadn't even targeted me. A relaxed message followed from Noel, telling me not to be shaken by the press and saying he was looking forward to seeing me back at Bryant Park for the big "Fashion Dogs on the Catwalk" show tomorrow afternoon. The other messages were from tabloid and TV reporters, including *Access Hollywood* and the *National Enquirer*. I couldn't think how they got my private number.

The temperature had dropped precipitously by the end of the day, as I dashed across to the yoga studio, where I had a good workout with the skinny, dough-eyed substitute. Exhausted, I went home, showered, had a high-protein low-carb dinner, and dove into my layers of comforters and sheets. I had just fallen asleep when my cell chimed. The display said *Angry Bastard*, the name I'd assigned to Bernie's number.

"What's up?"

"I . . . I . . . not f-f-feeling too g-g-good," I could hear his teeth chattering.

"Where *are* you?"

"Near . . . p-p-precinct." He sounded drunk, but before I could ask him anything else, his phone cut out. When I tried calling back I got his voicemail. I was worried he'd freeze, considering his constantly congested lungs, so I called the station. When the desk sergeant picked up, I introduced myself and explained that Detective Farrell was intoxicated nearby in his parked car.

"Old Bern's fine," the sergeant replied. "He sleeps there all the time."

"But it's really freezing tonight. Can't somebody just bring him inside. He can sleep on the sofa in his office."

"See what I can do."

Fifteen minutes later, I still couldn't sleep, so I called the precinct again. The overpaid armed receptionist said he still hadn't been able to get anyone to track Bernie down. So much for watching each other's backs.

I got dressed and headed outside. When I exhaled, my breath was white. I caught a taxi, and five minutes later I was up by the precinct on Thirty-fifth and Ninth. I walked around the corner and there, in front of one of the few remaining 24-hour porn video arcades, illegally parked, was Bernie's battered Buick.

He was curled up in the front seat, and didn't wake up even when I opened his door. It was easy to see how he had gotten mugged. He was shivering beneath a polyester and cotton sports jacket. His lips had turned blue. I tried to turn on his car engine, but it wouldn't start.

"What's going on?" he muttered.

"Come on, stakeout's over."

I helped him to his feet, hailed a cab, and pushed him into the backseat.

"Where to?" the driver asked.

After fruitlessly interrogating Bernie for his home address, I ended up taking him back to my humble abode. He obediently staggered upstairs.

"Where was I when you were my age?" he asked drunkenly as I opened my apartment door.

I pulled out the pullout in my living room and pushed him onto it, then gingerly removed his shoes. Maybe because he was freezing, or because my nose was stuffy, his foot didn't smell quite so bad. As I covered him with a blanket, I could hear Maggie in her apartment, laughing it up with her latest French tickler. I jumped back into my bed for the second time and fell asleep right away.

Around three in the morning I was woken by the delicate sounds of Bernie retching his guts out in the bathroom. Once he stopped, I went back to sleep.

When I awoke a while later, I realized he was in bed with me. Considering he was probably still more drunk than awake, and my bedroom door was next to the bathroom, it seemed like a genuine mistake. I tried to get him awake enough to move back to the sofa bed, but he seemed totally out of it, even more so than I had been with Noel. I peeked under the sheets and saw he was wearing his boxers and T-shirt. A gold Saint Christopher's medal was around his neck. Every godparent in the outer boroughs seemed to loop one around their godson's neck at confirmation.

There was plenty of space between us, so since he was already snoring away, I left him where he was.

A few hours later, when he flopped his arm over me, I woke up enough to push him back. As I was drifting back into sleep, I could hear little Maggie making noisy, squeaky love. I pulled the pillow over my head, ignoring the bumping and groaning, but slowly my sleep thinned out.

"Sueee—" I suddenly heard.

The cry was cut short, as if Maggie had abruptly covered his mouth. It couldn't be Crispin. Both he and Noel were out of town, though they were supposed to return later today for Fashion Dogs on the Catwalk. Yet it had to be Crispin. Who else could it be? Then I remembered her asking about dating Noel. Maggie just didn't seem like Noel's type. But then I recalled her saying she was going to break up with Crispin and clearly remembered her confidently asking if she could sleep with Noel, as if he had already made advances.

As her bed hammered against our common wall, the fear was driven deeper into my skull that she wasn't with Crispin at all. I recalled Noel's astounded face when I mentioned that Maggie had asked me if she could sleep with him and suddenly realized it wasn't outrage he was displaying but restrained joy. As her groans of ecstasy grew increasingly louder and shorter, I found myself bouncing between terror and fury.

It would explain why Maggie had told Noel about my brief encounter with Eddie O'Ryan. More particularly it accounted for her sudden change of style: until recently she'd been a shapely brunette who never made too much of it. Suddenly—*voilà*, she'd transformed herself into a flamboyant blonde, more in the Venezia Ramada mold.

What was wrong with me? Wasn't I sexy enough? Or feminine enough? Too tall? Too tomboyish? If I got electrolysis and coconut-shaped implants, perhaps then I'd hold onto Noel.

I had a sudden impulse to clean and organize my clothes right now, but before I could act on it, I heard Maggie's front door creak open. By the time I raced to my door and peeped through the eyehole, her lover was gone. I rushed to my window in time to see a cab zoom off. I returned to bed pissed and lay there for about an hour, churning and stewing in my own angry juices. Finally I just tried breathing, Kundalini-style, in a series of short shallow breathes, to release my anguish. This must've been the reason that Artemis, who I'd learned was the Greek equivalent of Diana, had asked Zeus to spare her the temptations of the flesh and grant her a life of serene spinsterhood.

The hyperventilation must've stirred Bernie, because he suddenly turned over and pulled me firmly toward him. I was about to shove him away, but it felt surprising good to be held tight, despite the strong smell of cheap alcohol.

Bernie was a decent, sensitive guy masquerading as an asshole—most men were just the opposite. Although for some reason I trusted him, I couldn't help but think that the IA boys had a point. Either he was going to wind up hurting someone, or he would get hurt himself. With his partner's death and his own impending divorce, he must've felt humanity itself had left him high and dry. He was long overdue for a break. Maggie's lusty moans were still ringing in my ears, which was undoubtedly one reason why I felt as sensitive as a blister about to burst.

As I reached around into his boxers and felt his coiled masculinity, I knew I was making a massive mistake. Still I gently rattled it like a roll of quarters until it outgrew my hand.

"Huh?" he uttered as I rolled him onto his back. "What's going on?"

I knelt and pulled my underwear to one side, then stretched over him and slowly took him in.

"You?" He squinted at me.

"If you don't mind. . ."

"Uh, well . . ." He didn't resist.

As I continued working him into me, he said, "Hold it a minute. If you keep doing that, I mean, I won't be able to . . ."

"You want to . . ."

I shifted positions so I was on my back, and let him slowly assume the dominant position. Once his bad foot was carefully placed like a scaly tail behind him, so that he was safely on his knees, he started moving quickly, breaking out in a sweat like spring rain.

He pounded away for a few minutes then suddenly had to dismount. Before I could towel off all his sweat, he stumbled out of the room and quickly returned with his inhaler. He took three deep breaths from it, then got back to work as though he had just taken vaporized Viagra. In addition to enjoying the wonderful sensations, I loved the fact that the head of *my* bed was slapping against *Maggie's* wall for once. I let out some retaliatory moans.

Given how much booze Bernie must have drunk, as well as his reduced lung capacity and sore hoof, I was really impressed with his stamina. As he hastened toward liftoff, I couldn't resist shouting: "FUCK ME BABY!"

Then I suddenly realized I didn't have protection: "Wait! Don't come in me!"

He pulled out and, one jerk later, spewed his DNA all over my belly. Then he collapsed next to me, covered in sweat. We both lay still for a few moments as if after a car crash. Then, through the wall, I thought I heard the muted cry, "Fucker!"

I wiped off and listened intently.

"Everything okay?" Bernie asked, watching me listen to the wall.

"Glorious," I whispered and went into the shower.

Afterward, as I toweled off, I felt reluctant to go back into the bedroom. When I finally took a deep breath and opened the door, wrapped in a towel, Bernie had pulled on his boxers and was sitting on the end of the bed.

"If the world wasn't spinning, I'd hold you in my arms and tell you how gorgeous you are," he said, which didn't make me feel any better.

"I just figured we could both use a little pick-me-up," I replied with my back to him, pulling on my bra and panties.

In another moment, he lumbered into the shower and I was already dressed.

I couldn't make eye contact with Bernie as we put on our coats. He joked that it was "a good foot day" as I rushed us out the door and along the slippery intersections to a nearby diner on Seventh Avenue. Bernie grabbed a booth. Without looking at him, I asked the waitress for a black coffee, even though I always had tea in the morning. He ordered a full egg-and-sausage breakfast.

"Either you've inexplicably fallen in love with me and want to go to City Hall right now and get married, or you'd like to pretend nothing happened and never mention this again. I'd be fine with the former, but by the fact that you can't make eye contact I'm sensing you'd prefer the latter."

I didn't utter a sound.

"Sooo . . . Since nothing interesting happened lately, what shall we talk about?" he said calmly.

"Actually there is something that's been nagging at me for a while."

"I can't imagine."

"How did you know it was him?"

"How did I know who was who?"

"We dragged O'Flaherty to the precinct, locked him up, checked his room, and got zilch. Then, based on a brief conversation with a Con Ed worker, you had us go over to his room, wait several hours, and stake it out. What made you do that?"

He shrugged. "Intuition."

"See, that's the kind of thing that drives me nuts," I said. "I've been trying to sharpen *my* intuition, but all I came up with was this insane idea."

"What insane idea?"

I knew I shouldn't bring it up, but since this was our final day working together, it didn't seem like I had anything to lose.

"Do you remember that postcard he had on his wall, of the goddess of the hunt?"

"Yeah, the *not* Evelyn Nesbit statue."

"Well, the killer's name, O'Flaherty's first name, is Nessun."

"So? It's a typical Irish name."

"Except there's a Greek myth featuring a centaur called Nessus. He was responsible for the death of Hercules."

"Oh God, you're not going to say he went to the Hogwart Academy or some crap like that?"

"No, I'm just saying there was similarities between the Greek myth and—"

"Only I'm not Hercules and he didn't try to kill me? No, wait!" He was mocking me. "He tried killing you, so that means you're Hercules."

"Actually, it was your old partner I was thinking of." No sooner had I said that than I remembered Annie had asked me to keep the story from Bernie.

"How'd you know that?" he said, surprising me.

"Know what?"

"Did you go through the boxes in my office?"

"No. You mean, the files from your old cases?"

"Not just *my* old cases. In fact, they were mainly Bert's. The man always made copious notes. After we first interviewed O'Flaherty, I was going through the files and happened to find something Bert wrote about the son of a bitch long ago."

"What did he say?" I wondered if Bernie had already learned what Daisy had told us about Juanita Lopez, whom his partner would eventually marry.

"He didn't *say* nothing, he simply underlined the man's name three times. But for Bert, I knew that was it. He knew the man was dangerous."

"How long ago did he write that?"

"Decades ago, before O'Flaherty even went to jail. But Herbert Kelly was the real deal. Talk about intuition—that man had a super-human power. On that night when the Con Ed man mentioned him, I just thought this is worth following."

"Amazing."

"But he didn't kill Bert," Bernie said.

"Yeah, it just all struck me as odd."

"But how did *you* know that Bert knew O'Flaherty?"

"I didn't," I said simply and sipped my coffee.

"Why do I sense that there's something more to this that you're not telling me?"

"Okay, there is," I bullshitted. "But it's not easy to talk about."

"Just say it."

"All right," But there was no way I was going to try to launch into all the myth stuff again. I took a sip of coffee and said: "If you don't cut the shit, you're going to get into big trouble."

"What the hell are you talking about?"

"Two cops from IA interviewed me yesterday."

"I warned you. Everyone saw that news item about you at the fashion show—"

"Actually, they were asking me about you."

"Huh?"

"They said they'd racked up a bunch of complaints about you."

Without looking at me, he slurped down the remainder of his coffee as though it were hydrochloric acid. He'd completely forgotten about Nessun and his old partner.

"I told them you were fine, but you're not, and you know it."

"Okay, my foot makes me a little cranky and—"

"It's not just your foot, or your cough, or Bert's death, or your wife leaving you . . ."

Without hearing another word, he dropped a crumpled ten on the table without even breaking his victory yolks and stomped out the door.

I pulled on my coat and ran after him. We walked together in silence for a while. After a few blocks, I was surprised to hear him listing a number of tasks he wanted me to finish up with Alex and Annie. I'd assumed he knew.

"Bernie," I interrupted him. "This is it."

"This is what?"

"Today's my last day."

"What?"

"I'm leaving in five minutes for my ophthalmologist's appointment. And tomorrow I've taken a personal day to have my eye surgery."

"Okay, when you come in on Monday—"

"My thirty days are over," I interrupted. "Monday I'm back in Neighborhood Stabilization."

"Oh fuck, I meant to extend your assignment," he muttered. When I didn't respond, he added, "Look, all the bullshit aside, you've become a significant part of this task force. And there's still a killer out there."

"Bernie, I know you've recently gone through a lot, and now your department's trying to push you out, but I'm just saying, maybe if you considered going to AA or anger management—"

"Arrivederci, kid," he said and limped away faster than I would have thought possible. It must've hurt like hell.

I watched him hopping north toward the precinct and felt bad that in trying to help, I'd only added to his pain. I headed east and caught a subway uptown.

Twenty minutes later I was at my doctor's office. His assistant brought me into an examination room and told me to sit in an upholstered chair. The doctor put drops in my eyes to dilate my pupils, then swung a large black armature plate over my face that was fitted with a series of lenses. Through a tiny eyepiece he seemed to stare into my very soul, seeing all the guilty little secrets I had accumulated there. As he carefully measured the different parts of my eyes, I couldn't stop thinking about the events of the past month.

"Try to take it easy," he said. "Stay away from bright lights until your pupils have time to return to normal." He gave me a pair of sunglasses to wear that looked like they were meant for welders.

I went home and lay down for a few minutes. Without intending to, I dozed off. I was briefly awakened by my cell phone's chime, but I saw it was Carl and let it go to voicemail. When I awoke, it was six p.m. and I realized I was late for the fashion show.

I got the train to Times Square, then pushed through the busy midtown streets toward Bryant Park. Fearful that I wouldn't be able to find him, I called Noel.

"I just arrived," he said. "Meet me at the stone stairs on the east side of Sixth Avenue and Forty-first."

CHAPTER NINETEEN

I was relieved not to see Eddie O'Ryan among the officers assigned to the back steps of Bryant Park. Noel emerged just beyond the French doors where photographers were lined up to catch any stars. Flashes exploded as Noel dashed outside and gave me a quick kiss.

"Do you plan to arrest any more models?" some asshole reporter asked me.

Inside the doors Noel handed me a large scarlet box with a beautiful golden bow. It contained the brand new dress along with a pair of black pumps.

"You look very Jackie O in those sunglasses," he replied, "all you need is the white headscarf."

The frames hardly looked glamorous. "My pupils are dilated," I explained. "That's why I have to wear them."

"I just hope you'll be able to see *me*," he said.

He led me through a wide lobby to a smaller venue area within the park. A banner read, "Welcome to the Fashion Dogs on the Catwalk."

People were running around sporting various laminates, screaming into phones and headset walkie-talkies.

"So what's the drill?" I asked, swept up in all the hullabaloo.

"The whole thing should be over in a second. I just hope Venezia makes it on time."

"You said she *wasn't* coming!"

"Crispin persuaded her to, because he's not going to make it. But don't worry, you won't have to see her."

In the distance, I could hear dogs barking.

"Oh, they want me to spend some time bonding with a goddamned mutt before the show. We better get a move on."

He asked some slim blonde usher wearing a headset if she could show me to a changing room, and told me he'd be back shortly.

While Noel went off to bond with his bitch, I pulled on the Roberto Cavalli dress. It was a little too loose up top and too tight in the bottom. The pumps were too long and narrow, but I squeezed into everything and put my own clothes into the scarlet box. Noel greeted me when I emerged.

"I feel like Cinderella," I confessed. "But I'll turn back into a cop at midnight."

"Just don't arrest anyone," he said, only half-kidding.

"So where's your canine?" I asked, hoping to see one.

"I hear it's a French Bulldog, but they still haven't located it. Come on, let's find your seat. It should be in the front row. Be sure to back away if one of the dogs lift a leg."

"Has Venezia shown up yet?" I asked nervously.

"No, she's still in the kennel," he quipped. "Crispin is going to be furious if she misses the show. They've put gowns aside for her."

Suddenly someone paged him. Noel told me where to meet him after the show. Loot and his wife Sheba were throwing an after-party bash we had to attend. He gave me a kiss and vanished.

Inside was a huge banner publicizing *Fashion Dogs*. It showed a bare-chested Noel Holden, dressed only in tails and top hat, following Venezia, who was in a two-piece bathing suit. *This bitch runs with style,* read the tag line. The catwalk was painted and modeled like a city sidewalk, complete with faux street signs, occasional parking meters, and at the very end a large cardboard fire hydrant. Along the far wall was a huge, stark cutout of a dramatically lit New York skyline. It was the first time I'd ever seen an image of the skyline without the Towers.

An usher checked my ticket and led me to an uncomfortable folding chair in the conspicuous front row. Half the row was already occupied with spectators, and the photographers were already clustering at the front too. I wasn't sure, but I feared that some of the photos being snapped before the show were of me—the catfighting cop who was dating Noel. Black-vested caterers began circulating with trays of white wine. I really wanted some, but I passed.

In a matter of minutes all the seats were taken. I think I spotted Jack Black, Courtney Cox, Ivana Trump, and one or two of the newer comedians on the *Saturday Night Live* cavalcade. A fanfare of Loot's unintelligible rap along with strobing, colorful lights signaled that the show was about to begin. With bouncy steps and arrogant stares, a succession of young, incredibly tall female models strutted forth. The pooch walk was evidently for later. The regimented way they jerked forward, moving each leg in conjunction with their hip and shoulder, was both amusingly absurd and stringently sexual. As their shoulders dropped and thigh crossed over thigh, each kept her head and eyes focused militaristically straight ahead. They marched like heat-seeking robots.

Then came the men. To my undiscriminating eye, Loot's gangsta wear looked no different than Phat Farm and all the other loose gangsta wear—pants missing the hips and revealing the waistbands of colorful underwear, yet defying gravity by clinging just above the ass cheeks, while bunching up at the ankles to reveal odd, wedge-shaped sneakers, worn with plastic bubble jackets that were inflated like balloons. As a cop, my first thought was: they were good clothes for concealing weapons. Hoodies and sweatpants bore Loot's distinctive logo, a drunken thunderbolt.

Once the human show was over, it was the canines' turn. Several supporting actors from *Fashion Dogs* were set to walk first. Reading the preface in the show's catalog, I learned that the pack of modeling mutts had only been paroled from the local pound for the duration of the show. Charitably, each dog was listed by name and all were up for adoption. Pit bulls seemed to be the most prominent breed on the runway, but German Shepherds and assorted terrier mixes were also present. I kept my eye open for Venezia, but that particular bitch never showed up.

Finally Noel emerged to loud applause wearing a T-shirt that was cut off above the waist to display his flat, six-pack abs. He must've just executed a thousand high-speed sit-ups. He held a short leather leash that restrained a Rottweiler, not exactly the adorable French Bulldog he'd been expecting. He'd told me the dogs had been given several trial walks before the show to test their suitability, but obviously this was different. Perhaps it was the bright lights and throng of spectators that made them jumpy. Or that the inexperienced dog handlers didn't hold the leash confidently enough. In any case, some of them bolted skittishly back and forth. Several barked and tried to fight with other dogs. Occasionally they leaped up at their disaffected human companions.

When the show finally ended, the models playfully pulled the reluctant designer out onto the catwalk, where he displayed a modesty that wasn't present in any of his clothes.

As soon as people stood up to leave, the next show began loading in. Noel rushed me out through a private exit and into an awaiting car on Fortieth Street.

"Crispin's plane just landed. He's going directly to Cithaeron's from the airport."

"Is Maggie meeting him?" I didn't particularly want to see her, either.

"I think they broke up a while ago."

"Can I ask you an odd question?" I began cautiously.

"I'd expect no less."

"Where were you last night?"

"In LA," he said. "I arrived at 3:30 this afternoon Why? Was another girl murdered?"

"No, it's not that."

"I can show you the airline ticket."

"You've officially been removed from the list of suspects."

"How exciting. Do you know Ji Andersen?" he asked, referring to a recent "break-out star" from some WB tween show.

"Wasn't she at Miriam's party?"

"Oh, right. Well, Crispin's bringing her. He's trying to get her into his next film."

"What kind of name is Ji?"

"It was Jill, but first she dropped one l, then she pulled the other."

When we pulled up to the curb in front of Cithaeron's, a bullfrog-chested, bling-blinged doorman opened our car door. Photographers snapped away.

A bulge of would-be gatecrashers was being kept at bay on the sidewalk. We walked along the red carpet through the lobby and around an indoor fountain, and were led into the grand ballroom. Loot and his beautiful blonde Asian wife, Sheba, were greeting everyone as they entered.

Noel shook Loot's hand. Sheba, a former model, complimented my Roberto Cavalli.

"But isn't it it's a little dark in here for sunglasses?" she asked. When I explained that I'd just had my pupils dilated, she chuckled as though I'd used a euphemism for sex.

The DJ was mixing Loot's music with the classics. Attractive, well-dressed youth mingled. Noel, like a politician, was shaking hands, pecking cheeks. Hugs all around. Everyone seemed to be in the middle of a laugh, as though the world was just one big private joke that everyone knew but me. Noel spotted a group of film people behind the sizable VIP lounge and we headed there for shelter.

Usually I didn't mind the bullshit. In fact, I had come to love the artificiality of it all, the world in the clouds in which beauty and popularity were richly rewarded and protected, where facelifts were the self-evident remedy to aging. And even after death, it seemed, you could live on through fan-based web sites—on a strange, velvet-roped summit, where doormen and bouncers protected you from the vulgarities of cloven-footed types like O'Flaherty and Bernie, along with all the rest of the world's victims of deprivation.

Crispin entered the grand ballroom with Ji, who rose to a sheer height of about thirteen feet and had the misshapen face of an eternally angry teenage boy. When she turned around, all beheld a thick waterfall of luminous blonde hair that dropped straight to her perfect ass like golden rays from the heavens. As I stared at her jealously, I could just imagine her with a majestic bow and a quiver of arrows hanging from her back—I was clearly out-Dianaed here.

"Loot's wife just chewed me out cause Venezia's a no-show," Crispin yelled, "Where the fuck is her fat ass!"

"Who knows?" Noel said. "I just tried calling her publicist."

"Loot personally invited her, for fuck's sake!"

"Well, she missed it," Noel said.

"This is fucking lame. These fucking actresses get a little fame and they think they're the Queen of the Nile."

"Not all of us are like that," said Ji, the figurative and literal pillar of post-adolescence.

"You know who Noel is, and this is Gladyss." Crispin made the introductions. "Everyone, this is Ji."

When we shook, her fingers were cold and oddly vestigial, like gills. She didn't even look at me, just Noel.

Music started blaring. Loot and Sheba took to the floor and

danced flatfootedly, as if they were stomping out flames. Noel asked if I wanted to dance. We slowly rocked and rolled through three songs before Crispin and Ji started vibrating next to us.

"Hey, sexy!" Crispin called over to Noel. "Let's swap."

"Why not?" Noel replied.

"You dance marvelously," Ji said to me, then I thought she added, "like Liza."

"Who?" I asked.

Just as Ji broke out in squeaky giggles, Noel grabbed her and swung her around onto the dance floor.

"Who did she compare me to?" I asked Crispin.

"Liza Minnelli, I think," he replied while leering at his freakish date. "Look at her boogie!"

I wondered whether Ji was implying that I was fat, or old, or drunk. As I politely danced with Crispin, I sensed that the sleazy director kept trying to move me away, to a more distant place from where I couldn't see Noel. Finally I walked away from Crispin and found Noel doing this slow, lurid number with the blonde freak.

They clung together as though for dear life, tiptoeing tightly around the dark outer perimeter of the dance floor as if searching for a way out. I wasn't sure, but I suspected Ji was the instigator.

"So," Crispin said, coming after me. "I wanted to ask you about this fingerprint thing."

"What about it?"

"Noel said that I'm a suspect."

"It's nothing to worry about. It'll only take a sec," I said, still unable to take my eyes off of them.

"I'll tell you right now, that's the wrong way to get your man," Crispin finally whispered into my ear, as if caressing my brain. "There's nothing more unattractive than clinginess."

Completely vexed, I let out a loud, long sigh.

"Hey, I might not have throngs of suicidal fans, but spend a little time with me and you'll find loyalty and true love," Crispin said. He gently took my hand and swung me back toward the bar. I continued to try and keep Noel in view, and finally he turned toward us and waved. While I was frantically waving back, I knocked my sunglasses off. Crispin hastily picked them up before someone could step on them.

"I thought you were getting some sort of operation to be rid of these?" Crispin said.

"Tomorrow," I replied, watching Noel laugh and sway across the vast floor.

"So why are you wearing sunglasses anyway?"

"Eye doctor appointment."

"Oh wait, I think I saw you earlier today."

"Where?" I noticed Noel had stopped dancing, even though the music played on. He seemed to be talking to Ji about something urgent.

"Madison and Thirty-third Street?" Crispin said.

"Nope, wasn't me," I replied.

Ji was giggling and nodding eagerly. So was Noel. They were agreeing on something, perhaps a rendezvous.

"My doctor is on Seventy-second and Park."

"So what's the deal?" Crispin shouted over the music. "First I heard that you'd solved your big murder case, and now you're rounding up Miriam's senile bedwetters."

"It turned out to be two different murderers." I yelled into his ear. I knew I shouldn't say anything, but it was pretty much all in the papers by now anyway.

"What exactly do you know about this new murderer?" he asked.

"Nada," I said, not giving out any details.

"Check out Noel," Crispin said, as if I could look away. "Seeing his face sixty hours a week, having to press it on celluloid, I sometimes lose track of exactly how handsome he is in the wild. Then I see some young kid like Ji getting wet off just dancing with him, and I remember the man is a living god."

"Yeah."

Crispin turned to me and said, "The best way is to do it is quick, like you're ripping off a Band-aid."

"Do what?"

"End things." Then, under his breath, he muttered, "That's how I did it."

"What are you talking about?" I asked as he grabbed a glass of vodka off the bar and swigged it down. He didn't reply, so I asked him again. "What the hell are you talking about?"

"When?" He looked confused.

"Just now?"

"Hey, cut me some slack, I've just downed about six frozen Absoluts," he replied. I wondered if he was mocking my Rocmarni fiasco.

"You just said, 'That's how *I* ended it.' "

"Have a drink, Gladyss." As he handed me a glass of champagne, he squealed, "Suwee!"

"A regular stag, aren't you?" I guess I meant stud.

"Actually, that's a horny little pig, remember?" He grinned.

I tossed the drink in his face and headed out onto the dance floor. I was planning to grab Noel in the middle of his creepy sex shuffle and ask him what the hell was going on. But then I realized it didn't even matter. Whether he had screwed Venezia in LA, or Maggie here, or whether he was planning on seducing Ji later, none of it mattered. Without even knowing it, I had ceased being an investigator when I got sucked into the whirlpool. I was no better than my neighbor, pathologically infatuated with vapid celebrities.

"Gladyss!" I heard Noel shout as I sped down the front steps, around the velvet rope, and past the blinding flashes of the paparazzi. I grabbed a cab and headed home.

CHAPTER TWENTY

I got back to my apartment roughly fifteen minutes later, and before I even had time to take off the Cinderella dress my cell started chirping. I answered without checking, assuming it was Noel asking what was wrong.

"Is this Officer Gladyss Chronou?"

"Who is this?"

"I'm a reporter for the *Daily News.* I'm calling to get confirmation that you and Noel Holden have officially split up."

"How did you get my fucking number?"

"I don't mean to be a pest. I just thought perhaps you'd want the opportunity to tell your side of the story."

"Sure, here's my side of the story." I turned off my phone.

I stripped, lay down, and turned off the lights. I wanted to go to sleep, but I couldn't get off that easily. I lay in bed alternately feeling used by a lying scumbag, and stupid for letting the most handsome and perfect man in the world slip away. Finally I tried watching TV, but I couldn't get off this awful roller coaster of uncertainty. First I'd think that he really hadn't done anything wrong, and whenever I envisioned his perfect face and sexy body, I'd feel myself go soft all over. The goddess Diana wasn't weakened by frail human urges, but it shook the very core of my being to imagine life without him.

At nine the next morning, after only a few hours of shallow sleep, I heard frantic knocking at my front door. Before I could say anything, I heard Maggie call out, "Are you in there, Gladyss!"

She must have heard about my breakup with Noel. After a minute or so she stopped banging, and I tried to sleep some more. My eye surgery wasn't until the afternoon. After about an hour of floating face up in a small pool of misery, I heard my doorbell buzz. My first thought—perhaps hope—was that it was Noel wanting to apologize. Then I realized it would just be another fucking reporter. Again I decided to wait it out. It would be just a matter of time before they left me alone. After five minutes of repeated buzzing, though, I finally looked out the window.

A RMP was parked out front.

"Hello?" I said into the intercom.

"Officer Chronou?"

I buzzed the patrolman in, but he buzzed back.

"Yes," I said into the intercom.

"Detective Sergeant Farrell asked us to remain here until you got him on the phone. He's at the precinct."

"One second." I turned my phone back on and called his direct line.

"Bernie?"

"Ah, Officer Sleeping Beauty,"

"Hold on." Then I yelled into the intercom, "Okay, I'm on the phone with him. Thank you."

"So why was I awakened by two uniforms on my day off? I'm all done with Homicide, remember?"

Suddenly my call waiting beeped.

"Get down here immediately," he said.

"Am I in trouble?" I asked, half-fearing that someone in IAD was finally on to me—and only me.

"We arrested your boyfriend last night."

"Who? What?"

"Noel Holden is in Central Booking."

"What!'

"He killed Venezia Ramada and those others."

"Venezia? And what others?"

"He's our second killer, Gladyss."

"You're crazy."

"Just get down here immediately. Oh, but you might want to disguise yourself. The entire Mickey Mouse fan club is camped out in front of the precinct and they're asking for you."

He hung up.

I couldn't believe what he'd told me. Venezia dead? And Noel had killed her, as well as Jane Hansen and Caty Duffy? It was impossible.

But obviously they'd arrested him. That explained the massive number of messages I now saw had accumulated in my voicemail. My next thought was that I didn't want to miss my eye appointment, but it wasn't until later in the day, so I got ready to leave for the precinct.

It was about five degrees outside, a good excuse for overdressing. Twenty minutes later, buried under layers of clothes with my hair piled under a knit cap, I saw for myself the three-ring circus parked outside the precinct and knew that someone would undoubtedly spot me, despite my disguise. I headed around the corner. On Thirty-sixth Street, the rear of the precinct was surrounded by blue wooden barricades. I passed the patrol cars and scooters parked in the driveway and went in through the garage. Some hard ass from the 1-9 stopped me. I showed him my badge, but he shook his head.

"Enter on Thirty-fifth," he commanded.

"I can't, it's mobbed."

"Well this ain't the Bat Cave," said the little shit.

"Do me a favor and call homicide. They'll confirm that this is an extraordinary situation."

He got on the phone and called Annie, describing me in unflattering terms. She told him to let me up pronto.

When I walked into the squad room, Alex silently held up a page from the *Daily News* that I hadn't seen. It bore a photo of me walking out angry and dejected from Cithaeron's last night. A few seconds of flashbulb fame seemed to cast twenty-four hour shadow. I smiled thinly and went into Bernie's office.

"So what happened?"

"I got a personal call from the police commissioner this morning, asking about this." He held up a *New York Post* story with the headline: NYPD ROOKIE DATING SERIAL MURDER STAR! Alongside it was a photo of Noel and me kissing on the steps of Bryant Park.

I couldn't believe it. "What the fuck is going on?"

"You didn't want to break up with him—okay, fine. But you told me you had checked the son of a bitch out, didn't you?"

"Yeah."

"Well what the fuck did you do exactly?"

"Myself and another officer went to the airline that he took from Spain and confirmed that he was on the plane when the third murder happened."

"So you checked out his alibi for one of *O'Flaherty's* kills?"

"Yeah, but I also ran his prints against all—" I said, as I suddenly recalled that we were never able to actually check his alibi.

"Last night when I got home, you know what I did?" he replied with an angry smile. "I wasn't completely shitfaced for once, so I sat at my computer and thought, Gee whiz, I wonder what would happen if I plugged Noel Holden's name and Marilyn Monroe's name into Google at the same exact time—and guess what came up?"

"What?"

"After a little surfing in the archives of some internet magazine called *Suicidal Pearls*, I located a long interview with Noel Holden. Apparently he played Joe DiMaggio in a TV movie of Marilyn Monroe in 1993. Did you know that?"

"No."

"There's nothing suspicious in that in itself, of course. He's an actor. Actors get picked for roles. It just struck me as an odd coincidence."

"Good, because I'm sure that's all it was."

Noel couldn't butcher two women, I was convinced of that. Not because of any feelings on my part, I just couldn't see him dealing with the huge mess.

"Then I noticed another odd coincidence. The producer credit on the biopic read Miriam Williams."

"Well, that's probably how they met."

"Then I took the time to read the interview. In it Noel Holden said," Bernie picked up a printout from his desk: "'I used to believe Marilyn Monroe was my mother and that she gave me away. Not just because I was adopted, but because I was born at Los Angeles County Hospital'"—Bernie stressed the final words—"'*on the very day she was there to have her spleen removed.*' "

"Holy shit!"

"Holy shit is fucking right. In fact, in one of the killer's poems he referred to himself as a spleen."

"So what are you saying? That he killed these women to get back at his phantom mother?" The whole thing sounded ridiculous.

"No, I think all the crazy shit was just to mislead us. He had other reasons to kill."

"Like what?"

"Actually, that brings me back to what I read last night on the internet. Being a voyeuristic creep, I decided to have a gander at this Venezia sex flick. Have you seen it?"

"I was told you can't see who the man is," I said nervously.

"True, but you can see his penis. And it occurred to me that we've got someone right here on the force who might be able to ID the prick in a lineup."

"Suppose it is Noel in the video? What would that prove?" I didn't want to confess to having seen the tape, or admit that I hadn't a clue as to the erection's owner.

"Motive," he said simply.

"Motive for what?"

"This morning all three desk clerks at the Times Square Hyatt saw Noel Holden exiting the lobby. Half an hour later, the cleaning lady knocked on the door of Venezia Ramada's room, walked in without noticing the Do Not Disturb sign, and found her mutilated body."

Taking a pause he held a terrifying crime photo.

"If the tabloids had any doubt, I can vouch for the fact that she had implants, 'cause they were surgically removed by the killer."

All the air was suddenly sucked out of the room. I looked at the vivisected and duct-taped remains of the starlet who until now had only made me angry and jealous.

"Are they sure Holden was in the room?"

"Hell, yeah. He admitted it. He says he freaked out when he saw her body, and instead of calling the police he ran."

"I just can't believe he'd . . . I mean, why?" I felt myself trembling.

"Did you know that a couple of days ago he lost the voice role of Kangaroo Lou in an upcoming Pixar project? Because of that porn flick with Venezia."

"So what do you think? That he killed Jane Hansen and Caty Duffy just to hide the fact that he was going to kill Venezia—and he did all this because of losing a single film role that he hadn't even lost back then?"

"Look at his record. Over the past few years, Holden's roles have gotten increasingly mainstream. He's been cultivating a more wholesome image. You probably know more than I do, but I'm guessing he met Venezia a while ago at one of those booze-fueled Hollywood parties. He beds this nutjob, and I'm guessing she'd set up a webcam and filmed the two of them bumping uglies."

I was too embarrassed to tell Bernie the whole weird truth—that Noel had actually slept with Venezia as an act of revenge against Crispin, who had previously slept with *his* girl.

". . . Next thing he knows," Bernie continued, "he can't get rid of her. She's now his best friend's girlfriend." Again Bernie had the chronology wrong, but I guess it didn't matter.

"If she was one of the little people, he could probably ignore her, but she's an heiress, if a disinherited one, and she becomes this low-grade celebrity, she's in movies now, and Crispin is getting her through all the same velvet ropes and into the celebrity bashes he attends. I mean, he's got to be thinking, this is worse than extortion. Not only can I not pay off this bitch, but she's nailing my buddy. Next thing he knows, she's uploaded her little fuck tape of the two of them going at it. I mean, this is the kind of shit that can cost a mainstream star his career, Remember Fatty Arbuckle!"

"So you think the sex tape was his trigger?" I asked, cutting to the chase.

"I think he didn't know how to get rid of her. He'd probably known she had the footage for some time, but he didn't know what she was going do with it."

"But why wouldn't he have killed her *before* she brought the tape out?" I asked. "I mean, you've got a point—if that is him in the film and he didn't want the tape to come out. But now the damage has been done and the reason is clear."

"I think he stumbled over you, Gladyss. He found out about these pre-existing murders, and that's when he planned it. Tossed down a couple of girls to lay the groundwork—girls with similar, uh, physical attributes to Venezia, of not quite on the same scale. Then, before he can off Venezia as well, the fucking tape comes out! Nevertheless, he sticks with his plan . . ."

"It's too farfetched," I said. "I mean, who's going to go through all this just to kill that bimbo? He could've done it a lot quicker and easier out west a month ago."

"Still, he had opportunity, motive—"

"You really think this sex tape is sufficient motive for three violent murders? Look at all the actors today who have survived crazy sex scandals, not to mention those who've appeared buck naked on film. Even if they could ID his dick, that tape on its own would hardly cause a ripple in his career."

"Thank you, rookie," he said, reverting to his old condescending self.

"Look, you're forgetting that I do have access to him. I was with him the day after the sex tape hit the Internet. He was genuinely amused by it all. In fact, he spent the evening consoling Venezia, who appeared to be truly upset."

"Which would be the smart thing to do if you hated someone and didn't want to draw attention to the fact that you're about to cut them into little pieces."

"But why would he kill Venezia *after* we caught O'Flaherty? And if he was trying to blend into the O'Flaherty MO, why would he introduce the whole Marilyn thing?"

"We're still filling in some of the blanks, but the main thing is: he left Venezia's hotel room just *before* she was found murdered."

"You better have a strong case," I said, "because you can bet that he's going to assemble a team of lawyers that will rival O.J.'s."

"Oh, one more thing! Forensic went back to the evidence collected at the Jane Hansen crime scene, and they found a hair that matched Holden's."

I didn't say anything. I had gone to that crime scene directly from my date with Noel. Even if he'd left the hair behind after committing the murder, a crack defense team would spot that connection and claim I had inadvertently brought it with me on my clothes. I took a deep breath as I could already see how this was going to have a serious backlash on my career.

"He's a big celebrity! Wouldn't he have been spotted going into the hotel?" I argued.

"He's an actor," Bernie replied." He knows about costume, make-up. He knows how to take on a role. Is acting like an innocent man so difficult?"

"I could see him committing a crime of impulse, maybe. But you're saying he researched O'Flaherty's case and then elaborately, patiently built on it?"

"Maybe that's why he was getting close to you, so he could milk you for inside information on the killings. Ever think of that?"

Instead of trying to convey to Bernie how insulting that insinuation was, I asked if Noel had confessed to anything.

"Other than seeing her dead body and running away, no."

"So what happens now?"

"He's in Central Booking, awaiting a bail hearing. The DA is trying to hold him in custody, but he's got lawyers working to get him released."

"This is crazy."

"We've checked his alibis, Gladyss. It's tight, but he was actually in town for the first two murders. Oh, also Alex traced a call that Holden placed around the time that the Jane Hansen photos were uploaded at the Midtown Manhattan library. It was made only blocks away from there, at his publicist's office."

"I can't believe all this is happening."

"Hey, you were the first to suspect him, remember?"

"Yeah and I ruled him out."

"Yeah, for O'Flaherty's murders. This is why I've got over twenty years in this job, you had just over twenty days."

He was right—it had been incredibly cocky of me to presume that Eddie and I could handle that by ourselves. Bernie could probably see me blushing, because he added, "Hey, you'd feel a lot more foolish if you'd woken up with him strangling you."

When I walked out of Bernie's office, I could feel the stares of all the other cops pressing against me. At that moment I felt responsible for the brutal deaths of three women. How could I ever have hoped to be a homicide detective? There was no way I'd be able to live this down.

Looking at the wall clock, I realized it was later than I'd thought. To have any chance of making it to my appointment on time I had to leave right now. When I reached the front door I saw there was a mob of reporters outside. I tried exiting through the back, but the guard had locked down the metal gate and vanished. So I buttoned up my coat, pulled my scarf up over my face, and yanked my little knit cap down over my hair. A trio of suits who were listening to a fourth were just leaving, so I tagged close behind. I stayed right on their heels and listened in as their leader talked about dollars and cents.

As the quartet pushed through the cluster of photographers and reporters, I saw him standing along the outer fringe, the cub reporter Bernie had given the frigid timeout. Before my little group had made it halfway down the block, I heard the kid scream, "That's her! The sex cop!" Turning around, I saw a small platoon of reporters charging forward like a disorganized swat team, wielding video cameras and boom mics.

As we reached Ninth Avenue, I pulled open the door of a cab as it was still moving, and we sped down Thirty-fourth and up Eighth to the eye clinic. As the taxi headed uptown, I couldn't help but think that my plainclothes days were over. Regardless of any disciplinary action that might follow, the worst thing for me was that every detective on the force would undoubtedly hear about the bimbo rookie who had an affair with the serial murderer she was supposed to be investigating. I'd be stuck directing traffic at the Holland Tunnel for the rest of my working life.

And even if none of this happened, I'd still be back in my uniform blues next week, pounding the icy pavement with O'Ryan, who in his quiet, dysfunctional way would never let me live this down.

When I arrived at the clinic, the receptionist asked if I had an escort to take me home after the procedure. Yesterday, at the fashion show, it had actually crossed my mind to ask Noel if he'd do it, because it seemed like a boyfriendly thing to do. Now I lied and said my mother was going to pick me up downstairs.

The nurse gave me a Valium and a cup of water and told me to relax. Because I knew I'd have to get home on my own, I bit it in two and swallowed one half, discreetly slipping the other into my pocket. My thoughts immediately began to drift. No matter how hard I tried to imagine the gruesome details, I could not envision Noel strangling and mutilating those women.

Some time later I was brought into the operating room, placed in a big chair that folded down flat, and slipped under a large machine. The nurse fitted a brace around my chin, and then the eye doctor slipped a cold metal suction cup over my right eyeball. It was unbelievably uncomfortable. He fiddled around with some controls, then he pushed a button and zapped my eye. Then he repeated the procedure on my left eye. Immediately I realized I could still see to some extent, but that didn't stop the nurse from slapping large bandages over my eyes.

"Go home and rest," he said. "Just take it easy for the next seventy-two hours, and no physical activity for a while until your eyes fully heal and your vision is clear."

I was escorted to the reception area out front to wait for my fake ride. When the receptionist was occupied answering the phone, I discreetly peeled off the adhesive bandages and slipped on my welder's glasses. Through the window, the street looked streaked and blurry. When I saw a large, jellyfish-like person passing out front, I said "There's my Mom!" and dashed for the door.

I walked until I was out of view and waved my hands wildly until a cab stopped. When he'd driven me down to my place on Sixteenth Street. I handed him a twenty and, since I was unable to read the meter, told him to keep the change. I opened my front door, and instead of chancing the elevator, I grabbed the banister tightly and walked up the stairs to my apartment. Once I was safely inside and all alone, I locked my door, put on the little security chain, and stripped. Although it was still early, I felt woozy and just wanted to sleep. Tomorrow I would start thinking about the possibility of finding a new career. I lay down and quickly dozed off, only to be awakened some time later by a sharp knocking on my neighbor's apartment door.

"Maggie, it's me." I recognized Crispin's voice in the hallway. "You okay in there?"

I heard her door open, and instantly there was a short scuffle, followed by a cry, then *boom!* The next thing I heard was her front door opening and slamming shut again. As I pulled on my clothes, I envisioned Crispin attacking Maggie. Feeling absurdly confident because I'd been able to make it home unassisted, I fumbled for my Glock then went and tried Maggie's door. Locked. I went back into my apartment and called 911. I told them I was a police officer, gave my address, and asked for immediate backup.

I planned to wait for them, because my vision was still foggy, but then I heard a muffled scream. Fearing Maggie was in danger, I located the spare key she'd given me, and used it to safely unlock her door. When I pushed it open, I saw a blurry form that had to be her lying slumped on the floor. The TV was on, but the volume was turned way down.

"Maggie!" I yelled at her. She didn't budge. I knelt and tried to find a pulse in her neck with one hand, while holding my pistol in the other. I couldn't quite figure it out, but she seemed to be in an odd position, and was wet; it smelled like fruit juice. On the floor was an empty plastic jug and lying next to Maggie was a large, black book, face open. When I stooped to peer at it closely I saw that it was her Bible. Even with my limited vision, I could see that a cavity had been carved into the pages. I was trying to figure out what could have been hidden inside when a heavy blow from behind sent me sprawling, and I blacked out.

CHAPTER TWENTY-ONE

"Gladyss!"

I came around slowly . . . to complete and total darkness! When I finally pulled myself off the floor I saw absolutely nothing. I was totally blind.

"My fucking eyes!"

I heard a tense male voice say "Gladyss, talk to me. What's the situation?"

It was O'Ryan, somewhere behind me.

"Eddie!"

"Where is he?" O'Ryan asked softly.

"I can't see!"

"What do you mean?"

"I just had an eye operation . . ."

I tried not to panic.

". . . and he hit me . . . and now I'm . . . I'M FUCKING BLIND!"

"Fuck! Let me see!"

I felt his hands nervously hold my head and tilt it back. He must've been staring into my eyes.

"Did you call for backup?"

"Before I came in."

"Your eyes look fine. Just stay calm. Backup should be here in a minute, along with an ambulance." He ran his fingers across the back of my head.

"Ow! What the fuck!"

"You have a bloody contusion." I had my hands cupped over my eyes, hoping and praying that my sight would flip back on, like a light switch being thrown.

"I was up on Twenty-third when I got the 10-13," Eddie was saying. "I recognized your address. But then as I was coming in . . . I guess it must've been him . . ."

"Who?"

"Your actor buddy, Noel. I saw him on the corner of Sixth Avenue. Just now."

"Shit! He must've made bail."

"If it wasn't him, it sure as hell looked just like him."

"What was he doing?"

"Getting into a cab on Sixteenth Street."

"For God's sake, check Maggie!" I said feeling around for her.

"Relax," he said. "She's right here and she's breathing, no apparent injuries. From her pupils, it looks like she's been drugged. And she has this . . ." I heard an odd crinkling sound. "Her ankles and wrists were bound up."

"But she's not cut in any way?" I didn't remember any blood.

"No, she looks okay."

I heard a faint thump that might've come from a neighboring apartment.

"Did you check the bathroom?" Eddie asked quietly.

"No, didn't get a chance. I heard Crispin Marachino knock and call Maggie's name, then he went in and it sounded like there was a scuffle and a loud bang. The door opened and slammed shut again, and then a minute or two later I thought I heard a scream."

At that moment there was another loud bang. I heard Eddie announce, "Police!" and kick open the bathroom door.

"What's going on?"

"Oh shit!" he said.

"What do you see?" I yelled.

"It's Marachino. He looks pretty bad. Holden must've attacked him too."

Eddie spoke into his walkie talkie. "Patrol post thirteen, civilian emergency. Need a second EMS forthwith." He then relayed my address and other information.

I was crouching next to the TV set, which was turned to CNN, and over Eddie's voice I could just hear the newscaster: "*We're live on Centre Street, where movie star Noel Holden is about to be released on two point five million dollars bail.*"

274

Presumably Eddie could see Noel's picture on the TV, because he paused abruptly. For a moment I thought he had simply made a mistake. We both listened as the newscaster finished talking about Noel's imminent release.

"On New Year's Eve, when you told me you were a virgin, it was snowing outside. Do you remember that?"

The coldness in his voice, its air of stark finality, made me realize it wasn't an error. I was in serious trouble.

I heard the doorbell buzz in my apartment next door.

"As pure as the driven snow in this filthy, fucked-up city, that's what I thought. I should've just shoved my thick cock into your tight little snatch right then. But . . . I treasured your purity. The fact that someone as beautiful as you, who must've had to fight off countless assholes trying to fuck you, had chosen me to give me your gift—"

"I *did* choose you Eddie!" I tried to focus just on breathing in and out, trying to re-enter the moment, even though I knew he was going to kill me.

"You were so tall and strong . . . and pure of heart . . . I just thought, this blonde beauty is mine to protect and cherish. I know it's a cliché, but I thought that we really were destined for each other . . ."

As he was talking, I could hear other buzzers being rung from downstairs. They were trying to get into the building.

"I mean, *no one* is still a virgin at twenty-three. But then what do you go and do? You take your beautiful little rose . . ."

"Eddie, just listen to me, please!" I was still on my knees, my weight resting on my calves. My fingertips slowly stroked the ground around me until I could feel the muzzle of my gun, lying where I had dropped it.

". . . and you go and find the lowest of the low, and you part your beautiful strong thighs for that vile scumbag. You sacrificed your purity to jackals!"

"Please calm down, Eddie" I managed to say.

"I know I must sound crazy, but here's the kicker—I'm not."

"NYPD!" I heard a voice outside the door, and the crackle of radios.

"I want you to put down . . . your weapon," I said with a tremor. It crossed my mind that if he did shoot me now, at least he'd get caught.

"You don't even . . . I was still on duty *after* that fashion show. . . Remember that awful night? Everyone booing you even though you were the only one doing what was right! I should've killed all of them right there."

"Calm down," I said, to him and myself.

"*I* was the one who brought you home that night, when you were drunk off your ass and you tried to arrest that dumb crack whore."

"Tell me that you didn't kill those people, Eddie."

"You were so wasted that night, you didn't even realize that *I* was the one who put you in a cab, brought you safely home, and carried you up the stairs in my arms."

"Eddie, I'm grateful for that, but . . ." My hand was trembling. All I could do was focus on his voice.

"I was the one who undressed you and put you to bed like you were my own."

"Eddie, I . . ."

"I abandoned my post to bring you home, then once you were asleep, I went back to the precinct to sign out."

"I'm very grateful, but . . ."

"And when I came back to make sure you were okay, what do you think I found?" Now his voice was boiling with rage.

"I don't care!"

"I found that disgusting creep was *doing* you!" he screamed. "And I would've *married* you!"

The blast from his Glock knocked me flat. I grabbed my gun and fired three times into the blackness until I heard a gasp, and then a thud.

Feet began kicking at Maggie's door.

"Hold on!" I fumbled my way across the room until I located the doorknob. I unlocked it, held my hands in the air and said, "I'm a blind cop, don't shoot."

"What the hell—" one of them said, presumably seeing Eddie's uniformed body. I explained what had happened.

"You can't be blind," said one of the cops. "He took three bullets to the head."

Since O'Ryan was in uniform and I wasn't, they cuffed me. The cops were from the one-zero; none of them were from Midtown. Over the next few minutes I heard more cops pour into the apartment.

All of Eddie's radio calls had been fake, so we had to wait another five minutes for the paramedics to arrive for poor Maggie. Crispin was dead. One of the officers said his skull had been cracked open like an egg. When Annie showed up and my identity was verified, the cuffs were removed. The medics gently taped bandages over my eyes, and I was finally rushed to Saint Vincent's Hospital.

An eye surgeon was waiting for me in the ER. When he heard that I'd had Lasik surgery just hours earlier, he examined my eyes and then explained what must have happened, something about rods and cones. I was too frazzled to take it in.

"Will I be able to see again?" That was all I wanted to know.

"Oh yes," he said. "It'll just require a brief operation."

I was sedated, and when I awoke the next day, I could see images again, though they were still blurry. I was told that would soon pass. But because of my head injury, I wasn't going home any time soon.

During my convalescence, Annie told me later, a variety of forensic evidence quickly came to light that proved Eddie was definitely our second killer. For starters, the same roofies that had been used to drug both Jane Hansen and Caty Duffy were also found in Maggie's system. And although we couldn't find his knife, blood residues from all three Marilyn victims were found on shoes in O'Ryan's apartment, though he hadn't been on duty at any of the crime scenes. In addition, after the news broke about the killer cop, a honeymooning couple from Toronto came forward to say they'd seen a cop going into the Kings Court Hotel at roughly the same time as Caty Duffy's murder. It had to have been O'Ryan.

But the most damning—and saddest—evidence was found in the meticulously handwritten journals Eddie had kept. Barry said it looked like they had been written in calligraphy. Not only had he kept a diary of the killings, the back pages contained early drafts of the menacing poems he had sent to the Marilyn web site.

Apparently, since I'd been transferred to homicide, Eddie had been lurking in my vicinity every moment when he wasn't at work or asleep. He kept a watch on my building so he could monitor all my comings and goings. Each time I went to yoga or the corner market, he wrote it down.

His artistic handwriting betrayed a discontent that went way beyond being jealous of Noel; he'd developed paranoid conspiracies about the power of the cult of celebrities, who he felt were constantly undermining American society and morals. I had concerns of my own about the negative effects of our celebrity culture, but I also realized that I had only myself to blame for succumbing to it.

Like Bernie, Eddie had done his research and discovered various details about Noel Holden, including his odd comments about Marilyn Monroe being his mother, and his on-again, off-again affair with Venezia. It appeared that his motive for the killings was to revenge himself for the "abrupt withdrawal of my affection." That was the phrase he used. Though as I remembered it, he was the one who had done all the withdrawing.

O'Ryan might have been able to continue his murder spree undetected if it hadn't been for his insane fantasy that Noel and Crispin had worked together to rob him of my virtue. This was what had fueled his final rampage: the murder of Crispin and the attempted murder of Maggie, which was to have been loosely timed to Noel's release. He hadn't figured on my walking in on him.

"Not only did you get a plum assignment in Homicide," Barry said. "At the same time you met and got involved with a Hollywood star. The combined impact of those two things was probably what set him off. There's evidence in earlier journals that he'd long exhibited a pathological level of envy—now he undoubtedly felt he had been cheated out of his girl and a prospective job at the same time."

Since we'd never be able to interrogate O'Ryan, it would all remain open to endless speculation.

Despite the ordeal that had landed me there, I fondly remember the time I spent healing in St. Vincent's back in 2003. Sadly, it's gone now. After generously serving the Lower West Side of Manhattan since 1849, the hospital abruptly went bankrupt in 2010, prompting an investigation by the DA. Now there are plans to tear it down and build luxury condos—one more thing for O'Flaherty to have gotten mad about, except he died in prison back in 2007.

The evening before I was released from the hospital, Bernie, Alex, and Annie came to visit me and we found ourselves reviewing the case.

"The more I think of what O'Ryan did, the more I appreciate the opportunism of it," Alex said. "He plugged into an open case that you were assigned to, then subtly twisted the crimes, hoping that we'd arrest Noel, who he believed had displaced him in your heart."

"And don't forget, Gladyss," Annie added, "You were the one who said that Noel was a suspect in the first place. He was just giving you what you were initially looking for."

It was a painful realization. "Shit, if I had never told him that I suspected Noel, the murders of Jane, Caty, Venezia, and Crispin would never have happened."

"Don't be too hard on yourself," Bernie said. "A psychopathic killer is a psychopathic killer. If it hadn't been this, he would've eventually gone after someone else, and instead of four murders it might've been forty."

Annie and Alex headed home after a while to be with their families, so that left me alone with Bernie.

"I talked to Internal Affairs," he said. "Long story short, I'm back on modified duty pending an investigation."

"That doesn't sound good."

"They say they have enough evidence to make a case for dismissal and bring me up on charges."

"So what are you going to do?"

"There's something called forced retirement—I get three-quarters disability pension if I leave quietly." He sat on the edge of my bed, looking down. "I guess I'm taking it."

"I'm sorry, Bernie. "

"No, it's probably for the best. Hey, I was ready to go last year, but after Bert took sick, I felt like the department wanted to be rid of me too. And I don't like being pushed."

"You've got to get your health back," I replied.

"The pulmonologist said my lung capacity is forty percent, and there's little I can do about that. The last doctor I spoke to recommended having the foot amputated."

"I'm sorry."

"He said that's why it always smells so bad. It's permanently infected."

"They can do great things with prostheses nowadays."

"Smell or no smell, I'm keeping my fucking foot!" he shouted.

"Bernie, you have to do something about the anger."

"When I came on the force twenty years ago, I was like you,

Gladyss—a smart, sexy young cop. Back then, the city was more like I am now— bitter and damaged. It smelled rotten. Midtown was loaded with guys like O'Flaherty. And we all thought the city would only get worse. I never thought it'd turn around like this."

"But it did. New York's actually a great place now."

"Have you traveled much?" he asked.

"Yeah, I went to Europe after college, traveled around the Mediterranean."

"What did you see?"

"What are you getting at?"

"There was a time when, if you went someplace, you saw distinctive things just there. People dressed a certain way, each place had different music, different food, people spoke a different language. People even behaved a certain way that was their way. I mean, once you homogenize the world until every place is just like every other place, you destroy those distinctions, you destroy the beauty of the place. Yeah, New York was dirty and dangerous back then, but that kept the rich assholes away. And it allowed for a very unique style and character all its own. Times Square was the epicenter of that, at least for me."

"But surely it's better now overall," I argued. "safer, cleaner."

"It was like some crazy, intense, unique character who was suddenly . . . lobotomized. And now it's happening to the whole city."

He rose slowly to his feet and smiled. "Anyway after years of working with Bert, I know for a fact that he never would've got out of a warm bed on a freezing cold night, pulled me out of my car, and taken me to his home. Thanks for that."

"I would've taken you to *your* home if I knew where you lived."

"More than anything in the entire world, I'm glad that you didn't know where I live. Otherwise I never would've been date-raped. Thank you again for that."

He gave me a kiss on the cheek, then limped out the door.

Over the course of the next decade, as New York seemed to steadily drain of its New Yorkishness, Bernie must've grew increasingly less comfortable, until he finally gave up and tried joining other retired city workers in the relatively neglected outer boroughs. But without a family to put up with him and help him assimilate, what recourse would there be for the old curmudgeon but simply to retreat and become ever more reclusive.

More terrifying still is the realization that I might be on a similar path myself. Initially I liked the fact that New York was getting cleaner and better behaved, but one day I began to realize that the process was continuous. Slowly, as it kept changing, I found myself growing steadily crankier over the years. Whenever I would find myself ranting about how things used to be just a few years earlier—how the glamour of the big city that drew these revolving-door natives here is all bullshit—my current boyfriend, who arrived in the city only five years ago, accuses me of "olding."

"You can't look at the city as a finished piece," he once replied. "You should think of it more as a continuous work in progress."

After her attack, Maggie had recuperated across town at Beth Israel Hospital, recovering from mild concussion and a damaged voice box. Apparently O'Ryan, while trying to strangle her, had dislocated her larynx. I'd apparently interrupted him when I knocked on her door. Even though her injuries were greater than mine, my insurance was much better than hers, so she was released before I was.

When I finally came home from the hospital, Maggie greeted me with a big hug. In a hoarse whisper she said, "Thank you for saving my life."

This was the first time I had seen her since the shooting, so I asked her if O'Ryan had surprised her while she was alone with Crispin.

"No, it wasn't like that," she began. "In fact, Crispin and I had broken up the day before."

"Then how did he happen to get you?"

Speaking in a soft, methodical voice that made me wonder if she was overmedicated, she described how O'Ryan had knocked on her door holding a paper bag while I was getting my eye surgery. He claimed to be looking for me. She'd told him where I was and invited him into her place. He'd taken a plastic jug of fresh apple juice out of his bag, saying he'd just bought it at the farmers market in Union Square and didn't want to drink it alone. She'd brought two glasses and they drank. When she started feeling woozy, he'd pulled out his gun and forced her to call Crispin, who was still in town, and plead with him to take a cab right over.

"Did you wonder why he wanted to see Crispin?"

"I thought it had something to do with the photos. I figured you'd told O'Ryan about them and he was pissed. I sure didn't think I'd wind up getting Crispin killed," she whispered sadly.

"What photos?"

"Oh." She looked away. There was clearly something she had never told me. "Crispin was a freak."

"A freak how?"

"He knew I had a crush on Noel and kept dangling him in front of me."

"Dangling him how?"

"Manipulating me."

"How?" I pushed, but she just looked away and tears started rolling silently down her cheek.

"Just tell me, Maggie!"

"He told me that he wanted to punk you."

"'Punk me how?"

"Remember that Bible I had with me when I came over that one time?"

"Yeah." It was the same Bible I'd seen when I went into her apartment and found her unconscious, only then it was open, revealing that it had been hollowed out.

"Crispin gave it to me."

"What for?"

"Well, don't get mad . . . It had a miniature camera in it."

"Why?"

"Remember that night when we kissed?" she asked.

"Uh huh."

"He was behind all that."

"Behind *what*?"

"Crispin gave me the Bible with the camera hidden in it and told me how to position it. He said it was just going to be a prank. I was going to show it to you later."

"So there are photos of us kissing?"

"There were. I deleted them."

"Some joke."

"He'd wanted me to go all the way."

"All what way?"

"You know, seduce you."

"How exactly did Crispin—?"

"He told me to say I'd gotten the role in that soap. And I was suppose to be teaching you to kiss Noel."

"I remember that. So it was all a lie?"

"Yeah."

"But I'd been out on a date that night with Noel."

"Yeah, he called me later and said you were on your way home. And that you'd be tipsy and randy. Those were his exact words."

I remembered that evening now. I'd arrived late at some ridiculous premiere party on the South Street Seaport; I had forgotten about it, but Maggie talked me into going. Crispin had handed me a tall stein of beer and a Bushmills chaser when I walked in, and he more or less dared me to drink it. Then I remembered her kissing me—and all the while she was photographing it.

"How could you do that?"

"I'm so sorry," she said. "People do dumb things when they're in love. I mean, that's probably why O'Ryan did what he did, right?"

"I guess so," I said tiredly. Sadly.

"Could you do me one favor?" Maggie asked. "I mean, if you don't mind."

"What?"

"I just need to talk to Noel one final time. When he calls you, can you ask him to give me a call."

"Sure," I said, half-disgusted, half-embarrassed by her pathetic request.

While I was still banged up and medicated, I had rebuffed a half-hearted attempt Noel made to come and visit me in the hospital. I just didn't want to be seen like that. Given what I had learned about celebrity behavior, I never expected to hear from him again. So I was startled when I woke up one morning roughly a week after I got back home to find a lengthy message from him on my voicemail. He told me he was at a hotel in Saint Bart's, down in the Caribbean, recuperating. He said he was sorry about my suffering, and grateful that I had spared him a long and costly trial. He claimed he knew there was something off about Eddie when he first was knocked down by him that day we met.

"So I really want to thank you," he said. "The DA was planning on going after me with everything they had. Hell, they had a witness who was ready to testify that I had left Venezia's room just prior to her being . . . What I'm trying to say is, I'm deeply grateful."

He rambled on a while longer, as though I were actually on the other end of the phone. Then he must've spotted a sexy girl out his window, because without any transition he abruptly hung up. He didn't even say goodbye, let alone leave a phone number I could pass along to Maggie. When I checked my phone to see if his number was listed among the incoming calls, I was actually happy to see it said RESTRICTED.

Maggie and I stopped hanging out and just became hi/bye friends, who passed one another in the hallway. Three years later, when she was invited by some casting director to do a fifteen-minute audition for some TV show, she gave up her apartment and moved to LA. Ultimately I think we both were relieved we no longer had to pretend.

As for Noel, after his final phone call I made a point of changing the channel or flipping the magazine page whenever I glimpsed his sharpened face. I just wanted it all behind me. One night in 2007, I accidentally spotted him on a talk show and all the expensive make-up couldn't hide the fact he'd had a nip and tuck and a dye job. Like all glamour figures, he'd begun his long slide down.

As commercial rents kept rising in the neighborhood, the little yoga studio across the street finally had to say Namaste and fold. When I checked it out online, I found there was more to the story: a sexual harassment suit had been filed by Penrose, the yogarexic instructor, against the owner. Evidently he had not quite renounced everything.

A short time later, a shiny new fitness franchise appeared just around the corner, complete with four yoga classes per day. It had all the old poses I enjoyed without requiring me to think about my seven spinning okras as written in the tantrums, or whatever.

While lying with my eyes closed during final relaxation one day, I tried to summon up the image of the statue of Diana, but to no avail. Instead, an image of Noel in a leotard wearing a cape popped into my head; I had just seen it on the side of a bus. He was playing some comic book superhero. When I considered the Greek myth that best suited him, I didn't even have to use Google to come up with Narcissus, the legendary egotist. Later though, when I did look it up, a sad story emerged. Narcissus had a relationship with a wood nymph named Echo. But as much as she loved him, he loved himself even more. Slowly Echo withered away, leaving only her reverberating voice behind. It was a classic tale of unrequited love, with Maggie's name echoing all over it.

My brother Carl returned to New York for Easter, which was spring break for him. I was still on sick leave, and went back to Astoria, Queens, to celebrate the holiday with my family. They had all heard about the murders and my brief fling with the Hollywood Hunk. Over dinner, I filled them in on some of the more interesting details that had never made it into the press.

Toward the end of the evening, after most of my cousins had left and I was planning to do likewise, Carl gave me a hug, something he rarely did. I hugged him back and asked if he was okay.

"I guess I'm just afraid that we're both getting worse."

"Worse! I just helped catch a goddamn serial murder!"

"Well . . . which you, kind of . . . caused," he added sympathetically.

"I caused!"

"I don't mean deliberately! But for years you protected your virginity like Fort Knox! Then, on New Year's Eve, you impulsively decide that you're wasting your innocence, and that very night you go to bed with that creep. Of course, he turns out to be a psycho killer! And you don't even *do* it with him, instead you end up giving him a homicidal case of blue balls!" He laughed.

"*Because you called*! We would've done it, but *you* interrupted!"

"Oh right, blame it on me!"

"It was all just really bad luck," I amended for the sake of peace.

"Bad luck? Really. Well how about your flaky neighbor who tells

you about some mystical brand of yoga that gives you x-ray vision—
and suddenly you turn into the goddamned Goddess of the Hunt!"

Instead of pulling out my Glock, I grabbed my coat and left.

Eventually we made up, as usual, but over the last ten years he has
grown increasingly combative. He's always on the side of justice for
the little guy, and since I was a cop, what he calls "a security guard
for the rich," I invariably become a piñata for his growing rage.

By October of 2011, he'd become a regular member of Occupy
Oakland. The last time he called me was that November night when
Bloomberg shut down Zoo-cotti Park. He woke me up in the early
morning hours screaming, "The rich have decimated this country,
and when we protest that, you oinkers do their dirty work for them!"

I hung up on him. We didn't have any further communication
until a little over a year later at our family's 2012 New Year's Eve
party, which ended with me storming out the door as he yelled:
"Fascist Bloomberg is finally out this year! He can't buy any more
re-elections!"

Three months after Crispin's murder, I was back in Neighborhood
Stabilization doing foot patrol in uniform again. It was almost like
those four weeks in Homicide had never happened. To make mat-
ters worse, I'd been paired up with O'Ryan's old partner, Lenny
Lombardi. Under the circumstances, I was nervous about returning to duty—it's rare that people who kill their co-workers end up
returning to their old position. But when everyone read the news
reports of Eddie's lunacy, they were genuinely sympathetic. Still, that
first day back, I kept waiting for Lenny to ask about it, and he didn't
say a single word.

That evening we found ourselves all the way east on Forty-second,
passing through Grand Central Station. I looked up at the famous
ceiling and stared at those wonderful zodiac signs, drawn out from
their starry backdrops. Aries the ram, Taurus the bull, Gemini the
twins, Cancer the crab . . . I was amazed by the notion that three
thousand years earlier, people had extrapolated their gods from
seemingly random dots in the sky.

"You know," Lenny said, seeing my heavenward gaze. "Someone
once figured out that those images are all painted backwards."

"No fooling."

"Yeah, and when they asked the Vanderbilt family, who owned the building, what the deal was, one of them said, that's the perspective from the gods looking down at us."

"A good spin on a fuck up," I commented. And since it seemed a natural progression, I asked, "Did you know there's a Greek myth tie-in to the O'Flaherty murder case?"

When he said that he did not, I told him about the postcard of the Diana statue that was taped up over the killer's bed.

"That's it?"

"Well, he had been killing tall blondes, and I'm a tall blonde— which was why I had been brought in in the first place."

"So it's like you were the goddess Diana."

"There were other similarities," I added, without going into the matter of my recent virginity.

"Well, I guess that would account for your old partner," he said casually.

"Bernie Farrell?"

"No, Eddie O'Ryan."

"What about him?"

He pointed up at the constellations on the ceiling again. "Orion's Belt."

"Huh?"

"Orion was Diana's hunting partner. She ended up killing him, too."

ACKNOWLEDGMENTS

Thanks to the following people who helped with *Gladyss of the Hunt*. My cousin Patrick Burke 3rd; my Uncle Steve Burke; Coree Spencer; Jennifer Belle; Justin Michael Niotta and *Rabid Magazine*; Jeff Vargon, who has kindly videotaped so many of my readings; Johnny Temple and my other friends at Akashic Books. Among my yoga guides, first and foremost Sylvia Rascon, who patiently and generously gave so much of her time and expertise; Syama and Dhyana at the Stanton Street Yoga; Sandi and Yoga to the People on Saint Mark's Place. Sarah, Erik, Henry Hanson-Spence, and Jane. My friends at the Strand Bookstore, among them Nathan, Andrea, Justin, Peter, Anna, Aya, Martine, Michael, Jorge, Jeremy, Tom, David, Sheldon, Eric, Sam, Antonia, and of course the great Ben McFall. My friends at the Cooper Square post office, including Amy, Carmen, Brenda, Vincent, Shirley, and Cynthia. My many friends at the Jackson Heights Branch of the Queens Community House, and Delphi, who introduced me there. The great St. Marks Bookshop, the longest-running indie bookshop in Manhattan, worked by Shauna, Peter, Jessie, Anton, Benjamin, Jed, Margarita, and of course Bob and Terry. Two talented young writers who helped me with this book, Anjelica V. Young and Kyle Lucia Wu. So many friends I've met on Facebook in recent years who have become like a cyber family. Also special thanks to Paul Rachman, Mike McGonigal, and last, yet perhaps most, Steve Connell, a brilliant editor and friend.